King of Angels

A Novel About the Genesis of Identity and Belief

Perry Brass

Belhue Press

Belhue Press, First Edition, Second Printing

Copyright 2012 © by Perry Brass

Published in the United States of America by:

Belhue Press
2501 Palisade Avenue, Suite A1
Bronx, NY 10463

Electronic mail address: belhuepress@earthlink.net

The following is a total work of fiction. All the characters, institutions, and events in it are purely fictitious and have no relationship to actual specific personages, living or dead, or business entities except when described as part of a fictional narrative.

Cover and interior design by Tom Saettel. TomSaettelDesign.com

Cover art by permission of Wes Hempel
("A New Beginning," copyright Wes Hempel. For more information about
Wes Hempel please see the note about him at the end of the text of this book.)

ISBN: 978-1-892149-14-5

ISBN: 1-892149-14-1

Library of Congress Control Number: 2011941459

Other books by Perry Brass

Sex-charge (poetry)

Mirage, a science fiction novel

Works *and Other 'Smoky George' Stories*

Circles, the sequel to *Mirage*

Out There: *Stories of Private Desires. Horror. And the Afterlife*

Albert *or The Book of Man*, the third book in the *Mirage* series

Works *and Other 'Smoky George' Stories*, Expanded Edition

The Harvest, a "science/politico" novel

The Lover of My Soul, *A Search for Ecstasy and Wisdom*
(poetry and other collected writings)

How to Survive Your Own Gay Life, *An Adult Guide to Love,
Sex, and Relationships*

Angel Lust, *An Erotic Novel of Time Travel*

Warlock, *A Novel of Possession*

The Substance of God, *A Spiritual Thriller*

Carnal Sacraments, *A Historical Novel of the Future*

The Manly Art of Seduction, *How to Meet, Talk to,
and Become Intimate with Anyone*

And then the Deer and the Birds were told by
the Maker, Modeler, Bearer, Begetter:
". . . Name our names now, praise us. We are your
mother, we are your father. Speak now:
'Hurricane,
Newborn Thunderbolt, Sudden Thunderbolt,
Heart of Sky, Heart of Earth.
Maker, Modeler,
Bearer, Begetter.'
speak, pray to us, keep our days."
—Popol Vuh, Translated by Dennis Tedlock

To name something is to praise it, through the
naming of it. It is also to destroy it. With the
consciousness of Names, comes the burden.

For Hugh, and also for Tony Adams, Jerry Kajpust,
Steve Parelli and Jose Ortiz, and all the people who
believe in the power of love to form the world.
With great thanks to Patrick Merla and Tom
Saettel, and also for the memory of my beloved
friend Jeffrey Lann Campbell.

Part One:
In The Beginning

1

Somehow Or Another, It All Begins Here

It's only right that I should tell you about my beginnings. My name is Benjamin Rothberg and I grew up by the water in Isle of Hope, a sunburned marshy suburb about fifteen miles from downtown Savannah, Georgia. The natives call it "I'll-a-'ope," with the same kind of stretched-out, lazy-sounding vowels you hear in words like "calliope." Still, it was the most ravishing name in the world, the Isle of Hope. You head out on a twisting curlicue of a road to where the marshes and rivers soak into each other and dense hammocks of palmettos watch over the sea grasses with their salty-sweet stink of oysters, shrimp, catfish, and turtle shells. I grew up there with my younger sister, my mother, and my father, a salesman and a Jew. To me even at an early age, the two seemed indistinguishable: Jew. Salesman. The fast-talking Jew who never really stands still in one place and lives off his own spew of words becomes a salesman. What else could he do? What else could *they* do, since they were never to-the-land born?

My father was short, Mediterranean dark, and chunky, you might say, but good-looking in a distinctive, large-featured kind of way. He had dark, thick wavy hair and eyes like opaque disks of cobalt-blue glass, the sort found in old Roman ruins, that pulled you in and warmed you, and went well with his tanned skin. Dark glistening hair grew on his chest, legs, feet, and arms. It appeared like the curling leaves of anthracite-black field flowers on his hands, up to the first joints of his fingers. A lightning field of pure electricity seemed to swim around him. Men were drawn to him not simply because he could talk more than they could (any fool could do that), but because he listened as hard as he talked. My mom was almost too ridiculously his opposite: all fine length, with beautiful, streaky, ginger-ale blonde hair and long, smooth arms and legs. She'd been athletic and habitually stayed in motion, which bothered my father, who was kinetic enough to need to some kind of balancing gravity around him.

When I was very small, tired, and on the verge of tears, he would squat down, look at me with his intense blue eyes, and nod. "Yeah, Benjy," he would say. "That's the way it is. You need to go to sleep now." Or, "You need to stop doing this, and act like a big boy. Like a *mentsh*."

And I would. I'd stop, not because I was scared of him as solid as he seemed—certainly next to my mother—but because I wanted to be a part of him, an extension of him really, because he was the most amazing thing I'd ever known.

He would hold me in his gaze with the pure tension of his attention, and now I, too, was swimming around him, with all of that lightning-bright electricity. It's difficult to say how much you love a father when you're that tiny, or even later, when you're maybe seven or eight. He can eat you like a dinosaur or an ogre out of a fairytale, or hold you like a cleft in a mountain supporting a small sapling tree. I felt held like that when he was near me. He had a smell, too, I can't forget. Men smelled then of perspiration, salt, liquor, unfiltered tobacco, and the profound, lingering scent of their hair that absorbed the smoke of winter log-fires and the earthy mist of summer nights.

I remember his smell distinctly, from when he took me on his lap and taught me how to read at the age of five. I'd been trying to figure out words, and my father said, "Why should he have to wait till school?" So he taught me how to sound each letter out phonetically, and group them together into words and then short sentences. I picked up reading almost immediately, making him very happy. By the beginning of the third grade, I could read on a sixth grade level and was already bored with primary school books; I was bumped up to the fourth grade in the local public school. The problem, then, was to keep how smart I was hidden from the other kids, because they made fun of me.

He was known to us as Robby and Robby was always the name my mom, Caroline, called him. I think he'd actually invented it some time back when he was a kid up North. He didn't tell me a lot about his childhood, but Robby was his *goyishe* name, the one he used socially and for business in the South. He used Leon, the name he'd been given at birth, with other Jews, almost automatically falling into it; my head would fairly spin when it happened. Out of the dense cobalt of his eyes, his smile would seem suddenly more real. Hidden delicious parcels of medieval-sounding, melodious Yiddish and even more fragrant, ancient Hebrew would spring out into his vocabulary; his voice reverted to a richer, special "Leon" timbre: younger, deeper, more flexible, sometimes softer;

as if the words were incantations from some hidden source, siphoned from a secret life, that of the distant Sephardic Jews to whom he at various times alluded with pride—"the real *nobility* of the Jews," he called them—now pouring openly, simply, through him as Leon.

Still the Robby voice was the one I knew mostly, and when without warning the Leon voice would appear, I'd get anxious. What had happened to Robby, my daddy, the man who had taught me to read as he held me on his lap?

If they were having a serious conversation and I happened to be there, and she was buzzing around like a mosquito, he'd say, "Caroline, can't you just stay in one *farkakte* place for a sec and listen to me?"

Mom would stop, cock her beautiful blonde head, look quizzically at him, and smile that smile—half Mona Lisa, half spy from another world—that never really let anyone know exactly what she was thinking.

"OK. *Robby*. If that makes you happy."

The truth was, for most of those years I didn't really know her, any more than I knew Robby, who was also known in other places out in the big adult world as Leon. Even worse, they didn't know me, either.

At one point, Robby/Leon Rothberg wanted me to be brought up as a Jew.

I guess they'd been noodling about it for it years, and finally he'd become adamant. Caroline didn't care one way or another. In her wonderfully breezy world of tennis, martinis and Salty Dogs, canasta with girlfriends, and the assorted good-looking, smart people she liked to associate with, God was pretty much like food. It all amounted to sweet, sour, salty, lumpy, greasy, or crunchy; there were certain things at a certain point you wanted to stick in your mouth, but you could always eat something else—so why make a big deal out of it?

The two of them drove me one Saturday into Savannah, to the big orthodox synagogue that Leon himself distantly knew because of various business connections. It was an overpoweringly strange, dimly lit, frigidly air-conditioned place where the women, looking overdressed, sat in an area separated from the men. Everyone was standing when I walked in, and some were up on a raised platform, praying loudly in a language that I recognized was Hebrew. I noticed immediately that all the men looked vaguely like cousins. In fact, many actually looked like Robby, or approximations of him, wearing dark suits and little black caps and long, blue-striped white shawls, swaying back and forth like trees in a brisk wind: talking to God, I guessed.

A short time later, I began elementary Hebrew lessons. The other kids thought I was strange because Mom didn't look like anyone they knew—she was *obviously* a *goy*, and even though I looked somewhat like her, I took too much after Robby/Leon not to be anything *but* a Jew.

Still, I was told flat out by Esther Fein, "Your mama's gotta be Jewish before anybody can call you a Jew."

Esther was nine like I was, and a spoiled little bitch already, as Mom, into her third Salty Dog, declared. We didn't keep kosher either, which according to my classmates made me even less a Jew. When I brought that detail up to Mom, she threw up her hands. She was never going to give up her bacon, shrimp, fried oysters, catfish, and barbeque pork for anyone, not even God Himself, even if He came down and looked exactly like Robert Mitchum.

"Benjy, if the Lord didn't want us to eat stuff like this, He *never* would have made 'em so darned good," she said, munching on a pork rind.

I shrugged; she had a point. After a few Hebrew lessons I got tired of being treated like a freak, and my formal Jewish training as well as Saturday mornings at the synagogue ended.

It hurt Robby horribly. He had this very special, heart-tugging way of show-ing pain on his deeply-tanned face so that all the wrinkles came out and he looked like a sad old hunting dog. I didn't want to ask him any more about it; it was too obviously distasteful for him. He was set so deeply into himself, into his own mysterious world of business deals, and even farther back, into that empire of his own "noble" Jewishness, that I just stayed away from it, as any intelligent Southern kid would have done.

The sad fact was, Robby was hardly ever around. He'd disappear for weeks sometimes, working for companies in small towns like Valdosta or Macon, or somewhere up in South Carolina. Sometimes he kept books for them, or sold for them, or met with distant customers from up North. Catalogues for things like cheap plastic raincoats or bedspreads and wind-up toys were scattered all over the house. When I asked, "Why is Dad gone?" it was met by evasions or silence.

"He's only providing for us," Caroline would answer, looking more Mona Lisa than ever, giving us her closed "Don't ask any more questions" expression.

So I didn't.

Our house was big, airy, always freshly painted white, and pleasant in its marshy, outlying setting. We lived well, with a full-time maid and two large comfortable cars. It was easy to see our position, because most of the kids around us didn't live that way. Their dads fished for a living, or worked on shrimp boats, or did menial work in seafood restaurants or in small stores. Some pumped gas or even did lawn work for those people who lived like we did.

I was going, like I said, to a small public school where I tried to pick up the way the local kids talked and to act the way they did. In the beginning, everyone stared at me, and I was afraid even to open up my mouth. And, from almost the beginning, I didn't feel like an authentic, *bona fide* regular male child. I felt more like an imitation of one, as if all the other boys were in fact, *real.* They had nothing to hide; they were never thinking about something else, or questioning it, or even ever bothered by *knowing* they were questioning it. Jesus, Santa Claus, the Easter Bunny, and the Pledge of Allegiance were what they believed in, as well as the unalterable fact that the cowboys were forever more deserving of victory than the Indians. They were white kids and that, in itself, was very important. In fact, that was the biggest thing of them all, except that you didn't talk about it. It was simply there, like the air or the sky. Almighty God and my schoolmates were melded together. You saw it imprinted on their faces when they prayed at the beginning of every class.

I was a Jew, or, at the very least, something resembling one. In truth, I wasn't sure what I was, or, even worse, if I *was* a real boy.

One day, in the beginning of fourth grade, by the big oak trees at recess, Russell and three other boys ran up to me. Russell was about half a head bigger than I was, freckled and blond, with some hair already sprouting on his arms. He had very pale, very clear blue eyes, not like the denser blue of Robby's. Although like me he was only in the fourth grade, already he seemed like a recognizable big boy. He stared at me, sizing me up, and finally demanded, "We wanna know if you a' *real* boy."

I was terrified. I knew sooner or later this was going to happen. It seemed only inevitable because, inside, I wasn't sure myself. I didn't answer.

Lance, a kid my actual age in the third grade, cried out, "He ain't!"

They all laughed hard, except for Russell.

"If you a real boy, show us your *polliwog*!" Russell insisted. "Right now!"

I pretended not to know what he meant. Lance smiled, like he had *all* the answers. "He don't know what it is, 'cause he don' have one. He's a Jew. They ain't got *polliwogs* like we done."

Scared as I was, I looked Russell directly into his clear, swimming-pool-blue eyes. I'd learned this from Robby. "Just look at people," he told me. "It always makes them think you're not afraid."

"I don't have to," I said emphatically. "I don't have to show you *anything*."

"Cause he don't have one t' show!" Lance declared, his small face grinning ear-to-ear.

Russell looked away from me, shrugging.

"He got a *polliwog*. I seen it. I jus' wanted t' fool wit' him."

Suddenly Mrs. Smith the young teacher came up to us. Everyone pretended nothing had happened. I kept my mouth shut, but from then on I was scared to go to the boys' room. I was scared they were going to take my pants down and do terrible things to me. I'd heard stuff like that went on in there, when no adult was looking.

After that, Russell stared at me, and sometimes walked up to me to demonstrate he was still bigger than I was. He was curious about me; I could tell. But he'd never seen my penis, that was for sure. And, no matter what, he never became my friend.

I knew Jewish boys didn't show off their penises to everybody. I'm not exactly sure how I knew it, but it ultimately made sense. Your penis was something God gave to you *especially*, so you didn't just show it off. I had seen Robby's, but that was different. It was dark and bigger, and surrounded by shiny black hair. We went swimming together at the beach and sometimes took our bathing suits off in the shower. There was never any word about it, but it seemed ridiculous to call it by some childish name like a "polliwog." It was a definitely a *pee-pee,* or a *peter*. Sometimes Robby referred to it as a "shmuck" or a "putz," but it was *never* a *polliwog*. That was a kid's name and I knew it; it was part of the silly kids' world where I was supposed to live, although there were times when that world seemed as cut off to me as even the more intimidating and monstrously large adult one.

Then soon enough, it happened: I learned how to discard some of the more usual aspects of Robby and Caroline—characteristics that made me the child of a certain set of parents—and act in a regular, acceptable, *local* way. Some of it was like not being scared of ugly things anymore simply by choosing not to get close to them, or pretending I was really someplace else when the situation came about. So I learned how to pick up slimy frogs in the schoolyard without fear, and not to show how unstomached I was and revolted by a dead cat; or that I was nervous when it was time to play baseball because I was scared I threw like a girl. I would just act like I was totally somebody else, and let the act take over. Also, I learned it was important *not* to act smart when you didn't *have* to be—not to stand out, or "show off," or be noticed in any way and get laughed at. I learned not only how to imitate the other kids, but even, more important, to quickly forget that it was only an imitation. I also learned how *not* to look smart and yet to look "busy" instead of stupid.

All of this was difficult, because receding into the background took more effort from me than showing off. It was like somebody had put a big stick labeled "Dumb" into my mouth, and clamped my teeth around it. Or had blindfolded me, while I still had to pretend that I could see.

I was afraid of being the only Jew-boy out in the sticks, who came from a home where his parents voted for John F. Kennedy who, everybody said, was a nigger-lover and a Catholic. I'd heard at school that Kennedy was going to turn the colored people on us, but I never heard that kind of talk at home, or even among Caroline's more worldly friends who climbed up to our second-floor porch at home (which we called the veranda) to smoke cigarettes and drink Salty Dogs. So I learned how to play with the other kids in Isle of Hope and not be scared, or admit that I was only *acting* in a way that might have been labeled as purely "idiotic" by some of Caroline's fashionable friends. Still, I knew this was only an act, and one I didn't have to do at home. At home Robby appreciated that I was actually smart, and I could be myself, even if I wasn't sure exactly *what* that self was.

It was strange; sometimes I felt all tangled up inside, and Robby and Caroline only added to the tangle. I was this sort-of Jewish kid—even if I wasn't *exactly* Jewish. But I felt Jewish; it felt like something I couldn't put my finger on, but it was there, an almost *namable* shadow, even if I could not name it and it didn't represent the complete outer shape of me. Nevertheless, we were comfortable in Isle of Hope in a Southern way. It was very nice, if you didn't think about it a lot, which most people didn't; at least not enough to talk about it. Josephine Thomas, the young black woman who worked for my parents, came in every day, and she was like one of us except that she wasn't. Josephine couldn't be Jewish, no matter what; that was the one thing I was sure of (even though that might not have been absolutely true, which I learned later and which confused me even more).

Still, as much as I wanted to, I knew almost nothing about Robby when he was gone for so long. I'd look at the strange catalogues and even some of his business papers if I found any lying around. They could have been written in Chinese. When kids at my school asked me what my dad did, I'd answer, "He's in business," and when they responded, "Is that 'cause he's a Jew?" I would just turn away. How could anyone answer that?

The fact that he was a Jew was known to most people there; there was no way around it. We didn't go to one of the local churches, and I guess word got around very fast about that. So even I began to connect his business, secret as it was, with the simple fact of him being a Jew.

It all seemed like a secret; part of the big adult world, a fortress we kids were not supposed to approach except in the most fearful way. The big adult world was painted in deeply enticing colors, like the silent old buildings at sunset around the squares in downtown Savannah, or the garish "Coming Attractions" of a grown-up movie with Eddie Fisher, or Elizabeth Taylor in a slip. I sneaked up sometimes to it when Mom had her friends over to drink martinis or Salty Dogs, while they smoked cigarettes on the veranda, which had a nice upper view of the water beyond the treetops. I would huddle behind the screen door as they talked about girls who got "knocked up" and had to "have it fixed." Or husbands who had girlfriends. Or, in an even lower, more *adult* voice, they would talk about men who were "like that."

"You really think he's . . . *like that*?"

Mom's voice suddenly went kind of funny, with this strange upward tilt in it, as if she were talking about cartoon animals instead of people.

Lucy Boyd, one of her friends, broke in.

"Y' know, come to think of it, I think John's cousin Peter's *like that*."

That brought on a big laugh.

"His *peter*?" Jane Wilson shrieked, cigarette in hand. "Ya'll think it's his *peter*? Girls, lemme tell you, it's never just ya peter that's like that!"

Lucy gulped an impatient sip of her drink.

"His cousin's name is *Peter*! And he *is* like that. I know, you can smell it on him. And he's got those . . . weak hands and he paints pictures and he—"

"Come on!" Mom injected. She shook her head softly, exhaling a slow curl of cigarette smoke. The smoke kept the gnats away. "Just 'cause you're *dreamy* and paint pictures, doesn't mean you're *like that*. I know lots of normal guys who are like that, but aren't *like that*—if you know what I mean."

Her voice lowered a bit. It sounded somewhat unraveled now, but without the funny tilt in it.

Sometimes Liz would sneak up and join me. When we heard this, Liz and I looked at each other behind the veranda door, and shrugged.

But a short time later in school I learned exactly what "like that" meant. The kids talked, and they weren't nearly as kind as Mom and her friends. They used words that hit hard and scared me—*queer, sissy, faggot, pansy, fairy, fag, lightweight*—words meaning something despised and to be avoided. I was never sure when one of those words might explode like a hand grenade directly in front of me. But who had actually seen a *fag, queer, sissy, fairy, pansy,* or *lightweight*? I definitely hadn't.

Still, the words were there, and I heard the very same ones by the marina docks, spit from the mouths of the men talking at the fishing boats. One minute it was baseball, next the "coloreds," and then "them pansy-asses is snappin' up places in I'll-a-'ope, spending good money on 'em! But who wants them kinda fairy-queers around here?"

I got the message, and even Caroline and her friends weren't exactly letting it rest either. A group of men "like that" from *way over* in Savannah *were* buying up old places nearby and spending good money to fix them up. Still, as Caroline admitted to her friends, the "local white trash is not happy. Oh, they like the money—just not the light-weights."

Then the truth dawned on me: no matter how much I tried not to, at a certain point, I actually *saw* them. It couldn't be helped; you had to be *blind* not to see them. They were out on the streets near the market at the boat landing, wearing clothes you didn't *normally* see in Isle of Hope, or you'd see them driving around in bright sporty two-seaters, which, I was informed, only "pansy-ass light-weights" would drive.

Mom's attitude toward them was decent and friendly in an offhand, never actually mean way. They were "artistic." "Interesting." When other people, especially the folks whose kids I knew from school would ignore them or whisper about them, she'd even go straight up to them and maybe address them by their names, passing the usual time of day but little else. It was a custom, a formality of Southern friendliness, and that was all: it was really distant.

We never went into their houses, beautiful places with fine furniture displayed inside big picture windows. But, amazingly enough, really up-close, some of these men looked like they were no more "light-weight" than, say, my dad.

I seriously thought about that, putting it all together as best I could, and it did make me look at my father differently. I could see already that he was two different people—Robby and Leon—which made me wonder, actually, what he was really like *inside*. Inside that adult world I was not supposed to know about; inside his own world, and of course, inside himself. Then, because there was too much else to think about, the thought would simply vanish. I guess this was the beginning of me straining to get into this intimidatingly distant, adult fortress with its secrets, the ones I was yet to understand.

Some of the men working on the fishing boats pointed out the "fairies" in voices nowhere near a whisper, and it was like a dark shadow had drifted over the faces of those being pointed out. The fishermen and shrimpers scared me, because I knew from school what it was like to have people say things I didn't want to hear, and then to have to pretend I didn't hear them. The "fairies" (or whatever they were called) also pretended they weren't hearing it, but their faces hid nothing, certainly not from me. I was able to see it, and I wished I could do something about it, small as I was, but I couldn't. I wanted to admit I was a Jew who wasn't a Jew, and still wasn't sure what they were. But it was OK; it had to be. It was like with Robby: there was stuff about my dad that wasn't *real,* and surely I knew it, as surely I was alive.

The men they talked about wore nicely starched white shirts and striped silk ties. Sometimes they wore expensive casual knit shirts or sweaters; things that Robby also wore. Some even wore their hair the way he did, carefully, as if he really thought about it. But there was something definitely peculiar about them—like they were paper dolls cut out and pasted into the local picture, instead of *real* living men. So they weren't actually a part of this corner of the world, any more than my own father was.

The guys from the boats at the landing wore sweat-stained, soiled T-shirts, and had work-coarsened hands and wind-bitten faces. My shoulders jerked out of fear—like danger was stalking me—when I ventured around them. Something might happen I couldn't stop. I wanted the men they were talking about to disappear and take my fears with them. But they went on shopping or walking together, or looking around, stopping in their cars at a light. Sometimes their softer faces took on protective reflections from the big live oak trees or the patterns of palmetto fronds; then they got blasted almost blind again by the sweaty glare from the road from the scorching sun above, reflected by a covering of sun-bleached white oyster shells.

But soon these men were gone, and with them those shadows. The shrimpers and locals would talk about other things. Negroes. Baseball. Jesus. Women. And I felt better, as if Leon, my Jewish father, were no longer in danger. I'd go back home, where I didn't have to put on the school act in front of Caroline, Liz, Josephine, or Robby. Soon enough, there'd be school again and the act would have to come back on. Then quick as summer lightning, I'd have to pretend to be like everybody else, when I knew I wasn't.

It was getting frankly more difficult. The worst part was that by the time I was ten or eleven *I* realized I didn't look like the other kids, either.

One day in the seventh grade Judy Beasley, a cute little auburn-haired girl who sat across from me announced, "You look like a nigger! You got dark skin, and your hair don't look like white people's hair."

"I have blue eyes," I answered defiantly.

"So? They got blue-eyed niggers. I seen 'em."

"I don't care what you *seen*," I said, trying hard to keep from either crying or exploding, when in fact I just wanted to disappear. "I'm not one of them!"

I hated her, but I wasn't sure what to do about it. I resented being called a nigger, a word we definitely never used at home, where we often sat down to dinner with Josephine Thomas. I gave Judy the cold shoulder for a while, but couldn't tell my parents. I was too humiliated even to speak about it, which hurt even more.

Judy soon enough took back her words, and even cottoned up to me, telling me at recess, "It's OK. My daddy told me the Jews in the Bible were darker than us. So that means you *ain't* a nigger. You jus' look like a Jew in the Bible, and we need t' respect that."

I nodded at her, pretending I'd forgotten everything. But it did make me look differently at Josephine. Perhaps after all, she could be Jewish.

Then, just before the start of eighth grade, when I was ready for junior high school, my parents came to an earth-shaking decision: public school was no longer working for me. I don't know exactly how they'd figured it out—nobody asked *me*; I was just a kid—but in any case, they had a meeting up on the veranda. Josephine, in one of her very attractive yellow dresses, brought up two small shakers, one each, of martinis and Salty Dogs. Robby smoked and I, hidden again, listened, making sure they didn't see me.

"He needs to be with another kind of people," Robby asserted, his dark brow knit. "I'm talking, Caroline, about *smart* people with *real* flush toilets and real books in their homes."

Caroline put down her Salty Dog and looked squarely at him.

"Robby, that's unkind. We have plenty of friends out here and none of them have toilets that don't flush."

"The public school children, Caroline, are not from the same class as your friends. Your friends are more like those kind of guys who're movin' out here and buyin' up houses. Besides, they're *your* friends, honey, and not mine. I'm gone too much, trying to make a livin' for us and keep us in this damn house. My feeling is we should send him to Holy Nativity Military Academy out there on the other side of Savannah. It's a high-class place run by an order of Catholic guys called 'Sebastianites.' They're known to be pretty liberal in their beliefs towards other people, but still strict. If he can't be Jewish, at least he should get some kind of moral discipline one way or another to keep him out of trouble."

My ears popped up: I was totally interested. Mom gave Dad her special smile: Mysterious, utterly knowing; definitely skeptical. I could see it from where I crouched, but I couldn't see Robby.

Then her smile loosened a bit, getting broader, like she was holding in a joke.

"So that's what being a Jew's all about? Keepin' out of trouble? No wonder you Jews got the short end of the stick f'so long."

"Caroline, you're being hurtful. Please don't make fun of us Jews. I don't make fun of your own people and you know it."

"In a pig's rear end. You think they're all stuck up. You do, Robby."

"I don't. Honest. I just know sometimes there's a barrier between us."

Mom exhaled.

"Like you're hairy and circumcised, and don't look like them?"

He chuckled deeply, sounding like an almost empty oil barrel rolling down a bumpy hill, with a bunch of stones in it. It was an extremely resonant chuckle for a short man; it made you feel that Robby was on top of everything. Robby could do that, just like Caroline could do her smile.

He settled down. "It's an easy choice," Robby insisted. "Benjy's a smart kid—God, they let him skip a whole year in school out here. But he needs morality and discipline, and he's definitely not going to get either with a bunch of yokel kids who carry ringworm. So—far as I'm concerned, there's no argument."

Mom lit another cigarette. I watched the smoke curl up to the ceiling of the veranda. Liz suddenly snuck in next to me behind the door, and whispered into my ear, "What's goin' on?" I shushed her with a finger on her lips, but inside I was smiling.

Oh, how I was smiling.

"Holy Nativity's not cheap," Mom said thoughtfully. "You gotta buy him shoes and uniforms and that kind of stuff. And they'll make him go t' chapel. You want that? He'll practically have to be a little Catholic to go there."

No, I won't! I thought, shaking my head.

"No, he won't," Dad echoed my thought, adding, "I'll do a deal with them."

"Holy effin' crap! You're always doin' deals, Leon."

That did it! Dad got up and I could see his face, with all sorts of deeper frown-lines etched into it.

I supposed he didn't like Mom using that kind of language, even if we kids weren't supposed to be hearing it. But even worse, she'd called him *Leon*, which he did *not* like, especially if there were some sort of Jewish reference in the conversation. As in "deals." Even *I* knew Jews and deals went together like ham and eggs.

Mom's long body stiffened up a bit; her Mona Lisa turn of face returned.

"OK ... *Robby*."

"Better. Thank you. And please, Caroline, none of this *effin'* stuff."

"Sure. Whatever you effin' say, Robby."

Dad smiled.

"I'll give 'em the tuition money up-front and then give 'em some more, and tell the head father I don't want Benjy to be forced to go to no chapel. I mean—God's-honest-truth, Caroline—the kid can go if he wants, I'll tell Benjy that. It's up to him. It'll close to break my poor heart, but if being a Jew jus' doesn't do it for him then he can try Catholic for a while. For cryin' out loud, they ain't gonna bite him."

Caroline poured herself some more Salty Dog from its shaker, and gave Dad a refill on his martini.

"I think Josephine didn't put enough gin in this," she observed, tasting her drink, then added: "Don't bet the ranch on that, Robby. Catholics *do* bite. They can bite your sweet ass off. I'm not crazy about Catholics. Jus' call me some ol' hick WASP, but I don't like being told by Rome what movies to go see and what TV shows t' watch."

Liz and I were now cheek-to-cheek listening behind the door. She was puzzled; her eyes wide open. I put my hand over her mouth to stop her from interrupting anything.

"Honey," Robby assured her. "We hardly ever go t' the movies and who cares what you watch on television? It's all the same bull. A bunch o' lies to keep you sittin' till the commercials come on. Holy Nativity will make a man out of Benjy. Just you watch!"

2

Holy Nativity

And so, gratefully, I began attending Holy Nativity, a small Catholic military academy housed in sprawling Southern-Gothic stone buildings on the other side of Savannah. It meant getting up extra early to be driven in, and each day after classes, Mom would pick me up and drive me home. The Sebastianite brothers who ran Holy Nativity took the name of their order from St. Sebastian, who, I learned, was the patron saint of soldiers. There were all sorts of pictures of him around the school. Young and exceptionally good-looking, he looked like a Hollywood teen heartthrob, with beautiful wavy hair and lots of arrows stuck in him. The story was that he'd been a captain of the Praetorian Guard in Rome, and a secret Christian who performed miracles and was liked by tons of people. When Emperor Maximian, a disgusting pagan, discovered Sebastian's secret, he ordered that the saint be executed. Sebastian survived the arrows and was finally beaten to death by the Emperor's own personal detachment of thugs.

When I heard this story, all I could think of was Robby and myself—trying to pass as *something* or other in Isle of Hope—and smile. A secret Christian? How about a secret *Jew*? The all-too-obvious connection was certainly not lost on me.

Holy Nativity was called by the boys "Holy Smokes" or "Holy Nate." The story about how the school (with its name Holy Nativity; that in itself was peculiar for a military school) got to Savannah, Georgia, was also of interest. It seems a certain Father Joseph, an abbot of the Sebastianite order who had been brought over from England in the mid-1900s (prior to the Great War), was motoring alone down to Florida to visit his sister, a nun named Mary, who'd been teaching impoverished Seminole Indian children in a certain backward village called Miami. It was late at night on a chilly, starry Christmas Eve. Without warning, his T-Model Ford broke down in a rather dreary, non-descript district of Savannah. Nervously, Father Joseph set out on foot in this strange landscape and, to his amazement, stumbled onto a church—Catholic, of course.

It was all locked up, but next to it was a half-lit tavern. From there he was directed to a local priest, who cheerfully got out of bed and had Father Joseph put up by some excellent people, recent Irish immigrants. Even though he was a proper English gentleman (albeit *Catholic*), Father Joseph held no animosity *whatsoever* toward the Irish—who, it turned out, were extremely hospitable to him and offered him generous amounts of the local cheer. And so, when he woke up the next morning—with a headache—he decided it *must* be a sign he should start a school, right there in that dreary precinct of Savannah, to raise up with gallant military bearing Southern gentlemen of all persuasions (or, at least, to include Irishmen) and call it . . . what else? This made sense even to a half-Jew like me: Father Joseph *plus* Sister Mary at *Christmas* equals . . . Holy Nativity Military Academy.

Either you hated everything about Holy Nativity—the iron-hard discipline; enough homework to kill; going out way too early for military formations when you could barely keep your head up, and desperately needed to take a piss, a crap, or blow your runny nose; push-ups in those scratchy uniforms in the cold dirt for punishments—and got so down-at-the-mouth, screwed-up *miserable*, you washed out fast; or, you smartened up and learned to take it all in stride. And then everything, *pretty much,* just went along with the flow. And also, please keep in mind, for me, after being at school out in the sticks, Holy Nativity was a *breather*; I actually liked the place. I didn't have to think so much about being different at Holy Nate like I did in Isle of Hope, because, well, the whole southern Catholic military school thing was just . . . so *effin'* strange. That was the only way to put it.

Not "light-in-the-loafers" strange, but real damn *odd*.

The monks who taught us never seemed completely human. It was like they'd fallen in from another planet. They were smarter than regular men in some ways—and softer; and, in other ways, they were revoltingly harsh and hard. They could snap into a discipline that made your head pop, then suddenly make you feel that they were on your side. The fact was they were not there to be our buddies, yet we had a sense that many of them did like us. And then, out of the blue, something would happen that made you realize they actually had human bodies under their well-tailored, one-piece olive drab habits ending in flowing skirts, although most of the time we were supposed to pretend that this wasn't the case.

The first time they took us swimming at a pool, I saw Brother Alexis (known, behind his back, as Brother Alex), a handsome young geography teacher from Montreal, almost naked. He was tall and fair-skinned, as though the sun didn't hit him, with muscular arms and a big chest sprinkled with dark hair. When he realized my eyes were not moving from him, he sternly demanded, "Rothberg! *What* are you doing? Where are you *now*?"

I stumbled out, "Here, sir?"

"Good. Keep it that way."

I did a quick about-face and hurried to the other boys at the edge of the pool, who were all laughing. Tim O'Neill, a small, freckle-faced wise-ass, slid up next to me and whispered, "Yeah, Alex's got a big one. Hard to think what a priest does with it, but it's there."

I'd made friends faster than I'd thought I would. I had a feeling some of the kids were ordered to befriend me by the brothers (going along with Father Joseph's desire to raise stouthearted Southern gentlemen) who figured that, as a half member of the Chosen People, I should not be ostracized at Holy Smokes. In history class the brothers went on a lot about the Holocaust and what a wonderful job the Catholics did protecting the Chosen People, and how the Jews were no longer to be blamed for the death of Our Lord Jesus Christ. I got the feeling this speech was done specifically in my honor, and I squirmed when I heard it. Far ahead of their time, the Sebastianites were especially proud that Holy Nativity was one of the earliest schools in Savannah to be racially integrated.

The monks spoke in a very formal manner that men normally did not, at least not the kind of men I knew back in Isle of Hope. So, if I hadn't known better, I might have figured there actually was something *lightweight* about them; but I did know better, or at least I wanted to think I did. The boys wavered back and forth between idolizing them and at the same time making secret fun of them.

Robby was happy. I saw it in his face that had become even more lined and concerned in the last year or so. Something was going on, and I didn't want to be the cause of it.

"I'm *qvelling*," he admitted, pulling me closer to him.

I asked him what that meant.

"It's Jewish. It means I'm really happy you're finding Holy Nativity so good."

"It's not *so* good," I told him, wanting to sound adult and not go overboard. "But sure, I don't mind it."

"D' ya miss girls?"

I nodded and put a lot into the next sounds I made.

"Uh-*huh*!"

Robby smiled broadly.

"Am I glad to hear that, boychik! You need t' meet girls. An all-boys school is good for you. It'll shoot some steel up your backbone. But you need a few girls around you, for your own sake. We're gonna start takin' you to some dances at the Jewish center."

He pulled me onto his lap and hugged me. I was getting too big for that, but Robby still had not figured that out.

There was going to chapel.

At first when the other boys went, I stayed in the classroom reading and studying by myself. The boys would pile back in, full of stories about what had happened—who held the plate at Communion, who got yelled at, what the priest blabbed about; there was lots of smirking about all the dirty jokes they'd whispered while they should have been praying. I felt left out; this went on for weeks. Then, one day I just popped up out of my seat and joined them. As we walked slowly in line down a long, narrow corridor, I became nervous, clenching my fists with no idea what was going to happen, sweating profusely and imagining myself suddenly in the Middle Ages, during the Inquisition when they used to burn Jews. A pang of regret shot through me. What *was* I doing? I felt like I was going to pee in my pants. But I told myself *I* had decided to do this, and anyway I was sick of staying alone while the other guys were having fun (even if they weren't supposed to be).

Several of the brothers in their long olive-gray habits stared at me. Their gaze almost made me feel naked. One of them, Brother Ulrich, pulled me aside. Ulrich looked about a hundred years old and was notoriously stern. Most kids tried to steer away from him; they could never figure out where his shifty eyes might land and stick. The joke was that he was ready to retire—in the next century! Another joke was that before he took his final vows and was given the name Brother Ulrich, after St. Ulrich, he was called Mr. Mahoney. So he was *actually* the TV dummy Jerry Mahoney's brother and had a wooden head, too! Amazing, how kids had a way of finding out everything.

"Mr. Rothberg!" he growled. "Are you s'posed t' be here?"

Suddenly Tim O'Neill popped up beside me. I hadn't even been aware that he was nearby, occupied as I was trying not to pee on myself.

"Beg your pardon, Brother Ulrich," Tim said. "But I asked him to. I thought it'd be nice if he came with us. That way he ain't left behind. He won't receive Communion. I promise. He'll just be here with me."

Brother Ulrich lowered his face for a second like a bulldog thrown a bone, then his baggy eyes shot up again. But Tim had already grabbed my hand and I quickly jumped into a place next to him in the pew. I needed to say something to him.

"Thanks, Tim," I whispered as Brother Ulrich moved on, frowning.

He flashed this wonderful, wide-open, dimpled grin full of teeth, his freckled nose a half inch away from mine.

"You Jew-boys need to learn somethin' about Jesus too," he spoke into my nose. "Right?"

I shrugged. Who could argue with that?

"Jeeze," Tim went on under his breath. "Ol' Mahoney's just a dummy anyway. But ya gotta watch out for 'im."

"Why?" I whispered back.

"Cause he hates anything that ain't *pure*. You know, like fun. He *hates* fun. Some-a th' monks are like that."

Tim was small and scrawny; his wool uniform never fit him properly. A strong dose of sunlight from an ordinary windowpane streaked with dirt up close to the ceiling hit him. It wasn't stained glass with Jesus and the saints on it, but the streaking still made it interesting. The clear light seemed to go straight through him; I could see the veins in his pale neck and face, then I felt this feeling about him hit me as well. It was warm; I could feel it in my heart, but I didn't want to stare at him anymore—so I grabbed his forearm.

"Gotcha," I whispered.

"Cut it out," he said loudly.

We were stuffed into the middle of a row of boys who were all acting like something had been forced on them but they were OK with it for a while. I could smell their breath. It didn't smell like Jewish kids' breath, whose dads must have all been dentists. They had their teeth straightened and their mouths minted. Catholic breath was different: milky and dense. A priest at the altar said something in Latin and the boys chanted back. (Vatican II hadn't come into full effect yet.) Then the priest switched to English and welcomed us like we were all guests.

"That's Father Edward," Tim whispered. "They bring him in just for this. He does the sermons. If he starts doing this talk about 'impure touching,' he means jerkin' off. Ever done it?"

Since I was still a Jew or something close to it, I didn't want to say another word. Another boy shushed Tim who ignored him.

"Anytime you get a boner they make a big to-do of it. Truth is, I don't pay it much mind. My folks have six kids. I betcha anything my dad does it sometimes."

"What?" I asked, as low as I possibly could.

"Jerk off, Doodyhead. Wha'd' ya think? Everybody does it 'sept the priests and the monks and they get blue balls."

Tim smiled to himself, then grabbed my hand and thrust it directly to his groin. He was hard. I was shocked. I'd never felt a boy hard before, much less in chapel.

"Just want'd you to know what I was talkin' about," Tim said, grinning towards the altar. Turning serious, he said, "Father Edward is gonna *consecrate* the Host soon. That means he turns it int' the body of Jesus. I'll have to go up and receive the Host, but you gotta stay here bein' a nice Jew-boy."

Brother Ulrich started lurking by, staring at Tim and shushing him. He fingered the air in the out-the-door direction to show that he was going to have Tim ejected if he continued blabbing. Tim made a show of clamming up, and Brother Ulrich moved on.

Now I wanted Tim to talk in the worst way. Nobody had ever done anything like that with me before: let me feel his boner. Mom would have called it *audacious*. I liked the word. Tim was definitely *audacious*. I realized I liked him. It simply hit me; as if there were only the two of us there, although some of the other boys were squirming and whispering, trying hard not to laugh, like a punchy wave of silliness was hitting them. Then everybody shut up.

That was when Father Edward invited them to get up and receive

Communion. I wasn't sure why the wafers were the Host when a host was someone who had a party. At the seder I went to at Hebrew school, a rabbi led the service. "He's the host," Dad had explained. Now these boys were eating the Host. Was it, perhaps, pay-back for something the Host had done?

It made no sense at all to me, but I wasn't Catholic. The Jews had never mentioned impure touching to me. I'm sure it was in the Bible somewhere, but they didn't talk about it. It seemed the Jews had enough to think about, what with World War II and the Holocaust, without worrying about stuff like that.

After chapel, Tim sidled up to me at "free play," the thirty-minute break we had instead of recess. We were all in uniform, but ties got untied and shirttails were pulled out of pants.

"I'm glad you were at chapel," he said, offering me his hand. "I can't talk to a lotta these kids—they're too fuckin' Catholic! Everything's a sin, sin, sin. Even when they joke about it, they're still scared stiff o' hell and stuff like that. You're lucky. My dad said Jews don't believe in Catholic sin. They have sins of their own, like eating pork. D'you eat pork?"

"I do."

"Shit, that's no fair! You don't even have fuckin' Jewish sin! How lucky can you get?"

"Pretty lucky," I agreed.

We were off to ourselves. I liked that. When I extended my hand back to him, he held it for a moment.

"I want you t' be my friend," he offered. "Would ya? My folks asked me to be friends with you. They felt it was the good Catholic thing to do. They're liberals, know what I mean? They like Negroes and Kennedy and unwed mothers. My mom says we shouldn't judge, period. I know she does it, but only to people she don't like. They'd be cool about you being my friend, my Jewish friend."

He stopped for a second, then said: "Jesus! Fuck! Here's Storch!"

Horace Storch, disgustingly big and short-necked, walked up to us. Like Tim and me, he was also in the eighth grade and had a square jaw and an overbite. He loomed over Tim like a tyrannosaurus rex; he was a fat reptile. But he was only a bit bigger than I was. Storch was famous for being a bully. Behind his back, boys jokingly called him "Horace the Homo" and he hated it and would kill anyone he caught doing it. He started to pick on Tim, grabbing at him and punching him.

I told him to lay off.

"Suck my dick," Storch spat out. "You can suck it any way you like, Jew-boy!"

It didn't hurt me when Tim called me a Jew-boy, but when Storch did it was painful. I raised myself up to my full height.

"Shut up!" I told him.

"Gonna make me?"

"Yeah," I answered and hit him hard in his face.

Robby had taught me how to fight. "The worst thing you can do is hit a guy in his face," he said. "It scares him. It makes him wonder what'll you do next."

Storch grimaced, looking like he was fighting back tears. Another young monk, Brother Andrew, hurried towards us.

"Split up right now!" he ordered. "I don't want to see you two *near* each other again. Understand? Are you hurt, Mr. Storch?"

"Yes! I'm hurt!" Storch cried. "Call my parents! This Jew-boy almost knocked my tooth out!"

"You're not to use that kind of language," Brother Andrew insisted. "I won't allow it."

Storch lowering his eyes and tried to look smaller. "Sorry, Brother Andrew," he said, feigning contrition. "I shouldn't have cursed like that. I'm so sorry. Will you call my folks, please?"

I realized Storch could be an excellent actor. Brother Andrew asked him to open his mouth, and peered into it.

"Looks like your teeth are OK, Mr. Storch. There's no bleeding. I think your pride's hurt more than anything else. You walked up to them, I saw it." Brother Andrew shook his head. "You pick on smaller boys, Horace, and one day you'll pick on the wrong one. Just because a boy's small does not mean that he can't defend himself. Remember the story of David and Goliath? I think it's only appropriate that both of you go to the office and wait there."

Storch's eyes flared back up.

"But he—!

"I said the *office*, Mr. Storch. Now follow me!"

Father Greer was Holy Nativity's Commandant, the military school equivalent of a headmaster. He'd been a chaplain in the Navy, so he had been a real military-type guy and still had the posture and attitude to prove it. I had met

Father Greer when Robby brought me over to Holy Smokes to sign me up. He and Father Greer had had a confidential meeting while I waited outside the office, and then Father Greer had asked me to step inside, and asked me if I really wanted to attend Nativity. I told him that I did. (The fact was, I didn't *not* want to go, but I didn't say that.)

Brother Andrew left Storch and me alone in Father Greer's office, after a warning that God would be looking *directly* down at us, "So don't do anything the Lord would be ashamed of." At first, there was only God and Father Greer's secretary, an old maid named Dora Pilkin, who was out of earshot, but wore her glasses on a long chain around her wrinkled neck and could look in on us.

Father Greer's office smelt of furniture polish and tooth paste; I wondered if the Commandant kept a toothbrush in his desk drawer. Robby had mentioned to me once that guys who drank at work usually did that, to cover up the smell. "They always have great teeth," he confided smiling. But nothing seemed funny now. If Storch's parents made a big deal out of me hitting their son, Robby would have been hurt and maybe even angry at me. He'd said it before to me: "As Jews, remember, son: We have to act better."

Storch glowered at me; any previous niceness act had ended.

"I'm gonna knock out every fuckin' tooth from yer Jew-head, *Rat*berg, and kill you," he hissed.

Now I didn't feel so bad. In fact, I wanted to hit him again. I wasn't the bullying type; it had taken a lot of gumption on my part to stand up to Storch. Suddenly I was standing a lot taller in myself, which was perhaps the reason *why* I was at Holy Smokes to begin with.

I took a deep breath and released it; that felt extremely good.

"You're an asshole," I said calmly. "You're just mad 'cause I punched you *and* I'm a Jew."

"Fuck you. You ain't a *real* Jew. If you was a *real* Jew, you wouldn't be here with a bunch of fuck-ass Catholics. I was just fuckin' with you 'cause you were with that little queer Tim O'Neill. He's a cocksucker, y' know that?"

Now I felt truly lost. What was he talking about? I'd heard *sissy, fag, queer, fairy, pansy,* and *light-in-the-loafers* out in Isle of Hope, but never the term "cocksucker." Maybe I'd just been over-protected, living in our nice white house; but this didn't make any sense at all to me. How could Tim O'Neill be a cocksucker? I liked him so much. I felt lost. I didn't know what to say, so I said nothing.

Storch's face lit up. "Yer a cocksucker too, ain't ya?" His reptile face glowed with satisfaction.

Now I knew what to say.

"I'm not, Storch. *Not* at all!"

"Prove it, *Rat*berg. After school, beat up Tim O'Neill!"

I looked at Storch's face. I had seen better-looking mugs on voodoo masks in *National Geographic*, the ones that had naked pictures of black guys in Africa in them. I hated him. But suppose he got boys believing I *was* a cocksucker, even if I weren't? Even if I'd never actually heard the word before, just because Tim was. I was in a pure quandary. I put my head in my hands and covered my face.

"You *are* a cocksucker!" Storch said triumphantly. "Look at you, stickin' yer fuckin' head in your hands. Like yer cryin', Crybaby!"

Now I got truly pissed, I could hear Robby say, "You're not going to let this little *mumser* bother you." *Mumser* was Jewish for bastard and Robby used the word a lot, even with Caroline.

I grabbed Storch by the throat, just as Father Greer walked in. I let go of Storch, but Greer saw it.

"Gentlemen," he said, his very deep, dramatic voice dragging a load of gravel with it. "I've heard we've had some kind of altercation here. That's very *unseemly* of two gentlemen like yourselves. I hope it's not something frivolous, like a girl or a football match. Those things come and go, but sportsmanship and excellent conduct follow you the rest of your lives."

"Rothberg said something evil," Storch blurted out. "He said—'the Jews were right to kill Jesus Christ.'"

Greer looked at me. "Did you?"

I was shocked, even though I shouldn't have been. This *was* like the Inquisition, just without the funny clothes.

"Is this the truth, Benjamin?"

Now I was so angry it took me a second to calm myself. "No, I didn't say anything like that."

"He's a liar!" Storch asserted. "A liar and a Jew."

Greer swiveled his chair toward Storch.

"That's enough, Horace!" Father Greer snapped. "I'm sorry, Benjamin, that you've been involved with this. We've had trouble with Horace before." He turned back to Storch. "We're going to put you on probation, young man, if we have any more instances like this."

"He hit me in the teeth!" Storch cried, pretending to be hurt and close to tears. I had to admit it: anyone would be impressed with Storch's acting ability.

"Brother Andrew told me," Father Greer acknowledged. "But I have a feeling you provoked it. Benjamin, I heard you went to chapel today. It's most gentlemanly of you to want to know more about our faith, but no one here will force you to go if you don't want to. I gave your father my word. We are proud that Jewish students want to come to our school and show support to it. Horace, I want you to apologize to Benjamin for the lie you told."

"It's not a lie," Storch maintained. "I swear it."

Father Greer shook his head. "Don't swear, Horace. I'm not going to bring your parents into this. But I want you to start using your conscience more. Just remember the Golden Rule applies to all of Christ's children."

"He ain't one of 'em," Storch said resentfully. "He's a Jew!"

"Go back to your class, Mr. Storch. I'm sending Mr. Walters a note about this incident."

Mr. Walters was Storch's homeroom teacher, a lay teacher; in other words, not a monk or a priest. There was something even more humiliating about getting a lay teacher involved.

"Yes, sir," Storch said. Glowering filthily at me, he got up and left the office.

"I apologize again, Benjamin," Father Greer said. "We've had trouble with Horace before. Frankly, I don't like anti-Semitism. It's as bad as anti-Catholicism, both of them are irrational feelings. We want Holy Nativity to have a reputation as a school that welcomes anyone. Be they Catholic, Jew, or of any other faith. We are all God's children, like I told Horace, no matter in what form He takes."

I nodded. I wanted to say something like "thank you," but felt funny about doing it. Something told me that Robby would have just advised: "The less you say to *goyim*, Benjy, the better off you're going t' be." So I just sat up straight in my chair. The Inquisition part was over and I felt lucky to have escaped it.

Father Greer was starting to sweat some. I wondered if he really did have a bottle inside his desk. He closed his tired-looking eyes for a second, then reopened them. "You may leave now, Benjamin," he said.

I got up.

"Oh!" Father Greer jolted up suddenly. "Please give my kind regards to your father. He's been most supportive of Holy Nativity. It seems we're going to have to come back and ask him for an additional bit of generosity soon."

I dreaded every change of class after that. I was sure the bigger boys were talking about me, egged on by Horace Storch, even if he was only in the eighth grade. But they weren't. I was still fairly invisible, and that was good.

A few days later, Tim O'Neill met me after school, while I was waiting for Caroline to pick me up.

"I want you t' come for dinner at our house sometime," he said. "I have three bothers and two sisters, and I want you to meet 'em."

Two of his brothers went to Nativity. I had seen them around, but never talked to them. They were twins, sophomores in the high school section. They were tall and very good-looking with clear skin and athletic bodies. Everybody liked them; it must have been hard for Tim to be their goofy, runty kid brother. Against my better judgment, I told him I'd do it. He looked at me with this sweet face, and didn't say a word.

I extended my hand to him. He shook it and for a second didn't want to let go of it. I felt funny about that and removed my hand. Caroline showed up, and Tim disappeared.

"Who was that little kid?" she asked when I got in the car.

"Tim O'Neill."

"He a friend?"

"Yeah … a friend. I'm making friends. It's really good."

"I'm so glad," she said, lighting up a cigarette from the car lighter. "Want to invite him out?"

I hesitated. I wasn't sure how close I wanted to be to Tim O'Neill if guys like Storch said he was a cocksucker, even if I wasn't sure what that meant. It had to be evil though. Of that I was convinced—and you're only as good really as the reputation of your friends; Robby had informed me once of that.

"So, d' you want to?" Caroline asked again.

I shrugged. "Sure."

3

"Transubstantiation"

I started avoiding Tim after that. I felt bad about doing it because he was taken with me, and in the eighth grade having anyone so ardently taken with me was *un*usual—take it from me. He always seemed to find a way to sidle up close to me, and I'd be nice to him but not too nice. I had made other friends and we comprised a small group of our own: William Manion, a chinless math wiz with revolting, dead-stale kind of breath, whom hardly anybody liked; Melvin Harris who was from a rich family and always very upright, but pretty clueless about most things; and Alfred Johnson, a shy, smart black kid. Then I met a ninth grader named Arthur Gomez. His real name was Alberto, but it just didn't work at Holy Nativity; the boys would have joked too much about it. A Puerto Rican, he already had a good build which kept him from getting into serious trouble with bullies at Holy Smokes, even though he was only of slightly more than average height. Gomez had deliciously creamy skin a shade darker-complected than mine, and was immensely serious; he knew I was Jewish and in a very real way I think he liked it.

His family had come to Savannah through the fishing industry. There were few Puerto Ricans in Chatham County and the Savannah area then, so they were a novelty. He was smart and very good looking with a handsome face, like every feature on it was beautifully formed, reminding me of something out of an art book, or a photograph from a cherished period of time. Your eyes went to him, and wanted to linger. One day at free play we ended up alone at the end of the yard and he told me that he questioned the Eucharist.

I did a double-take. I actually thought that was a dirty word, like uterus.

"You know, receiving the Host. Transubstantiation," he explained. I was still blank. But at least I knew it had nothing to do with a girl's private parts, which I really wasn't supposed to know much about anyway. I didn't say a word. Arthur smiled.

"It's when you take God in your mouth and *eat* His body."

That still meant nothing to me. But it sounded queerer than anything I could imagine. I'd heard Storch say "cocksucker" enough to be wary about taking any part of a guy into my mouth, unless he'd just had a snake bite. Snakes did not seem to be a part of the equation here, but luckily we were by ourselves, so nobody could hear him.

"I know about the Host," I said. "But I never knew about this. You're saying it *becomes* God? How's that happen?"

Arthur exhaled nervously; his face became flushed. "It's—it's like magic," he stammered. "This teeny piece of bread . . . the *wafer*, becomes God. You take Him in your mouth and it becomes *you*. I guess you can do it because the priest, who's ordained by God, offers it to you. He has to give up girls in order to do it. So he's pure and holy; it seems that's why he can do it. That's why it's magic."

I nodded. As Robby would define it: it was a trade-off. But I was still lost. I flashed back to what Tim had told me about Brother Alexis having a big one, but what would a priest do with a big one? However, if he was so pure and holy and could turn a tiny piece of bread into God, then even having a big one wouldn't get in the way.

"Sounds pretty cool to me," I said mostly because I liked Arthur too much not to say anything. I wanted him to believe I was interested. "But you don't believe in it? You doubt it, right?"

He nodded, smiling.

"You get it, don't you? I *knew* you would! Cause you're Jewish. Doubting it's a sin; we're not even supposed to *think* about it, just believe it. Other guys question it, but most try not to think about it. You just have to believe it until it becomes a part of you, like Jesus's body does when you eat the Eucharist. You take it into your mouth, and then it becomes you."

"It is pretty *weird*. Kind of like a horror movie," I said, smiling and pleased with how smart I sounded. *Religion—horror movie*. I could see Caroline giving me one of her little nods, thinking how did *I* ever have such a smart kid?

I looked at Arthur, and he looked at me. I could feel it now, plain as day: there was suddenly a strange, but deliciously jokey kind of link between us. Like something I'd be secretly afraid of inside the showers at gym. He turned from me quickly, shaking, and I was scared another dumb kid would jump in and see us. You had no privacy at all at Holy Nativity; there were always kids or lay teachers or brothers around—or, even worse, the priests. That was the problem in a no-girls school. Girls, I was sure, gave you some little edge of privacy.

He calmed down, straightening up, and returned his gaze to me.

"You're a Jew so I can talk to you about all this. OK?" He had the deepest, darkest, most magnetic eyes and shiny, coal-black hair like fine silk. "My mom or dad would go crazy if they thought I questioned the Pope or anything like that."

"Sure," I said. "You can say anything you want to me. Just—don't tell anybody else about it."

Now I did feel grown up, more so than I'd ever felt around Robby. I also felt warm suddenly; this warmth came straight up me, starting in my legs. It went to my stomach, even directly to my heart. It was like a ray of sunshine on the beach; I was glowing but embarrassed by it, and I didn't want Arthur to see it. I was scared he'd realize how much I liked looking at him.

His face became utterly serious; I'd never seen a kid look so totally, beautifully serious. Usually kids wore this dopey blank expression of stupidity, and they didn't change it until something made them do it. Now he had stopped all that, right in front of me, like it wasn't all that big of a deal. I didn't smile at him. Finally I lowered my voice and said:

"You can say anything you want to me, Arthur. It's a promise."

There was a great silence between us which made the noise from the other boys at the end of the yard seem like distant explosions. I wanted to leave before some other kid came up and ruined everything, but Arthur put his hand on my shoulder and squeezed it gently. It was not something the Irish kids or even the Italian kids could do, but he was Puerto Rican so I guess he could get away with it.

"Benjy," he said, his voice almost choking. "I'm glad you said that. I feel pretty out of it here. Don't you?"

Arthur had no idea how much I did, but it was stupid to admit it. The truth was only dawning on me that I wanted with all my heart to fit in, to mingle with the other boys and never even think twice about it. But something always kept me from it and it wasn't just the Jew part or that I lived in Isle of Hope with two parents who didn't really fit together. What I wanted was something I was sure Robby knew about. Even the half-hidden "Leon" inside Robby knew about it; my dad and I both knew. But unfortunately, neither of us could ever say it.

I wanted to be like the O'Neill twins and the older big cadets I saw in their uniforms. That was what I wanted, but how could you say it in the eighth grade? I turned my head a bit and could see Storch and his buddies off yakking. My reflex now was to get the hell out, but I didn't.

"I've always been *out* of it," I told Arthur. "I don't think about it a lot,"

He smiled at me and more delicious waves of warmth flooded my body. I couldn't help feeling them even though I was terrified someone would recognize it. Just then, Brother Alexis strode over to us, wanting to know why Arthur wasn't with the other ninth graders.

"I asked him a question about geography," I answered, lying immediately for Arthur.

"And he's helping you?" Brother Alexis inquired.

I nodded.

"That's wonderful, Mr. Gomez. Great! So you're helping a younger boy? I like to hear that! But we don't like to see two kids socializing together too much." He pointed to the other boys. "Go on now. You need to be with your *whole* class."

Arthur shook my hand again, and we split up.

After that, however, Arthur and I hung out whenever we could. We talked about stuff most people would never talk about, like Evolution (which Arthur believed in) and integration (which he did not).

"I'm not sure everyone should be integrated," he stated emphatically. "That's why my parents want to keep us in Savannah, and not go back to New York where all my cousins are. There are a lot of bad people in New York, and my folks don't want us *integrated* with them."

I wasn't sure what he was talking about, but I remembered Robby telling me, "You have to listen harder than you talk," I wanted to listen that way to Arthur Gomez, when he told me things he couldn't say to other guys. But he never talked about sex, and if I dropped a word like *fuck* or *dickhead* or *asshole*, his brow wrinkled and his jaw clinched. Sometimes Tim O'Neill sailed up to us and went into his dirty jokes routine. He knew dozens of them; he informed me that his brothers told them all the time. It was hard for me to imagine the glorious, unfathomable O'Neill twins cracking filthy jokes by the mile. They were both halfbacks on the Holy Nativity football team and looked like a pair of Greek gods to me. I could imagine them carved in stone on a temple, then coming alive. I was amazed simply looking at them; then, as word got out that their goofy kid brother had become my friend, they started to say hello to me in the hallways. When they did, my heart raced and the other boys in my class did this funny little half-step away from me. I was no longer the Jew-boy from the sticks, but a friend of the gods.

I needed that because there were times out on the drill field (everybody had to do drill at least three times a week, even the kids in the eighth grade) when Storch and his pals would approach.

"It's that cocksucker Rothberg," Storch would say and I'd get furious, but could do nothing. First because we were out there in "military discipline" and everybody knew it, even the brothers in their robes did, and second because I'd had the *cajonies* to hit Horace the Reptile in the kisser once, but lost them when I was alone and he was surrounded with his pack of disgusting creeps who all had prick names like Ken, Pete, and Mike. They pretended on one hand to ignore me and on the other to know just what to do: like kick me in the butt when they were sure no one else was looking. I had to pretend that nothing had happened because if I didn't, it was all over with.

Of course, if I didn't do *anything* at all, I was labeled pussy. But there were limits to this, because sooner or later the brothers noticed and came over and ordered Storch and his gang of *shmucks* (a totally great Robby-Leon word) to go back to their squads. We were assigned squads for drill and the brothers were smart enough to keep kids like Storch away from anybody he could bully too much, in the same way they tried not to put too many pals in a squad. A squad was eight boys, and I was quickly made assistant squad leader. I loved that. So did Robby.

"I told you you're gonna do *great* at Holy *Nate!*" Robby rhymed, hooting with pride. "My boy's already an officer!"

"An *assistant* squad leader, Robby," Caroline corrected. "He's not an *officer.*"

"Gimme a break, Car—" Robby blew out a great big cigar-smoke oval, one of his special tricks. "If I say he's an officer, *he's* an officer. I'm going to tell everyone I work with that, so please keep the fine print to yourself. OK?"

I detested drill, but then everybody hated it. If you liked it there had to be something wrong with you, like you were pussy *and* gung-ho at the same time. It was always too cold in the morning or too hot in the afternoon when we did it, and our wool uniforms felt like something out of World War One. They could stand up by themselves, itched all over, and smelled like a wet dog. Luckily, my squad leader was my friend Melvin Harris. His dad was a prominent lawyer, which was probably why he was made squad leader, and he had this ridiculous Catholic-lawyer's-son, stick-up-the-butt attitude. Melvin had big clumsy feet and a funny way of still not knowing left from right, so sometimes I'd have to correct him when he ordered us to "Right face!" and led everybody into a wall. As eighth graders we did not carry rifles, which, with Melvin as our squad leader, was a profoundly good thing; I can assure you of that.

Tim O'Neill was not in my squad, but sometimes he would come rushing up to me just to smile and I couldn't help smiling back. He had an outrageous amount of energy, and always seemed so happy to see me. His hair wasn't red by a long shot, but out there in direct sunlight it became extremely red, like it almost burst into flames. Once, out of the blue, I just started running my hand through his hair. I just felt this impulse and did it, mussing it up like Robby had done God-knows-how-many-times to me.

Tim backed away.

"Don't do that, Rothberg," he said, his voice almost at a squeak.

Every eye on the drill field was suddenly on us.

Tim walked back to his squad, slowly, like he did not want to appear uncool. Out of the corner of my eyes, I saw him put his hair back in place.

Ken Ferris, one of Storch's reptilian friends, slid up to me. "Rothberg's got a boyfriend," he hissed. "I saw you two guys being pussy t'gether."

"Shut up!" I snapped. "You're a dickhead."

"Sure. But I keep my dick to myself and don't stick it up some guy's ass."

Ken was ordered to go back to his squad. He turned around and shot me a bird and grinned; I ignored it.

I wanted to vomit. I hated everybody. Why'd I done that? Why had I just let myself go and stopped being—well, stopped being *something*? I just wasn't exactly sure what it was.

I realized I was in deep shit. Like every boy in the school had seen me out on the drill field playing with Tim O'Neill's hair. And probably most of the brothers and even some lay teachers, too. I'd wanted so much to belong at Holy Nativity. Now it felt impossible.

I pretended that nothing had happened for the rest of the drill. Melvin Harris was such a stick-up-the-butt that nothing actually registered on him. The truth was, he probably had some genuine sense of Catholic morality, like you don't judge people harshly and everybody deserved Christ's grace and that kind of stuff, so he wouldn't make a peep out of it.

I spent the rest of my classes in a deep fog: A fog of uncertainty, even of self-rejection. I wanted to go back to Isle of Hope and be with my sister and Mom, and of course Robby. He would have told me not to make a big *megillah* out of it. He had said that when I'd sunk into a real black hole sometimes, when I was a really small kid.

Just before the final bell, I was pulled out of Algebra I by Brother Alexis who asked me to follow him into his "office," which was in a hive of teacher cubicles not far from the principal's office. It was about as big as a janitor's closet, with only a desk for him and one chair. He motioned for me to sit down.

"Sounds like you had an incident with Tim O'Neill and then Ken Ferris. Is that true, Benjamin?"

I glanced down and nodded without looking up. I could see the headline in the Savannah paper: "Jew-boy Goes Bad at Catholic Military School." I was ready for Brother Alexis to chop my head off and tell me to leave Holy Nativity, pronto.

He put his hand on my shoulder for a moment.

"It's OK, Benjamin. All boys get into things with other boys. Sometimes they're good and sometimes they're bad. My job is to see that you don't get hurt by it. Storch and his gang have been warned. We can't throw them all out, but we can make it tougher for them if they keep hurting other boys. I want you to feel that you can tell me if you feel that something really bad has happened. You don't share the love of Christ," he said seriously. "But you will have *our* love, I mean it."

"Thank you," I said softly. I hadn't expected Brother Alex to say something like that to me; that awful fog I'd been in lifted as he looked at me with his soft brown eyes under his beautiful dark eyebrows.

"Sometimes boys get very close to each other here," he said. "Especially later in high school, and sometimes they bully and hurt each other. The important thing is that you come out of Holy Nativity and love the experience."

He got up and put his hand on my head, and kept it there for a moment. Then he escorted me out of his office. The final bell rang, and suddenly boys were running all over the place. Despite being as stern as he could be at times, Brother Alexis was very popular and almost every kid said something to him.

He smiled and that made me smile as I walked over to the front of the school where Caroline picked me up.

"Anything nice happen today, Sweetie?" she asked after I got in.

"Yeah," I said. "I had a nice talk with Brother Alexis, one of the teachers. He said he wanted me to love Holy Nativity."

"That's sweet. Why'd he talk to you?"

I just shrugged. How could I tell her that some of the boys wanted to make sure I was a *cocksucker*? The whole thing was crazy. I had no idea what they were actually talking about. It all sounded too dirty, and now even Tim O'Neill didn't want to get close to me. He'd shun me...but he didn't.

Two days later, he started telling dirty jokes again. We were in the hall, and Arthur came along, and seeing Tim just walked away from us. I watched him disappear and wanted him back with us, but couldn't say a thing.

"What's up with that guy?" Tim asked.

"He just doesn't like jokes," I tried to explain. "He's serious."

"Shoot! He's gonna stay a virgin for life!"

"I don't think so."

Arthur was so good looking, how could that happen?

Tim went into this joke about a Mexican named Poncho, who had a dick big as Texas, and the Mexican's boss's pretty wife Lucy who gave Poncho pussy— pronounced by Tim "pooh-see," with a Mexican accent—and I saw why Arthur hated Tim's jokes. Many of them featured Mexicans as characters. (There were no Mexicans at Holy Nativity, so everybody felt free to tell off-color Mexican jokes.) As a Puerto Rican, Arthur might have felt sensitive about it, but something else also was going on. Arthur was too sweet and sensitive of a kid to like coarse jokes. Maybe there was something about them that he felt insulted his parents and himself as well. And if he thought seriously about the Eucharist and "Transubstantiation," a word that was too big for me even to get out of my mouth, then he must have been thinking seriously about a lot of things. He was a quiet boy, and his quietness at times came close to breaking my heart.

I liked being around Arthur and looking at him. He was so different from the other kids at Holy Smokes. I could imagine a clearing around him, some dimension of calm and peace where I might seek shelter in a threatening forest. When I saw him in the halls or at free play or on the stupid drill field, my heart did this rapid little dance and I had to slow it down just to hide how much I wanted to run my fingers through the thick waves of his jet-black hair or place them on his already wide shoulders. I was in the eighth grade at a Catholic military school in the Deep South and you weren't *officially* supposed to fart with a thought all your own, and I didn't want to—indeed, *couldn't*—admit that I already had a huge crush on him.

The O'Neills

A few weeks later I was in a tent with Tim O'Neill. We were in his back yard on an overnight he had invited me over for. First there was dinner with his family. His two younger sisters were away with friends, but his big, god-like twin brothers were there, and also his really small brother, Joe, Jr. Catholic families seemed more spontaneous and real than Jewish families (not that I'd actually had that much to do with Jewish families either—or Catholic ones, for that matter). My own family seemed to stick to itself, but I could tell that Catholic families didn't have that funny, over-conscious Jewish thing: like you can never forget for a moment that you're Part of the Chosen People and therefore know the *real* words for everything. I always got that from Robby, even when he was trying hard not to be Leon. Dad just couldn't stop being a Jew, it was too deep inside him. And Mom, basically she was a Southern girl who liked to drink Salty Dogs and smoke on the veranda with her friends. There was a contradiction there, with me always somewhere in the middle.

Tim and I were in sleeping bags. He farted, then giggled.

"Sorry. Beans. I told Mom not to make 'em, but she's always got t' open a can of 'em. 'They're good for you, Son,'" he mimicked her perfectly. "'Everyday thank Jesus we have enough t' eat. Your grandparents came over from th' Old Country, County Limerick, and they knew starvation, believe you me. You kids don't know from anything like that, and you're blessed not knowin' it.'"

"You guys OK?"

I looked up. One of Tim's twins was at the tent flaps. He hunched down and stuck his head inside the flap.

"Je-zus! It's hot in here," he said. It was Neal. I thought that was extremely funny, naming a boy Neal O'Neill. Tim told me he was named for one of his mom's brothers who had died in World War II, so it *had* to happen; there was no way around it. "If you're going to do sleeping bags, are you naked inside 'em? That would be cooler."

"No, dork-head," Tim said. "We ain't naked."

"Then you should be."

Neal reached in and goosed the hell out of Tim.

"Get your hands off me, you big homo!" Tim squealed.

Neal put his big palm over Tim's face, pretending to suffocate him. Tim used as much force as he had to jerk Neal's palm away.

Neal started laughing, and Tim joined in.

"I'm gonna fuck you in the ass!" Tim squealed again.

"Shut up or they'll hear you!" Neal threatened. "And don't say stuff like that 'round your company, you little piece o' shit. I was just trying to make sure you're OK."

Tim looked embarrassed.

"Sorry. I was acting stupid, wasn't I?"

"Z'OK," Neal said, getting up. He looked at me. "If you need to pee, just do it in the bushes. We been doing it for years on sleep-outs. I think it's good for the roses and the gladiolas. Mom loves her gladiolas. Don't she, Tim?"

Tim nodded. Neal asked us if we wanted some water. I told him no, but Tim said yes. So Neal went in to get us some water.

"He's bein' real nice t' you," Tim explained. "Cause you're my friend. Pat'll probably come out with the water, 'stead of Neal. They really love me. It's great to have brothers like that."

I was wearing pajamas inside the sleeping bag, and Neal was right. It was getting hot inside the tent. I unzipped the sleeping bag. Now I was thirsty, and glad one of the twins was bringing water. It was pretty dark in the backyard that went on for a long way. It was fenced in, but nothing like the backyard we had out in Isle of Hope that actually disappeared into real woods, the kind with raccoons, skunks, and sometimes even foxes. I would never sleep back there. First because there were too many skeeters around and second because Robby had told me, "We didn't buy this house so you could sleep in a tent." Boys liked sleeping in tents; there was something secret and wonderful about it. It made sleep-overs special. But I couldn't do it in Isle of Hope with all the animals, mosquitoes, big trees, and chigger-infested Spanish moss nearby.

Tim was right. Pat did come out with the water, in a jar, with ice cubes in it.

He knelt down. They were so identical in their looks that it made people smile: Like two kids could be that handsome. Tim was cute and squirty, but he would never be as beautiful as his brothers. I was sure of that. Pat did not smile the way Neal did.

"I didn't want to do this, but Neal made me," he explained.

"Thanks," I said and guzzled the water as he retreated from the tent. Some of it spilled on my pajama top. The backyard was very dark now, although I could see several tall street lamps beyond the wooden fence, with swarms of gnats flitting around them.

"They spray here a lot," Tim explained in the dark. "So you don't get a lot of mosquitoes, but you do get gnats. Neal's right. It's hot in here."

He squirmed out of the sleeping bag, cast off his pajamas and then peeled off his briefs. He was all bone and muscle, with very small nipples and a little uncut dick with no hair around it.

"I bet you've got hair by now," he said.

I pretended innocence. "Where?"

"You know. On your dick."

"Some."

"Lemme see."

"Why?" Then I realized it was a stupid question. "OK." I took off my pajama top, and rolled my bottoms and jockey shorts down a bit past my hips, so that the hair on the edge of my crotch showed.

Tim jerked down my shorts with his hand, snapping them hard against my skin.

"Why'd you do that?" I asked, flinching.

"You want a handjob?"

"*Whaa?*"

"I asked if you want *me* to give *you* a handjob?"

"No!"

"Why not?"

"I dunno. Guess I'm . . ."

"Scared what people'll think? Neal and Pat have been doin' it to each other for years. They taught me how to do it."

"But you got so upset when I just put my hand on your head—"

"I have enough problems at school. Like you ain't figured that out? That dickhead Storch wants to kill me."

"He's a piece of shit," I said. "I hate him."

"Good," Tim said. "So do I."

He pulled off my pajama bottoms all the way, and I pushed down my jock-eys. Tim touched me and I got hard instantly. I was bigger than he was, but I liked the way his dick felt when I touched it—which suddenly seemed like the right thing to do—smooth and thin and kind of cold. The small head came out of hiding. I had never felt an uncut dick before, or for that matter any other dick except my own. Robby had told me that some men, "especially *goyim*," didn't keep themselves clean down there. But Tim was clean. It had a very nice feel to it, as his foreskin slid back and forth close to the head.

"You really know how to do this," Tim said in a low, dreamy voice."

"It's my first time," I said. "I mean with anybody else."

"I figured that out."

Actually Robby had told me about jerking off. He told me it was time we had a talk about stuff like that. I was surprised, but so much about my father surprised me. He had no qualms about me seeing him naked. I remembered that we used to take showers together a lot when I was smaller. Then we stopped; I kind of missed it.

Tim started stroking me harder. Then suddenly, he put his mouth on my dick.

"Hey!" I said, and stopped him.

"It's OK," he said. "I liked you the minute I saw you. I wanna do it."

"Sure?"

"Yeah, just don't tell—"

"You know I won't. Besides, who'd believe me? I'm a Jew and you're a Catholic at a Catholic school."

I stroked Tim some more and then he put his mouth on me again—just for several seconds—but I made sure I got him off me before I came. We didn't know what to do with it, so Tim suggested we wipe it on the grass, down by the roses and gladiolas. We walked naked over to a spot where the grass got taller and it was easy to wipe our hands on it. I loved being barefoot on the thick lawn. Suddenly Tim grabbed me for a second, and hugging me close to him put his head on my chest.

Back in the tent, he said, "You like that guy Arthur, don't you?" Then he added: "He's strange. I feel sorry for him."

"Why?" I asked. I didn't want to tell him how much I liked Arthur. He'd really think I was queer then.

"His dad drinks. And I think he hits him. My mom's on the Parent Committee at Holy Smokes. She gets to see everyone's records. Some she's not even supposed t' see, believe me."

"What'd she say about me?"

"She knows your mom's not Jewish and your dad is and you think you're Jewish but you ain't really a Jew too much. My parents told me I should be friends with you. They're that kind of people. You know, liberal Catholics. In Savannah you got your Catholics and your rednecks. So you're better off with your Catholics."

"That's the way my dad felt. His name's Robby but his real name's Leon."

"He sounds cool. Can I kiss you goodnight?"

"Sure." I didn't flinch now.

Tim leaned over and kissed me on my cheek quickly. Then I kissed him on his cheek and briefly hugged him, suddenly feeling the way I had when I ran my fingers through his hair on the drill field: like an electrical impulse had run through me. I wasn't sure what to do, but didn't have to wonder very long, because in a second Tim was asleep.

He was almost snoring, completely peaceful, still naked, half-way zipped into his sleeping bag. I couldn't sleep. Too many questions filled my head. What was I going to do now—with Tim? That creep Storch was right: Tim was a cocksucker, but what was so bad about that? But, maybe, Tim wasn't really *like that*. Maybe he'd sucked his brothers at some point, but maybe they'd *made* him do it. The beautiful O'Neill twins made me feel kind of aflutter—just the way they came outside one by one to do things for us. There was something nice about it, but weird too. The O'Neills were strange, but I should have been used to strange people, living out in Isle of Hope with all the rednecks and now the rich light-in-the-loafers types and me not being either of them.

Restless, I got up completely bare-assed to look at the stars, the wet grass tickling my feet. Looking up at the night sky, I started thinking about Arthur Gomez and this whole stream of happiness, wonder, and delight came through him to me. Arthur was beautiful inside and out. I could feel it. It wasn't even a mystery to me. I couldn't avoid it. Would I feel that way about girls? I had no idea, but all I could think about was Arthur. I wanted him right there, and I had to admit something to myself: I wished I *had* done something with Arthur, instead of Tim.

The feeling turned my head upside down. For a second, I felt like I was hanging by my heels from the Milky Way, way up there in Outer Space. OK. You ready? I'd even *blow* him.

I was *that* overwhelmed with him, and that time in the tent with Tim opened up to me how much I was. I was glad I had found out a little bit more about him. I had no idea what to do about it, but I was glad I knew. It made me feel good about myself, and I liked that. I stopped wondering about a lot—like, Godzilla, was I actually . . . queer? And Robby: What would he say? Probably something *very* smart that would have put everything in the right place, even if I didn't understand it exactly.

"Choose your friends wisely," he'd say. "They're the only things beside *mishpacha* that really stick with you."

I started feeling chilled; my feet were all dew-wet. I had to pee, so did it by the roses, then got back into the tent where it felt comfortably warm and dry. I snuggled up to Tim for a second, then released him and fell asleep.

In the morning Mrs. O'Neill made pancakes for breakfast, flipping out about ten a second. Pat was still asleep, but one of the little girls, Margery, showed up, and Neal.

"You guys sleep OK?" he asked me. "Tim didn't do anything crazy, did he?"

I panicked for a second. Did he really want me to say yes?

"Sometimes he talks in his sleep," Mrs. O'Neill explained. "It's not crazy, Neal. Some children do it. You and Pat used to take turns when you were Tim's age."

"Heck, Pat used to sleep walk," Neal said.

"Enough. We don't have to tell Benjamin everything about this family. We're getting ready to go t' Mass, Benjamin. I know that's not part of your religion, but—"

"I don't mind," I shot in. "I can go. I just don't take the Eucharist."

"You mean," Mrs. O'Neill suggested, "you don't receive Communion?"

"Yeah, it's like Transubstantiation, isn't it? That's when Jesus turns into wine and crackers, right?"

"You been listening to Gomez too long, Rothberg!" Tim said. "It's what happens at the end of Mass, like at chapel. Sure, Benjy can come with us. He's almost a Catholic now anyway. I was showing him a lot about it in the tent last night."

Beaming, Tim winked at me.

"Were you?" Mrs. O'Neill said. "And what did you think of it, Benjamin?"

I looked at the pancakes on my plate. If I ever needed any kind of Transubstantiation and be turned into something that knew all the answers, it was now. I hesitated, then said:

"It's interesting."

"You passed with flying colors," Tim whispered to me after breakfast. "Mom's crazy about you. She loves the idea that we're gonna have a Jewish friend. She loves Israel. You know, it's where *He* was born."

We all took quick showers. When you have that many people in a house and only two bathrooms, and one's in the parent's bedroom, off-limits to the kids, showers are fast. Tim got in as I was stepping out of the shower; his small dick was obviously hard. He reached for mine.

"This is how nudists shake hands," he joked. "Neal taught it to me."

There was a knock at the door. It was Neal.

"You guys better get out of there quick. Mom's half-way in the car already."

"Shit!" Tim whispered to me. "I wanted more time here."

"We'll be right out," I called out to Neal, and decided to do it. I went down on Tim very fast.

"Now *that* was the Eucharist," Tim said, low enough for only me to hear. "Now you're one of us. Welcome to the club—*our* club."

After Mass there was lunch—tuna sandwiches—then Caroline picked me up. She was glowing that I had made friends with the O'Neills, a nice solid Catholic family in Savannah. She was smoking and we were listening to pop music on the radio. She sang along with it. ("My boyfriend's back and you're gonna be 'n trouble…hey-la-dey-lah-*deh*!") Mom smiled while she sang, feeing like she was still a kid who knew the words to every new song. But I was hardly interested; I was thinking about all the ghastly homework I needed to do, and of course about Tim and Arthur.

I tried not to make a big deal out of my being friends with Tim O'Neill, but the fact that he had two handsome big brothers helped. Neal was always friendlier than Pat. I thought Pat was the handsomer of the two, but maybe that was because he seemed more serious. There was something about him that glowed enticingly, like a distant star. I could joke with Neal, but never with Pat.

"You always shut up as soon as Pat O'Neill comes around," Arthur observed. "I guess 'cause he's bigger than us. Right?"

I just nodded; that wasn't it at all.

Then something really interesting happened: Pat started becoming friends with Arthur, in a very sweet and knowing way. He didn't smile at him, but dallied around him during change of class. They would shake hands and just look at each other for a moment. It was like there was this kind of strange, barely mentionable bond between them. Pat was not as popular as Neal, nor nearly as outgoing, and maybe that was part of the bond, because Arthur was shy also. Even Storch saw this. It burned him up, but he couldn't say a word. After all, Pat was bigger and everybody liked the two O'Neill brothers—when you think of it, isn't that what twins are for?—so even Horace Storch knew to keep his mouth shut about either of them, and Arthur Gomez.

Storch, I could tell, particularly detested Neal, but he drew away from Pat. Pat's self-contained solidity repelled him. It put Storch in his place, an ugly territory Horace Storch, like most bullies, hated to be pushed back into. Storch could sometimes put on his snarly, over-bite smile around Neal—after all, Neal was a great joker, too—but that smile dropped as soon as Pat was around. I think he envied Pat's quiet security, his handsome shyness. It burned him up when Pat befriended Arthur.

"Hey, Mex!" Storch would shout, strumming on an invisible guitar, like a Mexican band musician, and singing, "Aye, y'eye-y'eye-y'eye!" when Arthur turned up in the halls.

I hated it. I thought about telling Brother Alexis, but feared being labeled a tattle. Also, I wanted to keep Brother Alex on ice for a big-time fuck-up, like if Storch and his group of troglodytes (big word, I know: refers to apes) tried to attack Tim, Arthur, or me in the boys' room. They were famous for that, and I had stopped them when they had once cornered Arch Flanders, who was even smaller than Tim, and tried to push his head down into the toilet.

"He's gonna tell the *Prin*-ci-*pal*!" Storch screamed in a high voice. "Ain't-cha

*Rat*berg? You Jew-ass bastard!"

I didn't say anything else, but they let go of Arch, and I put my hand on his shoulder and led him out of the boys' room. I felt so good about that that I told Robby about it that evening out on the veranda. He was back, after being away for another three-week stint in Valdosta where he was working for a company that turned out aprons, kitchen curtains, and other stuff. "Home fashions," he called it. Sometimes when he was gone for so long, he would take quick trips up to New York, to "grab some *gelt*"—Jewish for money—for these companies, but it was still a strange thing to me. He had just lit up a cigar. He had a beautiful new box of them with him. Caroline did not like the smell of cigar smoke, and she stayed off the veranda when he was smoking one; so it was only the two of us there.

"When you grow up, I want you to enjoy a good cigar," Robby said to me, exhaling the rich smoke. "One of man's greater pleasures."

He showed me the box. It was of dark wood, with rich red and gold lettering all over it.

"Cuban," he explained with pride. "Smuggled in from Canada. One of our big suppliers got it for me. He's always trying to give me something under the table. He likes my business, and I love his cigars!"

I was drinking lemonade and Robby was sipping scotch. "You were going to tell me something?" he asked, sipping and smoking.

I told him about Storch's gang and Arch Flanders.

His face lit up and he smiled, all smoky blue eyes and deep lines around them; suddenly I remembered when I used to crawl into his lap.

"Don't go to Brother Alexis unless it concerns you directly, son," he said, flicking the cigar ash over the railing, then pointing its red end at me. "That's one of the first rules of business. If it's not your fight, you don't bring out your big guns. Keep 'em for when it's your fight. I'm proud of you, Benjy. I knew this Catholic school would do great things for you. You're making friends. I heard about the sleep-over at the O'Neills. They're a good family." He winked at me. "I heard they have two sons who play football for Holy Nativity. Fantastic!"

He leaned towards me, ruffled my hair up and blew some cigar smoke over it. He got serious.

"I know you've been going t' chapel and Mass. You don't believe that *mischigas*, do you? I mean, look—Jesus is just a figure. Like Hercules or Paul Bunyan.

He might have lived, but people made up a lot of stories about him. Jews have their own stories too. See, it's really all about legends and what people want to believe even if their brains tell them it's a no-go. The problem is, their hearts take over and, human nature bein' what it is, they get crazy when that happens."

I nodded my head. I tried to understand what he was saying, but it still made little sense to me. I was just glad he was there. Just like I was glad Arthur Gomez was, and Tim and his brothers were.

Robby looked at me. I could tell that his full attention was on me, like it used to be when I was tiny. He was looking at me with those blue eyes that could almost look straight through you. I was glad they couldn't actually; I was scared what they'd find there, and if he'd ever be able to understand it.

"You have a wonderful heart, Benjy. But you need to have a wonderful *kop* also." Robby tapped his left temple with two fingers. "That's Yiddish for head. You need to keep your good *Yiddisher kop*. Do you still say the *Shema Yisrael*, the prayer I taught you?"

I had to admit that I didn't. He smiled.

"It's OK. God hears the prayers in your heart as well those as on your lips. The prayer in your heart, Benjy, is that you're a fine kid, and you have goodness and decency. Look what you did for that Arch kid. Anyone else would have just said t' hell with him. You need friends at school, but don't try to be too popular. Don't sell yourself out for popularity; it's a mistake a lot of people make. I'm so proud of you, son. Just remember that God looks inside you because He *is* inside you."

I nodded, and he took my hand and we said the *Schema* together:

A few minutes later Robby snuffed out his cigar and we went in for dinner.

It didn't occur to me, even for a second, that I could tell Robby or Caroline about what Tim and I had done in the tent, or what I did in the shower to Tim, or had thought about doing with Arthur Gomez. But what was there to tell, really? It was *cool*; I'd pretty much stopped being *too* afraid of it. When you're a half-Jewish kid in the salty sticks outside Savannah, there's a lot you keep to yourself. I had no way of comparing myself to the other local kids, some of them from redneck families who seemed all big-time Jesus. Caroline joked that a lot of them smelled funny, carried ringworm, and ate dirt, but I never believed that. I thought they were just funny things people said about other people. Still, the wariness I had about the locals in Isle of Hope knowing too much about me spilled over into not wanting anyone to know what I'd done with Tim.

The O'Neills were definitely not like the people out in Isle of Hope; I was taken with them, though worried about letting other boys at Holy Smokes know just how taken I was. I didn't even tell Arthur Gomez whom I should have been able to tell almost anything, except of course my own secret thoughts about him.

Tim and I developed a telepathy between us. I would look at him and he'd know to get lost, such as when Storch and his gang came around. I didn't want everyone to think that Tim and I were pussy together. That would have been real shit, even though after a couple of more sleep-overs in the tent, we were just about that, if you had to know the truth—but then who has to, *really*?

Tim was always cool about it, acting as if what we did together was a joke. (It was a *lot* frankly, although we never, on purpose, climaxed *into* or even that close to each other. Sometimes something would spill onto him, or me, but that was about it.) I guess because his folks were liberal Irish Catholics from the South, he didn't have the kind of hang-ups that Southern Jews had, at least the ones I met at the big Jewish community center where Robby had become a member (and was known as Leon). With a pool and nice grounds, the center served as a kind of country club for Savannah Jews. As the son of a Jew, I was a member too. Caroline never went.

"Not my kind of people," declared Caroline, about the ladies at the Jewish center. "They want to wear mink in the damn summer. Effin' air conditioning up to freeze level! I wasn't raised that way."

I wasn't exactly sure how I was raised, especially now that I was doing things with Tim O'Neill that could have got us both killed at Holy Nativity if anybody had found out. On one hand, it certainly scared the hell out of me, but—on the other hand—I liked it. What else can I say? I'd wanted it, *maybe*. OK—I did. Boys were always talking about what they did with girls, but you couldn't talk about what you did with another boy. Tim egged me on, and before I knew it we were both hard and playing with each other, and then he would put his mouth on my dick and I'd do the same thing to him. Tim made this wonderful noise, like wind going through the trees outside, except it was coming from inside him, and he kept playing with my hair, and rubbing my chest and I liked it. Then I stopped. I was not going to let him shoot inside my mouth and we never went into actual kissing. I mean, *kissing* a guy? How queer could you get—a question that, in fact, I never wanted to ask myself.

All this time I knew Neal and Pat were pretty much aware of it, maybe even in cahoots with the whole thing. I could tell this just by the way they looked at me, when they saw me the next morning, or at school. Pat could hardly look at me; but Neal was much warmer about it, with this sly, strange grin that was extremely neat to a kid like me, but still had a kind of evil in it that made shiver. One morning he caught me as I was getting into the shower. He popped into the bathroom supposedly to comb his dark wavy hair. He smiled at me with that smile, and then suddenly his hand reached inside the towel around my waist and was feeling my butt.

"I'm glad you're friends with Tim," he said with his killer grin. "We like having you here, Rothberg."

I didn't say a word but tried to shift away from his hand. Instead, he reached over to my dick and felt it. The door was closed, but it wasn't locked. I panicked. Suppose somebody walked in on us, like Mr. O'Neill, or one of the girls?

"Don't worry. We always knock first," he whispered, reading my mind. "You have to, in this kind of house."

He smiled at me again. I looked at him. My heart was beating hard. The truth was I didn't understand any of this, not being Catholic or even actually Jewish. I wanted to be something—and know something, too. But what it was, I couldn't put into words.

We heard footsteps coming outside. Neal took his hand away and left. I took off the towel and jumped into the shower. My heart was still racing so fast I could feel it inside my ears. They had this odd, painful ring in them, and my balls hurt too. I decided I didn't want to go to morning Mass with the O'Neills. I called Caroline and asked her to come pick me up soon. Then I thanked everybody and told Tim that I'd see him at school.

5

Arthur Gomez

While all this was happening, I tried to get closer to Arthur Gomez. It wasn't easy. Sometimes he clammed up around me, like he didn't want me around, though he never said a word about Tim or the even the idea that Tim and I were pussy, which I knew some boys were saying behind our backs. How'd I know? You can just tell when you're in a small world like Holy Smokes. Storch and his buddies would laugh at me in the hallways, and once Ken Ferris pushed me into Tim, and yelled, "Now you two can get married!"

I told him to go *eff* himself real quick, and he changed his attitude pretty fast because he knew I'd once hit Storch in the teeth and I was ready to do it to him—at least in their eyes I was. Not being a bully myself, it was not exactly second nature to me to be a fighter.

"Why y' think some guys are so mean?" Tim asked me once at a sleep-over.

"Don' know," I said. "Maybe they're just born that way."

"Think their dads beat 'em up too much? My dad's never once beat us. Maybe that's why the O'Neills are good people. Think so, Rothberg?"

"Yeah. Sure. The O'Neills are good," I agreed, not wanting to think any more about it.

But it made me think about Gomez. If it were true what Tim's mom had found out, that Mr. Gomez beat up on Arthur, that didn't fully explained why he had become the way he was—secretive, serious, too quiet. Arthur was no bully. He was beautiful to me, and so mysterious that all I wanted to do was just look at him. Leaving school one day, I asked him where he was going.

He shrugged, like he didn't want to say anything.

"Home?" I asked. "Need a ride? My mom can drive you."

I figured he took a bus there. I never once saw anyone come and pick him up.

"No," he said, his head kind of cast down. "I don't need it. The bus'll be here soon."

"Sure? I'd like to take you. Really."

I smiled at him. Now I wasn't sure what to do because I hadn't said a word to Mom about it, but I was pretty sure she wouldn't mind.

"I'd rather not, Rothberg. I mean it."

As much as I tried for it not to happen, my face must have fallen; I hated showing my disappointment so much and tried to shrug it off, but suddenly saw Mom and grabbed his arm, in the same impulsive way I'd ruffled Tim's hair before.

"Come on," he said sharply. "*Let go*. I don't want anything from you, Rothberg."

I dropped his arm, but this time felt a little more steel in myself, as in no more dropped face.

"OK."

I saw Caroline's face looking at us through the windshield. She'd probably been wondering what was going on.

"I'm sorry, Rothberg," he apologized softly. "I'll see you tomorrow."

Caroline had the radio going on full blast when I got into the car. There was this new English group called the Beatles and she was nuts about them. She knew a lot of their songs in her head and sang along with them.

"Hi, honey," she said, cutting the sound down a bit. "You OK? Who was that good-looking kid? A friend of yours? A lot better looking than that Tim O'Neill, I'll say. What was going on with you two?"

"I just thought he needed a lift," I said blandly. "I don't know where he lives. Nobody ever picks him up. His name's Arthur Gomez. He's Puerto Rican."

Caroline smiled her sweet, kind of inward, knowing smile.

"Like in *West Side Story*?"

I looked at her blankly

"Musical. Leonard Bernstein. Based on *Romeo and Juliet*, about New York. There are two gangs. One's Puerto Rican and the other's your basic New York white kids. Kind of like Isle of Hope in a distant funny sort of way. Y'know, we have the rednecks and the other folks like us."

She smiled again, looking at me. I loved that Mom and I had these kinds of jokes together, something Dad and I didn't really have. He was too serious.

"Bernstein's a Jew," she went on. "So your dad likes him, you know how Jews are?"

I chuckled loudly and realized something: I had Robby's distinctive chuckle. Even she knew it. She smiled her smile, and lit a cigarette with the car lighter. "Jews are always sticking together—listen, anytime your friend Arthur needs a lift, let me know. He's so good looking, I'll be happy to drive him home."

"Thanks," I said, looking down at my feet. "I want t' invite him out to Isle of Hope. But I don't know if he'll come."

"Why? He thinks we have some kind of disease?"

"No, it's not that! I don't know what it is. I feel bad for him."

"That's sweet, Benjy."

She leaned over and ruffled up my hair, like I'd done to Tim on the drill field, just more of it. Her hand stayed there for a second, and I leaned over and kissed her on her cheek. She turned up the Beatles again, and started singing along to them—"'*Listen, do you want to know a secret? Do you promise not to tell? Whoa, oh! Closer—let me whisper in your ear—Say the words you long to hear, I'm in love with you—*'"

Suddenly, I thought, suppose she can figure it out? And she knows I'm—*women were like that*. Dad always said women knew things men just *didn't* know. The Beatles song about being secretly in love hit me like a brick on the head, but I had to pretend it meant nothing. She went on singing: "'I've known for a secret for a week or two. Nobody knows, *just we two*—'"

I tried to pretend nothing was happening, putting on a really dumb-kid smile. Now I knew I wasn't crazy about the Beatles, not if they could sing about stuff like that that hurt so much. I knew girls liked them a lot; even the girls at the Jewish center were nuts about them, although a lot of them still liked Paul Anka, Frankie Avalon, and especially Eddie Fisher, because he was a Jew.

For the next couple of days, Arthur avoided me during free play, either keeping to himself or hanging around a couple of other brainy ninth graders. Sometimes I saw him in the library, or with Alfred Johnson, the only Negro kid in the eighth grade. Skinny and athletic, Alfred was also my friend. I always thought he and Arthur shared the same kind of telepathy Tim and I had, except I was sure they didn't fool around with each other. The idea seemed impossible. Like I couldn't imagine either of them doing it, as much as I wanted to imagine Arthur doing it.

Finally, I got up the courage to talk to Arthur.

"How y' doin'?" I asked him during free play.

"I've made a decision," he said decisively, moving away from me.

Uh-Oh! I thought. That's it—*I'm over*! He knows Tim and I are pussy, and it's totally bad news. I was sure Storch had got to him. But I couldn't see Storch anywhere, or even one of his pimply-homo pals who preyed on good kids like Arthur. Suddenly I hurt all over for a second; the hurt hit me, kind of like the way it did when I heard the Beatles song.

That tiny painful moment felt like an eternity, as Arthur moved slowly away, but I knew something at that instant: I wasn't going to just *let* this happen. Robby would have been ashamed of me. He was the real truth teller in my life; I knew it. That's what a dad actually is for: To be the truth teller in your life. I pulled myself up—I mean it. I stayed with him, and made myself become as tall as I could, almost as tall as Arthur was.

"So tell me: what'd you decide, Arthur?"

His eyes suddenly misted over and hit the ground. Finally, he looked at me squarely.

"I don't believe in God."

(I stood stock-still for a second, and just exhaled, then I said:)

"Oh?"

(I wanted to say like hell, "Is that all?" But I didn't, believe me.)

"What made you decide that, Arthur?"

He started to tremble. His eyes were close to crying, and I knew he couldn't do that at free play. He walked away from me, but not before saying, "I gotta get outta here."

After that, I felt much better. I felt terrible for Arthur, but good for myself and also for Tim. I decided to tell Tim about it after school, and made him swear not to breathe a word about it to anyone.

"OK. Sure," he said, shrugging. "What difference does it make? One more secret. The O'Neills love secrets, but you know that. Is that Storch-creep blackmailing you?"

I wished we had more time together. But we couldn't do another sleep-over for a while, it was getting close to finals and we were both supposed to be studying our brains out over the weekends. I was up to my ears in work. Caroline was going to be there any second; I also wished that I lived closer in town like Tim and his family did. I had to spill it out fast.

"Arthur's going through shit," I spilled out. "He doesn't believe in God anymore."

Tim grinned his gigantic, dimpled grin. It wasn't evil like Neal's, but it made you absolutely adore him.

"*So*? Every kid goes through that," he said.

"I dunno, Tim. It seems to mean a lot more to him; I can tell it does. Does your mom know where he lives?"

"If she does, she wouldn't tell me. She can't tell me everything. I shouldn't have told you about his father, Benjy. I think it was wrong."

"No, it wasn't. I've got to do something."

"Why?"

I couldn't answer and I saw Caroline drive over. Tim put on his "nice kid" smile, the one he could slide into so easily around adults. Caroline saw it, and smiled at him through the window. Tim looked at me, and muttered, "You're crazy about him. Aren't you, Rothberg? Just nuts about him."

I grabbed his hand and shook it hard.

"Go fuck yourself," I whispered, and dropped his hand and sped off to Caroline.

"What are you and Tim O'Neill up to?" she asked in the car.

"Nothing," I answered crisply, and not in the nicest way.

"Come on. He's like your best friend at Holy Nativity, isn't he?"

I didn't know what to say. Suddenly grown-ups seemed like a total pain in the ass. But I could use the pain, I knew it.

"He asked me to come over tomorrow," I lied.

"Tomorrow's Thursday. Don't you have a lot of work to do, finals and all?"

"I'll have dinner with him, and we'll study together. Tim's a wiz at history. He's got every date in the world in his head. He's going to explain to me the Revolution and the War Between the States."

"How will you get home?"

"His mom'll drive me. Or else I can just take the bus."

"That's a long way. And I don't like you taking the bus late by yourself. You don't know what kind of people get on those city buses."

"You mean like light-weights from I'll-a-'ope?"

She laughed. "Shut up!" But the next morning, when she dropped me off at Holy Nate, she gave me a ten-dollar bill for a cab, just in case Mrs. O'Neill couldn't drive me home.

My plan now went into action. I would follow Arthur after school. I would see where he lived and what was going on. Doing anything otherwise seemed ridiculous to me, down right unthinkable. In fact, there was no other plan.

After school I snuck up to where most of the boys who lived in town took a city bus home. There was a special student pass that they used it. The buses had just been integrated, but there were very few colored people in the front of the bus. Just from habit, I guess, they still sat in the back, especially the older ones. The bus Arthur got on was very crowded, and I felt funny getting on it and trying hard not to be noticed. Arthur found a seat in the middle, past a group of old ladies at the front who always talked to the drivers—it was like a regular Southern old lady tradition—and I squeezed in, on the other side of him, through the packed aisle, heading all the way to the very back of the bus where an older Negro man was sitting. He smiled cautiously at me.

"We don' want no trouble," he warned.

"Yes, sir."

"Just keep t' yourself. Be cool."

"Yes, sir," I repeated.

I did that, and tried hard to keep an eye on Arthur at the same time. We started going through some pretty rough areas, shacks in the inner city, in a run-down section of town. Suddenly a big white man dressed in jeans and a work shirt, appeared and stood over me. I felt really tiny, even in my Holy Nativity uniform.

"What you doin' sittin' in the back for?" he asked, the lines in his face hardening into a squint.

The black man who'd talked to me earlier turned away from me, his face out the window, like he had suddenly disappeared. Strange: How could you disappear and be there at the same time?

I saw Arthur stand up; it was time for me to leave so I didn't have to answer that man. I felt like I had just escaped something evil, although I wasn't sure what it was. I just knew I didn't like that man; he was what Robby would have called a real *yokel*. I should have said, "Mind your own business, you *yokel*!" but instead I hurried out the rear door as Arthur left from the front.

It was not hard to follow Arthur. I could see the back of his uniform, and in it he was big enough and distinctive enough not to disappear into the sur-roundings, which were getting darker and more menacing. Most of the people I saw—some Negroes, some hard to tell what race they were—looked beaten up and poor. I could smell the Savannah River with its acrid sulfur-chemical odor from a paper bag plant not that far upstream; a nearby sugar refinery increased the stench. This wasn't like the familiar scent of Isle of Hope, with its gentle, sweet marshy fragrance that appealed so nicely to you.

To make sure he didn't see me, I ducked into an alley for a split-second, then emerged again. When I did, I felt as if I had disappeared too, exactly like the Negro man on the bus. It was an amazing feeling, being invisible, certainly *if* you wanted to be. And I did; I wanted to enjoy it. I decided I'd see no one on the street—just pretend they weren't there; except of course for Arthur. But be-ing invisible slowed me down. I was spending a great deal of effort not seeing what was going on, and determining that no one saw me, even though I was in uniform.

So soon enough, I lost Arthur.

He vanished, and I felt utterly strange; after all, he was the reason I was in this difficult part of town at the end of the day. Feeling lost and directionless, I stopped moving. My face dropped; I must have looked terrible.

A woman strode right up to me. At first I couldn't tell what race she was, in that she was what they called a "high yeller," or mulatto, with regular white fea-tures and very straightened-looking hair. She was dressed nicely in a short, red-flowered cotton outfit, but there was something about her that just didn't seem like any of the other ladies I knew, certainly not like any of Caroline's veranda friends, or even like Josephine's nice Negro friends I had met.

"What you doin' here, boy?" she asked. "Lookin' for somethin'?"

"I'm looking for a Puerto Rican boy," I said, not knowing what else to say.

She smiled knowingly. "Ah, boys! So, you lookin' for a boy?"

I wanted to keep walking, but she grabbed my arm. I tried to make her let go of it, but she only grabbed harder while smiling wider.

"I know a place where we can go find yourself that Puerto Rican. Just a li'll bit over here. Come on, Sugar. You gonna go with Q-Tee. That's my name, Q-Tee Johnson. What's yours?"

"Benjamin Rothberg."

"That's a real *nice* name. You a Jew? You sure look fine in that uniform."

We were now through a doorway, and in a very dimly-lit establishment that seemed part grocery store, part bar, and maybe even part some kind of a dance place, as there was a big open space in the middle like a dance floor. It was semi-dark, yet I saw shelves stocked with canned goods, loafs of white bread, and some vegetables piled up in baskets, like okra, wilted green beans, tomatoes, and onions. It all seemed extremely peculiar, like who would know what you had walked into *until* you had walked into it? There wasn't a sign visible outside to inform you what this strange place was, but I immediately noticed several men at the bar, all young and white and not dressed like the people I'd seen on the street. They were drinking beer, smiling and talking to each other like close buddies. A jukebox was playing soft, rhythmic Negro music, the kind Josephine listened to on the radio when she was working in the kitchen.

Q-Tee pulled me up to the bar. The slightly chubby man wearing a white apron behind it was about Robby's age, and like Q-Tee, if he had a race, I wasn't sure what it was. He could have been part Chinese and part Indian, too, for all I knew. He was very bald, more bald than any man I'd ever seen and had a striking face, like I'd seen in the movies—often in the role of someone you'd want to run away from. I thought, maybe he's a pirate, and they're going to kidnap me like they used to do to sailors on the old waterfront in Savannah.

"Hi, Louie," Q-Tee said. "This boy's lookin' for someone."

One of the men at the bar stared at me, his eyes fixed on my uniform. I felt funny for a moment; like I was in a circus and couldn't tell who was in the audience and who were the performers, or even if I myself were part of a freak show inside it. Then, suddenly, everyone turned and *all* of them stared at me.

"Here in the Grocery Store?" The bartender shrugged, then winked at me. "Come on, Q-Tee! He's kinda young ain't he?"

"Give him a Coke, Louie. I'll pay for it."

"I can pay for my own Coke," I said. "I'm looking for a Puerto Rican boy named Arthur Gomez. He lives around here."

Louie got a bottled Coke and handed it to me.

"It's on the house. That way no cop can say we sell t' minors. Anyway, how old's this boy?"

"About fourteen," I said.

"Sure too young to be comin' in here."

Suddenly all the white men at the bar laughed.

"Give 'im five years," one of them predicted, his eyes sparkling. "Yesterday's trade is tomorrow's—"

"Shut up!" Louie said. "This kid wants some information and, you, Mr. Destiny, are not helpin'!"

I stared at the man for a moment. He reminded me of some of the men I'd seen down at the boat landing, just not quite as well dressed. He was in an old wrinkled white shirt, and a blue tie that looked fairly cheap, too.

"Where do you live?" Mr. Destiny asked.

"Isle of Hope."

"Beautiful place. Some guys are movin' out there, buyin' up houses. They're gonna make it pretty *pissy* one day, you can tell."

"Destiny, why don' you keep your big fuckin' mouth shut," Louie said. "This kid's looking for a friend and you're—"

"Aren't we all?" one of the other men interrupted, grinning. He also had that look like he automatically knew more than kids did. I didn't like it, but decided I wouldn't be taken aback by any of this. There were things I needed to know, and I'd find them out. I swallowed some of the Coke, then asked:

"Why, *Sir*, are you called Mr. Destiny?"

"He's gotta be called somethin'," Q-Tee responded in his stead, as Mr. Destiny just smiled, hanging his head in an embarrassed way. "Why are you called *Benjamin*, and why is yer daddy called something else?"

I nodded; Q-Tee had a point. My dad did have two names that were used in different locations, although she had no way of knowing that. I finished my Coke and several Negroes came in, looking like they were more from the neighborhood, swaying to the music the way that Josephine did at home. I liked looking at them. Louie left the bar, went up to them, and whispered something. One approached me.

"You lookin' for the P.R. boy Arthur? He lives close t' me. I seen him and his family sometimes. He wears a uniform like you got. His dad's a fisherman sometimes. He been havin' problems wit' work. I'll take you to him, if you want me to."

"Ain't that nice?" Louie said. "This guy is Samuel, Benjamin. He lives around here, and he's trustable. Some folks might take advantage of a kid like you, but Samuel won't. Right, Sam?"

"Yes, sir!" Samuel replied. "But I sho' would 'preciate it if Benjamin made it worth my time."

"Samuel!" Mr. Destiny shot in. "I'll buy you a drink when you get back, if you take this young man to see his friend. That's the only decent thing to do. He wants t' see his friend and you'll take him. OK, Sam?"

"Samuel ain't gonna try nothin," Louie insisted. "Right, Sammy?"

Now I was starting to feel queasy. Suppose Samuel tried to rob me, or beat me up, or kidnap me? I'd heard all these terrible things about colored people at the school out in Isle of Hope, even though I knew some nice boys like Alfred Johnson at Holy Nativity. Anyway, I had to do something, so I quickly decided that Samuel—or Sammy or Sam—was known at the Grocery Store, among these obviously presentable white guys, too. So everything, as Robby might say, had to be *kosher*.

I put on my best "Z-OK!" kid-smile; but Q-Tee must have seen right through it.

"Don't worry," she assured me. "You go wit' Samuel." She turned to Samuel. "Sam, you do anything t' harm this boy and I'll cut yer dick off and you know it!"

"I hear you, Q-Tee," he said.

"You know I'll do it," she said matter-of-factly.

"Yes, Ma'am," he replied politely. "Let's go, Benjamin."

A chill shot through me as I followed Samuel outside and saw that the dark street was totally empty. What had I done? Suddenly I missed the Sebastianite brothers at Holy Nativity and the way they took care of me. This *was* the adult world, and it was no movie. Dad and Mom were right. I was still only a kid. Samuel moved quickly, and before I knew it we were at least six blocks away from the Grocery Store, passing an open field piled with rubble and all manner of disgusting garbage. Close enough to hear, a train sped by on its tracks, shaking the ground. Its whistle blasted out a shrill noise that cut through my ears like a power saw.

At the end of the field there were some scraggly trees, then a lone desolate building that looked like an abandoned hotel or an old rooming house.

"Yer friend lives here on the third floor, with his momma and some other kids. He's a good-lookin' boy, but keeps t' himself. I'd be obliged if you gave me a dollar for showin' you this. Nobody's gotta know about it."

Now I felt really rotten: If I showed him I had money, he might do something really bad to me; all I had was the ten-dollar bill Caroline had given me.

I reached into my pocket and found two quarters.

"That's all I got," I said.

"Tha's cool," Samuel said and took them. "Guess you know how t' get back home?"

I nodded, and watched him speed off. Gazing up at several rows of windows that looked dingily yellow from the street, I focused on the third floor, hesitating. Suddenly I saw Arthur at a table, looking at a book. I felt immensely better; now at least I knew where he lived. But aside from that, I wasn't sure what else to do.

I remained on the street a few more minutes, then nervously walked through the unlocked front door and climbed up two flights of splintering wooden stairs creaking with every step. On the third floor, I knocked. No answer. I knocked some more; finally it opened.

There was Arthur, dressed in an old, sleeveless white undershirt and a pair of ragged wash pants. I'd never seen him out of uniform. His eyes widened, like he couldn't believe it was me.

"Rothberg? What're you *doin'* here? How'd you find out where I—"

"I . . . uh, want'd . . . " I stammered.

"Oh, shit—you think I'm—"

"Arthur," I cut him off. "You told me you didn't believe in God. I just want to talk with you about it. Sometimes I feel the same way."

His face flooded with relief.

"OK," he said. "Come in."

The living room was covered with very old, cracked, though diligently cleaned linoleum in a faded rose pattern; its sagging furniture was horribly frayed. Arthur's mother appeared. Tiny, barely five feet tall, she had a light-brown, care-creased face and lustrous black hair in long, thick braids. Arthur explained she spoke almost no English. She smiled at me, holding out her work-swollen hand, and I briefly took it. Arthur introduced me to the four other children, all younger than he, then he led me through a narrow hallway, with two small bedrooms connected to it for the other kids and a closed door that I presumed was his parents' room. His was the last, at the very end: a narrow bed, desk, and bookshelves. He shut the door.

I went to the desk chair and he got on the bed, drawing his knees up to him. His large feet were bare but beautifully clean, and I noticed the way they looked with fine small dashes of black hair at his perfectly shaped toes.

"I'm lucky," he said. "I've got a room of my own, 'cause I'm at the big school with all the priests. That means a lot to a Catholic family like this."

I could tell he was nervous; I looked around at the small room. His wool uniform was hung neatly on a hanger from a nail in the wall; I felt like it was witnessing us. I saw several pictures of him that might have been taken at Sears, with their kind of imaginary background of fake studio clouds and too-bright lighting. They always made you stare at the camera to keep from blinking. Arthur didn't look nearly as good in those pictures as he did sitting on his bed. We looked at each other for a second and without even trying to, I started smiling. I couldn't help it after thinking so much about him at those sleep-overs at Tim's. Now I was in his bedroom; all I could do was exhale softly from relief.

He smiled back at me, cautiously.

"It was good of you to come, Rothberg," he said. "Sorry if I wasn't so nice t' you at school. Remember how I said I felt so out of it at Holy Nativity? Well, Jesus-*fuck*, I feel worse now."

He stopped smiling. I looked into his eyes. They were so dark and sad; they reminded me of his small mother's.

"Why, Arthur? Tell me, please. I want to know. I do."

He nodded gently.

"I believe you," he said softly. "I never had a friend like you."

I felt myself reaching out towards him, even though I stayed glued to that seat by the desk. But it was like my soul was suddenly right there on the bed with him. I had to say something, even though I stayed silent for several seconds, just absorbing the moment.

"Maybe it's the Jewish thing," I said, trying to make sense for both of us. "It makes you understand what it's like to look at the world from a different place. I mean, I like Holy Smokes. I feel close to some of the brothers, like Brother Alex—Alexis. He kind of makes me feel like my dad does."

After I'd said the word "dad," Arthur started to shake, then cry.

Tears came from him; I felt simply awful. I didn't want him to cry. I got up, and without thinking went over to him, but still didn't touch him or anything like that.

"My dad hates me," he said, trying to sniff away his tears. "I disappoint him. He gets so fuckin' angry, he hits me just for breathing. We had nothing in Puerto Rico. We were like dirt. He had ten brothers and sisters and most went up to

New York, but Dad said he *didn't want to live on welfare in no barrio.* 'Least I gotta chance here. I can fish, do some work.'

"But he started drinking and beating my mom. He'd beat me and tell me, 'You think I'm jus' a dumb spic cause you goin' t' school with the Anglos, the Upper Crust, and you know more than everybody!' I *never* thought that. He accuses me of being a *puta*, a *maricon,* because I don't have any interest in girls now. Is that so bad? Benjy—are you interested in girls?"

I had to say something; I had to lie to him.

"Sure," I answered. "I guess I'm interested in girls."

"Some guys at school think you and Tim are pussy. Is that true?"

"You mean Storch?" I shouted, unable to control myself. "He's only a turd with a name attached to it. That's all he is!"

Now I felt really bad. I hadn't wanted to get so angry. As I tried to calm myself, I heard a loud knock. The bedroom door flew open, and a very big man in a torn undershirt appeared.

Arthur jumped off his bed and stood up.

"Papi, this is Benjamin Rothberg—from school," he said, wiping his eyes, flustered.

Arthur's father had dark brown features and arms like a heavyweight boxer, attached to wide shoulders and a puffed-out chest with a huge belly stuck under it.

"Hello, Mr. Gomez," I said, extending my hand to him

He ignored me.

"You two studyin', Alberto?" he asked his son.

"Sure, Papi."

"Good. It better jus' be studyin'. You need t' make those grades, boy. You lose that scholarship and it's all over with. Things is bad enough, right?" He turned to me. "You got a little color in your skin, Benjamin. Anybody ever give you problems with that?"

"No, sir," I said. I wasn't sure what else to say.

"How you like Savannah, Georgia?"

"I was born here. I don't know anything else."

"People here don't hate the Spanish people the way they hate th' coloreds, but it still ain't good. When I got here, a lotta people thought *I* was colored. I jus' didn't have the kinky hair. They didn't even want t' let me work on a damn shrimp boat, just t' do the kinda work colored guys do. Now some coloreds own their own boats and I'm glad for it. But things they get tough and"—he paused, embarrassed suddenly— "I start drinkin'. Guess you know 'bout that. Alberto tell you his *papi* drinks?"

"No, sir. I don't know anything about you."

He stared seriously at me again, then broke into a smile.

"OK! You two go on an' study."

Suddenly he laughed, but it was a brutal, forced laugh, like the guys at the docks made.

"I don' wanna hear 'bout you two gettin' into no kinda trouble. Hear?"

He turned and left, slamming the door behind him.

"I think you'd better go," Arthur said.

I realized he was right. First, because it was getting late, and I'd have to get back to Isle of Hope; and second, because some part, deep inside me, wanted to get back on the bed with Arthur and simply touch him—even after meeting his father who, I knew, would kill both of us for doing that. How did I know it? I could just *look* at Mr. Gomez and know it; but how would I go about touching him—I had no idea. I wasn't Tim; *he* would know about these things. I wasn't sure where I'd touch him, either. Maybe his hair: It was so dark and in such thick waves, throwing off an almost bluish streak of light, reminding me of evening tides on the beach. But there was no way even to think about touching it, and I knew it.

"I wish we could talk some more," I said. His face fell. I could see that, although I was sure he didn't want me to notice it. "Maybe you can come out to Isle of Hope sometime. I'm sure my mom would like that." But somehow I knew, it would never happen.

"How are you going to get back home?" he asked.

"I have money for a cab."

"That's good. I never get money like that. Guess you can see why. I'll walk with you down the street. Maybe we can find something."

He put on his shoes. His father was not around as we left the apartment. We could hear his mom talking in Spanish to the other kids who were jumping around every place. I liked hearing Spanish, the way it sounded. As we passed the Grocery Store, I noticed there was only a small sign for Pabst Blue Ribbon beer in the window. I asked Arthur if he ever went inside.

"Why would I do that? My dad says it's for perverts. People around here talk about it. Some colored guys go in there, but they'll do anything. It's just a part of their nature, I can't figure it out."

We walked about ten blocks, getting closer to the downtown district. I didn't feel scared anymore with Arthur next to me; there was something so beautiful and solid about him. Suddenly I wished I could hold his hand, but it was out of the question. I hated that he asked if Tim and I were pussy. I'd hoped that he wouldn't be a part of that kind of thinking. But I figured it was just something any boy would ask; the real difference would be in how he might take any truthfulness in the answer. On a street close to a movie theatre showing a Marilyn Monroe movie, we saw a cab parked with a driver in it. I was glad to see the cab, then thought: suppose one of the older boys from Holy Smokes saw me in my uniform walking with Arthur at night, what would he think?

Well, maybe nothing. I flicked the idea away and approached the cab. The driver looked like he was about a hundred-and-two years old. He was smoking and listening to country music on the radio. I looked into his window.

"I need to go t' Isle of Hope," I said.

"That's gonna cost you, kid. Least about eight bucks."

"OK," I said. I turned to Arthur and shook his hand again.

He pulled me closer to him, but without hugging me.

"I'm really glad you came, Rothberg. I'll see you tomorrow at school."

6

Andy Geyer

In the cab on the way back, the old man yakked and yakked, mostly about how the Negroes had taken over Savannah, and a decent white man could not get a job anymore because of Washington and the strange notions they had up there. I didn't say a word to him, but when we drove up to my house, Caroline was waiting by the door with all the lights on outside. She hurried over and met the cab.

"Thank God you're back. I was getting scared about you. I thought about calling the O'Neills."

When she said that, I thought my heart would flip over. I handed the driver the ten-dollar bill.

"You want change from this, kid?"

"Sure he does!" Caroline said. She grabbed the two dollars from him, and handed him back one. "That's enough."

With her arm around me, she led me back into the house.

"Andy's here," she said. "We've been wondering when you're going to show up. Liz is already in bed, and you should be, too."

Andy Geyer was Robby's business partner. He appeared on the front porch as Mom and I approached. A few years older than Dad, much heavier and balding, he reminded me of a warthog, with a habitual look of disapproval on his face. He and Dad had been friends since the Korean War, the "Forgotten War," which they were both in. Dad never talked about the war; he hated it. He had been wounded and sent home early. All he could say to me was "Thank God you'll never have to fight in one. I don't care if those Koreans eat each other like dogs, I don't want you in something like that."

(It was funny, though, that he had sent me to a military school and a Catholic one at that, but Dad was full of contradictions. He was all contradictions, really. Maybe we all are.)

"Hiya, boychik!" Andy shouted at me. He pulled me away from Caroline and started fake-punching me. I hated that, but at least he wasn't bear-hugging me with his big B.O.-cheap-cigar smell. Robby smoked cigars, expensive ones, every now and then, but this man smelled like a filling station urinal, one with old stogie butts floating in it.

"Wha-cha been up to?" he asked. "Hear you been gettin' military schoolin'. Great! Met any nice girls there?" He laughed this rude belly laugh that sounded like it came from a cartoon pig. Even his laugh seemed to have big, fat, gross pig hairs sticking out of it, the same way Andy always had a cheap cigar sticking out of his mouth. I pretended to smile.

Andy put his fat arm around me. I flinched, but he kept it there.

"There's something I gotta talk t' you about. Caroline, please forgive me, but we got some real man-talkin' to do. We'll go in the den."

"Do you want a scotch with you?" she asked.

"Sure. I'll have it after we talk."

Andy came by regularly and virtually had his own room, the den, set up for him. After he left, it stank of cigars and his smelly feet and his underarms. Robby was so different, with a smell I liked. Even his cigars and breath smelled different. Still, when Robby and Andy were together there was something about them, like Robby really became *Leon* again—this very different man, from another world. The *big* world, the world of Jews and money and some kind of shared past that went from the crowded streets of New York to Korea to Savannah, Georgia, to beautiful Isle of Hope, then it circled back to New York money again.

Josephine had already made up the fold-out bed in the den. Andy had his suitcase open, and there were shirts and socks out. A striped tie was draped over a side table, next to an ashtray already stinking with his cigar butts. I hated the smell, but with Robby gone so much, there would be Andy around. That was a fact of life. Actually, we didn't use the den a lot. My folks stayed up on the veranda or in the backyard unless the weather was bad. Sometimes we'd watch TV in it, but there was another TV upstairs in their room and we liked watching it better in there, especially if Dad were away.

Andy plopped down into one of two big stuffed, blue-chintz upholstered chairs. He tried to pull me onto his lap, but I dove onto the other chair to escape him.

"I guess you're too big for my lap now," he said sighing heavily. "Benjy, you know your dad and me been friends for a long time. Fact is, I can't remember when we weren't. After the war, he came here and he brought me with him. He was sick of being up North. You know, there are good Jews and bad Jews, and frankly he didn't like the bad Jews up there. Know what they call bad Jews?"

I thought hard for a second. "Christ-killers?"

"No, Benjy! Where'd ja get *that* crap! Is that what they teach you in that Catholic school?"

"No, I heard it out here," I said.

"Makes sense. Yokels! 'Tween you and me, I prefer *shwartzes* any day. The black people, they have soul. And dignity. A lot of Jews don't even have that. No, my friend, they call bad Jews *kikes*. It's a' evil word, and they have lots of 'em in New York. All they care about is money, money, money. I'm glad you're not one of 'em, and neither is your wonderful dad. He's decency itself. I love every hair on that man, I mean it."

He took out a big handkerchief that looked like it was stained with tobacco and blew his nose. Andy was an emotional man. He and Dad used to get into big arguments and end up hugging each other. He recomposed himself and gave me a big smile. At that moment I realized, it was possible to *like* Andy. I knew Caroline did, although grudgingly and in spite of his smell. He lit another cigar and shaped the smoke into a series of fuzzy big rings wafting up into the ceiling.

My eyes followed the rings. Andy could blow beautiful smoke rings, not easy with a cigar. I had to give that to him.

"Your dad wants you to get *bar mitzvahed*. Know what that means?"

My head left the smoke rings.

"Sure."

I'd heard about it at the Jewish center. All the boys my age were getting bar mitzvahed. They loved the presents, but you had to take the lessons and stuff seriously, and since Caroline was a non-Jew and, Jewish-wise, I was kind of sitting on the fence, the idea had not seriously entered my mind.

"It would mean a *great* deal to him, Benjy," Andy went on. "It's his great wish right now. See, things ain't goin' real good for him. I think you should know that."

"What do you mean?" I asked cautiously. I still had no idea what Dad really did. Money was like this strange magical material to me. He pulled it in, and

Caroline spent it. I knew Mom came from money. Her people, my grandparents, the Blakelys, were well off. I'd been told they went back a long, long way and had never, ever been poor, like Arthur was. The Blakelys didn't come out to Isle of Hope often. I wondered if they ever really liked Dad. They liked Liz though. For some reason I thought they liked her more than me; I could feel it, especially from Grandma Blakely. She always had her face powdered, her lipstick perfect, and looked like she'd never gone out in the sun. She wore very nice clothes but was slightly chubby; Mom said she was born in a girdle.

Now I had to listen. I wanted to know more.

"It's like this, Benjy. Several years ago your dad and me put together this business out in the sticks in the South. We worked for smaller companies that wanted to hire real *kops*. I mean brains like Jews have for business. We'd tell 'em what kind of loans to take out, how to expand, look at their books and tell 'em where they were going wrong, what kind of stuff to buy for their factories. And we'd stick around and guide 'em. Honest, you got no idea what we did for people down here. There was nothing like this until you got to Atlanta, or maybe Nashville. It used to be hard for some of 'em to get money. So your dad and I kept the big Yankee banks from robbing some of these little companies blind, and we kept a lot of people in work. Now the South is growing. Even Savannah's growing. Our problem is, at the moment things ain't going so nice for us. So it'd mean a lot to your dad if you got bar mitzvahed."

"What do I have to do?"

"You gotta study the prayers and be respectful of people. That ain't hard, you're a respectful kid. I'm just not sure where to do it, 'cause the big synagogue in Savannah may not be too keen on this. Technically, you're not a Jew, and your mom, if you get my drift, just ain't too hot to convert."

"Would I have to convert?"

"No, boychik. Far as I'm concerned, you're more Jew than I am. I mean it. I'd give up my blood for you. I did it once for your dad, during the war. I opened up my arm for him and he knows it. He was gonna die, see, and I dragged him back to the medic's tent and kept him alive."

I knew nothing about that. Dad was always reticent to talk about the war. I looked at Andy eye-to-eye now, seriously, just like Robby would do. But all Andy could do was nod at me, his eyes blood-shot, with a slightly crooked grin.

Caroline appeared at the doorway of the den. She had two drinks in her hands.

"Do you want that scotch now?"

"Sure. Caroline, you got yourself one great kid here. He's gonna go for it!"

"The bar mitzvah?" she asked.

"What else? I got a friend whose son will prepare him. His name is Solomon Bernstein. He's a cantorial student somewhere up in Baltimore. Truth is, he wanted to be a' opera singer, like Jan Pierce, but got cold feet. But he takes on students. Boychik'll like him. He's young and he's a patient teacher."

(That, he was not; but I learned that later.)

Mom looked at me seriously. She handed Andy a scotch and sipped on one that she had started for herself. How grown-ups could drink scotch was beyond me, but a lot of what they did also was. For instance: why wasn't Dad there, and why had he sent Andy to talk to me about the bar mitzvah?

"Are you OK with this?" she asked. "You really don't have to do it, if you don't want to."

"He wants to!" Andy said. He looked at me without smiling. "Don't you?"

The way he looked at me was peculiar. I can say that up to that point in my life, I'd never had an adult look at me in exactly that way: It made me feel that I was in control, but if I didn't do what he wanted me to do, I'd hurt him too much. And hurt Robby as well, and that idea seemed as revolting to me as telling any of them what I'd done with Tim O'Neill.

"Sure, I want to do it," I said eagerly. "The problem is, I don't know no Hebrew or nothing like that."

"*Any* Hebrew," Caroline corrected me. "Will that stand in his way?"

"Naw," Andy said, drinking down a lot of the scotch like it was Coke. "This is good, I mean the hooch. No Hebrew is not bad. Mostly you'll learn it by heart, and you sing most of it, so it's like singing the 'Star Spangled Banner.' Who the hell knows what that means? I always thought it was about some *shlemiel* named O'Say and what he could see. 'O'Say, can you see?' Anyway, you'll get the hang of that fast. The important thing is that you do it right after your thirteenth birthday, and Leon's there—I mean Robby. Y'know it means a lot to him, so you'll do it, *right*?"

7

Bar Mitzvah Lessons

My birthday was in the fall, which didn't give me a lot of time to prepare, and it meant that the summer ahead was not going to be as carefree as I'd thought. Andy gave Mom Solomon Bernstein's address and then set up an appointment for us with him. That weekend, Mom drove me over to his house. He was living with his mom in a nice section of Savannah. It wasn't splurgy, just a pleasant section of older bungalows with big front yards showing lots of azalea and camelia bushes in front of them. She dropped me off and stayed in the car, and I knocked at the door.

He came to the door wearing a t-shirt, some cheesy, cheap shorts, and flip-flops. He was about twenty-six, and kind of squishy looking, like he was still half baby-fat, even though he was already losing some hair on his orangy-blond head. I waved to Mom, and she drove off.

"You must be Benjy," he said. "I'm Solomon, but you can call me Solly. Sounds Chinese, I know, but everybody does it. Come in."

He offered me some water to drink, and that was all. Usually people in Savannah offered you ice tea or Coke and maybe even some cake. It was the Southern thing to do, but he wanted to get on to business.

"So you don't know any Hebrew at all?" he asked.

"I remember a couple of letters," I said. "Hebrew school just didn't work out for me."

"That's OK. The important thing is, can you take instruction? If I show you something, can you repeat it?" I told him I would try.

"Good."

He went to an upright piano in the living room, and started playing notes. He asked me if I could identify any of them; I couldn't. Then he sang something and asked me to repeat it. They were just a bunch of sounds in strange patterns

I'd never heard before, and I couldn't understand them. Obviously I didn't have Caroline's talent for singing along with the radio. He repeated his singing several times, and I listened as hard as I could. Then he asked me to sing along with him. I tried really hard but the sounds still evaded me. He kept correcting me, until finally he stopped and announced, "This is not going to be easy."

I could see the frustration on his face.

Andy had told me that he was going to be patient, but I figured I was just too dumb at this for any sort of human patience, including Solly Bernstein's. Then I thought: this is going to be like Robby teaching me how to read. At some point, quickly enough, it'll all makes sense. I just had to jump in fast to get to that point.

"I know you really want to do this," Solly assured me. "Mr. Geyer told me about your family. I feel sorry that your dad's stuck someplace out of town. You're the eighth young man I've prepared for bar mitzvah, but all the others came out of Hebrew school and went to *shul*, so they knew things before they got here. You won't have to do the whole service. You'll just go up to the Torah and sing some of the prayers, and then do the first couple of paragraphs of your part of the Prophets reading for the week. It'll be pretty straightforward and simple. I'll make a tape of the lessons and prepare a transliteration of the words for you. You'll have the whole Hebrew text, but it'll be in English letters. How does that sound to you?"

I nodded but, nevertheless, felt pretty stupid. Still, I decided that, somehow, Solly and Andy would get me through this.

"Can you get a reel-to-reel tape recorder? I know they're not cheap, but it'll be worth it."

I nodded again. I was sure Andy or Robby could come up with something.

He left the room, and lugged back a heavy piece of equipment that came in something that looked like an old suitcase. He put a fresh reel of tape onto one of the tape heads, and then fed it through several contact points until it was poised to go around the other head.

"Thank God for these," Solly said smiling. "Can you imagine learning this back in the old country, when the *rebbe* just did it once, and if you didn't get it they beat the crap out of you?"

I shook my head mutely, and Solly sang the whole lesson into the tape mike. He ended looking very pleased with himself. Actually, he was glowing as he handed me the tape. A few minutes later, Caroline came back and blew the horn for me. I said goodbye to him, and hurried out to the car.

I was quiet.

"What's wrong, honey?" she asked. The radio was silent.

"I'm just not sure how t' do this," I said. "Why didn't you want to come in and meet him?"

"Cause I'm not sure myself, honey. I feel like the *shiksa* wife who's the cause of all this. I never thought I'd feel like this when I married your father. Maybe I should have thought more."

"Don't feel bad, Mom," I said, sidling up closer to her. "It'll be OK. But I'm worried about Dad."

"So am I," she said and lit a cigarette. "There's a lot they don't tell me, Benjy, and for years I was happy not knowing. But I guess being dumb and happy are two things that shouldn't go together."

A few days later, a reel-to-reel tape player came by messenger from Valdosta, where Dad and Andy were working. I quickly learned how to operate it, and listened to Solly's voice over and over again until I got sick of it. I tried singing the notes and the sounds, but they never sounded the way he did. I asked Caroline to listen to me, but she always feigned a headache or was too busy. I think she felt I was being forced me to do something I really wasn't cut out for.

I had several more lessons with Solomon Bernstein over the next few weeks, in the early afternoons, after classes at Holy Nativity. Mom would drop me off without coming inside, and Solly would meet me at the door, smelling like he'd already had a couple of drinks before the lesson. I thought adults normally didn't drink at that hour. Maybe it was just a Jewish thing to do, although I remembered that Caroline and her friends sometimes had Salty Dogs on the veranda in the afternoon. Still, it seemed odd for me that Solly had been drinking that early.

He was supposed to be a man of God, yet he was always in flip-flops, some pair of cheesy shorts, and a T-shirt. I wondered why he didn't get more dressed up to go over prayers with me, like a real teacher would. I was working hard, listening to his tapes until sometimes the sounds "came out of my ears," like they say. But, even so, the problem was they weren't coming out of my mouth.

I tried not to get discouraged, but I could tell he was quickly losing whatever patience he had. Finally, after I had gone over one of the prayers about five times and he had even replayed the bar mitzvah tapes, he lost his temper and cursed in about six languages, including Yiddish. I'd heard Robby and Andy use words like that, but never so loud. Maybe there was some French and German thrown in, too.

"Shit! *Merd*!" he screamed. "You little *shmuck*! What are you doing to me? I'm not getting paid enough to do this! None of this means anything to you, does it? You're just . . . *machen falsch* with the words—faking it! These prayers, Benjamin, mean something. It's you approaching Jewish *manhood* and responsibility. Why are you doing this, if it means nothing to you?"

"My dad means a lot to me," I said, sucking back some tears into my throat to keep from crying. "He wants me to do this. That's why—"

Solly sank heavily onto the couch next to the piano, his face screwed up with anger and now with other feelings of frustration as well.

"I'm sorry," he said, exhaling. "I shouldn't be so hard on you. This isn't easy for you either. I know it. It's just—I've got an opera audition soon in Philadelphia. That's what I really want to do. The cantor business is just to keep me from starving—like who wants a starving opera singer? Trouble is, Benjy, I'm having to go to Baltimore next week to finish my work there before I graduate. I thought you'd be far enough ahead by now not to worry about me leaving. But you're not. So what do you want to do? You and Andy Geyer can try to find someone else to coach you. Maybe I'm just not right for you, see what I mean?"

I stood up. *Yes*, I did see what he meant. I knew exactly what I was going to do: I picked up the tapes he had made for me, shook his hand and walked out.

"I'm through with Solomon Bernstein," I announced to Caroline in the car. "He wants to throw in the towel, so do I."

She smiled completely, flooding the car with sunshine.

"So what about your bar mitzvah, honey? Do you want t' just say the hell with it? If you do, that's fine. You'll always be a man to me, regardless."

I told Mom I wasn't going to throw in the towel, and that I'd find somebody else to teach me, maybe at the Jewish center. Things had to have a way of working out; I wanted to believe that more than anything else.

"You're very resourceful," she said. "You must have got that from both of us." She tossed her head back and closed her eyes, and that mysterious, almost unknowable look she had returned to her face. "You know how to invent your own way, Benjy. Keep that. I mean it."

My shoulders and the tips of my ears wrinkled with pleasure, that child-glee that takes over your whole self. I liked what Mom said about "invent your own way." It made sense. It would be *my* way; I'd invent it myself. After all, no one had decided exactly where the bar mitzvah would be, or even how it was going to work. I decided, then, exactly *who* was the person I needed to see.

Tim O'Neill.

We were sitting naked in his tent when I told him about it. He was smoking a cigarette. He had stolen a couple from Pat who had started smoking even though as a good Catholic boy, Pat O'Neill wasn't supposed to. His parents objected to it (they were both ex-smokers and hated nicotine), but Pat had started smoking, and, I thought, drinking as well. Something was going on with the twins, and of course I wondered what it was. They were both dating girls and probably *fucking*, for all I knew. When you got down to it, wasn't that what it was all *really* about? Suddenly everything appeared to me to be about fucking, one way or another, although I wasn't exactly sure what *fucking* was all about, either. Still, I wanted to seem mature, so I asked Tim about it.

"Oh, sure," Tim said. "Pat's fuckin' 'em. They both have big ones, y'know. So why shouldn't they?" He put his hand on my dick and giggled. "You're getting real hair there."

"Cut it out," I said. "I need to do something about my bar mitzvah."

He started coughing from the smoke.

"Your *whaa*?"

"Bar mitzvah, you asshole! It's when a Jewish boy becomes a man. Kind of like your Confirmation. My dad wants me to do it."

"But you're not even all-Jew."

"He is, and he wants me t' do it. I was seeing this guy who was teaching me the prayers, except that since I dropped out of Hebrew school—"

"What's the matter, y'couldn't find any 'Hebes' to brew?"

He laughed, then squeezed out the cigarette into the ground. I was glad. I didn't like smoke in the tent.

"No, asshole, that wasn't *it*. I dropped out and I can't read Hebrew, except for a few letters. And the guy who was teaching me was so damn Jewish he got pissed off at me. Mom said he should have been singin' opera instead of givin' lessons. Anyway, I need t' find somebody else, and I need you to help me with it."

"Why? I ain't Jewish, that's f'sure."

"But you know me a lot. You know me really good. We can trust each other."

"That's for shit sure."

He impulsively kissed me on the cheek. I got hard for a second and I have to tell you I was embarrassed.

"Maybe your mom could help. She knows people in town, and I don't want someone who's so Jewish they get pissed off at me 'cause of what I have to do. Which is, basically, do the whole fuckin'-thing from memory."

He nodded seriously. His face took on a whole new look, like the kid part had dropped off.

Suddenly Neal popped his head in. "You guys kosher?" he asked smiling.

"Sure," Tim answered. "Rothberg's gonna get bar mitzvahed."

"Cool," Neal said. "I know guys who did the bar mitzvah thing; they got lots of swell presents and loved it. It's a big day. You know, moms came with their mink coats. Stuff like that."

"Again with the effin' minks," I said. "I need someone to teach me the prayers. Since I dropped outta Hebrew lessons and am a zero at it, no one wants to do it. And it'd make my dad real happy if I did."

Neal hunched down outside the tent. There really wasn't room inside for the three of us.

"You been smokin'?" he asked Tim disapprovingly.

"No," Tim lied.

"Good. I know Pat smokes. I wish he didn't."

"Come on," Tim said. "You got any ideas for Rothberg?"

Neal started drumming his fingers on his head.

"You should ask Brother Alexis to help you."

"He's a' effin' monk," I said.

"So? I bet he knows Hebrew. Lots of the brothers do. They're smart. You have to be to hang your balls up in the closet and become a monk. Kind of makes me happy I'm not that smart. I'm having too much fun with mine."

He stuck his hand in and groped me.

"Hmmm," he said. "A little tumescence here."

"Shut up, homo," I said.

But I liked the Brother Alex idea. It made sense. He was really smart, and I realized I could ask Brother Alexis almost anything. I thanked Neal.

"Glad I could help," he said. "You guys need any water, or something like that. How about some beer?"

Tim's eyes lit up.

"You're gonna bring us beer? You're the best brother in the whole fuckin' world, I swear it!"

"I like Rothberg. He's cool. Dad's got a bunch of bottles he's been hiding in the garage. He knows Pat and I steal 'em sometime. It's part of being Irish. If your kid didn't drink beer, you'd think there was something wrong with him, but he and Mom are too righteous just to give it to us. I'll be back in a sec."

Tim smiled. His tongue wet his top lip. I loved the way he did that.

"Christ! Isn't it wonderful having twin brothers?"

"I wouldn't know."

"Neal likes you," Tim said. "I'd be jealous, 'sept how can I be jealous of my brother?"

I didn't want to say anything about the times Neal had got too close to me. I didn't think it was right that he did, but I could never be sure about it. I don't know why it was so hard for me to tell right and wrong; maybe that was why Robby had sent me to Holy Smokes in the first place, to get some *morality*. But everything about the O'Neills seemed, actually, so totally moral in any *big* picture of the world. In a way that I had no idea you could be, I was in almost in love with them. My own mixed-religion family seemed so strange; but despite their quirkiness, the O'Neills didn't seem that strange to me at all. That was what puzzled me: how accepting of me they were, like I was of them.

Neal came back with two cans of Schlitz and a church key opener. He opened one for Tim and started drinking the other one. Tim took a gulp, and passed it on to me. I wasn't used to beer.

"Tastes, uh, strange," I said, trying to keep from either burping or puking.

"Think of it like liquid sunshine, with a little salt in it," Neal said. "It's got a kind of pecan-nutty taste. But mostly I like getting blasted on it."

Tim's eyes started rolling around his head, making like a drunk guy.

"Yeah, you should see him when he gets that way. Watch out!"

"Oh, shut up, fuck-face! You ain't never seen me that blasted."

He put his fist up to Tim's stomach and pretended he was going to drill his way through it. Tim only giggled and drank more of the beer.

"I better not have too much of this," he said. "We gotta go to Mass tomorrow."

"Cheap date," Neal said. "You're getting tanked off a quarter can."

He grabbed Tim's Schlitz and chugged it immediately.

"Didn't mean for you to hog the whole damn thing, Neal!"

Neal burped into his face.

"Sorry, young brother. I know thy need is large, unlike thy tool."

Tim looked hurt, and turned his head away.

"I think we need to go to sleep," I said. "Thanks for the idea, Neal. I'll talk to Brother Alexis on Monday."

Neal put his head into the tent, close to me. I could smell the beer on his breath, and frankly liked it.

"Good night."

Tim did not say good night to him, and I watched Neal go back into the house with the two empty cans.

"Why are you so upset with Neal?" I asked.

Tim looked at me. There were tears in his eyes.

"I hate it when he makes me feel tiny and small. It's stupid, isn't it?"

"No, it isn't. It's OK."

I kissed him on his cheek; he smiled.

"For a Jew, you're a really good guy. In fact, Rothberg, you're *just* a good guy."

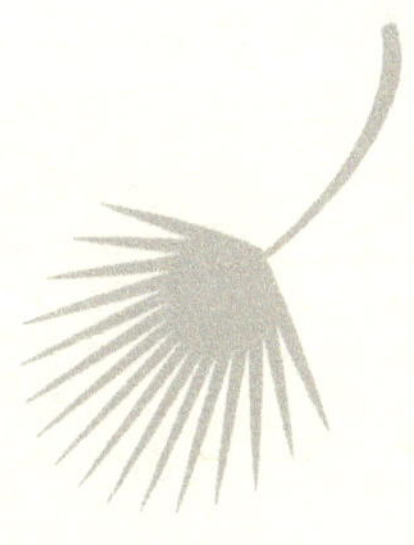

Part Two:
Rite of Passage

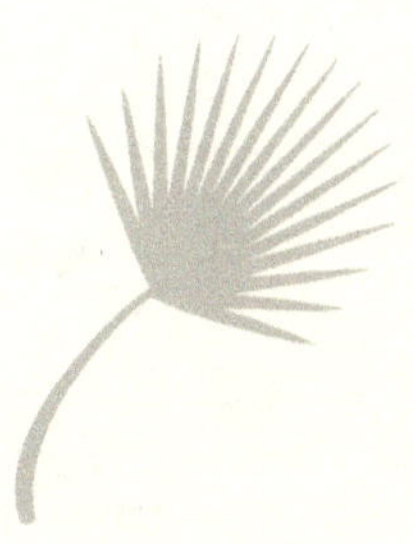

Brother Alexis And What Happened After That

On Monday at free play I asked Brother Alexis if I could speak with him in private. He asked me if something were wrong and I told him no. We went back to his office and I told him about my bar mitzvah problem and how much I wanted to make Robby happy.

He looked very concerned at me.

"It's wonderful that you feel that way about your father. Catholics have a thing about the family and fathers and sons. After all, who is our father except God? But what would you like me to do?"

"I need you to help me learn the prayers," I said. "Do you read any Hebrew?"

"Actually I do," he answered. "I took several classes in biblical Hebrew at seminary, and I know about the system of notes that cantors use; I was fascinated by that. But why are you asking me, a monk, to help you?"

I nodded; I had something to say to him and it was very important.

"I'm scared somebody else is going to say I'm just not *Jewish* enough. And I know you won't."

"No, I wouldn't do that," he said, smiling. "You say you have tapes of it, and this man Solomon prepared a transliteration for you? Suppose I showed you a short cut to learning Hebrew? It really isn't that difficult to learn, since every word is sounded exactly the way it looks. You just have to get over the fact that it uses an alphabet other than English."

"That would be great," I said. "When do we start?"

"Whenever you want. I have other work to do, obviously, but certainly as a teaching Sebastianite that's what I'm here for: to teach you."

"Thanks, Brother Alexis," I said. I could barely look at him I felt so good.

He really beamed at me, no longer the stern monk who'd confronted me that day at swimming.

"I'm glad you're here, Benjy. Tell me, you're friends with Arthur Gomez? I have him in one of my classes. His grades have been falling lately. Do you know if he's having problems at home, or is it only something to do with him?"

I didn't want to rat on Arthur, but I felt that Brother Alexis and I were now speaking man-to-man.

"I think he's scared that he can't come up to what his father wants."

"We all are," Brother Alexis said. "One way or another. Sometimes it depends on whom you consider to be your father." Suddenly he looked very bashful, and then began again. "I wish I could find a way of reaching him. It's hard to explain; he's a bright kid. I don't want him to wash out of Holy Nativity. Neither does Father Greer or any of his other teachers. We all like him. Would he allow you to reassure him? Peer counseling can be wonderful, even with younger students."

"I'll try," I said.

Brother Alexis got up, looking handsome even in his drab Sebastianite habit. I looked up at him. At the beginning of my time at Holy Nativity, I'd been nervous about how to keep from giggling at a man wearing something that looked like a dress. But Brother Alexis was so good looking that anything on this tall, attractive monk would have been appealing.

I told Caroline about Brother Alexis and what he had offered to do for me.

"Wow!" she said, tossing her head back and smiling intensely. "What a load off my mind. I don't know how you did it, Benjy, but I approve. I never did like the guy Andy hooked you up with."

"But you never met him."

"I saw him when he came to the door, and there was something just too—I think the word's *shleppy*, isn't it? He was just too damn *shleppy*."

"So it doesn't bother you that a Catholic monk is going to help me with my bar mitzvah?"

"Why should it? I'm a *goy* and you're only half Jewish. What's important is that you want to do it for Robby. He called today, while you were at school. I guess you know things are not going so great in Valdosta. But I told him about the bar mitzvah and he was so happy that you want to do it. You have no idea how much he loves you, Benjy."

I closed my eyes, and wondered if he'd still love me if he knew everything I did.

Brother Alexis, Caroline, and I agreed that the bar mitzvah lessons would take place after school, at least twice a week for a while. She wasn't sure how to arrange the actual ceremony itself, but decided to leave that up to Robby and Andy. And I decided to call Robby and tell him myself. I did, that coming Sunday.

"I'm so pleased that you really want to do this," he said. "You do, right?"

"Sure, Dad. I hope that doesn't bother you that Brother Alexis is going to help. He knows Hebrew, and he told me he knows the singing parts. I just want to know something?"

"What, son?"

"Why don't you come home? I miss you. So do Liz and Mom."

"I've got to make a living for us, Benjy, and these people are not letting go of me. When you get to be a big guy and have a family of your own, you'll understand."

"Maybe I'll never understand," I said. "Maybe I'll never be big and have a family."

"Oh, Benjy, that's why you're getting bar mitzvahed! It's your first step into manhood. Believe me, you'll understand when it happens."

I felt like I was going to cry and I didn't want to. I hated crying, but I felt like they weren't telling me the truth; and if my own parents wouldn't tell me the truth, who would? I knew I hadn't been truthful with them; I'd lied to Caroline about the night I had gone to see Arthur, and God only knew how much I was lying about Tim and his twin brothers. Still, all I could do was tell Dad "uh-huh," and say good-bye to him without sounding as numb as I felt with all the tears backed up inside me.

Dad didn't come home for another three weeks that seemed to drag on forever as the school year drew to a close. Brother Alexis arranged for us to have a room in the school that we locked, so no one could pop in during my bar mitzvah lessons. We both wore yarmulkes. He brought out books, and I had Solly Bernstein's tapes and sheets of transliterations.

"You need more than this, Benjy," Brother Alexis said, looking at the transliterations. "You really need to know what the prayers are and what they mean. The best thing would be to teach you to read Hebrew."

"We don't have enough time," I protested.

"Yes, we do. It's really simple," he said, and brought out a series of cards that he had made himself, with Hebrew characters on them. Below each character he'd drawn a figure, to illustrate how the character sounded.

"We'll start with the first letter in the Hebrew alphabet," he said. "It's called *aleph*. It's a dead letter. It has no sound at all. You use it to put a vowel in its place. You know what a vowel is: A-E-I-O-U, and sometimes Y."

So there was the aleph, and under it was an index finger at a pair of lips, as in "shush." It made total sense to me.

"Next, we have *beth*," he said. "The second letter. It has the same sound as B, but I want you to think of this picture."

"Why a house?" I asked.

"Because *beth* is the first letter of the word *bai-eese* which means 'house.' So when you see a *beth*, you'll think of *bai-eese*—house—and that way you'll get to know two things at once. *Bai-eese* was often shortened to simply *beth*, the way we shorten things like *goodbye* to just *bye*. That's what the name of the town Jesus was born in became—Bethlehem from *Beth-lechem*, the House of Bread, because it was a storage city. *Lechem* is Hebrew for bread. That's why it's important for Christians to know Hebrew, too. It brings up the Christian past just like it brings up the Jewish one."

I liked listening to what Brother Alexis was saying, just watching the words coming out of his mouth. Suddenly every word had a magical quality, like an incantation, something wonderful and secret between this handsome Sebastianite and myself. It was so different from my lessons with Solly Bernstein, who made me feel that everything was a test to see how smart or stupid I was. Of course Brother Alexis didn't want to be an opera singer, and I was sure he was doing this for me out of—

I realized, then, that I had no idea why he was doing it, except that it must have made him happy too. I could see it while he spoke; he had a real glow. Sometimes he would touch my arm or shoulder while we went through the Hebrew alphabet, and it was as if we were following a significant path, deeper and deeper into a secret code only the two of us shared. I began to vibrate with happiness, like I couldn't hold back all the energy inside me. At the end of that first lesson, he put his hand on my arm and, for a second, pulled me closer to him smiling.

"I think you're really going to get this," he said.

I nodded and only let out an "Uh-huh," trying not to go completely crazy. It might sound conceited but in the next few weeks I made *amazing* progress.

I could not have done it without Brother Alexis, even though there were moments when he admitted he was as lost as I was. This was despite the fact that he had been able to get a complete outline of a bar mitzvah service from a Jewish friend of his. It was a reform service; unfortunately, Robby did not go to the Reform Temple in Savannah, mostly because the Jewish men he knew in town were more orthodox Jews (although Southern orthodox was pretty reform by New York standards, something I learned later in life).

"I'm still not too sure what you do here," Brother Alexis said. "I guess you go up to the Torah and say this. But what do *you* do while they're reading the Torah?"

I had no idea. Caroline would not have been able to help me, and most of the time Robby was too busy making a fortune for us for me to even think about calling him. Maybe, I thought, Andy Geyer would know.

"When are you going to have this?" Brother Alexis asked me. "We have to know the exact date."

"Why?" I asked. "Isn't a bar mitzvah a bar mitzvah?"

"I'm afraid not, son. My Jewish friend told me you have to read a certain section of the Prophets that is assigned to each Sabbath service. It's called the Haftorah. Reform Jews don't read the whole thing if they don't want to, but I have a feeling your dad doesn't want you to be bar mitzvahed in the Reform Temple."

"You're right," I said, my heart sinking. "I'll ask Caroline to deal with this. It's getting more complicated, isn't it?"

Brother Alexis laughed.

"Nothing about you, young man, is going to be *un*complicated. I can tell that right now."

In the car, I told Caroline that we had to make plans. "Serious ones. Brother Alexis said that every bar mitzvah is different because of the week it's done in. Isn't that crazy?"

She shrugged. "I guess it's not like a wedding where they use the same service no matter what. I'll call Andy and ask him to do the legwork. I'm just not up to it—it's like real foreign territory to me, and you know how I feel: God doesn't care what you put into your mouth, or we'd really have a screwed up world—all those people eating pork, chitlins, catfish, and oysters." She smirked. "But I guess He does care what comes *out* of it on the day of your bar mitzvah."

The next morning Caroline told me that Andy said he'd take care of everything. My birthday was in September, so we'd have to get the bar mitzvah on the synagogue's calendar and Andy said he knew people there. "I guess he'll grease their palm with a lot of silver," she said. "The good news is that Dad's coming home this weekend."

"He is?!"

"Yeah. But, Benjy, I think you need to know something. This has been a really hard time for him. So don't expect a lot out of him."

9

Dad Comes Home

Robby did come home. I wanted to jump up and hug him, and so did Liz, but he hardly looked like my dad anymore. His hair was starkly gray and there were more lines in his face, around his eyes, his mouth, and his brow, than I could count. They were deep and dark like ink was etched into them. He walked slower, like it was painful for him, as if every step had to be measured and thought out. He smiled when he saw me and Liz. Then the smile fell, as if the effort was too wearing for him. Caroline was there, and she held him, like she was supporting him with one hand.

"Maybe you should just get some more rest, darling," she said. "Sit down. Would you like a scotch?"

"No, I'd like some water. Or how about some milk? You can put ice in it. I like cold milk."

He turned to me.

"So how are you, Benjy? How's school?"

I told him it was fine. Sure, I'd made a lot of friends I liked a lot. I didn't tell him about jerks like Storch and his buddies, or about Arthur, and I certainly didn't tell him *much* about Tim and the O'Neills. But I did mention that Tim had become my best friend.

"That's great. A best friend is the best thing to have until a girl comes along. Then your best friends stops being so best."

We were in the living room, because it was slightly chilly outside. Caroline brought in the milk.

"What about Andy?" I said. "Isn't he your best friend?"

"Sure, he is. We've known each other for so long. We went back to the war, the one in Korea. It was horrible. One day I'll have to tell you and Liz about it."

"You'll tell me?" Liz asked, excited. She liked being included in anything;

because she was younger and a girl, it was too easy to think of her as a baby. I hugged her. She got away from me and went to Robby.

"Sure," he told her. "But not right now. Now it's time for you to go to bed."

He winked at Caroline, who took Liz away. I was left alone with Robby.

"Why don't you tell me now?" I said. "I'm old enough."

"I think you are."

I remembered what Andy had told me, but I didn't want him to know how much I knew already. I wasn't sure Dad would approve of me knowing.

"So tell me."

"I can't. I swear to God, I can't."

He put his head in his hands the way I did, then looked at me. There were tears in his eyes. I had never seen him like that; it was hard for me to look at him. He was my dad, and I didn't expect him ever to cry. I went up to where he was sitting and put my hand on his head.

"Don't do that," he said, pushing my hand away. "I'm still your father. You have to respect that. That's the only thing I can give you, your respect for me. I hope you know that."

I was crying now myself. I left Robby and went up to my room. My pillow became wet with tears, and I had no idea why—it was just seeing him like that. And knowing inside, feeling it in every bone in me, that something terrible was going to happen.

He only stayed for the weekend, and everyone pretended that nothing out of the way was going on. Caroline had some of her friends for Salty Dogs and cigarettes up on the veranda and they all laughed with Robby. He looked fairly vacant but tried to smile. I was only allowed to stay there for a few minutes, then went to my room and did homework. On the last day, Andy came to drive Robby back to Valdosta, but first he took me aside.

"So we're having this bar mitzvah, boychik?" he said. "Wonderful! It's making Leon really happy. I called the synagogue and set the date. They wanted your family to join to do it, so I told the *rebbe* we would. I said I was your uncle. I hope that's kosher with you. You like having Uncle Andy around anyway, right? They'll call me up to the *bimah*, that's the place they keep the ark, and I'll get to bless the Torah, too. I'm lookin' so forward to this. Since I don't have kids of my own, you have no idea what this means to me *and* to Leon!"

I didn't like it when he called Robby Leon: It seemed like he really wasn't my dad when he was that. He was something different—that unseemly strange Jewish salesman, I guess, no matter how far back the Jewish salesmen went—just like I was this barely convincing Southern boy who'd grown up among the locals in Isle of Hope, going to a Catholic school run by monks. It all only proved to me how hard it is to see yourself as different, especially as something different from other people. I was used to seeing myself as an outsider in Isle of Hope, but I still didn't like seeing my father as even *more* of an outsider.

The date for my bar mitzvah would be two weeks after my birthday. We'd have to go through the summer first, and it would be very long and hot, like summers are when you're a kid. The only good thing was that it would be broken by the school retreat, and I'll have to tell you about that next, because then you'll understand how it *definitely* changed my life.

10

The Retreat

A few weeks after the end of the school year and the "fucked-up piece-uh-shit finals" as Tim called them, the whole lower school—that is, guys in the eighth and ninth grades—was scheduled to go on four-day retreat up at Mary of the Woods, a campground about thirty miles away, in an area where the mosquito-infested Ogeechee River makes a sudden turn into knobby Georgia pine woods. I don't know what happened if you failed your finals, I guess the Sebastianites would have to figure that one out themselves, but all of us were supposed to go. Anyway, I was told Catholics liked retreats. It was both a way to do a lot of praying to the B.V.M. (that's the Blessed Virgin Mary, for us/you non-Catholics) and her Son, the King of Heaven, and also to "foster school spirit."

Tim took me aside to explain it more fully.

"Retreats, Benjy, are a big deal to us. First, all the kids and the brothers get to let their hair down a bit—but only a bit—and then, if you gotta know, Catholics have this fear us kids are gonna join some blasphemous, anti-Catholic group, like the Y or the Boy Scouts. I mean, none of 'em are exactly hot-shit *anti*-Catholic, but they ain't exactly Catholic either, so that makes 'em more anti-Catholic than Catholic." He paused, as if to drill in his point. "See what I mean?"

Actually I didn't. I knew there was a Jewish Boy Scout troop at the Jewish center, so if *real* Jews, who didn't eat pork or mix their milk and their meat together, could be Boy Scouts, then why couldn't Catholics? The YMCA I wasn't sure about. It certainly wasn't Jewish, but it didn't seem *un*Catholic to me, either. But then the Catholics lived in a world of their own which sometimes didn't even seem really Christian to me. It was like they invented it all themselves and just let you in if they wanted to, a good case in point being my bar mitzvah lessons with Brother Alexis. As a Sebastianite brother, he didn't think twice about this, yet Catholic kids were not supposed to go to the YMCA? That seemed crazy to me, as a Jew, or whatever I was.

Still, so much of what Catholics did appeared to me to be secret and forbidden that even what Tim and I were doing seemed to fit nicely into it. Since Catholics appeared to have a whole lot *not* to talk about (masturbation; birth control; even sexy movies like *Baby Doll* and *Never on Sunday*) what Tim and I (and the O'Neill twins) *didn't* talk about seemed . . . well, just another part of it all.

I was excited by the idea of getting away from Isle of Hope, and also from Liz my baby sister, especially with Robby gone so much, leaving me the only male in the house now, very much outnumbered by females, if you include Josephine. So the approaching retreat, no matter what it was about, excited me. All the boys I liked at Holy Smokes would be there—as well as some guys I hated, but that was the price I had to pay—and there would be *no* bar mitzvah lessons.

"This is going to be *awfully* Catholic, Benjy," Caroline said when I gave her the retreat permission form. "D'you have any idea what's going to go on?"

I had some. "Sports," I said. "Swimming, boats. Hikes in the woods. Singing." Tim had explained all that to me, but beyond that, I didn't know.

"I'll sign it," she said, lighting another cigarette. "But promise me that if you get there and feel this is something you don't want to do—like it's just too *damn*-Catholic-crazy for you, pardon my swearing—you'll call me and I'll come and pick you up."

I tried not to let her see how much I was smiling. It hurt to suppress all those smile muscles that were working hard to come out: hell, I was going to chapel all the time and it never bothered me. I didn't do the Eucharist, or Confession. I mean, that would have been silly, and I wasn't sure what I'd have to confess. I certainly wasn't going to tell any man in a dress about Tim and me, and Tim had told me that he'd never tell anyone. ("They're all nuts with that self-pollution crap," he said to me in the tent. "I bet they do it back in their rooms, or else they get blue balls. That's a priest-thing, certainly. It must make ya nuts hurt like hell!")

I agreed to Caroline's promise. She packed about a week's worth of clothing for me (you know how Moms are), then on the appropriate Thursday— the weather already hot and sticky as taffy straight out the pot—she drove me through miles of remote backwoods to the retreat site. Even with a map, it wasn't easy to find. There were several campgrounds in the area. One, Camp Willow, was for Boy Scouts; another, Camp Holy Waters, for Baptist youth groups; both of which I guessed were avoided by the Catholics. Finally we saw a large wooden sign with a cross and stars circling it that read Camp Mary of the Woods. Dedicated to Our Youth and the Blessed Virgin.

"Must be the goddamn place!" Caroline swore. "Hard enough t' find it. You'd think the B.V.M. would have plopped down a bunch o' miracles just for unbelievers like me to follow."

"That's no way to talk, Mom," I said. "This is supposed to be a holy place."

"Full of boys!" Caroline screeched. "You gotta be kiddin', kid. God knows what kind of trouble you'll get into. And watch out for those priests. I have my doubts about them."

"I'm sure you know that Dad would not want to hear that," I said in my most adult voice.

Sometimes it felt like Caroline and I had exchanged places. Except that she could drive and I couldn't.

"You're right, Benjy. He's for this Catholic crap and he's not even Catholic. You've been doing great at Holy Nativity, so I should keep my mouth sealed. But like I said, if they start going off too much about hell and you burnin' in it 'cause you're not baptized and all that, please let me know. You don't have to believe everything that comes out of every Catholic's mouth. They're not Jesus, let me tell you. Or his best friends."

"Thanks," I said as she parked the car, and leaned over and kissed her. I was really lucky to have my parents. If—God forbid—word ever got out about what I had done with Tim, I don't think they would have been happy about it, but they probably wouldn't go totally ape-shit either. Some of the hard-shell-Baptist types back in Isle of Hope would have busted a gut, and God only knows what their kids were doing.

Brother Alexis came to greet us, in black shorts and a kind of priestly short-sleeve black shirt, but without a Roman collar. Despite my seeing him previously in a bathing suit, it was still hard to imagine him in shorts like that, but he was. Caroline quickly looked him up and down. I realized that despite my being at Holy Smokes for a year, the two of them had never met. I introduced them. Caroline looked flustered, but jumped right in.

"Brother Alexis, thank you so much for helping Benjy. I mean, for his bar mitzvah. You're a Catholic, and he's—well, you probably know I'm not Jewish—but it means a lot to me. His dad wants this, and—Jesus! What can I say t' you?"

She took his hand and kept shaking it and looking into his face.

I realized he was embarrassed, too. He managed to let go of her, take a step back and stand up straight.

"Thank you for bringing Benjamin to Camp Mary of the Woods, Mrs. Rothberg," he said formally. "We're very pleased having him here. And I'm happy that I can help him."

Caroline calmed down; I wondered what she was thinking. Brother Alexis was tall, good looking, and nicely built. Like Tim said, he must have had a big one. I guessed even Mom could imagine it. Suddenly this strange and amazing thought came into my head: Brother Alex was a *man* playing a priest, just like I was a kid playing a boy. I was supposed to be a regular, normal, "Grade-A" kind of boy, but that was certainly not what I felt like inside. With all my heart, I hoped that no one other than Tim O'Neill and maybe his twin boy-god brothers could see it.

Brother Alexis picked up my suitcase.

"He can carry that," Caroline said. "Benjy, do you think you can let Brother Alexis and me talk for a second? Which way is his cabin, Brother Alexis?"

Brother Alex told me that I was in Cabin Number Eight, and pointed me to it. Caroline kissed me good-bye.

"Remember what I said about calling me," she said.

I took off with the suitcase in the thick heat, turning around briefly to watch the two of them talk. Mom had become a grown-up again; it was written on the lower half of her face. Brother Alexis's face was serious, too, as if what she said had really got to him. I didn't want them to see me spying, so I turned back towards the cabins. A moment later I heard Mom's car as she drove off.

I was soon knee-deep in gnats and tall grasses. After several turns in the path, the cabins finally appeared, almost hidden in the pines. A latrine stood in front of Cabin Eight, with a shower and washroom. Everything smelled woodsy and fresh except for the latrine, which smelled of disinfectant. I popped inside to pee. Inside were six toilet seats with no partitions between them. I wasn't sure how I'd get used to that; I definitely didn't live like that at home and it made me wonder if I'd be calling Caroline sooner than expected.

While I was zipping back up, Neal O'Neill appeared and unzipped next to me. He had a ripe smile on his face while he took himself out and let wiz. I felt self-conscious and backed away.

"You in this cabin, Benjy?"

"Uh-huh."

"Great!" Finished, he turned to me. "I'm your cabin counselor. Every cabin gets two older boys, see? I'm glad you're here!"

He leaned over toward me and messed up my hair.

"This is gonna be fun," he said, grinning. "Pat's in another cabin. You coulda gotten him, but he's with the ninth graders. You have a friend in that cabin, Gomez?"

"Yeah."

"Nice kid. He's cute, too. Tim's told me some stuff about him."

"He's very serious," I said.

Neal winked at me. "Maybe we can change that. Isn't that what retreat's for—change?"

"I told you he's serious," I protested. "I mean it."

We were outside and the sun suddenly felt almost blinding, even coming through the pine trees. Neal picked up my suitcase. I tried to take it from him.

"What's your sweat, Rothberg? It's gonna be OK."

The good thing I could say about Cabin Eight was that it also smelled piney and was freshly cleaned. I guess Neal and the other boys who worked as counselors had done that. Brother Alexis showed up a minute later with another older boy whom he introduced as our other counselor. His name was Eugene Whitman; he was called Eugie. A Negro, he was not as tall as the O'Neill twins, but even better built.

Each cabin had ten boys in it, plus the Cabin Master and the two counselors. The other boys were all in my class. Billy Manion, the geeky math guy; Melvin Harris, my squad leader who led us into walls, and of course that asshole Storch. At least he was alone, split away from Ken Ferris and the rest of his gang. He pretended to be nice to me in a cold phony way. Tim was not in my cabin and I immediately missed him. I figured they were not going to put Neal and Tim in the same cabin. It made sense, but Brother Alexis and Neal seemed to wink at each other all the time, even when you could not actually see it, like they had some regular joke going on between them. Maybe it was something like the telepathy Tim and I had.

I overheard Storch tell another kid, "Guess they put all the *queer* boys in here. If one of 'em ever lays a hand on me, I'll—"

Storch shut up as Brother Alexis appeared, then went on talking when he left.

"Just don't let 'em catch you alone in the shithouse with yer pants down. Know what they wanna do with ya?"

The kid didn't say a word; maybe he was scared.

"Drown you in the toilet?" I asked.

"Shut up, you faggot Christ-killer," Storch growled.

I glared at him, raising my fist as if to hit him in the teeth again. Storch's eyes bugged out.

A lot of boys saw it and laughed. I felt great. Neal came over to us.

"You guys have *got* to get along," he said seriously. "At retreat we don't like bullies and we don't like kids who make fun of each other. I hope you understand that."

Brother Alexis joined him.

"Thank you," he said to Neal. "Mr. Storch, if you make another comment to Mr. Rothberg here about anyone killing Christ, and I hear about it, I'll have you sent home. And Mr. Rothberg, you'd better not raise a hand to another kid. I mean that, too."

I extended my hand to Storch and he shook it. But even I could tell it was only pretend.

We were given time to go to the latrine and wash up. Afterwards, we had lunch with lots of camp food to eat which always seemed to be variations on hot dogs or hamburgers. Then we went back to the cabin and changed into bathing suits and went swimming in the large camp pool. We were lined up according to height, and of course as much as I wanted Tim, who kept coming over trying to say something, I ended up with Horace Storch as my buddy.

Maybe I'd grown a bit in the last year, because we were now both basically the same height, which meant that whenever the lifeguard yelled "Buddies!" we had to find each other and join hands. I hated it, but Storch seemed to like it. The first time we joined hands, he pushed me down in the water. I got up and jabbed him hard in the stomach with my elbow. Robby had told me it was a great trick to use; after all, it wasn't a punch just an "accident."

"Do that again, Rothberg, and I'm gonna kill you," Storch growled in a low voice. "You goddamn Christ-killer."

I stuck out my tongue.

"Sure. Try it, Storch. I'll have you eradicated!"

"You'll *whaaa*!!!?"

The lifeguard blew his whistle.

"QUIET! Buddy count!!!"

"Storch!" Neal warned. "Keep your mouth shut. We're counting."

Storch looked at me, his eyes blazing. "Fuckin' queers stick t'gether," he growled under his breath but I could hear it. "Wudn't-ya know it?"

They finished the count, and free swim continued. Storch swam away from me, kicking water in my face but it made no difference. Bill Manion and Melvin Harris came up to me.

"Having a good time, Rothberg?" Manion asked. He had wallboard-dry white skin, no matter how much water or sun he got on it.

"Z'OK," I said.

"Crap luck getting Storch as your buddy," he commiserated. "But you show no fear of him. That's an excellent thing."

Tim appeared.

"I heard you and Storch already got into it. Serves that barf-bag good. I got Ferris in my cabin. He's like Storch Number Two. Fact, he is number two. And smells like it, too."

Tim started laughing.

"You don't need to resort to bathroom humor," Harris said.

Tim belched.

"Who ya think ya are, the effin' Pope? Go do some geometry problems, OK? I think ya mom gave birth to ya with a' effin' slide rule."

Harris didn't say another word, but glumly swam away with Manion. Then I saw Arthur and immediately abandoned Tim to go over to him, which was stupid. I turned back; Tim shrugged and turned away from me.

Arthur was hanging out alone at the other end of the pool. The boys were making sonic-level noise and spraying each other in water fights. I ignored everything and jumped up to sit on the ledge behind him, keeping my calves in the water. The toes of my left foot carefully nudged Arthur's back, but he didn't turn around to me.

"What's up?" I asked.

"Nothing," he said and turned to me.

"You look miserable," I said. "You're s'posed to be having a good time here. What is it?"

He was silent.

I got back down into the water and looked at him. The kids were so loud I could have said and done almost anything and no one would have heard me. It was wonderful

"Come on," I said, so close I could feel his breath on my face. "What is it? I want t' know."

Now he was breathing hard. I looked around. Asshole Storch and Ferris were no place to be seen. I watched Neal O'Neill's eyes land on me from afar, stick for a second, then wander away. He was minding the kids. So was Pat O'Neill, who never smiled. The two of them were standing together at the side of the pool, gazing around at the boys. The lifeguard had his whistle in his mouth. I was scared there was going to be another buddy check any minute.

"My dad threatened to kill me," Arthur said. "He's sure I'm a *maricon*. He was real drunk. He told me what a disappointment I am, that I'm never goin' to be a man. What am I gonna do, Benjy?"

My heart broke in two. "I don't know," I said.

Suddenly I needed to touch him. I reached out and put my hand on his warm stomach, just above his belly button. He let me keep it there, with all the crazy water spraying going on in the background. Unconsciously, my hand went up to his shoulder.

"It'll be OK," I whispered into his ear. "*Everything* is gonna be OK. I wouldn't let it be any other way."

"Thanks," Arthur whispered back. "You're the first person who made me feel good about being me. I'll remember that."

"I'm glad," I said.

He smiled and everything stopped for me, until from the corner of my eye I saw Tim approaching. I didn't want to talk to him, even though he was my best friend in the school and we had done all those things that I wasn't proud of but liked doing anyway.

Now I saw how tall and really good-looking Arthur was, how handsome in the water. And his beautiful quietness: it was like something that I couldn't keep myself away from. No wonder Caroline wanted to have him over. She must have seen it, too. It was like in the Beatles song about a secret love. Did she know I was already having this huge … I could barely name it; but whatever it was, was it something you were *only* supposed to have on girls? I had no idea.

Arthur eased away from me so that my hand no longer rested on the silky skin of his shoulder. But there was still this palpable closeness between us, like something maybe twins share. Except that he was dark and stood out against the white bodies in the pool (including my own that was darker than most bodies), but not of course against the few Negro kids. Arthur was like them. They never seemed to fully come out of their shells, no matter how hard they tried. There was always something about them that was different from the white boys, like they went back to a less enchanted part of the planet, away from our own stupid conformity, at the end of the day.

Tim stood in front of us. "What are you guys up to?" he asked.

Arthur looked away.

"Nothing," I said.

"Bet it ain't," Tim responded. "Bet you guys *are* up to something."

"So what if we are?" I said. "You sound like Storch."

"Get off it. I ain't like that asshole and you know it. Sorry, I should mind my own bee's wax, right?"

"No," Arthur said. "You're fine. Rothberg and I were just talking about the retreat. Like what's he going to do when we're all having religious practice. He can't receive Communion. I wish *I* didn't have to."

"Why?" Tim asked.

"Cause he doesn't believe in it," I blurted out.

"Really?" Tim smiled, loving it. It was like he now had a confederate in his shenanigans. I loved it when Tim smiled like that. It was almost like Caroline's smile, just not as grown-up. He pulled Arthur over to the side of the pool, and whispered something in his ear.

At the moment, the lifeguard whistled and all the older boys shouted "BUDDIES!"

Storch came up to me with that evil grin he had. I elbowed him in the ribs immediately. I wasn't going to stand for anything.

"You do that again, Rothberg, and I'm gonna kick your nuts in."

"Why?" I said, grabbing his hand and squeezing it until he winced. "Cause you don't have any of your own?"

He was going to say something, when the lifeguard yelled "Quiet!" and the count was made. As soon as it was over, I dropped the drip's hand and dashed over to Tim, who was now away from Arthur.

"So what'd you say to Arthur?" I asked.

Tim grinned.

"I told him *I* didn't believe in it either. It made him a lot happier. I also told him that Neal doesn't either and wants to be friends with him. Of course Pat believes it. Pat's always so serious about the Catholic stuff. I think he'd like to be a priest, 'sept he's still got a dick on him—and it's a big one, too."

Tim chuckled.

"I'm glad you told Arthur that," I said. "It must make him feel less alone. He's a wonderful guy, don't you think?"

"Sure. Neal wants to go canoeing with him. He can get a canoe while we're at Bible study. They can't make you go to Bible study, y'know?"

"Maybe I should go with them."

Tim looked around. It was time to do buddies again, then leave the pool.

"Naw," he said quickly. "Neal wants t' do this alone."

We had to separate.

"All right," I said. "Maybe that'll be good for Arthur, too." But I wondered what Neal was up to.

Dinner was OK. I sat next to guys I liked, and noticed that Neal managed to sit next to Arthur. He kept smiling at him and talking to him in a low voice. Arthur was smiling too, and for the first time I saw him really laugh. Storch was also eyeing them and boiling angry; but maybe that was Storch's thing, to get boiling-mad at people. Luckily, he didn't look at me at all. Brother Alexis came up and asked me to see him afterwards.

We met outside the dining hall.

"I've been talking to some of the other teachers, Benjy. We've been trying to figure out what we should do with you on this retreat. I mean, there are things you don't need to participate in because you're not Catholic, but things you might want to do anyway—like some of the discussions about morality. Would you like to do that?"

I nodded. "Is it all about movies and stuff?"

He looked at me quizzically.

"You know, like movies I'm not supposed to see? And TV?"

"No, we don't tell kids what kind of movies to see. Their parents do. This is about how you should treat other people, and how they should treat you."

My other thought was: How about playing with yourself? But I didn't say that. I told him the morality stuff would be OK. Then I made up an excuse that I wanted to have some time to myself, to go over the bar mitzvah stuff. He said that would be fine. The truth was, I didn't want to be surrounded by kids every single moment. Now, except for using the open toilets, I felt a lot better. I wouldn't have to call to Caroline. I was really having a good time with Tim, Arthur, and my other friends at Holy Smokes. I wondered if Tim and I would have any time alone, out in the woods maybe, but I realized that the brothers and counselors had probably organized every moment of the retreat, except for when I would be "studying" by myself for my bar mitzvah.

When Brother Alex left me to go over to some other boys, Tim walked up to me, then Arthur. Harris appeared and Arch Flanders and Alfred Johnson. I was so happy, I felt almost drunk with it. We walked back to the cabins with our arms around each other, singing crazy songs.

Suddenly Storch and Ferris were behind us.

"We'll get you fags yet!" Storch said loud enough for us to hear.

"Drop dead!" Tim said. "You fuckin' a-hole."

Storch stood stock still, even Ferris did. We were almost at Cabin Eight.

"It's that fuckin' Jew!" Storch shouted. "He's the cause of all this!"

Eugene Whitman appeared at the cabin door. "That's enough, Mr. Storch," he warned. "Any more of that and you'll be thrown out of the retreat."

"Like I care!" Storch cried out. "Like I damn care!"

Ferris left for his cabin.

Whitman approached Storch, pulled him aside and said something to him. I couldn't hear what it was, but I could see that Eugie's face was very determined, even though there were moments when he smiled, looking straight at Storch. Whatever he was saying, Storch stopped giving me hate looks. But because he was so good at acting, it was hard for me to tell what look he was giving me now.

The funny thing about retreat was that the first day or so seemed to last forever, then you got used to it, and the time just rushed by. I loved swimming and hiking, and games like volleyball and even touch football, although I had to be careful that Storch didn't try to kill me. He did a few times, but always made sure that it appeared to be part of the game without any real malice on his part.

I couldn't complain, or everyone would know what I was made of, something I wasn't even sure of myself. I also remembered what Robby had told me about not putting out your big guns until something especially bad happened. Mostly, I wanted to keep Storch "neutral" and away from me and my friends. It was amazing seeing them away from school, especially Arthur. He started to bloom, and smiled more.

Late one afternoon, I had ducked out of Bible studies or morality, I can't remember which, and took a walk by the lake. From a distance I saw Arthur out in the canoe with Neal. They were laughing. I wanted so much to be in that canoe, to sit so close to Arthur that I was almost inside his skin. Just to paddle out, with my arm around him, and . . . to kiss him . . . yes, kiss him.

But they were on the other side of the lake, and there was no way to reach them.

So I went back to the camp and listlessly read for a while, alone. When the other guys came back to our cabin, Neal and I looked at each other and I wondered if he knew I had seen him with Arthur. He came over and winked at me, then the two of us washed up together to get ready for dinner and for a moment I felt like Storch and his gang had just disappeared.

Finally, sometime before the end of the retreat, I got my moment alone with Tim. We snuck off into the woods for about half an hour after dinner, when all the other boys had gone out on a scavenger hunt. The sun had almost set and we found a place deep in some trees, behind a little hill. Tim hugged me, and then took his shirt off.

"What are you doing?" I asked.

"Just felt like having my shirt off. Do it, too."

"No. Suppose somebody sees us?"

"I'll just say I got hot doin' all this scavenger shit. Come on."

I took my shirt off, and he hugged me again.

"That feels good," he said. He reached down and felt my crotch. "You got a boner."

It was the truth. Part of it was just the excitement of doing something so forbidden. He pulled my dick out from the bottom of my shorts.

"Wanna jerk off?" he asked.

"Sure."

His small hand went over to my dick and he began to jerk me off. I didn't do anything to him at first, but soon was doing the same thing to him.

"This feels good," he whispered.

I didn't want to do anything more, but Tim put his mouth on my dick for a second. It felt great, doing this out there in the woods. I had no idea anything like that could feel so good, but then how could I at twelve? Well, almost thirteen.

A few minutes later I came. Then I had to figure out what to do with it. There were leaves around, but some of the sticky stuff was still on my hands. It was hard to believe that this stuff produced babies, even though you couldn't do it alone to make that happen.

I looked at Tim. I noticed that his small nipples had become tight on his chest, and extended out like tiny fingers.

"That's what happens to your tits when you get excited," he explained. "Girls do it, too."

"How would you know?" I asked him.

He grinned, all freckles and dimples.

"Neal tells me everything. Y'know, he and Pat have had girls together. I mean, the two of them with one girl, or even two girls, all in the same car or someplace. Neal says, 'That's the joy of being a twin.' He's told me all about girls. He really likes Arthur. He's been going out in the canoe with him whenever he gets a chance. Y'know, like after dinner or during some of the morality classes and stuff like that."

"I know," I said without thinking. I was glad Arthur had a friend at the retreat, especially an older popular boy like Neal. Then suddenly I got serious: "Are they doing *anything*?"

"What d'you mean?"

"You know what I mean. Something like, just *something*?"

"Oh, that." Tim's eyes narrowed. "Maybe."

"Jesus!" I said, too loud.

"Come on, don't bring Our Lord into it. So what? Neal's careful. He wouldn't do anything that Arthur wouldn't want him to do. He's not going to fuck him or anything."

"Fuck him? How do you fuck a guy?"

"God, you're dumb," Tim said with disbelief. "You *fuck* him in the butt. Ain't you never hearda that?"

"Sure," I said, trying to act blasé. Storch and his gang had talked about it, but

I never believed anyone actually did it.

"Gee, next you're going t' ask me where you fuck a girl."

"I am not," I asserted. "I know about that."

Tim put his T-shirt back on, and so did I.

"Good," he said, "You're a sexual wizard, Rothberg. I think Neal wants to fuck Arthur in the butt, but I ain't sure he'll do it. Arthur's nice looking, no denyin' it."

"He's handsome," I said too dreamily, and realized I was giving something away that I didn't want even Tim to have. But it was too late.

"You're really sweet on him, aren't you?" Tim asked seriously. "Are you in love with Arthur?"

"Is that possible? I mean to be in love *with* a boy?" I had no idea boys could be in love with boys. I'd never even heard of it.

Tim only looked down at the ground; he didn't answer. A moment later, Arch Flanders showed up with dorky Billy Manion. They were really surprised to see us.

"What are you two doing here?" Manion asked. "You jerkin' off or something?"

"Yeah," Tim said matter-of-factly. "Wanna eat my dick?"

Manion's pale skin blushed.

"Sorry, I didn't mean to be nasty. I guess you were just taking a breather from the scavenger hunt. Did you find anything?"

"Yeah, my dick in your ass," Tim grinned. "Manion, how could you find anything? You don't have a fuckin' clue!"

"That's not a nice thing to say," Arch interjected. Being small himself, he hated guys being rough with each other. I felt bad for him.

"They were just jokin'," I said.

"The brothers are looking for you two," Manion announced. "They noticed you were gone."

"I'll tell 'em we were talking about my bar mitzvah," I said as an explanation.

"Your *what*?" Manion asked.

"It's his Confirmation," Arch explained proudly. "We have Jewish friends. I've been to bar mitzvahs. They're fun. The guy gets up and says something in this funny kinda talk—"

"It's called Hebrew. The language of the Bible," I explained.

"Oh, fuck off!" Tim said. "He gets a lotta presents and everybody's nice to him, that's what it's all about." Tim beamed, like he knew everything about it.

"Sounds cool to me," Manion said. "But you two better go back and join everybody else, or they're going to think you're up to no good."

Back at the clearing, I explained to Brother Alexis and some of the other brothers that Tim and I had gone off to talk about my Confirmation. Brother Alex smiled at me. I had no idea if he believed me, or just wanted to. He put his hand on my shoulder.

"That's fine, Benjy. I'm glad you're including Tim. It's an important thing for a Jewish boy, and it's great that you're including some of your friends from Holy Nativity in it."

The next afternoon, during rest period, a short time for a nap after lunch, I got to talk to Arthur. I knew we'd be by ourselves only for a moment, so I came right to the point. But I didn't want him to know I'd been spying on him.

"Tim told me you and Neal have been going out canoeing together. How's that been?"

He looked around, like he was expecting someone to barge in any second.

"OK," he said. I could tell he was nervous.

"Just OK?"

"Yeah, it's been fine."

"Has Neal ever . . . y' know, done something t' you you didn't want him to do?"

"No," Arthur said. "He's never done anything to me I didn't want him to do. Never."

I didn't know what else to say. Except for what I did with Tim, I'd had no other experiences to do with this. Tim was small, but he seemed to know everything. Now I realized I did have to ask Arthur something, and it was something serious. But Arthur Gomez was a serious boy.

"Do you think, Arthur . . . " I hesitated, then made myself go on. "Is it possible for a boy to fall in love with another boy?"

Arthur smiled slightly, but so beautifully that it lit me up inside. I could feel this light from him coming directly into me.

"I think it is," Arthur said. "I don't believe in the Eucharist and in a lot of other stuff, but I think it's possible—sure."

Neal appeared and put his hand on Arthur's shoulder and Arthur stood really still. It was like they were the same person, like they were really joined. They both smiled in the same way at each other. Suddenly Storch and Ferris showed up, and Neal and Arthur both stopped smiling. It was as if a cloud had passed over their faces, the same cloud I'd seen at Isle of Hope on the faces of those men being talked about by the shrimpers and the rough guys on the fishing boats. I remembered Robby once saying to me, just out of nowhere, "Somebody always has to call your number." I'd had no idea what he meant then. Now I did.

I did have one bar mitzvah lesson during the retreat, in an empty office room in the administration building. Brother Alexis and I went over the prayers, and the part of the Prophets that I was supposed to read. We both wore yarmulkes. Andy Guyer had given me a bunch of them.

"You're doing really well," Brother Alexis said afterwards.

I decided that I had to ask him the big question that was on my mind. I felt I could trust him; after all, he, a Catholic monk, was helping me, a Jew, so it all made sense.

"Brother Alexis," I said. "Is it possible for a boy to fall in love with another boy?"

Brother Alex thought for a moment; his face became grave.

"Sure, it happens all the time. But that doesn't mean you won't find a girl and fall in love with her and marry her. When boys 'fall in love,' it's not like normal love, with girls and boys. You need to understand that."

"But if it happens all the time, why isn't it normal?"

Brother Alexis blinked suddenly, like he had not seen that coming.

"Good question, Benjy," he said, choosing his words carefully. "And I'm afraid I don't have the answer. I studied psychology in college, and there was some discussion that 'homosexual feelings'—do you know what that means?"

"Guys who are light-in-the-loafers, that kind of stuff?"

"No, that's prejudice, like saying Negroes are inferior and Jews are Christ-killers. It's all stupid—remember that, Benjy. I was going to say that there's been some discussion that homosexual feelings are more … anyway, more valid than people allow. That's about all I can say about it."

My next question just came out. I wasn't sure why, but I knew I couldn't ask Dad or Mom or anyone big I knew.

"Have you ever had that feeling—I mean, being in love with another boy? When you were a boy?"

"No," he said emphatically. "I've never felt anything like that, that I could tell you about. But I knew boys who did. It happened in the seminary I went to. I shouldn't say anything more to you, but you're Jewish and you need to know religious people have feelings, too." He smiled. "Heck, maybe only a Jew would know it. You're very smart for a kid, Benjy. Anyone ever tell you that?"

I blushed. "My dad does."

"He's lucky to have you, and I'm really glad he sent you to us. I am."

Late on the last afternoon of the retreat, I was by myself in the Music, Art, and Reading Room of the big rec cabin (called by some of the boys "the More Ass Room") reading a book about old-time knights and chivalry, when suddenly I thought about Dad. I was alone because I didn't want to go to another morality lecture, and I'd hardly been thinking about Robby during the retreat, even though I hadn't heard from him in a while. I wondered what was going on—Dad was in that big adult world that, defiantly, wouldn't let me in. He was missing from me, definitely, and something else was too. I couldn't put my finger on it. Then it dawned on me: there was definitely a line connecting Robby and me . . . and Arthur.

Arthur. King *Arthur*. Knights. And my *own* Arthur. He *had* to be mine. I couldn't imagine anything else. I felt weak suddenly, drained terribly, merely thinking about him.

There was something missing in me, something incomplete—and I needed to see Arthur and tell him. But tell him what?

I couldn't say it, couldn't even allow myself to know it. The way I felt about Arthur would never fit into any category allowed at the school, at least not one that anyone except Tim, or maybe Neal, might understand.

I closed the book, very glad that I was alone, that no one would know what I'd been thinking. Just as I was ready to return to my cabin, Tim burst in.

"Have you seen Gomez?" he asked.

"No, but I've been thinking about him."

"Shit, you're always thinkin' about him. You're pussy for Gomez, Benjy, you know that?"

"Shut up. What's the problem?"

"He wasn't at morality."

"So? That makes sense. He's not the *morality* type, neither am I. You can bet on it."

We walked back toward my cabin together, and on the way met Arthur. I was so happy to see him that I kept smiling at him, and circling him. I wanted so much to tell him. . . .

It was true: *I loved Arthur Gomez.* There was no way around it. But how could I hide it when I really didn't want to? I thought about Pat O'Neill, and the way he and Arthur had their own special, very quiet friendship with its own telepathy; they were both shy and sweet. I wished I had it with Arthur, that somehow I could have let him know what I was thinking, without even saying it.

I sat next to him at dinner, and while we were eating I put my hand on his bare knee. He looked over and smiled at me.

"What?" he asked.

"I just wanted to tell you I'm glad you're here."

"I'm glad you're here, too, Benjy. Neal wants to take me out one last time in the canoe just before it gets dark. I'm looking forward to it."

"I wish I could go with you."

"It wouldn't work. I mean, three in a canoe. It's just not how canoes work. Know what I'm talking about?"

"Listen," I said. "When we get back, I want you to come out to Isle of Hope with me. Please, will you do it? You can spend the night. Mom'll pick you up. Don't worry about your dad, if he gives us *any* problems—well, we'll do something."

He smiled and took my hand in his, squeezing it lightly under the table. Suddenly Storch lit in.

"Gee, you two *are* queers! I can see it on your faces."

Ferris was with him. I hated both of them. I exploded.

"Drop dead, Storch! I'll knock out *more* of your teeth."

"Try it, you—"

We were making so much noise, Brother Alexis and Neal approached.

"What's going on here?" Neal asked.

"Nothing," Storch lied. "We're just joking around."

"Doesn't sound like it," Neal said. "Are you being a bully again?"

"Let me handle this," Brother Alexis said. "Kids, cool it. This is the last day of the retreat, and I want all of you to leave with a positive feeling about it. I want you to remember this retreat all of your lives. I hope you will."

We didn't say another word. I couldn't rat on Storch and his turd-friend Ferris. It would have gone down badly, and nobody likes a rat, although I kept hoping Brother Alexis would catch the two creeps in the act of doing something malicious.

After dinner, I met up with Tim. We had a small amount of time to ourselves before we had to get back to our cabins, when of course Storch would be around. Neal and Arthur had disappeared in the direction of the lake. We walked slowly to the cabins, sticking close to the trees for privacy.

Tim had already heard that I'd threatened to knock out more of Storch's teeth.

"I'd love to be there when you do it!" he said.

"I can't," I said. "They'll throw me out of school. You can't just knock out some guy's teeth because he's a piece o' shit. We both know it."

"True, but I'd love to see it. Storch really hates Gomez, that's what kills me. Arthur's the nicest kid in the world and he hates him."

"What does he hate him for?" I asked.

Tim looked puzzled, like he was trying to put his finger on it.

"Storch is just a kid who has to bully other kids," he said, thinking out loud. "But Arthur's like an adult already. He's had to look out for himself, and it's made him grow up fast. You feel it when you're around him. And Storch knows that older guys like my brothers like Gomez. That's *it*! Storch is jealous!"

I felt bad for Arthur again, to be the object of Storch's hatred, like I was. I'd never told Tim about going to see Arthur. I'd always wanted to keep it a secret between Arthur and me. I just knew that if Arthur *were* king, like that other King Arthur, I'd pledge my complete faith to him, exactly as the knights of old did.

"He's like God," I blurted out.

Tim looked at me, baffled. "Like—what??"

"God."

"You *are* crazy, Rothberg. How could Gomez be *like* God? That sounds too fuckin' crazy *and* Jewish."

"So, what do you think Jesus was?" I said, laughing.

"Oh, man, that *is* blasphemous. Even I know it. You're in love with Arthur, aren't you? You're totally screwy-nuts about him."

"Are you jealous, too?"

"No. I ain't. Cause Arthur ain't never gonna do anything with you. He's too scared."

I looked around. We were getting into very serious territory, and I didn't want anyone to eavesdrop.

"How d'you know?" I whispered.

Tim also looked around, aware that what we were saying could get us killed.

"Cause Neal's been trying to get int' his pants, but can't," he whispered into my ear.

"He told you that?" I whispered back.

"Not in so many words. But you know how older brothers are. They don't tell you everything, but you start t' understand a lot."

I looked into Tim's eyes until I could see myself reflected in them. Suddenly I was scared. Suppose Neal did something to Arthur that made Arthur never want to get close to me again, like we'd been in the dining hall?

"I see," I said softly, trying to calm myself.

Bill Manion, Mel Harris, and Alfred Johnson caught up with us quickly afterwards, followed by some other guys. We all shook hands and pretended not to be kids for a few minutes, then played tag with each other. When some of the guys started pushing Arch Flanders around like he was a ping-pong ball, I put myself between him and them and realized, again, that it was a lot of fun to be a boy. Sometimes, when I was with Tim or some other kids besides Arthur, I felt that I had to pretend to be a boy. I wasn't sure what I was, but it wasn't a *real* boy. Real boys didn't think about being boys, they just *were*. It was unconscious, like being a dog. I was sure dogs didn't think about being dogs. They were *only* dogs.

Soon we were back at the cabins. I felt wonderful surrounded by my friends. Then Neal walked in, and I remembered what Tim had told me. Immediately, the smile on his face looked different to me. I wondered what was under that smile, that smile I liked so much on his clear, handsome face.

He was talking to Brother Alexis. Some other boys arrived later, and then finally Storch showed up alone—the last to come in—looking oddly secretive, like he had strangely grown up and was forced to be serious for a moment, more than I'd ever expected him to be. I watched him out the corner of my eye, with Tim's words repeating in my head: "What kills me is that Storch hates Gomez." It kills *Tim*, I thought—and Tim was not nearly as taken with Arthur as I was.

We all went to the latrine to brush our teeth. When we returned, Brother

Arnold from the ninth grade cabin was there, talking to Brother Alexis and Neal. Neal looked upset; I could tell he was trying hard not to let anyone know just how bothered he was.

Brother Alexis asked for quiet.

"I know some of you are friends with Arthur Gomez, a ninth grader," he said loudly. "Brother Arnold has just told me he's missing. Has anyone seen him?"

Manion came up to me.

"You saw him at dinner. You two sat together."

I held up my hand, and went over to Neal and the two Sebastianites and told them I *had* sat next to him at dinner. I didn't mention what we'd said, or utter a word about Neal and Arthur; it didn't seem right. Neal looked squarely at me, putting his hand on my shoulder. I didn't flinch.

"He's a great kid," Neal declared. "I'm sure he'll show up."

Brother Alexis took me aside.

"Benjy, is there something you need to tell us? If so, please do it now."

"We need to look for him," I said pleading. "Would you let me look for him?"

"No, I can't do that. It's dark outside. The adults will have to look. But if he doesn't show up soon, we've got to call the police."

Brother Alexis and Brother Arnold left us kids with Neal and Eugie Whitman, who both tried hard to keep order after they'd gone. Everyone was buzzing about what might have happened to Gomez. No kid had ever just disappeared at retreat, but some of the boys knew that Arthur kept to himself a lot, and thought maybe he had used the last day of the retreat as an excuse to run away. Certainly at some point all kids dream about running away from home.

"I bet he's hitchhiking now," Manion said. "He's out on some road getting picked up by perverts. My mom told me about perverts who pick up young boys."

"Would serve him right!" Storch blurted out. "He's only a queer anyway!"

Neal looked daggers at him.

"Shut up! I don't want to hear another word from you, Storch. You don't talk that way about fellow students at Holy Nativity!"

"Yes, *Sir*," Storch said, returning Neal's look in spades and putting it on thick. "Anything you say—*Sir*."

I could tell something was going on. Somehow, Storch knew about Neal and Arthur. He knew it, and he'd use it no matter what the outcome was of

Arthur's disappearance.

I could barely sleep that night; I kept tossing around, desperate to find out what had happened, and how Arthur was. Suppose he wasn't found, and just showed up years later, as an adult—and no one would know who he was anymore? I had never told him how much I'd wanted to pledge my whole faith to him, and that I would love him more than I'd ever *love* any girl, and that . . . .

I fell asleep thinking about that, but I wasn't sure it was *real* sleep.

The next day felt like a bad dream. There were cops all over and some strange men not in police uniforms. One was making notes; I guessed he was a reporter. No one would say anything to us.

Finally they got us all together in the large cabin next to the rec cabin, where they held Mass. Father Greer got up in front of us to speak. I had not seen him at all during retreat. He looked awful, like this huge weight was on him and he had not slept all night. No one made a sound.

"A terrible thing has happened here," he said. "A tragedy that only our Savior Himself will be able to explain, though as with all things of the world, we can only see it as God's will." He looked down, then said, "Arthur Gomez drowned last night in the lake."

I felt like someone had knocked all the air out of me.

Father Greer then told us that Arthur's parents had been notified and they had moved his body, and there would be a special Mass for him even before retreat was officially over, and I was crying so hard I couldn't stop myself. Everything rolled in front of me, refracted in my tears.

Everyone rose and they were saying the Lord's Prayer, and Tim came up to me. He was crying too, but he kept trying to comfort me. All he could say was, "There, there," and, "That's all right, Rothberg. It's OK t' cry. I know this is hurtin' you real bad, Rothberg."

We went over to the dining hall in complete silence for breakfast. You could feel the silence in the air like darkness, though the sun was out. I went back to the cabin and packed up in a deep fog, a fog of death and heartbreak. I had never really known this before, and now at twelve I was experiencing it. When Mom came to pick me up, she had already been informed. She was gravely serious, as we packed the car. Then on the drive back she said something.

"It's terrible about your friend, Benjy, but—"

I looked at her. She was smoking and looking straight ahead, not at me.

"But— *what?*"

Her shoulders tensed up at the wheel.

"Something bad's happening to your dad, Benjy. I'm afraid this has been really awful, but I need to tell you about it."

I swallowed hard. How could anything worse happen? I was scared to ask her what it was.

"He's having problems at work. Some people—" She paused. "Some people are telling terrible lies about him. That he used other people's money—he stole it. It's not the truth, Benjy. It's not the truth at all. He's been working like the devil to keep these companies going. He and Andy have done so much for them. These yokels have no idea what's going on, how he got money for them up North and kept their books and sold their stuff to the big stores and—I need to stop."

She was crying so hard that she pulled into the parking lot of a small luncheonette. I leaned over and stroked her hair. First Arthur and now my dad; it seemed impossible.

"Is it because he's a Jew?" I asked as a large man wearing a white apron came out of the luncheonette.

"You OK, Ma'am?" he asked.

She looked up at him through the window.

"I've just had a shock. A family matter."

"Sorry t' hear that. Why don't you come in and have a coffee? I can give the boy a Coke. That'll make you feel better. It would be my pleasure."

"Thank you," Mom said. "I'll be in in a second."

"People here are so nice when they want to be," Mom said as he walked back into the luncheonette. "I knew I'd have problems marrying your father. He had such ambitions. I never did. I guess when you grow up with some comfort like I did, you don't need to be that driven. I love Robby. You must never forget how much I love your father."

She took a tissue out of her purse, and looked at herself in the rearview mirror.

"God, I look a mess. I don't think I can go into that place, even as nice as that man was. I'll come by later and thank him."

She put the key back into the ignition. We were silent on the drive back to Isle of Hope, even as she turned into our driveway. After I had put my stuff away, we met on the veranda. It was a pretty afternoon; Liz was at a friend's house. Now, with just Mom and me out there, I felt very grown up. Mom poured herself a scotch and lit a cigarette.

"How did you find out about Arthur?" I asked.

"People started calling," she said. "I even got a call from the newspaper. They wanted some kind of statement from parents. I had nothing to say really. It's horrible, but kids drown. I'm only glad that it wasn't you."

She sighed, then pulled me to her and hugged me.

"When is Dad coming back?" I asked.

"Maybe not for a few more weeks. This is going to take a lot of money. I've already gone to my parents and Robby's seen a lawyer."

"Lawyer? Does that mean they're going to put him in jail?"

"I don't know what it means, Benjy. That's the terrible thing."

The phone rang. Mom almost jumped out of her skin. She went inside to answer it. A minute later, she came back to me.

"It's a policeman. He wants to talk to you."

I went in and picked up the phone.

"Hello, Benjamin. My name is Detective Whitacker from the Savannah Police Department. I guess you know we need to talk t' some of the boys who were close to Arthur Gomez. We believe that his death was a terrible accident, but we need to speak with you anyway."

"When do you want to do that, sir?" I asked, trying to sound adult.

"Can you come in tomorrow? We think it would be better to speak with you at the school rather than at the station. Kids don't like police stations, I know that."

"I've never been to one," I said.

"Good, keep it that way. Can I speak to your mom again?"

I got Caroline and she picked up the phone.

"I'll have him there at ten sharp," she said and hung up.

She was shaking. I could see it, and the drink and the cigarette probably didn't help, but I figured this was what adults did when they also needed to sound adult.

"This could not have come at a worse time!" she said, close to crying again.

"I'm sorry," I said. I *was* crying, thinking about Arthur and my father and how there was a very real link now between them. I hated crying; it seemed so babyish. I was glad no one from school could see me.

Caroline took my hand in hers.

"Your father's in terrible trouble, Benjy. I can't screw around with this, sorry for the language. I mean I've got to let you know something. But promise me you won't tell Liz. I think she's still too young to understand what's going on."

She took another sip of scotch.

"What's going on?" I said, sitting up as straight as possible.

"The truth is your father can't leave Valdosta, even for a minute. They're scared he's going to try to escape to New York. You know how yokels are in the South? They think that every Jew has family up in New York and he can just bolt back to where it's *safe*. Like New York is all Jews and Negroes, and the real people live here. Robby never did anything wrong, Benjy, I swear. It was all Andy's doing!"

I still didn't understand, but I felt stupid saying so. I could hear Robby saying, "It's your turn to be a *mentsh*, Benjy. You've got to be a grown-up." And somehow, it seemed that Caroline assumed that I would be. I realized there was a question I needed to ask.

"Then tell me, Mom," I said. "What *did* Andy do?"

"I don't know," she said, drying her eyes with a paper cocktail napkin. "They never let me into a lot of this stuff. Robby used to say to me, 'Business is tough, and the last thing I want you to do is get'—he used some Yiddish word—'*shmutz* on you.' Of course, I didn't push it. I wasn't really interested, and the *shmutz* was keeping us in this house, paying Josephine and your tuition at Holy Nativity. It's going to pay for your bar mitzvah, and later it will pay for your college and for Liz's. Speaking of your bar mitzvah, how's it going? You're still taking lessons with Brother Alexis?"

I told her I was.

"Odd isn't it?" she said. "You're somewhere between being a Catholic, a Jew, and everything else. You never seem to fit into any of the big spaces, and yet you're such a good kid. I couldn't dream of having a better kid than you."

I smiled, glad she didn't know about Tim O'Neill and the way I'd felt about Arthur, whatever that was called. I had never felt like that before, and was sure I wouldn't again. It was like he had made me glow inside. Really, my whole heart smiled when I was with him. I wanted to go up to Arthur and look at him and talk to him. But he was gone, and I didn't feel pain now as much as this huge emptiness.

I went into my room to unpack my stuff from the retreat, and wash around some before we ate. I needed to lie down to get my head back together. I felt as if it were coming apart, like there was just too much inside it to deal with. The phone rang.

"It's Tim O'Neill!" Mom called to me.

I picked up the extension in her bedroom.

"How ya doin'?" he asked me.

"I dunno. I feel like there's just too much for me to think about. How 'bout you?"

"Is anybody listenin' to you? Are you alone?"

"I think so," I said.

"Can you make sure?"

I ran downstairs and saw Mom in the kitchen with Josephine and Liz. She asked me what I needed, and I told her I was looking for something. She didn't ask me anything else and I was glad for that. I ran back upstairs.

"It's OK," I whispered to Tim. "What's up?"

"I guess you know about the meetin' with the cop tomorrow at the school."

"You, too?"

"Yeah, me and my brothers. You gotta do something. You gotta *not* tell anyone about Neal and Arthur and going out in the canoe. *Nobody*. Understand?"

"Why?" I asked, barely able to breathe.

"Cause they'll kill him, and he had nothing to do with Arthur's death. They *did* go out together and Neal *left* Arthur in the canoe. Arthur said he wanted to be by himself. He was scared of going home, scared of his old man. His old man was sure he was—"

Tim couldn't say it. I gave him the word.

"Pussy?"

"Yeah. He and Neal *never* messed around. You need to know that. Believe me."

"Is Neal with you?"

"No, but I know everything. Neal thinks Arthur killed himself."

"Jesus!" I said way too loudly. How could a fourteen-year-old kid kill himself? I wasn't even thirteen yet—how could that happen? I couldn't even penetrate the depth of Arthur's sorrow for him even to *want* to do that. Now I felt so bad.

"I won't tell 'em anything, Tim. I promise. I have to hang up now. I can't talk anymore."

I threw myself onto my bed. I needed to get hold of myself. Mom couldn't see me like this. Nobody could. Not even Tim.

I decided to take a shower, with really cold water and soap. But it was too cold, so I warmed it up a bit and stayed there for a while.

I missed Arthur horribly, but I had to pretend that the part of me that was missing him was simply not there; the same way I'd pretended to be like the other kids at my old school in Isle of Hope. A significant part of me was some other place, but I could do the things that I needed to *appear* normal, just like a regular normal kid, like the kid my mom loved so much.

After dinner Caroline, Liz, and I watched some really silly things on television, and I laughed like I normally would. Then I went to bed, where I decided that it was time to pray—*really* pray, not pretend prayers like I had seen too much during Mass at Holy Nativity. No wonder Arthur had doubted the Eucharist. Because I think Arthur really prayed—deep inside himself, he did. I knelt beside my bed, facing a window looking out on tall, dark trees.

"Hear O Israel," I said. "I know the Lord is One and I want t' ask You to help my father Robby—or *Leon*, his Jewish name—but most of all, I want you to bring Arthur Gomez into heaven with You. And please let him know how much I love him and miss him. I'm so sorry he drowned. I wish I could have been there to save him. I would have pulled him out of the water, even if I had to give up my own life to do it. I swear—no bull—I would have done that, just to save him. I can't believe he killed himself. I just wish he knew how much I loved him. But he didn't know; all he had was his old man. So please tell him, God. Please, just do that for me."

I felt better when I got up. Now I knew why people prayed and probably why Brother Alexis had become a monk, even though he was so good looking and he didn't have to become one. I kept thinking about Arthur, how much I wanted him there next to me. Then, suddenly, I felt that he really was. I could feel his face close to me in bed. I reached out and touched him, just like I had petted Caroline's hair. I was crying, but I knew he was softly smiling.

Then I fell asleep.

The Investigation

The next morning Josephine stayed with Liz while Mom drove me into Savannah for the meeting at the school. I was nervous and had no idea what to expect. I kept thinking about a large picture of St. Sebastian hung in the entrance hallway of the main building of Holy Nativity. He was tied to a post with arrows stuck in him, looking up at a ray of light that came from heaven. Now that ray of light reminded me of the light that had hit Tim, the first time I went to chapel with him. The light was from a dirty windowpane, but it seemed more beautiful and interesting to me than any light from stained glass might be.

The meeting was in Father Greer's office. Father Greer was there with another man, who I guessed was Det. Whitaker. My first impression of the place was always the smell of wood and fresh polish. I wondered if Father Greer polished all the bookcases, his big desk, and the big wooden chairs himself. He probably had people who came in with jars of wax to do it. Miss Pilkin shut the door behind us.

Father Greer, in full military uniform, stood up and thanked us for coming in, and introduced us to Det. Whitaker, who was about Robby's age, with a lot of streaky blond hair carefully combed back, with a very neat part on the left side. I wondered if he used Vitalis to keep it from flying around. It made him look younger. His face had a lot of wrinkles in it and was decidedly older-looking than his hair. But I had to admit, it was a nice face, not like some of the cops on TV.

"Benjamin, it's nice t' meet you!" he said, getting up, smiling at me, and shaking my hand. "And nice t' meet your mom, too. Mrs. Rothberg, is it all right with you if I talk to your son alone? As his mom, you can say no. But everything we say will be off the record. No lawyers, no court reporters around, as you can see. This is just a get-to-know-you session, and we need to get to know some of the boys who were Arthur Gomez's friends. You were his friend, right, Benjamin?"

"Yes, sir, I was."

I looked at Caroline, and tried to smile, but the truth was I was scared, unsure of what he'd ask me and if I'd be able lie if necessary as Tim had wanted me to.

"OK," Mom said nervously. "We're having a real problem at home, Officer. So I'm afraid this is just one more thing."

"Is there anything we can do?" Father Greer asked.

"It's personal and family," Mom said. "Families get into problems sometimes. You must know that."

"Certainly I do," Father Greer replied. "And I hope that God will grant you the serenity and grace to accept and persevere with all that happens, Mrs. Rothberg."

"Thank you, Father," Mom said softly. She lit up a cigarette. "I'll take a seat outside."

"It's a nice day," Father Greer said. "Let me take you around the grounds."

After they had left, Det. Whitaker sat directly in front of me and stooped so that he was talking at my level, the way Dad would do.

"I've been told your father isn't around," he said. "Is that true?"

"Yes, sir."

"That must be tough. Do you miss him?"

I nodded my head.

"Yes. I do."

"My father died when I was fifteen. I miss him every single day."

"You do?"

"I do, Benjy," he said, reaching out and taking my hand in his. "Sometimes when you're a kid, you need a guy to be there. Moms just don't do it, as much as we love them. You do love your mom, don't you?"

"Yes. I do."

My eyes gazed around Greer's office. Among all the polished wood furniture and pictures of the school from way back, I noticed another smaller picture of St. Sebastian. Strangely, the picture made me feel really small, being alone with Det. Whitaker. My attention wavered as I thought about Arthur, and for a second saw him in that picture.

"I heard," Det. Whitaker said, "that Arthur didn't have such a good time with his dad. Do you know anything about him and his dad?"

My eyes clouded up. Det. Whitaker offered me a tissue from his pocket. I blew my nose.

"Benjy, do you know anything about Arthur and his dad?" he asked again.

"No, sir."

"Are you sure?"

"I met him once," I admitted. "I went to where they live."

"We already spoke to his father and he told us about that. Did Arthur have any relations with an older boy here at school that was, well, close? Maybe a junior or a senior who took an interest in him, somebody like that?"

"I don't know that, sir."

"My name is Morris, Benjy," he said, moving his hand to my shoulder. "You can call me Morry, if you'd like. I know what it's like to miss your dad—'cause he's away. Like I said, I miss mine all the time. Think about it: Did some older boy, not a whole lot older but *older*, take an interest in Arthur, maybe something to do with that lake where he drowned? Maybe they went out canoeing or swimming together during the retreat?"

All I could think about was his hand on my shoulder. I wished he would remove it.

"Does it bother you that I have my hand on you?" he asked.

I nodded.

"That's OK, Benjy." He removed his hand. "Boys sometimes don't like to be touched by other men, especially if they get touched in the wrong way. Tell me, was anybody touching Arthur in some way that wasn't right?"

His blue eyes looked intently at me, and I hated it. Not because it was an ugly look but because it made me feel that I needed to say something that I didn't want to say. Suddenly I had to pee badly. I got up.

"I gotta go to the boys' room, sir," I said.

"That's OK. I'll be here."

Alone in the boy's room close to Father Greer's office, I really felt like St. Sebastian, roped to that post. Except Arthur was there, roped together with me. All kinds of people were shooting arrows at us. It was like a pain inside me, that's how the arrows felt. Now I could hardly pee, but managed to do it. Det. Whitaker was smoking a cigarette when I walked back into the office.

"Feel better?" he asked when I sat down. He put out the cigarette.

I told him I did.

"Good. I want you to tell me about Arthur's other friends, and also if any of the other boys didn't like him."

"A lotta guys liked him," I said, trying hard to smile. "He had friends."

"How about boys who *didn't* like him? We need t' know this, Benjy. We think something happened to Arthur at the lake, that maybe he didn't just *drown* by accident. Does anyone really dislike him—or *you*?"

My heart was beating so fast I could feel it inside my skull. I didn't want to rat on anyone.

"I know this isn't easy, Benjy. But a kid is dead, and we want to find out what happened."

"There're some guys . . ."

". . . who don't like you or Arthur, or that you and Arthur were friends?"

I nodded.

"I'll tell you what. I'll read a list of boys' names. When I come to the name of the guys who don't like you or Arthur, just let me know."

He started with the names of every kid in Arthur's class, then went into my class. I didn't say anything either, till he hit—

"Horace Storch."

I flinched. I could feel my body jerk when he read Storch's name.

"So this guy Horace doesn't like you or Arthur?" Det. Whitaker pressed me.

I was sweating so badly that I was even starting to smell. Father Greer's office wasn't air conditioned. It had just windows open, and was in the shade. I looked down at my hands. They looked pale; I could see blotchy places where blood was flowing in them.

"Are you OK, Benjy?"

"I feel pretty hot," I answered.

"Sure, it's hot in here. I guess that's why they don't have school in the summer. Does this guy Storch, does he have any friends?"

"A guy named Ken Ferris," I said. I could not look at Morris Whitaker while I said it. "And some other guys, but I don't know their names. They think it's fun to bully smaller kids. They did it to Arch once, and I stopped them."

"Arch?"

"Arch Flanders, a runty kid I know, but I don't like to see anybody get picked on."

"That's nice of you, Benjy. Stay that way. I don't like seeing people get picked on, either. Some other kids are coming in soon, so I think we'll end this for now. You and I have had a full morning, young man. I want to thank you for our talk."

I felt a lot better as I left Det. Whitaker in Father Greer's office. I had never mentioned Neal's name, or Pat's, and that made me feel good.

Mom was outside with Tim and Mrs. O'Neill. The twins were not there. Tim looked at me anxiously, but quickly changed his expression to a very convincing kid's smile. I smiled at him, feeling proud of myself.

"What did you and Det. Whitaker talk about?" Mom asked in the car.

We were still in the parking lot in front of the office at Holy Smokes.

"Arthur and his dad, and stuff like that."

"Did you tell him a lot?"

"I told him what I thought I knew."

"Good. There's going to be a funeral at a church out by the water. His father worked on fishing boats, you know. Father Greer said they've taken up a collection to bury the boy; it seems his family is so poor they couldn't afford it. He was going to Holy Nativity on a full scholarship. He was really smart. God! If something like that had happened to you, I don't know what I'd do! On top of what we're going through with your dad . . ."

She was sobbing now. I was glad nobody was there. It's hard having people see your mom cry. I didn't want to say any more about what was going on. I knew that my family was falling apart, but I just couldn't ask anything else.

The funeral Mass was two days later at St. Lucia, a small Catholic church off Victory Drive on the approach to Tybee Island. Arthur's mother was there, sobbing, with Arthur's brothers and sisters. His father was wearing a brown suit and a big tie with flowers on it, and sweating terribly, like he had been drinking. Mom and I sat in the back. The coffin was closed and I was glad. I didn't want to think about Arthur in a box. I had spoken with Tim on the phone and he told me there would be a wake. When I asked him what a wake was, he explained.

"People get together. They hug each other and cry; sometimes the adults drink a lot. The priests maybe come in, too. They had one when my grandfather died, Dad's dad. I was really little, like eight. It was at a funeral home downtown and they had Grandpa in the box and you got to look at him. He looked like he was sleeping. But they put this kind of paint on him, so he didn't really look like Grandpa, just this *thing* kinda like him. It was creepy."

I didn't understand, but was glad I didn't have to see Arthur looking like a thing that was *like* himself. I didn't want to have to think of him that way. I was still thinking about him constantly, and despite that time in the boys' room when Arthur was like St. Sebastian, roped to a post, it was more like he was still alive and could walk in at any minute.

The church was filled with dark-skinned people, and some boys from school came with both their parents, like Manion, Mel Harris, and Alfred Johnson who came with his mom. All of the O'Neills were there, including the small kids. Neal hugged me really hard. But Pat just stood stonily in the background, with this distant look on his face that made him strangely more handsome. I wondered if he felt even more of a loss than I did, because he and Arthur had that kind of magic closeness where you could talk without saying anything. At one point, he stared at me, or was he just staring at something else? I couldn't tell.

Since I had been to Mass before and knew what was going on, Mom, who wasn't Catholic, kept asking me what they were doing. There were altar boys and the service was like a regular Mass, except that the priest kept talking in Spanish. Then he spoke about Arthur in English, saying what a good boy he was and a comfort to his parents, and that God's ways were indeed mysterious but we must never lose faith in Him and his Son. Then he seemed to repeat his words in a shorter version in Spanish, and the Spanish people started really talking among themselves, until the priest finished, after which they lined up to receive Communion. Then, for the first time, I really wanted to do it—to receive one of the Communion wafers, simply to be closer to Arthur.

Except I realized something that hit me like a bolt of lightning—he didn't believe in it.

He never believed in the Eucharist and in Transubstantiation, and I was just about the only person he felt he could talk to about it. I was sure some of the other boys didn't believe in it either, but they kept it to themselves, as I did the way I felt about Arthur and what Tim and I had been doing together.

You'll always be with me, Arthur, I thought. *I'll always love you and now you'll know it, even though I never got to tell you.*

After the Eucharist, the choir sang, then they put the coffin on a trolley and moved it out the church. We all walked outside into blazing sunlight that felt good after being in the dark church. Mom hugged Arthur's mother. Mrs. Gomez looked really small next to Caroline, who was tall for a woman. Mrs. Gomez was still crying, as if nothing could come out of her except tears. She spoke almost no English and Mom spoke no Spanish. Mr. Gomez looked at me, nodding.

"Young man, thank you for being here," he said.

The priest came out, and Mr. Gomez went up to him and they spoke in Spanish. Both of them lit up cigarettes and just smoked until it was time to move. Then Arthur's family and their friends went over to the side of the church where the hearse was parked and two men in black suits were waiting.

All the O'Neills came up to us, and Mr. O'Neill shook Mom's hand and introduced himself. Mom and Mrs. O'Neill pretended that they knew each other from school, the way moms do. Pat shook my hand and looked at me with that same serious, steady look in his eyes, which felt like he was going to bore all the way through me. He would see exactly how I felt, because he felt that way, too, though neither of us could talk about it. He looked pale in the sunlight. He had such clear, perfect skin, but I saw that his eyes had a film of tears on them, even though I was sure he wasn't going to cry. Maybe that was why he couldn't say anything and had such a stern look on his face, all to keep himself from crying. This made me feel good; I didn't want to cry either. I'd done enough crying when no one else could see.

Mom didn't want to go to the cemetery. "Do you feel like having lunch?" she asked on the drive back to Isle of Hope. There was a restaurant called Johnny Harris's, that served great barbeque and we stopped there. It was a very grown-up place, but I wasn't hungry. I told her I'd love to have a Coke and she said that would be fine. It was still early, not yet noon, but she ordered a Tom Collins.

"Is that all you want, ma'am?" the waitress asked.

Mom nodded and lit up a cigarette, as the waitress left. She waved the smoke away from me. "Promise me you won't smoke, Benjy. It's an awful thing. I wish I didn't, but right now a cigarette is really good. That funeral was so sad. That poor woman his mother, and his dad. I felt so bad for them. I kept thinking—suppose that had happened to you? That you had drowned at the retreat."

She started crying again; I felt terrible for her.

The waitress, an older lady with very big, teased-up dyed-blond hair, came back with the drinks.

"Is there something I can do, ma'am?" she said kindly.

Mom wiped her face with a tissue.

"Thank you. We've just been to a funeral. A boy—"

"The Gomez boy? I read about it in the paper. Horrible thing. That poor child."

"My boy went to school with him. They were friends," Mom said. "We're all broken up about it."

"Well, you just stay here as long as you want. And if you need anything, a' aspirin or 'nother drink, just let me know. I'm not going to charge you for the first one. I want it to be on me."

"That's really sweet," Mom said. "Do you have kids?"

"Two. T'ain't easy."

"Then let me pay for it. Please."

"OK," the waitress said, then walked off.

"I need to talk to you, Benjy," Mom said, putting on her dark glasses to hide her red eyes. "I can't talk around Liz. She's too little. Dad's in serious trouble. I have to go to Valdosta. We may have to post bail for him."

"Is he under arrest?"

She nodded sadly.

"It's not his fault. Robby just got sucked int' some business deals by Andy Geyer and he's taking all the blame. I know it's 'cause—"

She stopped talking.

"*What?*" I asked her directly. "What do you know?"

"Maybe this wouldn't have happened if Robby weren't Jewish. But then he wouldn't be what he is. He's always sharp as a tack. I think the gentiles looked up to him. They owned that factory and thought that Robby and Andy were going t' save it."

"Can I go with you?"

"I can't take you there, Benjy. I'm sorry."

"Why *not*?

"Because Robby's in *jail.*"

I thought I was going to stop breathing. I felt tiny and completely helpless, but I had to feel bigger. I pushed myself all the way up in the chair.

"What are we going to do to get him out?" I said.

"I'll go to my parents. They have some money. We may have to put up the house. Just remember that your father loves us more than anything in the world. Never forget that."

I nodded; I wouldn't forget. Mom paid for the drinks and left the waitress a large tip.

"Is there anything that happened on the retreat I should know about, Benjy," Mom asked before she started the car. "Something you didn't tell the detective?"

"No. I don't think so," I said, looking at her.

"Good. Give me a hug. I need it right now."

I hugged her, and we drove back to the house.

Dad Comes Home Again

It took several days for Mom to drive up to Valdosta. I'm not sure what went on, but she was out of the house often and I was left alone with Liz and Josephine was there to take care of us. Josephine and Liz were out walking by the boats near the landing, when Tim O'Neill called me. Now I could really talk to him.

"Anybody listening?" he asked.

I told him I was alone.

"They questioned me," he said. "I wasn't going to rat on Neal. I mean, y' know he had this *thing* for Arthur. He liked him."

"We all did."

"Yeah, but Neal *really* liked him. He was—Jeez, I can't even say it."

"Then don't, dickhead," I said sharply. "Who cares? He didn't kill Arthur. Right?"

There was a pause, then Tim said, "Yeah." But he wasn't convincing me.

"Do you think Arthur just killed himself?" I said.

"No!" Tim said sharply. "That's a sin in the Catholic Church. You can't even be buried a Catholic if you kill yourself."

"So what happens to people who kill themselves?"

"I dunno. I guess everybody jus' lies about it, like Confession. The priest asks, 'Have you touched yourself impurely?' He means, 'You play with yourself?' Shit! Everybody plays with himself except your mom. I can't imagine moms playing with themselves, can you?"

"No." I couldn't even imagine *Robby* playing with himself. The thought just seemed impossible. "If he didn't really kill himself," I asked. "Then what happened at the lake?"

"I dunno. That's the terrible thing. God, it's horrible. I mean, s'pose he did?"

"Did they question Neal?"

"Yeah."

"What'd they ask him?"

When Tim didn't answer me. I told him that I needed to know in case Det. Whitaker questioned me again.

"OK, I guess I can tell you," Tim said. "The detective wanted to know if Arthur had ever done anything 'funny' to him. 'Like *what*?' Neal said. So Whitaker came right out and asked him, 'Did Arthur Gomez ever give you a blow job?' Neal told me that himself.

"Wow. What'd Neal say?"

"He told him *no*, like big N-O. He was not gonna let this cop fuck up Arthur's name. Really, that's just *not* Catholic. Your name's everything to us. Ain't it to you guys, too?"

"I see," I said. "So Arthur never *gave* Neal a blow job. Did Neal?"

"Oh, *fuck*—what *are* you, dickhead? Y' think my brother would give Arthur Gomez a blow job? Neal's on the football team."

"Did he?"

"No," Tim said. "But he … kissed him."

"*Whaa?*"

Tim exhaled. "I shouldn't tell you this, but I saw 'em. They were down at the lake, by the canoe. I went there just t' look." (Suddenly I remembered that I'd seen them at the lake, too.) "They were on the shore, and I could hardly see 'em—but Neal was on top of Arthur."

"Maybe they were wrestling?"

"Yeah. Like you and I wrestle."

"But you said Neal never gave him a—"

"I don't know! Maybe he did. He was strange for Arthur; that's the only way t' say it. But you were, too. Right?"

I couldn't answer him; what could I say? I'd already told Tim that Arthur was *like* God.

"You still there?" he asked.

I could barely get the word out. "Yeah."

"I don't wanna talk about this on the phone anymore," he said.

"Neither do I," I said. "Maybe we can do a sleep-over."

"I dunno. It's too hot. The skeeters are all out."

"You're scared, aren't you?"

"Like I said, I don't wanna talk about it on the phone."

After I hung up, I wondered, suppose Brother Alexis or one of the other monks saw them? Maybe they said something to Arthur and it just destroyed him. Arthur knew his father would kill him if Mr. Gomez thought Arthur was a queer. What was the word, a *maricon*? I'd have to figure out some way to ask Brother Alexis about it, without mentioning Neal.

Then I realized something: there was also Pat, and Pat had acted awfully *queer* himself, like he knew something and he was holding it in so tight that it was going to kill him to keep it there.

I spent the next couple of days reading comic books and watching TV and being bored and scared all at the same time. When Mom was home I wanted to talk to her about Dad. And I wanted to talk to him on the phone so bad it hurt. But what would I say to him? Stupidly, I couldn't remember saying to him that I loved him. Dad said that to me sometimes, but it always came out sounding like something you'd just say to a kid anyway. I mean, he thought I was going to be crazy about girls, and boy stuff that I didn't really care much about. It was like he had a secret world—so did I. But his secret world was basically the adult world, and mine seemed so much darker and worse. One day, like it or not, I would enter the adult world and know its secrets. But I was sure Dad would never, at all, know mine.

Mom told me she had the money for the bail. She and Andy Geyer—Andy, again!—would go up to the sheriff in Valdosta and present it to him to get Dad out. I didn't see the Savannah paper in the house anymore. Mom probably took it away before I could see it. I was afraid there was news of Dad in it, and that was why she hid it. She even turned off the local news on TV at six every night. I always liked the weather report because it was announced by this guy named Captain Sandy who was dressed like an old sea captain, with whiskers and a captain's cap. When I asked her why we couldn't see Captain Sandy, she'd say, "It depresses me. All the news depresses me now. Sorry, but it does."

She went up to Valdosta at the end of the week and brought Dad home. He could only stay for the weekend. He looked awful. He had aged so much that I could barely recognize him, certainly not as the same person who'd left not that long before. He looked as if he'd been gone for years and years. I wanted just to jump into his arms when he appeared with Mom, but I couldn't. I was too old and I knew it.

"How are you, Benjy?" he asked.

I told him I was OK, but was afraid to ask how he was. I felt stupid. How do you ask your dad how he is when you know it doesn't mean anything?

"I'm glad you're back, I really am," I said.

He smiled his old smile. It was beautiful; it just glowed all over him, like he was drenched in it. The lines on his face didn't disappear but only added to the whole effect, like he was drawing everyone of them into this beautiful pattern of his being with me. I took his hand and he held mine. Mom left us on the sofa in the living room. He pulled his hand through my hair, then drew it away. Suddenly he put his head in his hands the way I did, when I was exhausted from too much happening and wanted to escape for a second to some safe, dark place, even if it were only behind my closed eyes.

I waited for Robby to come back to me. He pulled himself together and looked at me.

"You probably don't know anything that's happened, do you?"

I shook my head.

"Maybe it's best. You're too young to understand it, and I wish I could protect you from it."

"I'll try to understand," I said. "I mean that."

"I know you do. I don't know how I ended up with you as my kid."

He started crying. I didn't want to see him cry. I didn't want to cry myself. It was bad enough losing Arthur, and now seeing Dad cry was horrible. I started to stroke his head. He pulled away from me, then suddenly drew me to him. He extracted a handkerchief from his pocket and blew his nose. He lit a cigarette.

"I made some terrible errors . . . but I had good intentions," he said.

"Will you have to go back to jail?" I asked.

"Maybe, but it won't be for very long. The most important thing is that you and your mother and Liz get to stay in this house, and also that you get to stay at Holy Nativity. I feel like they've done good by you. And you like it there, don't you?"

I nodded. I did.

"How have you been doing with the bar mitzvah lessons? Mom told me about Brother Alexis. I can't believe my kid's being prepared for his bar mitzvah by a Catholic brother, but—hey!—we're different and we don't have to be the same as other people. D'you believe that?"

"Sure." I smiled at him. Now I wanted to be a kid on his lap again, and not think about his business or anyone's for that matter.

"I'm sorry to hear about your friend. I'm so glad it wasn't you. It would have ripped my heart out, Benjy, and killed me faster than a bullet. How did it happen? He couldn't swim?"

"I saw him at the swimming pool. Arthur was as good as any of us," I said.

"Mom told me about the investigation. Did they ever learn any more about it?"

"If they did, they aren't telling us kids."

Liz came out and crawled all over Dad. I was glad she interrupted us. I was afraid of what might happen if Dad kept questioning me about Arthur. He hugged Liz and kissed her. Then Mom called us in for dinner.

At first it was like everything was almost the way it had been before. Dad and Mom joked with each other and he used Jewish words and she laughed and pretended that she knew everything about them. They talked about my bar mitzvah. There was a date for it, and Andy Geyer had talked to the people at the big synagogue in Savannah who agreed to it. It would be catered by the local kosher caterer who catered everything Jewish in the city.

"They're German Jews. Been here forever," Dad said smiling. "I used to know them when I first got into town. Those people know how to throw a party. I want lots of good liquor, and some fantastic stuff. Just because we're having these problems—anyway, Andy's going to give us some money. He says, 'It's the best I can do for the *boychik*.' That's you, Benjy. Andy loves you like you're his own kid."

Mom looked at me with a glare that went straight through me. It was only too obvious how she felt about Andy. Most of the time, he was Dad's friend, not hers.

"My parents will give us something," she said.

Dad's face went almost white.

"Caroline, they've done enough! The bar mitzvah won't cost that much in the long run. I was being a bit crazy, I know. But I just don't want t' go to them after what they did for me."

"So where will you get the money? Not those same—"

"Quiet! Please, let's just don't talk about it."

He put his hands back up to his face, and I felt awful. I hated it—why did

I have to have a bar mitzvah anyway? But I couldn't open up my mouth; I couldn't hurt Dad any more. I was afraid I was going to cry again and excused myself and I ran up to my room. All I could think about was Arthur and my father, until suddenly for a moment they became almost the same person. It was stupid. How could they be the same person?

There was a knock on the door. It was Dad. He sat down next to me and ran his hand over my head.

"It's OK," he said.

Unable to speak, I just hugged him. I had forgotten how he smelled and it came back to me. His perspiration and the cigarette smoke; it was wonderfully clean, I liked it.

"I'm sorry," I said, straightening myself up.

"It's OK, Benjy. You're still a kid, you need to know that. This time is precious, and it's my fault that you're growing up a lot faster that you should."

"No, it's not."

"See, even that's grown up. Sometimes I miss the fact that you're not a little boy anymore."

"Isn't that what being bar mitzvahed all about?"

"You mean it's not just about getting another fountain pen?" he winked and gave me his great smile that seemed younger than I was. I couldn't help but smile back.

"You're right," he said. "Your bar mitzvah is going to lead you into manhood. Later you'll get married and have kids of your own. You'll like that, and so will I."

I nodded. All I wanted him to do was feel good. I walked with him back downstairs and we had dessert.

The next day Mom announced to me that she wanted to spend the day alone with Dad. There was a lot they needed to go over. She could either drive me into town to see a movie, or I could call Tim and see if I could spend the day with him. I called Tim.

"Sure! Come on over," he said. "My parents are out. Pat and Neal are here with us." I could hear some little kids saying something. They must have been Lisa and Joe, Jr. the two youngest. Neal said something I couldn't understand, then got on the line.

"How you doin'?" he asked.

"I'm OK."

"Good. Sorry to hear—"

"Shut up!" Tim shouted.

"I wasn't gonna say that!" Neal told him, then said to me in a low voice, "I want to talk to you."

"'Bout what?" I asked.

Neal exhaled; I could hear his voice clench.

"What d'you think, dickhead?"

Tim grabbed the phone. "Sorry, Benjy. See, our parents ain't here. So my beloved brother's actin' like a turd stuck in a sewer."

Mr. and Mrs. O'Neill *were* away; Tim's mom was on a lot of committees and his father played golf on the weekends.

Neal grabbed the phone again and shouted. "You piece o' crap!"

Lowering his voice, he said, "I didn't mean you, Benjy. Listen, I know you got things o' your own, but I *need* to talk to you when you get here."

"Sure," I said and hung up, puzzled.

Mom brought me over before lunch. The good thing about having a large family was that having one more kid over didn't mess up anything. The O'Neills always had something to eat.

When I walked into the house, I saw Tim's younger brother, Joe, Jr. and his two sisters Margaret, the older one at nine, and Lisa, the younger one at seven, watching cartoons on TV. Joe Jr. was really cute. He was only five, but very smart. He was reading already like I had been, and probably would be smarter than Tim. I noticed Pat going up the stairs; he looked at me, smiled briefly, then continued up to their room. Tim looked at him, shrugged, then grabbed me and shook my hand, like we were meeting formally. Then he hugged me.

Neal wanted to take me out to the backyard.

"Can't I just say hello t' him first?" Tim asked. "This has been real shit with Arthur dead and other stuff."

"One day I'm gonna wash your mouth out with soap," Neal threatened.

"Sure, Neal," Tim retorted. "'Specially considerin' what's been in yours."

"Shut up, fuckhead," Neal ordered. "Let's go out to the back, I don't want the kids to hear any more than they have to."

"Ain't you supposed t' be watching *us* kids?"

"Yeah, I'm watching!" He got more serious. "This is important. Anyway,

Pat's upstairs if anything crazy happens. He's probably talking to his girlfriend on the phone up there."

Neal grabbed a can of beer, and the three of us went outside. It was still pretty hot out, but shady enough in the back. I remembered pitching the tent back there and what Tim and I had done in it. I wanted to get closer to Tim suddenly to talk about my dad, without Neal around. Neal was too much like an adult, and adults were driving me crazy.

There was a wooden picnic table in the back, and we sat at it. Neal drank some more of the beer and then handed it to Tim who took a deep swallow. He passed it to me, and I pretended to take a swallow and told them thanks. I still wasn't used to drinking beer; it tasted like stale bread and salt water.

"Nobody knows about me and Arthur, right, Benjy?" Neal asked seriously. "I mean, none of the other guys know how much I liked him?"

"I guess so," I said. "But are you *sure*?"

"What do you mean, Benjy?"

"He means," Tim blurted out, "like some other dickhead like Ferris coulda found out—and blabbed t' people."

Neal looked at his younger brother and panicked. He looked at me, took another swallow of beer, and tried to calm down.

"You think they'd listen to them?" Neal asked. "Most people hate Ferris and Storch's guts. That's why I don't think anybody's really gonna listen to them."

"We know that," Tim said. "But some of the brothers like 'em—for instance, Brother Ulrich."

"Jesus-fuck!" Neal swore. "Brother *Dorris*?"

"Doris?" I asked, "Like Doris Day?"

"Naw," Tim said, "It's got two r's in it. D*ahhh*-ris. It was Mahoney's name before he became Brother Ulrich."

I nodded. I'd heard the Mahoney part, but not the Dorris.

"Saint Ulrich was known for his rectitude, or *e*-rect-itude." Tim grinned as only he could. "Some of the older boys found it out, and passed it on. Anyway, Dorris is sugar-sweet over those turds Storch and Ferris. He hates anything that's impure. Just 'cause those two are bullies, he thinks they don't jerk off and suck."

"Come on," Neal said, with disgust. "This conversation is getting too rank even for me. How did I ever get a younger brother like you, Tim?"

"Cause I had an older brother like you, Neal. Pat ain't like you, I'll tell you that. For twins, you two are completely diff'rent."

"True," Neal admitted. "Pat's disgusted by the whole thing. He thinks that I—"
Neal broke off. I waited, not wanting to pry open anything else.

"He thinks," Tim continued for him, "that our beloved Neal pushed Arthur to suicide."

"All I wanted t' do was help," Neal protested. "I loved Arthur. He was the sweetest guy in the world and his old man was driving him crazy."

"You jus' wanted t' get into his pants," Tim said, needling him.

"Not true—it wasn't just that. I mean, guys fool around with guys. Nobody talks about it, but we know it happens, especially at Holy Nate, an all-boys school. It's been going on forever. Even Dad knows it."

"You're kiddin'!" Tim said. "I thought parents were stupid about stuff like that."

"They're not," Neal argued. "Dad once told me when I first got to Holy Smokes, 'Watch out for some of the older boys. They'll try stuff with you.' He didn't go into any details, but some people know there's a john in the library way behind the stacks in the basement, and guys have been using it for years to fool around in. The brothers are weird about it. If you get caught red-handed, they have to make a stink about it. But mostly, they pretend it doesn't go on because it dirties up the name of the school. The public school kids think we're all queers anyway. It's not true, but some of us—well, y' know, we fool around, that's all."

"Do you think somebody might have known about you and Arthur?" I asked Neal. I didn't want to admit that I'd seen them myself at the lake.

"Maybe Brother Ulrich, or some other ass-face like him." Tim suggested seriously.

Neal looked extremely pained. He just let Tim speak.

"Ulrich—ol' Dorris," Tim explained, "has a' evil temper. He jus' manages t' keep it down 'cause it's a cardinal sin to have a temper when you're a monk. Some of 'em have it anyway. I guess that's why so many of the brothers drink, and the priests."

I felt terrible; I didn't want to talk about it anymore. I had too many questions, and there was no way to get to an answer. I couldn't say anything to Det. Whitaker. If I did, I'd spill the beans on my friends. I couldn't even talk to Tim.

Lisa came out and asked Neal to make lunch for them.

"Can't Pat do it?" Neal asked.

"He won't," she whined. "He's on the phone!"

"OK. Peanut butter and jelly time," Neal announced, and marched Lisa into the house, leaving Tim and me alone in the backyard.

"I'm real glad you came over, Benjy," Tim said. "Shit's goin' on at your house, and I know you're thinking about what really happened t' Arthur, aren't you?" He put his hand on my shoulder. "Know what I think? I think Arthur just gave up. Kids do it sometimes. Even me."

"You think about killing yourself?"

"Naw, I couldn't do that. I mean . . . just givin' up. I'm talkin' about being Catholic. You got all this rigmarole about all the stuff you gotta do and you gotta believe in, but all that does is keep you from being *desperate*."

"Desperate about what?"

Tim looked at me, exactly as he had looked at me the first time we went to chapel together and I saw what he looked like in that clear beam of light from the dirty upper window. It was like I could see straight through him, and inside he was beautiful.

"About dying," he said. "And about God really loving you."

"So you think Arthur gave up?"

Tim nodded.

Now I had to hold on to myself. I took Tim's hand; I was shaking and close to crying.

"You're still broke up about it, ain't ya?" Tim said. He drew me close to him and kissed me on my cheek, whispering, "I wish we could fool around, but we can't."

I looked over and saw Pat, who must have come down for lunch, watching us through the kitchen window, his face registering nothing. I let go of Tim's hand and we got up and went in for lunch, too.

Pat and Neal resided over lunch like they were our parents. Neal smiled at me and ruffled his fingers through my hair, telling me what wonderful dark Jewish hair I had. (It wasn't fine like theirs; it didn't just blow all over the place in the wind.) Pat said very little. Sometimes he looked at Neal like he didn't approve of him when Neal made a joke or laughed hard at something Tim had said.

Mom picked me up around five o'clock. I asked her where Dad was. She lit a cigarette with the car lighter and puffed on it.

"Andy Geyer came by and picked him up," she finally said when we were on the road back to Isle of Hope. "They're on the way to Valdosta. Andy said we couldn't take any more chances with Robby being in Savannah."

I looked out the window. Summer was coming to an end. The clouds had a distinct edge to them, darker, crisper. Soon it would be hurricane season in Savannah, when things could get unpredictable.

"What kind of chances?" I asked.

"Some cop could pick him up for anything, and find out that he was out on bail. A reporter called. The Savannah paper has done some stories on Robby. I didn't want you to know about it, that's why I hid the papers for a while. It was all just a bunch of bull crap, Benjy. You need to hear it from me, just straight like that."

"So that means everybody at school will know?"

"Maybe. Kids usually just read the comic strip. Did any of the O'Neills say anything?"

Now I knew what Neal meant when he said I had "things" of my own. But all of that got lost as soon as we had started speaking about Arthur.

"No," I answered firmly. "They wouldn't. Tim's parents wouldn't say anything. They're really good people, I know it."

"Sure, honey. I'm glad the O'Neills are your friends, but they're Kennedy Catholics. They're smart, they have class, and they don't believe all the b.s. people around here believe."

"What do you mean, the b.s.?"

She lit another cigarette and blew the smoke out the window.

"People here are so narrow-minded. If you aren't like them, they just shut down around you. But you're too young to understand that."

"No, I'm not," I said.

"Good."

She tossed her blond hair a bit; I loved it when she did that. I could see why Robby was crazy about her. She looked like a regular adult person for an instant, not like a mother or a parent.

"Mom," I said, "all those things people say, about those men in Isle of Hope—you know, the 'light in the loafers' type—is it true? Are they really bad? Is there something about them that makes them—"

"Repulsive, *queer*, is that what you want to say, Benjy?"

I knew I was treading on thin ice, but I had needed to ask it. She smiled.

"People have their own ideas and they cling to them," she said. "When I married your father, my parents flipped out. But they got used to it. To tell you the truth, there is a lot about him I never understood and probably never will, but he has more goodness and moral fiber in him than any of the good Christians I knew, the country club people my parents liked and all the young men I met. I looked at Robby and it was all over with. He could have led me straight to hell and I would have gone with him. At least for a while."

We were getting closer to the house.

"How much trouble is he really in?" I asked.

"It's hard to say, Benjy. Maybe I've already said more than I should have. You've had so much put on you, being the kid of a mixed marriage. Do you feel like you don't belong anyplace?"

"No, I belong at Holy Nativity," I said.

"Because of your friends?"

"Sure. But I'm not going to be Catholic. I couldn't hurt Dad that way. And I want the bar mitzvah. I really, really want it now."

"Good."

She leaned over and kissed me as we turned into the driveway. Josephine came out with Liz. Josephine was trying hard to be cheerful, and so was Liz. Young as she was, she was aware that something was happening and it wasn't good. Liz was a brave kid; that's what I liked about her. She looked more like Mom, just like I took after Robby, *Leon*. Something inside me was Jewish and there was no way I could avoid it or evade it. We walked into the house; Josephine had dinner ready. It was one of her great meals of fried chicken and potato salad and lemonade. Just as we were getting up, there was a call from Brother Alexis. I took the phone.

"How are you doing, Benjy?" he said. "I guess this has been a difficult time for you."

I realized he must have seen something about Robby in the paper.

"I want you to know that everyone here at Holy Nativity is behind you. I've spoken to Father Greer and some of the other teachers. We'll make sure that this remains only your business. If any kid says anything bad to you in the fall, let us know."

"Brother Alexis," I said. "We need to start the bar mitzvah lessons again *soon*. It's going to be in October and I need to do it for my dad. It means a lot to him."

"That's great, Benjy," he said, his voice warming to me. "We still have close to another month of summer, but I'll set aside an hour for you, three afternoons a week. Just let your mom know when you want to start."

I thanked him and hung up. Back into the kitchen, Josephine was talking to Liz. I found Mom on the veranda, having a drink as it got darker. She looked up at me and smiled. I told her about Brother Alexis and she nodded, distantly. She tried to light a cigarette, but the match kept blowing out. I lit it for her; she was shaking, I could tell.

"Do you want some more lemonade?" she asked, smiling her wonderful, mysterious smile.

I told her no, and sat down.

"What are you drinking?" I asked.

"Scotch. I've started to like it. Robby loves the stuff. I can see why."

"How will we get Dad to the bar mitzvah?" I asked.

"By that time things will be different," she said, shaking her head. "I'm not sure how we're going to do it at the big synagogue in Savannah. We're not members—I never even went. Maybe Andy Geyer gave them enough money when he set everything up. I'm not sure how he did it. I have to admit this is an alien world to me, Benjy. It's not like my friends out here; the ones I sit around with and we have a smoke and a Salty Dog. I never was one for Jewish women. It's like they have no real life; at least that's how it felt for me. That's why I couldn't convert."

"Did you ever think about it?"

"A little, shortly after we were married. We were married by a Justice of the Peace here, then went up to New York for our honeymoon. My parents were pretty good about it; they had this big church-wedding idea for me, but they got used to it. They even got used to Robby. It's not hard; your father's really wonderful."

"You mean for a *Jew*?"

She broke up laughing.

"Shut up! I mean for *anybody*! He just wasn't like people down here. There was something beautiful about him. In New York, well, it felt like Robby was more like everybody else. All so—crazy-Jewish! Like everything was the most important thing in the world and Hitler was still hiding around the corner. I met some distant cousins of his who kept looking at me like I had two heads. The women had no idea what to do with me. They kept wanting t' know about our kids—how would they be raised? All I could say was 'As nicely as possible.'

"Robby was embarrassed by them, and yet proud, too. He had cousins who still had heavy accents, like they'd just come over from Europe after going through the war there. I did feel bad for them. They'd been through hell with Hitler, and I'd just had this nice time in Savannah, with attractive people who weren't like Leon—I mean Robby."

"He didn't want to be Leon with you, did he?"

"No, that was another mysterious part of him, something he could never quite fit into and could never quite leave. I think there was something about me being the *goyishe* wife that your father found calming. He'd fought in Korea. Andy saved his life, and Robby's always been grateful for that. But sometimes I think there's more to it; it's like Andy's a part of Robby's life that he can't get rid of."

Things were happening around me I could barely understand. Mom was drinking more, and I wasn't supposed to ask any questions about that—or about Dad in Valdosta. Would he be put in jail? I could barely imagine it. How could my father be in jail?

Not wanting to fall apart in front of Mom, I went to my room. In bed, I thought about Arthur being there with me.

He was wearing shorts and a shirt that was mostly unbuttoned so I could see his chest. He was smiling at me and reaching over and touching my face. I wanted so much for him to say something, but he didn't. I thought about his doubting the Eucharist, and wondered if that had changed now that he was in heaven. It was impossible for me not to believe he was there. Strange, I'd never really thought about heaven. Death seemed so abstract to me, and scary. I knew Catholics believed in Everlasting Life, and in getting into heaven through Jesus and the Saints, but as a non-Catholic—and even a non-Jew—the idea of heaven seemed as unreal to me as one of those fairy tales in a Disney movie. Actually, Disney seemed more real. *Snow White* scared the hell out of me when I was small. That scene with the old hag with all the warts on her nose and the poison apple was terrifying, like looking directly into death. To me, death was old people and poisoned apples that made you sleep without waking up. Once I'd asked Robby what death was like, and he looked as if a jolt of pain had crossed his face.

"Sometimes it's like going to sleep," he said. "And then other times . . ."

When he didn't say anything else, I asked "Was that what the war was like?"

"Yeah. It was like the other times. But you don't need to worry about it. Death is a long way off for you, Benjy, and by the time you get closer to it—and I hope that doesn't happen *forever*—I'll be there to keep you from asking the bad questions."

"What are those?" I asked.

"The ones even I can't answer."

Now I wanted to ask Arthur the bad questions. Like, what was death actually like? But, even more important, how did you get there? And if you really did kill yourself, why—and *why* couldn't I have stopped it?

I knew no one would answer me, so I got up and watched TV with Liz, while Mom was still on the veranda. Then I went back upstairs and brushed my teeth and went to sleep.

I resumed the bar mitzvah lessons with Brother Alexis soon after that. They got my mind off things, and I realized that they got his mind off things as well. I could tell something was going on; there was just this connection I had with Brother Alex. It was as if he were covered with ice, and trying hard to break out of it. He was young, handsome, and troubled, but there was no way of me knowing how much the rest of the school was also troubled after Arthur's death. I learned Hebrew, the words, how to read them, and what they meant. Brother Alexis made sure that I knew what I was saying when I said the prayers, and the portion of the Haftorah I was supposed to chant.

"You can't just mouth it," he said. "You have to know what you're saying."

I looked at him. Now I wanted to know what *he* was saying. What was going on among the Sebastianites at Holy Nativity that summer?

"How's your father?" he asked.

"OK," I answered quickly. "I think."

"This must be hard on you," he said.

I was scared that I would cry; I didn't want to answer. He got up, walked behind me and put his hands on my shoulders, in a way that he had never touched me before. His cheek went down to my hair. I smelled liquor on his breath; I'd never smelled that before, either.

"We all go through bad times," he said. "That's why God's there for us."

"Is He?" I said quietly

Now I did cry. I couldn't help it. He hugged me from behind. I grabbed his hands, and held them.

"Why did He take Arthur?" I cried. "Why Arthur?"

Brother Alexis held me tighter. He was shaking.

"I can't say, Benjy. I really *can't* say. But He brought you to us, and that's what's important. You have to accept God's grace and human suffering through it."

"I don't want to. I'm Jewish, not Catholic."

"You're not totally Jewish, Benjy. And God is working through you, you have to accept that."

He pressed his lips briefly to the top of my head, then let go of me and sat down.

"I'm sorry I did that," he said. "You're a student and I'm a teacher. But I felt … well, I don't know what I felt. Will you please forgive me?"

I nodded, unable to speak.

All I wanted to do was go back to the lesson. Later I wished I could have said something to Robby about it—like, why did I really *want* Brother Alex to kiss me that way, and why was I so happy when he did it? I felt my nerves tingle when he did. Did it have anything to do with what I'd been doing with Tim O'Neill, or how much I liked the way Brother Alexis looked? Could Brother Alexis see that I wasn't like other boys, the same way Tim O'Neill knew he wasn't? I wished I could have just said something to Robby, but there was no way in hell I could, even if he'd been around.

Still, I was sure Robby would have answered me in the most truthful, frank, forthright—and Jewish—way, without any of the usual lies and bull crap. I already knew that much about Robby, or *Leon*. And it made me know that under my skin I was very much a part of him, I was very much his son.

13

The Blakelys

A few weeks into the lessons that summer, Mom got me all dressed up and we drove into Savannah to see my Grandpa and Grandma Blakely. They were her parents, Betty and William. Or to be more precise, William Wentworth Stragham Blakely. He had been a judge, way back when, maybe during the Civil War for all I knew, and was extremely proud of his distinguished Southern heritage, the one that he had wanted to give Caroline and she tossed away, I guess by marrying my dad the Jew. They lived in a genteel, slightly shabby part of Savannah, where the houses all had big live oak trees in front dripping with gray Spanish moss, thick rows of azaleas around them, and in the back, disciplined formations of delicate, dark-green camellia bushes that were rigorously nursed by Southern garden-club ladies.

Their colored maid Suzy, in a neatly-pressed black uniform with a crisp white apron, greeted us at the door. (Our maid Josephine never wore a uniform. She had asked about it, but Mom had told her, "I don't want you to look better than I do," and laughed.) They did not believe in air conditioning but had all the windows open and ceiling fans blowing lightly down on us. The fans messed up my hair and I reached up to put it back in place.

"Your mom and pa are waitin' in the back for you," Suzy said to Caroline.

Betty and William Blakely were on the back screened-in porch that overlooked the camellias, having cocktails of iced sherry, which they liked to drink, I knew, in the afternoon. There was a lemonade for me and Suzy brought another iced sherry for Mom. Grandma was wearing a nice navy-blue dress with a white collar and William was in a coat, tie, and freshly pressed pants, like I was. It had always seemed strange to go visit your grandparents and look like you're going to church, but that was the way we always looked when we went to the Blakelys. I'm not sure that Dad had ever gone with us. If he had, I'd been too young to remember it.

"Come here, Benjamin," Betty ordered.

I did, and she leaned over and kissed me. She smelled of face powder and perfume and some disagreeable smell that old people always seemed to have, that I later learned came from their dentures. William shook my hand and did his usual "How are you, young man?" after which I went back to sit next to Mom, who had already finished her sherry cocktail and was ready for another.

Suzy went to fetch one for her. There was a crystal bowl filled with dried peanuts and I grabbed some of them and chewed them while I drank the lemonade. For a moment no one said anything; they just made these strained polite smiles at each other. Then Mom said, "Benjy, do you want to go into the living room and watch television?"

I got up, thinking that was the thing to do, when Grandpa Blakely said, "No, I think Benjamin should stay here for a moment. Caroline, we want to help you with the . . . what do you call it?"

"The bar mitzvah," Mom said. "And Benjy doesn't need to hear this discussion."

The Judge, that was what Dad sometimes called him, looked at her seriously.

"His father is having problems, and I don't think this young man should be the last one to know. He's not a baby anymore."

Caroline looked defeated.

"OK. We need your help with the bar mitzvah, and Robby has—" She took a deep breath, then said, "you know, court fees, and of course a lawyer to pay for."

"Can you still pay for the house?" Grandma asked. "I don't want my grandchildren to have to worry about that kind of thing."

"They're not worried," Mom said, exhaling.

"But you are," Grandpa said. "I know it. Benjamin, your mom is going through some troubles. It's the kind grown-ups have to go through. I think it's good you know something about it. Your dad's in trouble with the law, and—"

Mom jumped up.

"Benjamin, I'd rather you don't hear the rest of this conversation. Please, for my sake, go into the living room!"

Judge William got up and grabbed my hand.

"I'll take you in there in myself. There are things guys need to talk about anyway. Do you like airplanes?"

I nodded.

"So do I. I have a collection of model planes upstairs. We'll go there."

I'd seen the Judge's collection of model planes before. They were in the upstairs den, were old, hand painted, and made out of wood; they looked like they were from World War One. The Judge had been an aviator, back when it was very special and I guess mostly rich guys like him had planes.

"My mother hated 'aer-o-planes,'" the Judge said when we were alone up there. "She never wanted me to fly one. So of course I did. Back in those days, in Savannah, there was a small private airstrip and my buddies and I got together and we flew the planes, and some of us bought some. You can't imagine what they were like. All made out of canvas and wood with an engine in them that should have run a lawn mower. But it was so exciting! You could see the world from a place no one had ever seen it before. You could see it like you were looking down at a map, with all the rivers and marshes and streams. The hills, the mountains further up in North Georgia. I flew up to Washington once. The capital! It was a huge thing to do … I was young then. I loved it."

He brought out some more models and let me touch them, and we pretended to fly them, taking them up in the air in our hands, stretching far up while Grandpa made grunting airplane sounds that came out of the bottom of his throat.

"I've got to go downstairs now and join in a serious talk, young man." He sighed. "At my age, talking so serious is ridiculous. Know what I mean?"

I shook my head.

"Good, you shouldn't. I mean the most serious thing I can do now is die, and I don't want to do that. I want to see you grow up, and become a fine young man who'll do something great for the world; that's what I want to see."

I smiled. I had never heard Grandpa Blakely talk like this. He'd always seemed so much stiffer to me, always Judge William or Judge Blakely. He had a large stomach that swelled out of him and extended beyond his chest. It was like you could land one of those model planes right there on his belly. It was hard to believe he was ever a dashing pilot in those early planes, like I had seen Jimmy Stewart in movies.

"People think I disapproved of your dad marrying your mom," Grandpa said. "That wasn't true. I disapproved of *why* my daughter wanted to marry your dad.

I think she just wanted to get away from us and Robby seemed as far away from us as she could get, without ever really leaving. She never really wanted to leave Savannah and the life we gave her here. But the kind of young men she met just weren't for her—it was a mystery to me. Your dad's fine. I'm not an anti-Semite. I have a lot of Jewish friends. You can't live in Savannah and be the kind of people we are without having Jewish friends. They are not the closest people in our life, but they are our friends. I hope you know that."

I nodded again, and he bowed towards me, shaking my hand.

"There are some *National Geographics* up here and some *Life* magazines if you get bored. I'll come back up and get you when we get sick of the grown-up talk."

I looked at the airplane models and heard his heavy footsteps treading down the stairs. I then looked through the *National Geographics* but couldn't find any pictures of naked people. What was the use of *National Geographics* without naked people? I didn't feel like looking at *Life*. I started opening up some cabinets, knowing that I would find some liquor bottles in them. I did; they had an almost full bottle of Canadian Club and some other bottles of darker looking drinks with foreign names that looked like cough syrup. I opened the Canadian Club, and took four quick swallows of it, swigging it directly out of the bottle, chugging one right after the other without even tasting it.

It felt warm going down my throat, and then hot somewhere in my stomach where something inside started punching at me. I decided I had better lie down flat on the bare floor. That felt better; it was cooler there. I looked over at the airplanes on a coffee table and some shelves. They were wobbling, doing this funny little dance that made me giggle. They reminded me of Grandpa Blakely. I could see him doing the same dance. Then the room started to wobble. I closed my eyes. Groups of images ran through my head: pictures of Isle of Hope. Boats. Rough men by the boats. Dad. Platoons of boys in uniform in formation at Holy Smokes. Tim. His cool twin brothers.

Then, slowing down . . . *really* slowing down: Arthur.

In his room, his silky light brown arms glowing in his white, sleeveless T-shirt.

Then at the pool on retreat. Bare-chested.

And finally . . . naked.

I could hardly catch my breath. My dick felt hot. I had a raging stiffie.

There was a bathroom by the den, next to Grandpa and Grandma's room, and it had their old people's stuff in it. I locked the door and took down my pants and jerked off fast into some toilet paper, flushed it, and ended up on the floor, almost passed out, but smiling. Like my whole body was smiling. Then I found a mostly squeezed out tube of Gleam toothpaste and passed a bit of it over my teeth with my fingers and gargled some with water. I made sure I was set to go out, and left the bathroom.

Mom was upstairs looking for me.

"Where were you?" she asked.

"In the bathroom," I said, trying not to smile or even be noticeable.

"Oh," she said nodding. "Grandpa and Grandma want to say good-bye to you."

I went downstairs and kissed Grandma Blakely and shook Grandpa Blakely's hand and thanked him formally for showing me the airplanes. But I wasn't seeing them; I was seeing Arthur Gomez smiling at me, just like he had smiled at Neal at the retreat.

We got into the car and for a moment I couldn't say a word. It was like I was locked inside myself, kind of buzzing around in my head. Later, I learned that was called "having a buzz," but then it felt strange and also kind of good.

"What did you do upstairs?" Mom asked while she was driving and smoking.

"Just . . . uh, looked at the magazines, and—"

"Drank? Dad keeps liquor up in the den. Did you find it and drink some of it?"

Now my heart was really beating.

"Listen, I used to do the same thing. I don't like it, but I know you did it. I could smell the old toothpaste trick on your breath. I don't want you to do that again. First, you're too young, and second when you're old enough to drink, I want to give you your first *real* drink and we can do it together."

I looked down at my feet. She reached over and patted my head.

"I'm not angry," she said. "I have too much to worry about to be angry with you, Benjy."

"I wish you wouldn't worry," I said.

"I know. You're really growing up so fast. In a little while you won't even have a childhood left. That's what I'm really afraid of."

I had to ask her: "Is it because of Dad? Because of his problems with the law?"

"That's only part of it, Benjy. You see, Robby's sick."

Now I knew I'd lose it. My head crashed to my knees. I started heaving. She stopped the car.

"How much did you have to drink?"

"Just a little bit."

"Of what?"

"Canadian Club."

"Canadian Club, straight? Hell, I couldn't get that stuff down until I was eighteen! Are you going to throw up?"

I nodded.

There was nothing around us except some bends in the road and trees and swamps beyond them. I got out of the car, went behind a tree, and accompanied by buzzing mosquitoes and gnats, heaved up something that was all spit and smelled horrible. She got out of the car, and put her hand on my head. It felt cool and wonderful.

A cop on a motorcycle stopped and walked over to us. He was not very tall, but in his black Savannah Police Department motorcycle uniform and mirrored glasses, he was terrifying.

"Everything all right, Ma'am?" he asked.

"My son had something bad for lunch, officer. He'll be fine in a minute."

The cop looked at me and I saw myself reflected in his mirror lenses, surrounded by what looked like scars from teenage pimples on his face.

"Not a good thing to park here, Ma'am. When you're ready, just get out as good as you can. Watch out for traffic, see? There're speeders here and y' know what they can do t' you when you're gettin' back on the road."

"Thank you, Officer," Mom said sweetly, smiling at him. He walked away, and gave her one last look before he got back on his cycle.

I felt better when I got back into the car.

"I'm glad you were here," she said. I asked her why?

"Cause I can tell he's the kind of cop who'd try something with a woman if a boy wasn't around. It's like an unwritten rule. If you'd been a girl, he might have even tried it, just a little feel or something. But he kept it to himself because of you."

I should have said we wouldn't have stopped but because of me, but didn't.

"You feeling better?" she asked after a short while.

I nodded.

"What's wrong with Dad?"

"He's just been sick. You probably noticed he doesn't look well."

I had noticed, but didn't want to say a word about it. My dad had been good looking. Maybe not the way some other boys' dads looked—Robby was shorter and darker looking despite his deep blue eyes, but he'd been handsome. I'd always known that.

"Is there something I can do?"

"He wants you to do the bar mitzvah. You have no idea what it means to him."

"I do know," I protested. "That's why *I* want to do it."

"Good. Andy's doing all the work, all the stuff I have no idea how to do—I mean, Jesus, I'm the *shiksa* wife"—she smiled broadly. "My parents will pay for a lot of it—don't tell Dad though. They really want to come. They've never been in a synagogue in their life. They're good Episcopalians. But nice people, you have to hand it to them. They gave me very little grief marrying your dad. Some grief, but not a lot. I guess that I'm not Jewish didn't bother them nearly as much as some of Robby's family. What's left of it."

"How come I never met them?"

"They're up North. They're Yankees, y'know."

I laughed. "That's no reason to hate them," I said.

"You're right. But they'll never act like we will, that's for certain. I met them once. They were such a bunch of neurotic Jews! They never stop worrying and asking questions. They already had you born and educated before you were even conceived. People down here don't take a lot out of you. But those people certainly wanted their pound of blood."

"I thought blood came in pints and gallons."

"I guess I wanted to say pound of flesh. It's from Shakespeare's *Merchant of Venice*. It's about this Jew who loans money to a Christian and asks for a pound of flesh if the Christian can't pay him back. The Christian's girlfriend dresses up like a man and acts as his defense lawyer. She discovers the loophole that gets the Christian, you might say, off the hook—that the Jew can get his pound of flesh, but he can't extract one drop of Christian blood."

"That's smart," I said. "It sounds pretty Jewish to me, actually. She had what Dad would call a Jewish *kop*. I guess she had to be cagey like the Jews, right?"

"I never thought about it like that—your dad *is* cagey."

That evening in bed, I stared up at the ceiling. All I wanted was for Arthur to be there with me, in any form he wanted to take. I didn't believe in ghosts (I didn't *dis*believe in them either), but even if he came to me as a ghost—beautiful, shimmering all over, his light brown skin and dark hair appearing out of… what, air?—I would have welcomed it.

Was I really *in love* with him?

That was impossible. He was dead *and* a boy, and even boys who fooled around with other boys didn't fall in love with them. Dead: that meant he was unreachable, in some place we can only imagine. Even what I'd done in the bathroom at Grandpa and Grandma's wouldn't bring him back to me. Still, I wanted to touch his skin, to kiss his lips, to see him as part of myself and as my own. But heck, I couldn't even define *myself*. Who was I? Was I a boy, or just a frightened girl in a boy's body? Was I a real Jew, or just a cowardly Christian who didn't believe in the Eucharist, just like Arthur didn't believe in it?

I kept looking up at the ceiling, seeing things revolve, if only in my imagination. I was sure I saw Arthur, and I believed in him. He was there with me, no matter how hard I tried to disbelieve it. Then I realized something.

I did believe in him—*more* than I believed in anything else.

Except for Robby.

14

School Again

There was a pall over everything when school began again at Holy Nativity. There were still too many mysteries clinging to Arthur's death to ignore it; it was like his body was still somewhere in the school. I saw him all over the place, smiling at me with that same almost hopeless smile he had when we walked out together to find me a cab. That felt like a hundred years ago. On the third day of classes I spotted Det. Whitaker in the hallway. He took me aside and asked me how I was doing. I told him OK.

"Sure?" All I could do was nod again. "I'm sorry about what's happened here," he said flatly. I guessed he meant Arthur's death. I looked up into his face that was lined like he didn't sleep very much. His hair, young looking and streaky blonde, had light bouncing all over it because of whatever he used to keep it down.

"You are *one* good kid," he said. "Your dad must be proud of you!"

He smiled stiffly at me. The dimples at the sides of his mouth looked like they could hide dimes in them. Then he shook my hand, and went into Father Greer's office.

"He's been poking around the school," Tim said when I told him about it later. "But you can bet ya nuts, they ain't gonna let us know what's goin' on. Something tells me th' old monks like Brother Ulrich are plenty pissed off. The effin' 'honor of the school' is more important to them than any dead Puerto Rican kid."

"How can you say that?" I said. "It's horrible."

"Cause it's true. They're convinced it *had* to be an accident. Arthur didn't kill himself or he couldn't be buried in consecrated ground. That way, see, it's all God's will, and he's up there now playin' with the Saints—where we'll all eventually be, 'sept for you, cause you're a Jew-boy."

He laughed and I started laughing with him. Then right there in the hallway I goosed him on his balls. No one was looking, but Tim got pissed.

"Don't do that," he hissed. "That asshole Storch'll start rumors. Y'know how he is."

I pulled Tim closer, and locked him under my elbow, with my arm around his neck.

"Come on, Rothberg," he said, squirming to get away.

I let him go. Then I said it; I had to—"If that turd bothers you, I'll kill him. I know he had *something* to do with Arthur. I know it."

Tim looked at me, scared.

"Not now, Rothberg," he said, lowering his voice to barely a whisper. "We gotta talk about this later."

I was still taking bar mitzvah lessons with Brother Alexis during the week. The Hebrew no longer sound strange to me. We were going through the prayers I would recite when Brother Alexis told me I needed to think about making a speech.

"What kind of speech?" I asked. "You don't mean in Hebrew?"

"No. But it's a Confirmation. So you need to confirm something. You should thank your parents and your family and the people who prepared you for this, and address God in some way. Among Jews, a bar mitzvah signifies that you are now equal to the task of being in God's presence. You're an adult male. You can count in a *minyan*, that's the ten men needed for a service."

"That's because I'm thirteen?"

"And because you've been confirmed. That's important no matter what."

"I guess that's why my dad wants this so much." I hesitated, then asked, "Could you be in a *minyan*, Brother Alexis?"

"Probably not. I never got bar mitzvahed obviously. Religions have a funny way of deciding who's in and who isn't. It's like you have to be baptized Catholic to receive Communion. But you knew that."

"What happens if you're baptized Catholic and you refuse to receive Communion?"

"It's a sin. You *should* receive it, Benjy. Why'd you ask?"

"Because Arthur told me he doubted the Eucharist, and it really bothered him."

Brother Alexis looked at me for a second, then his eyes clenched shut. He re-opened them and looked at me.

"You knew this?"

"Does it make a difference?" I asked.

"It might to some people, but not to me. The police are still trying to figure out what happened to Arthur. His death was a real tragedy, but I don't think that his doubting the Eucharist would drive him to kill himself. Lots of kids have doubts; it's a stage they go through. Arthur was only fourteen years old. I knew he was having a hard time at home, but he seemed stronger than that."

But not strong enough not to drown, I thought.

"I'll think about the speech," I promised. "I'll start writing it at home."

"If you have any problems, let me know. Let's go back to the prayer you say after you begin the Haftorah *parsha*. And then we'll go over your Haftorah section to make sure you know what you're saying. You have to know what every word means, I believe that."

On the way home, I thought about what Brother Alexis had said about knowing what every word meant. It seemed so vast: every word went back thousands of years, in a foreign language written in something that felt like a strange code. I liked codes; I was starting to understand things about them—like for instance, the way that Tim and I talked to each other was a code. His brothers used a code. Maybe it was the code of twins, or of brothers, or of Irish Catholics—it was hard for me to know. I suspected that the words used out in Isle of Hope for certain men who behaved in a strange way were also a code, and that there were code words for Jews as well. But what about me? What was the code for what I was, someone still at that undecided point between everything?

I grabbed Caroline's hand and held it. She squeezed it back lightly and drove with her left hand. "Something bothering you?" I told her that Brother Alexis wanted me to make a speech for my bar mitzvah.

"What'll you say, 'Today I am a fountain pen'?" she asked with a grin, then explained, "It's an old joke. I think Henny Youngman used to tell it on Ed Sullivan, I guess 'cause kids get so many fountain pens on their bar mitzvah. What else do you give a thirteen-year-old boy?"

She giggled and let go of my hand to light a cigarette.

"I want Dad to be there," I said, suddenly choking up.

"It's OK," she said. "This may be the most difficult time of your life. I've got to hold myself up for you and for Liz, but if it wasn't for that, I'd be a mess myself."

I let that settle in, then asked Caroline if I could spend Saturday night at Tim's.

"Don't you see him enough at school?" she asked.

"He's my friend."

"Sure, Benjy, but you need more than boy friends. Not *boyfriends*, I mean *boy* friends. I've been talking to Robby about it."

"You talked to *Dad*? How is he?"

"He's . . . about as good as he's going to get. You're really too young to understand what's going on."

"But you're always telling me how grown up I am!"

"Sure, honey. At thirteen you're going to go to war and start a family. Listen, you're too young to know everything, take my word for it. But you're not too young to go to a party at the Jewish center this Saturday. I want you to do that instead of spending the night with Tim. There will be *girls* there, your age."

"Whose party is it?"

"A boy named Allan Streitt. It's *his* bar mitzvah party. His dad knows Robby from a while back, so we got an invitation. Robby really wants you to go."

"He does?"

"Yeah, sweetheart. He's concerned you don't know girls. You know, there's always talk about all-boy schools."

"But he *wanted* me to go to Holy Nativity."

"Sure. It's been good for you. But this party will be good, too. You'll see things you won't see in Isle of Hope, and you'll meet some girls. Who knows? You might even end up with a little girlfriend."

15

The Party

It was a Titanic production: That was the only word for it. Mom decided the occasion called for a whole new outfit, so after school on Friday she drove me to Alfred Joseph Roote, a very preppy, "exclusive" oak-paneled men's store close to downtown Savannah. It had a tiny boy's department; we were waited on by a wrinkled middle-aged man with meticulously combed red hair who kept clearing his throat while he looked at me. He pulled out lots of stuff and I tried it all on. Finally he and Mom settled on some gray wool slacks, a plain button-down white shirt, a dark green silk tie with thin diagonal gold and purplish stripes on it, and, to go with everything, a twill navy-blue blazer. The blazer sported a pirate's wealth of twinkling gold buttons, stamped with something resembling the English royal family crest. I felt strange: was I really supposed to look like *this*? But Caroline was beaming. I could tell this meant a lot to her, because she knew I'd probably outgrow everything in a year. But it felt great buying new stuff, knowing it was just for me.

Except it wasn't. In the car she told me that I would be wearing the same things at my bar mitzvah, too; so I knew it was also for Robby.

Everything was put in boxes or on hangers with plastic film over it. When we took it back to Isle of Hope, I started to get nervous. I went out on the front porch and looked around. There were all the big trees with the water beyond it and you could hear some of the local kids playing outside, and the next night I was going to be with a bunch of Jewish kids I didn't know and they were going to start talking about me and I could just imagine what they'd say.

"Are you *really* Jewish?"

"Are you going to have a bar mitzvah, too?"

And, of course: "What's it like going to a Catholic school—with all those boys?"

I tried not to think about it too much, but I was hardly hungry at dinner, and even sleeping was difficult. I got up in the middle of the night and looked at myself in the bathroom mirror. I felt ugly and stupid. What would I say to them? I wished Robby were home, even as Leon. *Leon* would have known exactly how to handle everything. After all, they were Leon's people.

But not mine.

I felt better the next day. I liked the clothes; I decided they made me look *adult*. Still I felt strange as Caroline drove me into town and parked the car at the big Jewish center.

"I'm just going to say hello to the Streitt's, then leave you to make friends," she said as we entered the building. "Call me when it's over, and I'll come pick you up. Or maybe someone will be coming from out where we are, and can give you a lift back."

"Fat chance," I said bitterly under my breath. Caroline looked down at me.

"You OK, Sweetheart?"

I exhaled really hard.

"Sure."

The party was in the back, in the main ballroom of the Center. It was huge and dark, with lots of decorations and streamers, and loud music pumped in from a sound system. Mom went up to some adults who looked like parents, and shook hands and put on that public smile she could do better than anybody, then dragged me over to meet the boy's family.

Mr. Streitt was dressed in a dark suit, and was short and bald with very bad breath. He smiled at me with yellow teeth; I felt bad for him. I didn't know what kind of business he was in, but having a kids' party I could tell was *obviously* not his cup of tea. His wife was about a foot taller than he, and dressed in very pointy heels and a tight splashy floral-print dress. She was wearing a fur stole, which seemed strange because it was not that cold outside, or even inside. The stole looked thrown over her, but you definitely could see her boobies, which looked like they were going to pop out of her dress any second.

"Aren't you a darling!" she said taking my hand. "I'm Anita Streitt. I see where he gets his looks, Mrs. Rothberg. Come, I want you to meet our Allan. He's been dying to meet you."

She took me by the hand, and Mom waived good-bye to me.

Mrs. Streitt pulled me a couple of feet, and I glanced back. Mom had disappeared. Now we were in the thick of a bunch of young people, maybe five or even seven years older than I was.

"They're mostly friends of Allan's brother Nathan," Mrs. Streitt explained. "Sometimes I think this party was more for them than for Allan. You have any older brothers or sisters?"

"No, Ma'am."

"That's too bad. It can help—they've been through all the crappola, and can show you the ropes. Even I learn from the kids sometimes. When Eis, that's my husband Isaac, and I first came to Savannah—we're originally from New York—our older son Nathan went to public school, so he quickly figured out what things were all about down here—you know, about being Southerners and getting along with them." She nodded. "He taught us a lot actually. Funny, learning from your kids! Here's Allan's older brother now. Natie, I want you to meet Benjy Rothberg. He lives in Isle of Hope."

Nathan seemed tall, considering his father, even though he was only a few inches taller than I was. He was about seventeen, with good skin and features but with a thin neck, kind of like a goose or a crane. Still, he was remarkably good-looking in a pair of shiny dark slacks with a dark suit jacket over a deep blue Lacoste shirt.

"I didn't know Jews lived out there," he said.

"Natie! Jews live everyplace," Mrs. Streitt said. "They got Jews in Alaska."

"Sure, I know that, Ma. But that's different. It's a whole state."

His face twitched at me, then he said kind of blandly, like he didn't really mean it, "Nice t' meetcha."

I extended my hand to him, but he didn't take it and disappeared.

"I'm sorry. He's now at a funny stage," Mrs. Streitt explained. "The one where he's decided his parents are stupid. It's the whole *Rebel Without A Cause* thing. A lotta kids go through it; I just hope Allan doesn't land in it for very long."

Now Allan appeared. He looked more like his father, but without the bad breath. He was shorter than I was and seriously pudgy with a very beaky face, looking like a fat pigeon in a dark, chalk-striped suit that looked like it should have been on an old man. He smiled at me nervously, which made me feel much better. His mother introduced us, and left us to go back to the adults.

"Where d'you go to school?" he asked.

I told him. He just nodded.

"You like it?"

I told him I did; thank God he didn't ask me what it was like going to a Catholic school.

"What d'you like about it?"

"The guys are really nice. Some of them."

"How about the guys who aren't? Are they anti-Semitic?"

I smiled. That was an interesting question, but before I could answer, Nathan came over with a drink in his hand. I could tell it was a real drink. How he got it I didn't know.

"Hey, shrimp!" Nathan said. "What are you and the little half-Jew talkin' about?"

"Why don't you go fuck yourself with a nail?" Allan answered.

"Y'mean the one you keep up your ass?" Nathan started laughing. It was a funny, shrill, kind of barky laugh. "One of these days, shrimp, I'm gonna pound you int' the wall and keep you there."

Allan turned his back to him, and Nathan left. I could tell Allan was upset by this.

"You'd think on my bar mitzvah my nutty brother would give me some slack. I just wish I could get out of this damn suit. Do you dance?"

I thought: this is weird. Is he asking *me* to dance?

"Not with me!" he said, reading my mind. He chuckled. "Golly! There are girls here and you should ask one. Just don't try to go too far with one. Know what I mean?"

He pointed to a group of about six girls talking by themselves. They all looked between twelve and about fourteen but dressed like adults with their hair teased up and lots of puffiness under their skirts. He brought me over to them and introduced me. Fanny Cohen, Ilene Liebowitz, Rachel Some-other-Jewish-name, Rebecca I-forget, Susan I-forget-too, and finally Faye, who was dressed more like a real girl in a very nice, simple dress, rather than like a pretend adult.

Her name was Faye Jacobson and she had short dark hair and dark eyes and smiled at me like she knew me from somewhere. I asked her what she was smiling about.

"Just the way you look. You don't look like the guys here."

"How do they look?"

"Too Jewish."

I got really scared. Didn't I look Jewish *enough*? I wanted to ask her, but my mouth dried up. She smiled at me again with this expression that had a lot of warmth to it: like she was beaming at me. It was a look I had seen my mom give my dad.

"You're quiet," she said with that same look on her face, her voice low.

I was quiet because I didn't know *shit* what to say. Now I really wished I'd had Robby there with me. I liked her. She was cute, and she didn't make me feel squirrelly—y'know, like some strange animal that collects nuts?

She asked *me* if I wanted to dance. We went out to the dance floor. They were playing some fast songs, and I tried not to look too goony. I could tell she danced a lot, maybe with her girlfriends. Girls could do that, dance with each other. I could never understand why girls could dance with each other and boys couldn't, but she was good at it.

Then, they put on "Harbor Light," a slow dance, and I froze for a second.

"Maybe we should just wait this one out," she said.

I looked at her.

"No. We don't have to," I replied, pulling her close and holding her.

It felt really good having her next to me. She put her head very close to mine and had this dreamy quality, like she was sleepwalking, while I moved us about, making sure we didn't bump into anyone else. I didn't know how much of her I was supposed to touch, but touching her felt wonderful, just breathing in the way she smelled.

Allan was dancing with this skinny girl who was about half a head taller than he was. He winked at me.

"God, what a catch already," he whispered to me, but Faye heard him.

"Just because it's your bar mitzvah, Allan, doesn't mean you can act like a *shlemiel*," she said curtly.

He smiled.

"Sorry," he said, leading the skinny girl away; I watched them over Faye's shoulder. He had dipping down pat and doing other things, like making figure eights on the floor. Suddenly, the dreamy music turned into a Latin beat, and I knew here I was lost. I let go of Faye.

"Let's get something to drink," she said and took me over to the bar, where a real bartender in uniform asked me what I wanted. I wanted a real drink too, but thought better about asking for it. After all, I wasn't as old as Nathan. I asked for a Coke.

"I'll have some pale sherry," Faye said to the bartender.

He poured her something from a bottle, and she drank it easily.

"Jewish kids learn to drink early," she told me. "As long as we have it in moderation. You know, you have it on Shabbos. So you're not really Jewish? You don't look Jewish, at least not as Jewish as some of these people."

"My mother's not Jewish. But my father is."

"I've heard of your father," she said, sipping the sherry.

I had to ask. "What have you heard?"

"He's in trouble with the law. The whole community's talking about it. He's on trial in Valdosta. Is he guilty? I mean did he do it?"

I turned away from her. *I* didn't know if he was guilty. Suddenly I felt tiny, like a deflated balloon, as if all the air had been sucked out of me. The music got louder again. I heard Anita Streitt's distinct voice on the speaker system announce:

"It's the Hora, boys and girls, moms and dads. Everybody get into a circle and do the Hora!"

Faye grabbed my hand, and brought me up to a bunch of her girl friends and I took her hand, then realized I had Allan's hand too. Allan smiled at me.

"Having a good time?" he asked.

"Sure," I lied.

The music pounded in my ears. At first everybody pulled apart, then immediately dashed into a tight bunch. I felt as if my arms were being pulled from my shoulders as the crowd surged one way, and then another. Suddenly Allan separated from me into a smaller circle of kids and everyone was in a circle except me; I was left alone.

A pair of hands suddenly gripped my waist from behind, moving quickly up to my shoulders, then pushed me so hard I almost fell to the floor. It was Nathan Streitt. He thrust his face right into mine. From his breath, I could tell he'd been drinking a lot more.

"Having a *good* time?" he demanded. "You little half-Jew! Your dad's a *goniff.* A crook! Everybody knows it. You think you can just come here and dance with one of our girls, and act like you're one of us?"

"He's not a crook!" I answered, zooming from humiliation to rage. "You don't know what you're talking about."

I stared at him, and he pulled his face away. If he'd been my size and age, I would have hit him. I felt bad that I couldn't. Why was he such a shit, and his brother was so nice and everybody else was nice too; or were they just fooling me? Without a doubt I knew I didn't belong there, and Nathan was just a signpost telling me that. I didn't need any code for this. It was only too obvious. I didn't look like any of them, and now I felt more like Caroline and not like Robby—OK, *Leon*—especially in Caroline's ultra-preppy Alfred Root get-up.

Nathan was still red-faced and furious, but I could tell he was embarrassed. He could barely look at me. Several bigger guys closer to his age approached, glanced at both of us, and left without another word. I looked around. Allan was with his parents, at the other end of the ballroom. It was too noisy to hear anything, but for a second all three of them looked at me. His father looked away, and his mother shook her head sadly in my direction.

Allan hurried across the room to us.

"What are you doing, Nathan?" he said.

"Shut up, shrimp. You want it known that a crook is at your bar mitzvah party?"

"He was invited, Nate. Why don't you just go back over to your friends and leave us kids alone?"

"Because they're not *my* friends. Mom invited them. They just came for the free liquor."

"She wanted *your* friends to be here, too. That was all."

"Yeah, Mom always wants what's best." He caught his breath for a second. "Why don't you go back to them? Mom and Dad miss you. See?" He pointed to their parents. "They don't miss me."

Allan walked away. I started to walk with him, but Nathan grabbed me forcefully and pulled me out of the darkened ballroom, into the hallway. With too many fluorescent lights it seemed ultra-bright out there. He leaned me up against a wall and wouldn't let go.

He wiped his face. I realized he was crying.

"My so-called friends are talking about you," he said. "You know what that's like?"

Tears were streaming down his face.

I stared directly at him. "Sure. I get talked about a lot."

"I bet you do. You're not like other kids, that's obvious. These kids can be real shitasses; I'm talking about the popular Jewish ones. The ones Mom thought should be *my* friends. Listen, I don't hate you but you're getting all the attention here, and not in a good way. My dad's a *shtarker*, you know what that means?"

I didn't.

"It means he came up here and bulldozed his way through Savannah. So we have a lotta things to worry about, just fitting in ourselves. Anyway, I want you to leave, will you? I mean it. I won't hit you, but I will—if you don't get the hell out right now."

"I'm not scared of you," I said.

"I can see that. But you should know when you're not really wanted, just like I do. I'll tell Mom and Dad your mom came to get you. There's a pay phone in the lobby. Just go use it. Need a dime?"

"*No*," I said emphatically, almost spitting the word out at him.

He reached into his pocket, and fished out several coins.

"Take one anyway."

I threw them back at his feet, and walked away from him; he disappeared back into the ballroom. I could hear the music burst again then soften as I gathered more yards of floor between me and it. The lobby was not very big, but it had a pay phone that you couldn't miss. I took out a dime and started to call Mom, then knew whom I wanted to call.

Tim's mom answered the phone. I asked to speak with him. Tim came really fast.

"You OK?" he asked.

"Can you and Neal pick me up? I'm at the Jewish center. You know where that is?"

"Sure. You sound like you got into a fight or something."

"Hard to talk about it. I came to a bar mitzvah party, and I didn't know anyone—"

"Did they give you a hard time 'cause of Holy Nativity?"

"No, 'cause of other stuff. Please, Tim, d'you think Neal could pick me up?"

"Sure. He's here. Just wait outside the place and we'll come get you."

It was very dark out now, and it had started raining, one of those long drifts of steady rain that happened in the South in the fall. I waited under a long carport attached to the lobby, feeling damp and utterly self-conscious. I wanted to vanish anytime someone came out of the party, especially with their parents. Kids looked at me, then looked away. A woman, very nicely dressed but a little too made up, someone's mom I guessed, walked up to me and asked me if I needed a lift home, as if she knew where I lived; maybe she did. Maybe it was all over me, or the way I was dressed, or how my hair was combed. I told her I was OK, and she smiled knowingly at me. I felt like I had a big sign on me that said I didn't belong in *any* world, I was an outsider.

Finally, Neal and Tim drove up.

"Get in!" Neal said, smiling.

I got into the back seat. Tim turned around and looked at me.

"Neat outfit," he said. "All new?"

"Yeah."

"So what happened? Y'get anything t' drink?"

Suddenly I started crying; I'd been holding it in. I hated myself when I cried. Neal pulled out a Kleenex from someplace and handed it to me. I blew my nose.

"Mom always keeps tissues in the car," Neal said. "So what happened, Man? You're all bent outta shape over something. What is it?"

"Everybody knows about my dad," I said sniffling. "I think they know more than I do."

"Sure," Neal said. "He's Jewish, and the Jews are pretty tight here, so they talk. I guess your parents have kept a lot from you. Parents always do that. Our parents were thinking about getting a divorce once; we were the last people to know."

"I thought Catholics didn't get divorced."

"They do. It's just hard as hell," Tim explained. "'Specially when you got a lot of kids."

"Ours didn't," Neal said. "I guess they stayed together for our sake, which isn't bad, believe me. Pat was really screwed up over it. He holds a lot of stuff in. I don't. I must take after our mom. Maybe he takes after Dad, who just plays golf a lot."

"You think there was another woman?" I asked.

"Sure," Neal said. "At least it wasn't another guy!" He laughed. "I mean, *Mom* and another guy. Get it? Anyway, kids don't have to know everything, but it hurts when we're the last people to know. Why don't you stay with us tonight? You can bunk with Tim."

"OK. I'll have to call my mom and tell her."

Tim looked back and winked at me.

"Feeling better?" he asked.

I nodded.

"Catholics are really good guys," he said seriously. "I mean when we don't start the Inquisition and shit like that. Sorry about what happened at the Jew center."

"It's the *Jewish* center, dickhead," Neal corrected him.

"Go eat a fat one," Tim said and stuck his tongue out at Neal. Neal ruffled his hair up. I felt very good and safe, for a while.

Mrs. O'Neill was really nice. She didn't ask a lot of questions, but gave me the phone and I called Mom. I didn't tell her anything, except that I was at Tim's and that they had asked me to spend the night. She was actually happy that she didn't have to drive in to pick me up. I wondered if she had been drinking, and would now just drink more.

"Did you have a good time at the party?" she asked.

"I met some girls," I said. "One was really nice. I liked her."

"Was she pretty?"

"Yeah. Really pretty. We danced a lot."

"Maybe we can ask her to come out to Isle of Hope."

"Maybe," I said. The truth was I didn't get her phone number or know where she lived, and God only knew how many Jacobsons were in Savannah. But there couldn't have been that many. There weren't that many Jews; even I knew that. But it seemed like everybody knew about Robby, and even about me, my sister, and probably Caroline, too. I wondered if Catholics talked the way Jews did? I'd have to ask Tim.

Mrs. O'Neill asked me if I were hungry. I wasn't. All I wanted to do was just brush my teeth and go to sleep. We stayed up for a while, and Neal and Tim joked with each other. Pat came in, and briefly said hi, then walked up to the room he shared with Neal. I wondered where Mr. O'Neill was, and Mrs. O'Neill told me that he was in Atlanta, on business. She didn't say anything else. Tim's little brother and sisters were already asleep. Mrs. O'Neill announced that it was time for everyone to go to bed, because of Mass the next morning.

I used a spare toothbrush in the bathroom, then I got into bed with Tim.

This was the first time we weren't in a tent when I stayed over. It felt kind of funny, since Tim's bed was pretty small. He was in it already. He smiled, turned off the light, and reached over to me.

"Why are you wearin' your undershorts?" he said.

"Cause I'm not wearing pajamas."

"Oh, I see. Must be some Jewish thing; you guys can't sleep in the raw."

I took off my undershorts. He put his hand on my shoulder and then sat up.

"Didja meet any girls?"

"Yeah."

"Like 'em?"

"Yeah. One was really nice. I could tell she liked me a lot."

"Wuddja fuck her?"

"God, Tim! I don't even *know* her."

"Well, wuddja?"

"I don't know."

"You're so queer!"

He put his hand on my dick. I was hard. I couldn't help it. It was why I'd had my shorts on. Maybe it was just from being twelve, but almost thirteen. Truth was, I liked him putting it there.

Suddenly he kissed me. On my mouth.

"You mind?" he asked.

"No."

I kissed him back.

"Good," he said. Then he kissed me again, and this time he stayed there. I had to push him away, because I couldn't breathe.

"What is it?" he asked.

"I need some air."

I sat up, and looked at him. His blue eyes glowed in the dark. He was smiling like all over, like the way he looked the first time I went to chapel and he sat next to me. I put my hand through his hair, as I had done at the school. This time he let me.

"I realized something at this party," I said to him.

"What? You like girls?"

"No. I realized I am more Jewish than anything else. We were dancing the Hora, know what that is?"

"Sure. It's like this Jewish dance. Wasn't it in *Exodus*? Didn't they dance that with Paul Newman?"

I shrugged. I hadn't seen *Exodus*.

"So, the Hora made you Jewish?" he asked. "You *are* queer!"

"Oh, fuck you," I said, genuinely hurt.

"I'm just joshing. You can be as Jewish as you want. I don't care. You can't be Catholic because, well, you have to believe what Catholics believe."

"But even Arthur didn't believe that. And he killed himself."

The smile left Tim's face. His dimples disappeared. He started crying.

"I'm sorry," I said, feeling terrible. I didn't want to hurt Tim. I loved him, even I could admit that. "I didn't mean to say anything bad."

Tim sniffed. He got up and found a Kleenex from a box in his room. Suddenly he looked really small, like he had turned into a sad dejected doll. He got into bed and I drew him to me.

"Arthur didn't kill himself," he whispered hoarsely.

"How d'you know?"

"I can't tell."

"Why?"

"Neal made me swear not to. I can't tell anybody. But Arthur didn't kill himself. I know it."

"What happened? Can't you tell me anything?"

Tim went limp, like all the living spirit had left his body. I'd never seen him like that.

"I swear I won't say anything," I told him. "I'd say cross my heart, but you know I can't do that. But I swear, by everything that Jews stand for—"

"Cut that shit," he said. "What the hell d' Jews stand for any more than what Catholics stand for? It's all a buncha lies. My dad's not in Atlanta on business. He's got a girlfriend. Neal knows it. Pat's hung up like hell on it. Shit, fuck. Arthur's death had somethin' to do with Brother Ulrich—Dorris Mahoney, the dummy Jerry Mahoney's big fat brother. That's all Neal'd tell me."

"How does he know?"

"People talk. Kids talk. They whisper stuff. They know Brother Ulrich goes down to that bathroom in the library. He's been seen down there. I think he got Arthur down there with him once."

"But there's no proof, right? It's just gossip. Gossip's what's hurting my dad."

Tim's eyes narrowed at me. He was dead serious now.

"But with your dad, it's more than gossip. It's the fuckin' law. Us kids, we're kept out of everything. We're supposed t' be all innocent and not know nothin', like Baby Jesus. But we know. It's real shit, ain't it?"

I put my head down on the pillow, and Tim put his head next to me.

"I'm sorry," Tim said. "About everything. You're my friend, I mean that."

I leaned over and kissed him. He kissed me back. He put his hand on my dick. It was no longer hard.

"You don't wanna fool around?" he asked.

"I think I just want t' go to sleep now," I said.

"OK."

I wanted to go to sleep, but couldn't. The whole weekend had been so long it felt like a month, what with getting new clothes at Alfred Roote's and the party and what happened there. I thought about Faye Jacobson; she was nice and really pretty. Robby would have been happy about me meeting her, but I wasn't sure about the rest of what went on. "Sometimes people can be their own worst enemies," he told me more than once, often speaking about other Jews down South. They were clannish certainly and into everybody's business, but they stuck up for their own—or at least Robby wanted to feel that way. The question was, whose "business" was I?

I couldn't answer, but I thought about what Tim had told me about Brother Ulrich and the bathroom downstairs next to the library. And I realized what I had to do, as I fell asleep.

Mom picked me up the next morning after breakfast at the O'Neills, before they all went to Mass.

"I'm still not sure how you ended up at the O'Neills," she said as she lit a cigarette, her hand trembling. I wondered if she'd had too much coffee, or maybe too much to drink. One thing seemed certain to me: being without Robby was really getting difficult for her.

"I just wanted to be there," I said.

"It was nice of them to pick you up. It saved me the trip in the rain. But tell me, Benjy, what happened at the party?"

"I met a nice girl," I said, looking out the window.

"Yeah, you told me. What was her name?"

"Faye Jacobson."

"Is she your age?"

"Yeah, I guess. She's a friend of the boy who got bar mitzvahed."

"Allan Streitt? I hear he's a nice kid. He has an older brother—it seems like they had problems with him."

"How did you know?"

She smiled that wonderful Mona Lisa smile.

"Listen, I may be a *shiksa*, but I know a couple of things about Jews here. The older brother came close to getting in trouble with the law. When that happens with Jews in the South, everybody finds out about it. When he was fifteen, he stole a car and went out for a joyride. I think he made some of the wrong kind of friends who weren't Jewish, and had to prove something to them. Maybe back then his parents wouldn't buy him a car—but they had to spend a lot of money to keep everything kosher. My dad learned about it since he's a judge."

Suddenly I remembered what Anita Streitt had said about Nathan being in his *Rebel Without A Cause* stage.

"Anyway, Mrs. Streitt married ol' Eis for obvious reasons: He had the money, she had the looks. That story must go back to Abraham, or at least Jacob." She smiled again and released some smoke from her cigarette. "Jacob was the first truly sexy Jewish hustler—he got it on with all the girls and produced twelve kids. So did you have a problem with—what's his name?"

"Nathan." I nodded.

"Is that why you left the party? Mrs. Streitt gave me a call early this morning and apologized. They don't know what to do with the kid. She told me he must have been drinking and got out of hand. She's sorry that you had to deal with him on your own. She said she gave him a real piece of her mind afterwards. But I wish you'd called me, Benjy."

"I didn't want to bother you," I said lying. "And I missed Tim." That was the truth.

"So you'd rather be with Tim than Faye?"

Now I was totally embarrassed. What would she ask next: did Tim and I play around? What did we really *do* together?

"No!" I said emphatically. "It's just, well, he's my friend and I hardly know her."

"Why don't you invite her out to Isle o' Hope?"

I hesitated for a moment. "I'll invite her to my bar mitzvah. I want her to meet Dad anyway. That should make him happy."

She pulled me to her and hugged me with one hand while she drove. I loved Mom. There was no way anyone could not love her.

"Of course it will," Caroline said, almost giggling. "His kid's finally getting in with the Chosen People."

Another Investigation

When we got back to the house, Josephine was waiting for us. She was now with us constantly, like she was almost living with us. I wasn't sure what my parents were using to pay her with, but somehow they managed to do it.

"There was a call from Mr. Geyer," she told Mom. Mom's face fell. She went upstairs to her room to call him back. Tim had been right: the kids aren't supposed to know anything and yet we did.

She came down just before dinner with a drink in her hand. We were in the den; Liz was upstairs watching TV. I asked her what was going on.

"I think I should know," I said.

"It would kill your dad if he knew you were worried about him."

"But it's hurting me. That guy Nathan Streitt said some really ugly things about Dad. I hated hearing it from him."

"I know," she said, pulling me to her and kissing me. "The trial's going on. People are talking about it all over the place—even people in New York, Robby's people. It's not simply a trial about Leon Rothberg. It's a trial because he's a Yankee Jew in a small Southern town. Valdosta is a lot smaller than Savannah, and there are people there who still think Jews are salesmen working for the Devil." She laughed. "'Drummers for the Devil.' Neat idea. I guess he could use a few of those, because Jesus has certainly got enough salesmen, if you consider all the Holly Rollers and Jesus-mongers here. That's what's going on, and there's not a whole lot I can do about it. He's got a good lawyer, but he still has to face a jury there."

"Should I go and see him?"

"He's in jail, Benjy. They won't even let him out on bail now. They're sure he'll skip town and run back up North and maybe leave and go to—God knows where!"

She started sobbing. I got her a Kleenex.

"Thanks," she said. "My dad's doing what he can, but those people in that little town want to kill him. It's like he represents everything they hate."

"Did he do anything wrong?" I asked. She looked at me. "Did he?"

"It's complicated," she said, after blowing her nose. "I don't understand it myself. I grew up with money—Dad always had it, at least enough of it. So did Mom, your Grandma Betty. They were garden club people and country club people. Your dad wasn't like that, but he had such brains and class, I was crazy about him. It was like he had this light around him. He made me feel I had a soul inside me. Everything else had been just, well, going through the same motions with the same people. I'm sorry, maybe you can't understand that."

"Yes, I can," I said.

"God, you're as smart as he is."

"That's because I really am a Jew," I said.

"That's fine with me, Benjy. You can be anything you want to be."

"I *can?*"

"Sure. If you want to be Jewish and marry a Jewish girl, I'd love it."

"You mean like Faye Jacobson?"

"Yeah, like her. But just not till you graduate from Holy Nativity."

I didn't know what to say. I wished I'd been able to tell her that I felt the same way she had felt about Dad about Arthur Gomez. That he made me feel I had a soul inside me, too. But maybe I was just too young to know any better. Or, I hadn't met the right girl yet.

Later in bed that night, I made a pact with myself, and with Arthur. First, you have to understand, I just wanted him so much to be there with me. I could imagine kissing him the way I had kissed Tim and he had kissed me, but even more so—I was kissing Arthur like I'd *never* kissed anyone. Ever, or maybe ever would. I *had* to know what had happened to him; I needed to. So I made a pact that I wouldn't be scared to find out the truth.

The plan: I decided to station myself in the basement of the library between classes and studying at Holy Nativity, and even between my bar mitzvah lessons with Brother Alexis. I made up all kinds of excuses why I should be there, like I was writing papers and needed the reference books. I kept an eye out for that certain bathroom in the corner, the one that no one ever used. Sometimes Tim would come down and find me there. He knew what I was doing—Tim's not dumb—but he was sure nothing would happen.

"Brother Ulrich's too smart to do anything as long as somebody's psyching the place out."

"What would he do?" I whispered.

"Dunno," Tim answered softly. We were behind a big pillar; nobody could see us easily. The bathroom was around the corner, but we could see anybody walking in. No one did. I wondered, did everyone in the school have some idea about that bathroom, at least everyone up in the high school section? Tim and I were still in junior high, and I was sure that none of the smaller kids knew about it. I wouldn't have known myself if Tim hadn't told me, and he'd been clued into it by Neal.

"I need to ask Neal," I said. "Would you bring him down here?"

"No way. I'll get into holy effin' shit if Neal finds out what you're doing."

I tried to whisper to keep my voice down, but it was getting hard.

"Why?" I asked.

"God, you *are* a fuckin' Jew!" Tim's voice rose. "Why, why, *why*? Cause no one's s'posed to know about this. Neal'd cut my balls off if he knew you knew. It's like guys foolin' around. You keep it t' yourself. I wish you wouldn't do this. What are you trying t' prove?"

"I need to know what happened with Arthur. I *owe* it to him."

Tim sighed.

"He's dead, Benjy. You can't do nothin' for him. Except maybe pray, and I ain't sure that for a Jew to pray for a Catholic works. Even a Catholic like Arthur—"

I put my hand on Tim's mouth. There, around the corner, was Brother Ulrich in full Sebastianite garb, striding quickly towards the bathroom. We ducked behind the pillar but Tim accidentally hit some books with his elbow, causing the monk to turn in our direction with a start.

"Who's there?" he demanded, and launched towards us—"What are you do-ing here, Mr. Rothberg?"

There was enough anger in Brother Ulrich's face to boil a cup of coffee. That seemed funny to me. Robby would have said he wasn't holding his cards close enough to his chest; he was letting *way* too much out.

"Doing research," I said.

"On *what*?"

I looked into his face.

"Birds. *Dead* birds."

"And what about you, Mr. O'Neill. You doing *dead* birds, too?"

"No, Brother Ulrich. I'm simply keeping Rothberg company."

"Well, if you keep sticking around down here, you're both gonna be *dead* birds y'selves. The faculty uses this bathroom, not kids. Understand me?"

Tim could not say a word, he was shaking so much. I could feel his whole body vibrating next to me. But Brother Ulrich didn't intimidate me. I hated him.

"So no kids ever use this bathroom?" I asked.

"You got that right. This part of the library is off-limits to you. Now, scram."

"So"— I was angry, I was boiling the way Ulrich was—"how come I've seen kids use it, with some brothers?"

"Who! Who did you *ever* see down here?"

He was spitting, and some of it hit me in the face. But I figured, I'm in this far, what else can happen?

"You, Brother Ulrich. I saw *you* with a kid."

"Did you now?" he asked, smiling at me with a face that could have curdled milk. "And who by the way, Mr. Rothberg, was the young man in question?"

"Alberto Gomez."

The smile dropped from his face.

"You're lying, Mr. Rothberg! And I am truly ashamed of you, making up such a lie on the soul of that poor kid who drowned. Truly ashamed."

I glanced over at Tim. He was stone white, all the blood had left his face and his neck. He looked like he was going to faint.

"I gotta leave," he said. "I ain't feelin' good."

"That's all right, son," Brother Ulrich said. "Please leave. Leave this liar's presence, and give my love and the love of God to your parents and your brothers, too."

Tim grabbed his books and hurried away. Brother Ulrich grabbed my arm.

"I'm taking you right up to Father Greer. I'm telling him that you're a liar. Lying's an egregious sin. It's enough to have you expelled!"

I jerked my arm away from him, but he gripped me harder. Now I knew I had to make a stand, not simply for me, but for Arthur and also for my father. I had to show Robby what I was made of, even if he was in jail in Valdosta, Georgia. One day I'd tell him all about this. We'd be adults, having a scotch together and smoking a good cigar, and I'd tell him what he'd meant to me and how he had prepared me to do this.

I looked directly at Brother Ulrich, until he let go of my arm.

"I'm not lying," I said. "Maybe I got the name of the kid wrong, but I'm *not* lying."

He raised his hand, as if to slap me. I flinched. I was a kid and knew how much being slapped by an adult would hurt.

"If you hit me, I'll go to the police," I said. "I'll go to Det. Whitaker and I'll tell him everything."

"You would, would you?"

I just stared at him. Brother Ulrich was a short man, somewhere about Robby's size, but still bigger than I was. He was fat, and repulsive.

I didn't say anything else. He turned around to walk away, but first he looked at me with this look of unmitigated hatred. Still, it didn't scare me. I'd made up my mind: if he ever touched me, I'd kick him straight in the balls.

I saw Tim outside later; he was with Neal.

"You are *something*, Rothberg," Neal said, shaking my hand and smiling. "Tim's clued me in on what happened. You are one fuckin' ballsy Jew."

"He ain't scared of Brother *Dorris*," Tim lit in. "That turd's scared generations of kids here at Holy Smokes. And you ain't even scared!"

"Thanks," I said. "I was scared. I just didn't show it much."

"That's half the battle," Neal said. "Makes me want to go down there and psych out that john and see who does go into it. But if I got caught, they'd throw me out, and me and Pat wanna graduate and go on to college. So—"

"—you better not do it," I suggested.

"You really told Dorris the Dummy you saw him bring a kid down there?"

"He did," Tim said. "Scared me shitless. I thought I was gonna faint. Maybe throw up."

"Shut up, squirt. Rothberg, I can't believe it. They should put up a fuckin' bust of you in the hallways, along with th' pictures of Saint Sebastian gettin' arrows stuck in his keister. Lemme give you a lift home, all the way to I'll-a-'ope."

"Naw, I'm waiting for my mom. The thing is, we still don't know what happened. We still don't know the truth about Arthur."

Neal's face fell; now he wasn't smiling so broadly.

"You gotta let that go," Tim said. "He's in heaven."

"Yeah," Neal said seriously. "Where all good Catholics go, no matter what they've done. At a certain point, God forgives you as long as you believe in the basic stuff."

I nodded. "So what's the basic stuff, Neal?"

Neal resumed smiling, becoming incredibly flirty. I could see why Arthur had gone to him.

"Saints. Miracles," he said quickly. "The blessed history of the Catholic Church, and the basic goodness of th' Father, th' Son, and th' Holy Spirit. The Pope, he's like God's stand-in on Earth, but it's always about the basic goodness of the Holy Spirit, and how you should come up to it, and you *can* if you work hard enough. The real stuff of you—*it* can."

"That seems wonderful to me," I admitted.

Neal eyes brightened, like he was almost effortlessly pulling me in and convincing me of everything he'd said. Suddenly I wanted to kiss him—kiss him like I couldn't imagine ever kissing Faye. It was terrible; I knew that didn't make me very normal, but if it were really all about God's basic goodness and coming up to it, He'd understand.

Caroline drove up. I said good-bye to Neal and shook his hand and then Tim's.

"So what happened in school today?" Caroline asked.

"Nothing much."

"How are the bar mitzvah lessons?"

"Fine."

"Jesus! The whole damn thing's just a month away, and I'm not ready for it. Andy was supposed to make all the arrangements—the synagogue, a caterer and everything. It's on the calendar; Andy told me so. We're supposed to have a meeting with the rabbi next week. Andy set that up, too."

"What are we going to do about Dad?" I asked. "Suppose he's convicted?"

"I don't know, but I can't drive and think about it. If your dad's convicted we may have to leave the house. You might have to leave school."

She pulled the car over and started crying again.

"Please forgive me," she sobbed. "This is not helping you."

I patted her beautiful hair. I felt good doing it, but I had to ask her again.

"What are we going to do, Mom, if he *is* convicted? Won't the bar mitzvah be kind of … stupid?"

She stopped crying and smiled faintly.

"I guess the bar mitzvah then will be the least of our problems, won't it?"

When we got home, Josephine came out to the driveway with Liz. She told Mom that Andy Geyer had called, and had asked her to call him back as soon as she got home. Mom disappeared upstairs, and left me and Liz with Josephine.

"Would you like some lemonade?" Josephine asked.

She went back to the kitchen to get it. Liz and I settled into the swing in the front yard. It was nice being with Liz. She was starting to look a lot more like Mom. It was like she had Mom's genes and I had Dad's. I felt jealous: I really wanted more of Mom's. She was taller, leaner, and more athletic than Dad. I'd never get that, but my sister would. At least none of us looked like Allan Streitt, although Nathan Streitt was good looking, even if he was a *shmuck* as Robby would have said. Or would that have been Leon?

"Is Daddy ever going t' come back?" Liz asked seriously.

"Yes," I told her. "He is."

"When? He's been gone for so long. I was just a kid when he left."

I laughed. "You're still a kid."

"You know what I mean. Now I'm in fourth grade, and I know a lot. I can read and understand things. It all changes so fast, and I want him to be here before I get too old."

Josephine came out with the lemonade. She must have understood that we were talking about my father.

"You shouldn't worry so about Mr. Rothberg," she said. "He's gonna be OK. I been prayin' lots 'bout it myself."

"Thank you," I said. "You're wonderful, Josephine."

Josephine went back into the house; Liz looked at me anxiously.

"I hope Josephine's praying works," she said. We stopped talking. I had homework to do, so I went up to my room. A short time later Mom came in, sat down on my bed, and looked at me. I'd never seen her look so serious. I was afraid to ask what was going on; she had to force herself to speak.

"Your father's been convicted," she said. "They haven't sentenced him yet. But he's been convicted."

I sat down next to her. Suddenly I felt like I was a hundred years old, and I hadn't even been bar mitzvahed yet.

"Should we go up to Valdosta?" I asked.

She started wringing her hands, then stopped.

"No. I think they're going to let him come down here before the sentencing. I mean, he hasn't killed anyone. He'll be in a minimum-security place. Andy said that Robby wants more than anything in the world to come down for your bar mitzvah—that's what he really wants."

She put her hand on my shoulder.

"You're growing up so fast, and I can't stop it. I guess every parent wants to, just like every kid doesn't want them to. My parents didn't want me to marry Robby, then they just came around to it; sometimes I think more than his family up North did."

"Does he ever see them?"

"Sometimes when he goes up there, but there's such a gulf between them and us. It's like there's such a gulf between Robby and me sometimes: That Jewish part of him I never can be a part of. Do you know what I mean?"

I nodded.

"I guess I'm the thing between the gulf, aren't I?" I asked. "But what about Liz? What does she want to do? Do you think she feels Jewish?"

"I don't know. But we have to think about her, too. She just takes it for granted that she doesn't have a religion. She always says, 'I don't need to believe in Jesus, as long as I'm good, right?' She has a point. But what do you believe in?"

"I believe in Dad," I answered her. "I believe in Dad very much. He's innocent, I know that. And I believe in Arthur, too."

"The kid who drowned? Isn't that kind of morbid, Benjy? He's dead."

"Well, Catholics believe in an eternal soul, and—"

"Oh, please! That's the Catholic idea of the soul, sweetie; and you get that by swallowing the rest of their stuff, hook, line, and sinker. They believe in the Blessed Virgin Mary, but if it's a choice between an unborn child and the kid's mother, to hell with the mother. Sorry, my innate anti-Catholicism comes out. It was Robby's idea that you go to Holy Nativity, not mine. But you've done very well there, I can tell. You've got wonderful friends; it's made you grow up."

She got up.

"The meeting with the rabbi's going to be effin' weird, pardon my language.

The thought of it makes me want to have a good stiff drink. I think normally Robby should be there, or at least a *real* Jewish mother, which I know I'm not."

I smiled.

"Yeah, but you're my *real* mother and that's what counts."

"Sure, I guess you could have ended up with a *real* Jewish mother," she said, shaking her head. "The kind who complains all the time about their kids—'Oy! My son doesn't vant to be a doctor!' Frankly, you can be what you want to be, just don't try to stick around us, because there ain't gonna be a lot of money around here. Speaking of which, Andy said he'd completely pay for this shindig. He said it was the least he could do."

"What does that mean?" I asked seriously. "I thought your parents were going to pay for some of it?"

"I think their money'll have to go for Robby's lawyer, and other things. Like food and gas and stuff like that. I hate this—you're a kid and you shouldn't have to worry about things like this. I certainly didn't. I didn't know what money was when I was your age, but then Dad and his family and Mom always had it. It was nice, Benjy, I admit it, coming from the people I did. I just didn't want to marry one of them. Boring!"

17

Planning For The Bar Mitzvah

The meeting at the synagogue was awful. A thin, stooped old man, who looked to be a about hundred, but was probably only fifty, led us through a short hallway to the rabbi's office. A secretary outside with iron-gray hair smiled faintly at us, like it cost her something to do it. She opened his door, and Rabbi Silverman, short, chubby, and bald with large watery eyes, rose and motioned for us to come in. He was in a dark suit, like he was getting ready for a funeral, but I gathered that was what rabbis wore.

"Hell-*oooooh*, Mrs. Rothberg," he said like an actor, in a deep, resonant voice that never really seemed to come out of his throat. It was like he was impersonating someone else, maybe someone taller and better looking. "And you must be young Benjamin, Leon's son. We are *soooh* sorry to hear about your father's—" He closed his eyes theatrically, then re-opened them. "Anyway, a bar mitzvah is always *such* a joyous occasion. It means you are joining the community and the congregation as an *adult* young man. You are now part of a *minyan*. You know what that means, of course?"

"It means he can be one of ten men who make up a quorum for prayer," Mom said smiling, as if she had just passed the first section of the test.

"Yes, it does, Mrs. Rothberg."

"Please call me Caroline."

"Fine, Caroline. Now, we know that your husband is not a member of our congregation, but Mr. Geyer has made a donation in his name, which we are very thankful for. *Tzdakah*, charity, is an important part of Jewish life. So tell me, Benjamin, *whooo* has been preparing you for your bar mitzvah?"

He really stretched out that *who*.

"I've been having lessons at school," I answered cautiously.

"*School*? I didn't realize you're attending Hebrew School?"

Mom's eyes hit the floor, so I explained to the rabbi, as well as I could, that a teacher at Holy Nativity who was completely conversant in Hebrew was helping me learn the prayers as well as the part of the Prophets I would be called on to read; and that I'd also learned to read Hebrew and to understand what I was reading, which was more than I had learned with Solomon Bernstein.

"So you didn't stay with Solly?" the rabbi asked. "That's *most* unfortunate; he's a gifted bar mitzvah teacher. A lot of our boys go to him for preparation. I'm afraid I have no experience with your teacher. Let's face it, Mrs. Rothberg, it is *rah-ther* unusual."

"It was Benjy's choice," Mom said. "His father and I wanted him to make it."

The rabbi put the tips of his fingers together, and pursed his lips.

"I'm not sure this will do," he said a moment later. "There is a whole order of the service for a bar mitzvah, and we need to know that the person who's preparing Benjamin understands it. But let's get on to other things. You have a caterer, I hope? One who's *kosher*?"

"Yes, Andy Geyer said he would take care of all that."

The rabbi closed his eyes again, thinking. Then they popped open.

"Good! You are on the calendar, so everything in that vein is fine. I am, though, a bit concerned about Benjamin's preparation. Let's try to discern something."

He took a prayer book from his bookcase and opened it, smiling at me with one of those strange frozen smiles I could never quite figure out, kind of like he had barged into me on the toilet but was trying to forget I was there.

"Here, Benjamin. Can you just show me how *you'd* recite this prayer? It's the one done at every service. It's a variation on the Kaddish, the basic prayer of the Jewish people. It doesn't say anything except that it glorifies God's name. That's what Jews do. We glorify a God who has no Name, yet we still glorify His Name because in truth all of Creation is His Name."

I took the book from him and blanked out completely, like it could have been written in Chinese. My eyes couldn't even see the characters in Hebrew on the page. I wasn't looking at him, but I was afraid he was still smiling at me with that same interrupted-bathroom smile.

"Go ahead," he said.

"He must be nervous," Mom said. "I would be right now. Rabbi, is this necessary? I think you're embarrassing my son."

"Sorry, Caroline," the rabbi said firmly. "But if he's embarrassed now, what *will* he be like on the day of his bar mitzvah?"

Mom shot me a supportive look with her eyes, nodding. This was no Mona Lisa smile, just a "Get *him*!" expression aimed at the rabbi that made me understand she was right behind me.

I looked at the page again and now the letters came into focus. I remembered all of them, as well as the words. I began reading, hardly stumbling a second, then I chanted the words, remembering everything Brother Alexis had told me, about exactly what sounds went with what words, and what the words meant and how they were important because they affirmed God's presence—and that was what it was *all* about. The words were "transparent," Brother Alexis had said. "They see all the way down to the soul of the world, because that's where God is, no matter what your religion is."

When I was through, I handed the book back to Rabbi Silverman. For a moment, he didn't say anything, then he said, "You did beautifully, Benjamin. Just…beautifully. I'm just not convinced you'll be able to follow the rest of the service. You should start coming here every Saturday until the day of your bar mitzvah. That way you'll also get to know some of our young people, and feel more at home here."

He got up and shook Caroline's hand, and then shook mine.

"I hope you'll do that. We would like to welcome you here into our midst as a young member of the congregation."

"Thank you, Rabbi," Mom said. "That's very kind of you. I'll be happy to drive Benjamin here from Isle of Hope."

Rabbi Silverman cleared his throat.

"Well, I'm afraid that driving is *not* something we do on the Sabbath. Can he stay with a friend who lives close to the *shul*? A lot of people do that."

"Sure," Mom said. "I know lots of people around here. They'll all be happy to have him stay so that he can walk to the synagogue. Don't you worry about that, Rabbi. Come, Benjamin. I'm so proud of you. We'll plan—"

She grabbed my hand and we got out. Neither of us started breathing again until we were back in the car.

She lit a cigarette.

"God, could I use a good Coke and barbeque sandwich right now! That man gave me the willies. I'm sorry, but some of those Jews! I think they've forgotten how to be alive. Thank God your father's not like that, or I never would have married him. But then I wouldn't have you, so it was all worth it." She leaned over and kissed me. I hoped her lipstick wasn't on my cheek.

"For real about the barbeque sandwich?" I asked.

"Sure."

We drove up to a drive-in on Victory Drive where a cute young carhop in short shorts and a tight blouse took our order.

"She must get *some* tips," Mom said. "You really did great with that guy, a lot better than I did. I was ready to tell him to go cram it, except that it would have made your dad very upset and that's the last thing I want to do right now."

"What are we going to do about me going to *shul*?" I asked.

"I'll drive you in on Saturday. Why not?"

"He said you weren't supposed to drive on the Sabbath."

"That's his horse crap, Benjy. I'm sure there are Catholics at your school who eat meat on Fridays and who don't do their rosary when they're supposed to. All professional religious people have to push their stuff down your throat. It's part of their job. In the Middle Ages, they'd have you burned at the stake, but they can't do that anymore. The Jews were never in a burning position—usually, they were the ones getting burned. I mean they can barely hold on to Israel, so don't worry about it. I'll make sure that you'll look like you've walked—like I won't drop you off directly in front of the place."

"I don't know if I want to do this," I said. "I'd rather spend Saturdays with Tim and the O'Neills."

The carhop attached a tray with our food to the driver's side window. Mom had a barbeque sandwich and I had a B.L.T. We both had Cokes. They were big fountain Cokes with lots of ice in them, the way that Cokes always came in the South. Mom thanked the carhop and she left.

"It's sinful for girls to look like that at her age," Mom observed. "Can't they leave some of it for old ladies like us?" She smiled, tasted her sandwich and proclaimed how good it was. Then she said, "You really need to have some more Jewish friends if we want to go through with this bar mitzvah thing. And we do, don't we?"

I nodded while I dug into my sandwich, which came with french fries.

"Good. I'll call up that Streitt boy's mother. You can go to the synagogue with him."

"I like Allan. But I don't like Nathan."

"He's kind of a sad story," Mom said. "And his parents are—anyway, it's good that you like Allan. He can fill you in on all the bar mitzvah stuff I can't."

She put her sandwich back on the tray.

"The whole thing seems crazy," she said, almost in tears now. "My husband's in jail for something he didn't do. We don't even know if we'll be able to stay in the house and—" She stopped herself. "But you're getting bar mitzvahed. I guess that's a blessing, right?"

I told her it was, without asking her any other questions. All I could think of was Robby in a jail, in a cell, waiting for me to do this. I could see his blue eyes, his face and the lines on it. He was waiting in that cell just to walk into the synagogue on the day of my bar mitzvah, and be proud of me. I could feel it. And I wanted him to be proud of me, because in truth I was proud of him too. There was no way I could not be.

So, the next Saturday, Mom dropped me off a few blocks from the synagogue and I walked the rest of it. Although it was fall, it was still humid and warm. I didn't like being dressed up, but inside it was very air conditioned and everybody was in suits and fancy dresses. In the lobby I found a box of yarmulkes and put one on. When I entered into the sanctuary, the service was already underway, and the first person I saw was Allan Streitt. He got up and came over to me.

"I'm glad you're here," he whispered. "Come sit with us."

He was with his father, who looked the same way he looked at the bar mitz-vah party—not that he could have grown any or gotten any better looking. He had his eyes closed, like he was thinking about something or meditating. He opened them, looked at me, and smiled, then leaned over and shook my hand. I liked that he seemed open to my being there.

"Where's your mom?" I whispered to Allan.

"She's on the other side, with the women. Here's where we are in the service."

He handed me a prayer book. The cantor was singing something that made very little sense to me, in this very theatrical, beseeching voice that reminded me of someone like Paul Anka or Eddie Fisher asking for love. Except I guess he was singing to God. Then they pulled out the Torah from its ark, which had little curtains in front of it that they opened and closed, and they read from it. I was impressed. I had never heard anyone actually read the Torah. Allan showed me a book with the translation, and I was able to follow it somewhat, although not much because they read it so fast. A short time later, Rabbi Silverman got up—he was wearing a white robe with a large shawl that ended in fringes—and I figured it was time for his sermon.

He scanned the congregation. His large eyes hit me and I could tell that he recognized me as he smiled immediately, like a neon sign had turned on, flashing: *Pay Attention*: *Benjamin Rothberg Here*! His sermon was mostly about approaching the High Holidays, and I realized that my bar mitzvah would follow them pretty closely. I hadn't even connected my birth date to the High Holidays—what kind of Jew was I? That was always an open question.

He went into how important it was to be extra good, and observe all the laws you could—I thought about the B.L.T. I'd had with Mom at the drive-in, and felt suddenly really bad about it, but I also felt bad about not seeing Tim that weekend, and wondered what the O'Neills were doing. He quoted a lot from the Bible, and talked about Abraham and Isaac and how important it was for the world that God that interceded and Abraham had not had to sacrifice his only legitimate son.

"This is the basic tenet of the Jewish people: that God tested Abraham so severely that Abraham was set to sacrifice Isaac, and yet God showed compassion to Abraham, so that the patriarch did not have to make this sacrifice. Instead Abraham sacrificed a ram, which is why we blow the *shofar*, a ram's horn. Still, this was the beginning of God's choosing the Jewish people for His purpose—we all know that—because we have always been willing to make sacrifices for Him. We have bent our will to Him in a world that denies Him. And we will do this soon, as the Holidays approach, bending our will to Him, asking for His forgiveness, and allowing us to be inscribed for one more year in the Book of Life. Amen."

Of course the sermon made me think about Arthur: Why wasn't he spared, why wasn't some ram chosen instead—anything except this boy? I looked at Allan and tried to be politely genial, but my hands were clenching. I was hoping it would all be over with after the sermon, and we could get up and leave, but there were more prayers and singing. Allan made sure that I knew the right place in the prayer book, but frankly I was bored by then.

Finally, after one last song, Rabbi Silverman blessed everyone, shook the cantor's hand, and everyone got up. Allan smiled at me; I liked his smile. He was not a good-looking kid, but he was obviously sincere and I'm sure that being the squirt brother of Nathan Streitt had been a trial for him. He asked me if I wanted to come home and have Shabbos dinner with them. "Your mom spoke to mine," he explained. "So we're expecting you." Seeing me still hesitating, he added, "It's OK. Nathan's away. He's with *his* friends."

The Streitts' house was within walking distance of the synagogue, in an impressive new subdivision of Savannah. Allan jokingly called it the Golden Ghetto.

"See, the synagogue used to be downtown, but a few years ago a lot of Jews were moving out in this direction, away from the *shwartzes* I guess, so the synagogue decided to move with them. It's Orthodox, and Orthodox Jews are supposed to walk to *shul* on Saturday, although I'm sure you can see that Southern Orthodox isn't really as strict as the stuff up North, like in New York."

His mom who was walking with us, beamed. She was wearing another tight, flowery dress, pointy heels, and a stole which seemed really crazy in the weather.

"Allan, you're so smart," she said. "But he's right, we had to leave because the *shwartzes* were taking over the downtown area. It seems to be the flow of things. Not that I have anything against *shwartzes*, they can be nice like anyone. They'll soon be in all the schools; then I don't know what we're going to do. They're in the schools up in New York, but the *shwartzes* there aren't as backward as ones down here, if you know what I mean?"

Actually, I didn't. There had been Negro boys at Holy Nativity for several years; it was one of the first schools to integrate in Savannah. I thought about Alfred Johnson and how much I liked him. And of course about Arthur. In a really white world, he would not have fit in anyway. Sadness hit me. I realized that a lot of people from the synagogue were walking in the same direction as we were but no one would even look at me, as if they had already figured out who I was. They smiled at the Streitts, and some of them called out Allan's name, but no one said a word to me even after Allan introduced me to various kids, some our age. They simply continued walking.

The Streitts' house was very big and they had two maids working there on a Saturday. A large table had been set with dinner plates, and sparkling crystal glasses for water or iced tea and wine for the adults. Allan took me past it to his room, which was big and filled with books, games, and toys. I looked around.

"All of this is yours?" I asked.

"Some of it was Nathan's. I inherited it when he got tired of it—like a microscope set that he never touched. You wanna change clothes? I think you could fit into my pants—just tighten them with your belt. It's crazy to stay in *shul* clothes when you don't have to."

He offered me a pair of blue jeans and a T-shirt. He had no self-consciousness stripping down to a pair of jockey shorts in front of me. When I did the same thing, he looked at me.

"You're really good looking," he said. "I wish I was as good looking as you. I know I'm a real *mieskeit*, but there's nothing I can do about it."

"You have a great smile. It just opens up your face."

"Thanks. Girls like it. Did you see Faye today?"

I told him no.

"She must have left early. Sometimes she doesn't stay for the whole service. Her parents are not very *frum*. That means they don't care about all this Jewish stuff. She liked you a lot at the party. I'm sorry my brother was such an asshole. He gets crazy sometimes; I was embarrassed by him."

"*You* were?" I said while slipping into the jeans. He was right; I really needed to tighten the belt. The T-shirt fit OK. It was striped and made of really nice cotton. I liked the way it felt. "I—"

I couldn't finish saying anything.

"I know." He put his hand on my shoulder and kept it there. "Listen, I'm your friend. I know what it's like to be hurt by people."

There was more food on the table at dinner than I ever thought I'd eat in my life, enough to feed twelve people when there was only Mr. and Mrs. Streitt, Allan, and myself. The two uniformed colored maids brought out everything and served and then cleared things away, and even brought me a fresh glass when I asked for some more iced tea. Mrs. Streitt talked endlessly, mostly gossip about people I had no idea who they were. Mr. Streitt just ate, chewing very loudly. He had changed into a pair of slacks and a polo shirt, but Mrs. Streitt kept her *shul* dress on. She said hardly anything to the maids, but they knew exactly what to do just by following her eyes or gestures as she pointed to things. I could not imagine Josephine in that situation. She was more like a real person; sometimes she sat at the table with us when Dad was not around and things were less formal. But I thought that the Streitts' maids were more like something out of a play or a movie.

"How are your parents?" Mrs. Streitt asked me after dessert, as she dabbed her mouth with her napkin. "I mean your mom, how's she doing? It must be hard on her, what's going on. We barely know each other, just a bit through Andy Geyer. He's your dad's friend, right?"

"A lotta people know Andy," Mr. Streitt cut in. "He's a *macher*."

"Eis, that is not a good thing to say in front of this boy."

"He probably doesn't know what a *macher* is, do you, son? It's somebody who gets things done. A lotta people in this town don't like Andy Geyer, but if you have some kinda job that needs to happen, he'll do it for you."

"Dad," Allan said. "His father's in trouble. We know that. It doesn't help to bring up this stuff."

Mr. Streitt looked over at Allan sheepishly.

"Sure, son, we know that. I hate it when my kids are smarter than I am, but it's the truth."

"It's OK," I told Mr. Streitt. "I didn't know what a *macher* is. Or much about Andy Geyer. All I know is that he's my dad's business partner. My parents don't talk a lot about these things in front of me."

"Yeah, well your mother's a *goy*," Mr. Streitt said. "They don't know much from business. It's like a secret world that we Jews have the key to. They like the money, don't get me wrong, but they always have the attitude that it dirties their hands. So we're supposed to do the dirty work."

"Eis, that's enough," Mrs. Streitt said.

The front door opened, and Nathan came bursting in. He looked around scowling, but said nothing.

"Would you like some Shabbos dinner?" his mother asked.

"Sure."

He sat down and a maid silently brought him a plate.

"Did you wash your hands, Nathan?" Mrs. Streitt asked.

"Not since I had 'em up my ass."

"Shut up!" Mr. Streitt said. "I will not have that kind of language inside my house."

"Sure . . . I've lost my appetite," Nathan said glumly. "Especially with our guest here." He got up and walked away.

"Go to your room!" Mr. Streitt ordered, when Nathan was out of sight.

"What are we going to do with him?" Mrs. Streitt asked. "Benjy, I'm sorry about our son's behavior. He's a problem kid. He always has been. We've tried everything. Counselors, psychiatrists, even a special camp once for him. It all did no good."

"I should a' taken off my belt and gone at him," Mr. Streitt said regretfully. "But no, my wife was all for Dr. Spock and his bullshit. If I'd talked to my father that way, I wouldn't a' been able to sit down for a week. Still, he gets a car, allowance. It's nuts."

"He's a disturbed child, but he'll get better," Mrs. Streitt said. "Remember the way he used to be before the last counselor we got? People were still talking about the police, and you don't send the police to a Jewish home. It's just not done."

I had to get up. I just couldn't take the conversation anymore. I told them I needed to use the bathroom. There was one for guests near the dining room, but I'd seen another next to Allan's room. I hurried over to it, went in, and sat on the toilet seat. I put my head in my hands and started crying. Everything at the Streitts *was* like a play, a bad play. There was a soft knock on the door. I thought it had to be Allan so I opened it.

Nathan barged in.

"How are you, cutie?" he asked and grabbed me. "Y'know, I'd love to fuck you in the ass. I could fuck you in the ass right here. I bet those guys at that Catholic school do it all the time. Everybody talks about Holy Nate. It's a joke, right?"

I was crying uncontrollably now; I felt terrible. There was no way I could hide it. He let go of me, and looked at me silently. His whole attitude changed. I saw it—he was no longer the obnoxious person I'd seen at Allan's bar mitzvah party, or even the one who'd barged into the bathroom. His face fell. His eyes became soft, extremely so, like they were asking for something.

"Jesus, I feel like such a shit," he said, his voice close to cracking. "I was jus' trying to impress you, show you what a regular guy I am. Guess you can see I'm not. What's wrong, Benjy? Tell me, why are you crying?"

"I don't belong here," I said.

He nodded, shrugging. "Who does? God, I didn't mean that stupid crap about fuckin' you in the ass. I was joking; I get so fuckin' crazy—my parents drive me nuts. They just want to be good ol' Southern Jews in Savannah, Georgia, instead of Yankee kikes. I guess anybody can see what the hell's going on here and it's not a pretty picture."

He put his hands gently on my face.

"You're really a good-looking kid. I can see why Allan likes you."

He found some Kleenex and gave me one. I used it to dry my eyes and blow my nose. Then I washed my face.

"Would you do me a favor?" I asked afterwards. "I want to go home. Would you drive me back to Isle of Hope?"

"Sure, why not? I'd love to get out of here myself."

He told me he'd be in the TV room, a small room past the den. We left the bathroom and he pointed it out to me. I looked around. The living room was too full of porcelain tchotchkes and white-and-gilt Louis-Something furniture to actually live in; the den was smaller and more comfortable, and the TV room was filled with stacks of magazines and coasters for drinks. So I figured it was more like our veranda. These people did not live a lot outside; their life was definitely air-conditioned.

I told Mr. and Mrs. Streitt that I wasn't feeling well, and that Nathan had agreed to drive me.

"Finally, he's doing something worthwhile!" Mr. Streitt said. "Just make sure he drives slow and safe. That road out to Isle of Hope has a lot of twists in it."

"He's a safe driver," Mrs. Streitt said. "One thing you can say for Natie is that he's a safe driver."

Her husband shook his head. "That's not what all the tickets said. But it's good that he's doing this; maybe it shows a change of heart in him. Nathan's a good kid, really. But he has his problems."

"Thanks for coming to dinner," Allan said, smiling.

"No, thank you." I nodded to his parents and thanked each of them personally. Allan walked with me back to his room so I could change back into my clothes.

"Will I see you next Saturday?" he asked.

"I don't know. It all depends—"

"I understand. But if you need any help with your bar mitzvah, let me know."

Nathan's car, a sporty Karmman Ghia in a lemon yellow color, was in the

Streitts' four-car carport. The top was down, and I immediately fastened my seat belt as we got into it.

"You don't have to do that," he said. "I promised Mom I'd drive extra-careful."

"OK," I said, and unbuckled it. Once we were away from the house, he lit a cigarette and offered me one.

"Do you smoke?"

"I'm not even thirteen yet," I said.

"I didn't ask you your age, but if you smoked. It's OK. You don't need to smoke." He lit up from the car lighter and exhaled. After a short while, he turned on the radio to a local Negro music station, but lowered the sound.

"I like black music," he said as we left the city, and got further out into the country. "My mom keeps calling them *shwartzes*, like they're not even human. Sometimes I hate Jews, they're stupid and narrow-minded. You're lucky that both your parents aren't Jewish."

"At least you know who you are," I said glancing at him.

I looked back at the road as it passed behind us. The area around Savannah was so beautiful that you couldn't help noticing it. It was like being inside a beautiful song; the landscape sang to you: the big oak trees, the Spanish moss, the pines, the tall grasses by the marshes, the sand and red clay. It was all part of the earth that we came out of, that Adam came from. I looked at Nathan again, like he was Adam.

"You mean *what* I am?" Nathan said. "I know what I *am*, that's the hard part."

"Why?"

He wouldn't answer me. He just kept his eyes on the road, and we listened to the music. Then he asked, "Has any guy ever touched you?"

"Wha' do you mean?"

"I mean, like has he ever touched your dick, or tried to get to your ass?"

"No."

"Good. Keep it that way."

Suddenly I wanted one of his cigarettes. This wasn't like talking to Tim, or even to Neal. It seemed like such an adult conversation; I could never have anything like this with Allan Streitt or any of my friends. I didn't know Nathan, yet somehow he didn't seem like a stranger to me. He pushed in the car lighter and when it popped out, he handed it to me. I was able to light the cigarette because

I had seen Mom do the same thing. I took a very slow drag on it, but it still burned my throat. I tried hard not to, but coughed.

"First time smoking?"

"No."

"*Sure*," he smirked. "So, somebody has? I'm asking you."

"Why are you asking?"

"Because you're so good-looking. I figured that somebody must've tried to get t' you. That's why. You don't look like the usual Yid. Your mom must be gorgeous."

"She's beautiful," I admitted.

"So, who touched you?"

He put his right hand on my knee, and kept it there.

"Stop doing that."

"Why?"

"Because it scares me."

"You wanted me to drive you home. Why? You could have got my folks to do it, or called your mom, but you wanted me to. Why, Benjy?"

Now we were really way out, where the road simply meandered. At night it could be scary sometimes, especially if there were no moon. It was black then, and all you had were your headlights. There was just the tall swamp grass, the trees, and the distant sounds. I felt terrible, but I told myself I wasn't going to cry.

"Because," I said, "I thought you understood how fucked up I am."

"You mean because I'm fucked up, too?"

"No. I—I don't know why. I just felt something. I was scared of you at first. Especially when you came in the bathroom and said all those things to me. It's not like that at Holy Nativity. It's not like that at all."

"You sure? I've heard lots of things about Holy Smokes. Kids joke about it. Especially Jewish kids."

"It's wrong."

"How wrong? A hundred percent wrong?"

He kept his hand on my knee. He was stroking it and then gripping it harder. I tried to remove it, but he wouldn't let me.

"Why are you doing this? Why can't you just drive me home?"

"That's what I wish I could do. I wish I could *drive* you home."

He smiled. He spotted an unpaved country road that turned off from the main one, and turned into it. There was a deep stand of pines nearby. He stopped the car.

"I need to pee. You need to, too?"

"No."

"Come on," he said. "I know you need to pee. Come on."

He pulled me out of the car—it was easy, since he was bigger than I was—and led me to the pines and unzipped himself and took his cock out. It was big and hard. Then he unzipped my pants and yanked them down, almost breaking the waist button. They were my good pants, and I felt terrible. I didn't want anything bad to happen to them. My heart was beating so hard that I could feel it in my throat. He started jerking off, then went down and sucked me. A second later he came in his hand, and I shot down his throat, feeling like my whole body was pouring out of me. I'd never felt that way when I came with Tim.

Nathan wiped his hand on one of the trees to get some of the cum off, then used a pocket handkerchief. He pulled me to him and held me. I kissed him on his mouth exactly as I had wanted to do to Arthur; I'm not sure why. I sat on his lap, so I wouldn't get any of the pine stuff on me. We were quiet.

Then he said, "If you ever tell anyone about this, I'll kill you. I mean it."

"You didn't have to say that, Nathan. You really are fucked up. I wouldn't tell."

"You've done stuff like this before, right?"

"Yes."

"Kids at school?"

"Yes."

"But you didn't go this far?"

I nodded. I wasn't about to go into details I hardly understood myself.

"You're such a beautiful kid. Kids like you—like *us*—we grow up so fast. Because we know what it's like to be on the outside, and that's where you see everything. Those other kids at the Jewish center, those little Southern Yids, they're on the outside, too. You have to be to be if you're a Jew in the South, especially in a town like Savannah. But they have this fantasy that they're Southerners who just *happen* to be Jewish. Like they try to be all preppy-cool and still nice Jewish kids; you can't believe what they *say* about me. I tried really hard to be like them, till one day I just woke up. So I understand what you're going through. Hell, maybe I helped you wake up faster."

He smiled and we got up. Now I did have to pee. Nathan peed too, for a long time. We went back on the main road, and drove on some more until we came to a small store. He got out and came back with two cans of Schlitz. He was only seventeen, but no one asked him for ID. He handed one to me. I told him I didn't like beer.

"Too bad," he said. "There are moments when nothing's like it. Especially in the kind of heat you have in Savannah. You gonna go t' *shul* again next Saturday?"

"No," I said.

"Good. What are you gonna do?"

"I don't know. My dad wants me to be bar mitzvahed more than anything in the world."

"Then you should do it. Poor guy. He's in jail in fucking Valdosta, Georgia. No Jew in his right mind should end up there. I feel sorry for you."

He pulled me to him, and messed my hair up with his hand.

"You are such an amazing kid—but, boy! I can't ever see you again, not like this. It would be too dangerous, for me and for you. You should stick with those Catholic kids; they can get away with shit that I can't."

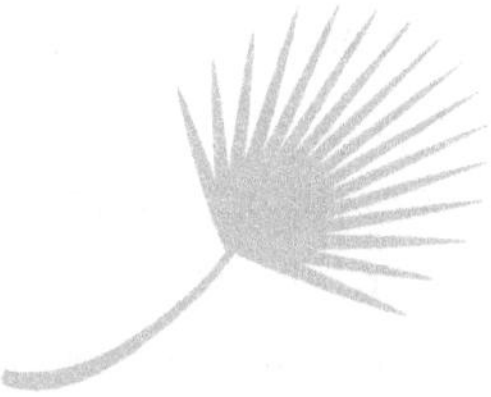

18

An Alternative

Evening was approaching. Nathan waved good-bye to me and drove away without coming into the house. Caroline didn't say a word to me about the cigarette on my breath; I told her I had homework to do and rushed upstairs and shut the door to my room. But a few minutes later, Caroline came in and sat on my bed.

"So, *boychik*, what did you think of the whole *shul* thing?" She laughed for a second. "God, do I sound Jewish or what?"

I broke into tears; I had been holding all this stuff inside me, and still didn't know what it was. There was no way I could say anything about Nathan. I put my head in her lap, and she stroked my hair and waited for me to tell her what was wrong.

"I don't feel I'm a part of those people at all," I said, sobbing. "All I feel is how outside I am. I don't know what to do about Dad."

"Not much we can do, darling," Caroline said. "But—I believe God makes things happen for the best. That's what Mom always told me. She still believes in Jesus, and she taught me that things really do happen for the best."

I could only hope she was right.

At school on Monday I was happy to be back with my friends and feel normal again. They liked me without trying to figure me out, and we knew how much we could accept of each other. The time at the synagogue and with the Streitts was like putting on another skin, and I didn't know whose skin it was. Was it Dad's, or some idea he had about me, or that I'd had of myself that didn't work?

The strange thing was, even without knowing it, I must have grown. I felt so much older than I had only a year ago. Horace Storch must have figured it out, too. He and Ken Ferris had recruited another kid named Joe Flauwerty, who was greasy-faced and kind of squirty but puffed himself up to appear big. Storch, Ferris, and Flauwerty tried to act like they were a regular Cold War menace, something all kids should be scared of, like Communism and fluoride in the water, but they avoided me in the hallways and left me alone at assemblies. Tim was fast to pick up on this. He came up to me, punching me in a friendly way in the arm.

"Looks like Horace the Homo's scared of you," he said grinning.

You could hear him in the next classroom. I told him to lower his damn voice and punched him back. He pretended to howl.

"I think it's cool," he said lowering it. "Wha'd'ya think the reason is? Didja threaten him or kick his butt in secret?"

"Naw." I was sure this did not come from me; I wondered if Neal or even Pat had got to him and done something.

"Think it's got something t' do with Mahoney the Dummy?" Tim whispered in my ear.

That was a thought. "Just cool it," I said very *sotto voce*, "with Brother Ulrich. I've got too much shit on my plate as it is."

Tim was close to bursting with his kid grin.

"Then scrape some'f it off."

Good advice I thought, and told him I wanted to see him this coming Saturday.

"I thought you gotta go t' synagogue and do penance or whatever you Jews do when the crap gets all over you. Ain't th' High Holidays comin' up? Mom's told me about it. She's got scads o' Jewish friends—she's very *ecumenical*. That's her new big word."

"I'm not going," I said. "High or not. I gotta tell you something, Tim."

"What—We gotta go. Class is startin'."

I held him back. "Jews give me the creeps; it's like they come from another world."

"So?" he smirked. "Y'think Cat'lics don't?"

He smiled and shook my hand.

Our next class was geography with Brother Alexis. I had been a map guy for years—Robby was crazy about maps and used to spread them out for Liz and me all the time. So I knew a lot already and didn't have to pay close attention; sometimes Brother Alex saw me drifting me off and he'd call on me just to get me back to earth, but I could fool everyone by answering the question directly from memory. Mostly, I was thinking about Nathan: I was hurt that he'd said he couldn't see me anymore—more hurt by that than by anything he had done. I mean, Tim and I had done stuff with each other, and Neal had made what I guess you'd call passes at me—even if always in a joking way. But what Nathan had done was different somehow. I wondered why he'd done it: Did he just feel he could? Did he see something in me he knew would make it possible? Strangely I felt that I could trust him, but in the *weirdest* way. It was like we had a common bond, that neither of us really fit into anything. But there was no way I could tell anyone about it, except maybe Tim.

At my next bar mitzvah lesson, I told Brother Alexis about meeting Rabbi Silverman.

"Was he bothered that I'm preparing you?"

"A little," I said. "He wants me to go to the synagogue on Saturdays and watch what's going on and pray—and meet other boys my age."

"That makes sense. Religion doesn't happen in a vacuum. It does take a community."

"But what about people who convert on their own?"

"What are you talking about?"

"Abraham didn't have a community. And how about Jesus? He knew he was the Son of God, without anyone telling him, didn't he?"

Brother Alexis leaned back in his chair. He was wearing a short-sleeved black shirt; dark hair glistened on his forearms. He looked at me intensely with his very deep dark eyes, then leaned in closer toward me.

"Is that what you think you're having, Benjy, an auto-conversion? Maybe you have a feeling for God that we have no idea about. Is that the case?"

I hesitated; the question was too big for me to answer and I was too aware of Brother Alexis's physical presence next to me. I could feel my heart pounding inside me.

"I don' know what I feel," I finally said. "I just want t' do this bar mitzvah for my father, before they take him away."

"I see."

His dark eyes glistened. He took my hand and held it; I relaxed and let him. I wanted Arthur to be there in the room with us; that would have made every-thing perfect. But I knew it wasn't going to happen, and I'd have to go back to being a regular, somewhat average boy again, or at least make an attempt at it. Brother Alexis let go of my hand, and I told him about meeting Faye Jacobson and how much I liked her.

"That's good," he said smiling. "You need to meet girls. I guess you'll invite her to your bar mitzvah, or will she just be there? Since it's a part of the service, anyone can come."

I nodded and we returned to the prayers and my Prophets portion.

Andy Geyer called in the middle of the week and told us that they had postponed the sentencing of my father. It was getting a lot of press up in Valdosta, and the judge did not want to be swayed by it, so he was taking longer than usual.

Mom told me this alone on the veranda. She was already half drunk, her words were having a hard time coming out, and she kept forgetting where she had left her Salty Dog. At one point she asked me to get her another one, and I told her that her glass was still half-full.

"Should we go to Valdosta and visit Dad?" I asked.

"Not you, honey," she said. "But I'm going tomorrow. Josephine'll stay here with you, and my folks will come out and make sure everything's OK. I'd ask them if you could stay there, but I'm sure you'd be happier here. My folks aren't used to kids, and you'd probably drive Mom nuts. She's got to have doilies all over everything, and her napkins folded perfectly. When I was about your age, I thought you weren't really supposed to *swallow* the food at the table. It didn't seem quite polite."

She started laughing very hard, like the joke was twice as funny as it was. Then suddenly the laughter stopped and she sat still for a second.

"I'll call a lot," she said, immediately looking more sober. "I know we promised the rabbi you'd to go back to the synagogue on Saturday. Is there some way you can get a lift, or would you rather I asked Mom and Dad to drive you?"

"I can ask Nathan Streitt to give me a lift."

"You mean he'd come all the way out here for you? That's wonderful, Benjy. The Streitts have turned out to be really great people. I guess Andy Geyer knows how to pick 'em!" Her eyes focused on me. "You've got to be a man now, no matter what. I'm counting on you."

Mom got into her car the next morning with her traveling bag, on the way to drop me off to Holy Nativity. I told her I could take a city bus out to Isle of Hope at the end of the day. After school, I took a bus into downtown Savannah, and transferred to the Isle of Hope bus. The buses were all pretty old, but clean. And, like I've said, white people still pretty much sat up front, and black people sat in the back. A sign at the front of the bus, next to the driver's seat, stated: "White Patrons Will Sit From the Front of the Bus Toward the Rear, and Colored Patrons Will Sit At the Back of the Bus Toward the Front."

I laughed reading that sign, because it was hard to imagine who would sit in the middle. Most of the riders were elderly, black, or poor, or kids like myself. The bus made many stops as it plodded through a long stretch of the city, and it was fairly crowded. Actually I ended up *in* the middle, next to an elderly white lady who smiled at me and asked me my name. I told her, and she said, "*Rothberg*? Do you live in th' I'll-a-'ope?" I told her I did.

She smiled again genially. Her teeth were yellow, but her face was chalk-white with powder. She wore white lace gloves and carried a white lace hankie.

"Your family's been abidin' in I'll-a-'ope for a while. Everybody out there knows it."

"Thank you, Ma'am."

"You seem like such a nice young man. I see you go t' military school at Holy Nativity. Is that so?"

"I do."

"But I thought your people were Jewish, not Catholics."

I didn't want to say anything else to her, so she just said:

"My! It is *one* beautiful day!"

"Yes, Ma'am," I agreed.

She nodded at me a couple of times, then her chalky face wrinkled when a young Negro woman took an empty seat in the midst of white passengers, directly across from us. There was a Negro college situated all by itself in the marshes on the way out to Isle of Hope, and she was probably going to it. She had books with her, and was nicely dressed. Very soon after she sat down, a tall, red-faced bald man in overalls stood up in his seat and said loudly to her:

"Cain't you niggers figure out where you 'sposed t' sit?"

She didn't answer him.

"Maybe," he went on, "if you had *uh-volved* more, you'd know yer place. You niggers still belong up *theah* in th' trees!"

He sat back down; you could have heard a pin drop. He swiveled his head, staring back at me, and the girl. I cringed inside, thinking about the time on the bus when I had gone to see Arthur—and how it then became part of that visit to him. I had heard about problems in places like Selma, Alabama, and I wanted to do something; I wanted to say something. But I was swept up with a combination of fear and hating that man. I felt awful for the young woman who kept her face directed out the window, pretending that he didn't exist.

Then a younger white man sitting in the window seat next to the girl pulled the cord for a stop. She got up so he could get out. The man in the overalls glowered at her as she stood for a moment, and after the other man had cleared the way and was close to the exit at the front of the bus, I got up.

"Good-bye, young fella!" the old lady said to me, forgetting we were not even close to Isle of Hope.

I took the place of the other man, and the girl sat down next to me.

"You a nigger-lover, too?" the bald man hissed at me. "Makes sense. You look it!"

I didn't answer, but my heart was pounding.

The girl looked down towards me. She was taller than I was. "Pay him no mind," she advised me quietly. "You didn't need t' do this."

For a moment that seemed to last a lifetime, everything was silence and I hated it all. I hated the man in the overalls, and that I couldn't say anything. I hated the polite but inquisitive way that old lady had spoken to me. But most of all, I hated being not quite thirteen: old enough to know stuff, but too young to do anything. Then, as it usually happens, out of nowhere people started talking again; things became almost normal. The man in the overalls rang the bell and got up. I could feel his eyes drilling through me, but I didn't look at him until he had reached the front of the bus.

"You have yo'self a good day, Lucas!" he declared loudly to the driver, more a boast than a greeting. The bus quieted again. The driver cleared his throat.

"We don' want no trouble here," he said.

"They askin' for it, Lucas. And we gonna give it t' 'em!"

The driver stopped and he got off, and with that, a huge, rippling sigh of relief made its way from the Negro passengers in back even up to the white ones in the front. It felt like some sort of deliverance from a too-evident ugliness that was as horrible as being cornered by Storch and his gang. Suddenly the Jews I'd met in Savannah started to make sense to me. They were scared like I was. But what were we all scared of?

That was the deep, disturbing question.

I don't remember saying anything else to the girl, but she smiled at me when she got off at her stop on the side of the road by the college. The old lady got off next and avoided even looking at me; I didn't care. But I was glad to get back to our house and find Josephine in one of her pretty dresses waiting for me.

I went home with Tim on Friday, and felt good about it. Caroline was still in Valdosta, so I felt like I was getting away with something. That night, after supper with his whole family—except for his dad, who was again away "on business"—I was in Tim's bed. We were in our jockey shorts and he sat up.

"You really gonna do this bar mitzvah thing? My mom's been talking about it. I've never been to a bar mitzvah before. What's it like? Is it like you get confirmed and then can go to Confession, that sort of thing?"

"Jews don't have Confession," I answered. "At least I don't *think* they do."

"Sure. Mom says you guys have Freud."

"Yeah," I joked. "We don't have priests, just places for crazy people to go."

He punched me on my arm. It hurt, and I punched him back.

"Stop! I didn't punch you that hard."

"Sorry," I said.

He put his hand into my shorts.

"You're always hard."

It was true. I was thinking about something and I knew I could tell Tim. I put my hand in his shorts and squeezed his small balls.

"I want to tell you something," I said.

"What," he asked, squirming in my hand. "How long are you gonna keep goosing me like this?"

"Till you promise you won't tell anybody else."

"I promise."

I took my hand away from his balls. Suddenly I was scared to tell him.

"Come on, what is it?" he insisted.

I wasn't sure where to begin, so I just jumped in.

"A man gave me a blow job."

Tim's eyes popped. "For real? Was it good?"

"Dunno. It was over with pretty fast."

"Who did it, one of the monks? It wasn't Brother Alex, was it? I always suspected he would."

"No, asshole. Brother Alexis is not that kind of man."

"How d'you know? Just cause he's got a big one and has hair on his chest, don' mean he don' think about givin' blow jobs. It's part of bein' a brother, y'know. Some do and some don't."

"Jesus, how do you know all this?"

"Neal tells me. He thinks that a lot of the priests fool around, just that they hide it a lot better than Brother Ulrich who's a turd. Nobody likes Mahoney the Dummy, not even the other monks. Well, maybe Father Greer does. He's the Commandant, he's got t' like 'em all."

I didn't want to say anything more, but it was getting to me that I couldn't talk about Nathan to anyone. Especially Allan Streitt. He didn't like his brother, and it would have just gotten everyone into super-trouble if I'd told him what had happened. Nathan was *really* screwed up; there was no doubt about it. But there was also something about him that I weirdly liked. Somehow, deep inside, I must have felt that—right from the *beginning*—exactly as he knew how out of place I was with the whole Jewish thing.

That was what was so strange: the Jewish thing was like something you couldn't be a part of, and yet, also, couldn't *not* be a part of. He must have sensed that about both of us immediately. That was why he'd caused so much trouble at Allan's party; now I remembered him crying outside the ballroom at the same time that he was threatening to hit me if I didn't leave.

"Didja have to give him one?" Tim asked.

"No!"

"Good, it's best if you keep it that way. And if you do, don't let it get around." He winked. "That's my advice to you."

Tim took his jockey shorts off, and started feeling me again. I knew what was going to happen, and while he was jerking me off and I was doing the same thing to him, all I could see was Nathan Streitt's face and also his body. At least the specific part of it that he showed me when we got out of his sports car to pee on the way to Isle of Hope.

When it was over and I went through that funny white moment when you don't know where you are for a short while, Tim broke the silence.

"Are you gonna tell me who it was?"

"No," I said firmly.

Tim accepted it. "Are you gonna see that girl, the one you saw at the dance at the Jewish center, what was her name?"

"Faye. Yeah, I'd like to see her."

"Think she gives a great blow job?"

"Oh, shut up!"

I punched him on his arm again, and he laughed this time, and then kissed me on the cheek, which he liked to do. Then we went to sleep.

On Sunday, after breakfast, I called my grandparents, the Blakelys, and Grandpa Blakely came by to pick me up. He stopped in front of the O'Neills' house and blew the horn and I came out. He had a big car, a Lincoln, and I felt small getting into it. He was playing soft old-time jazz, on the radio.

"Do you like this kind of music?" he asked. "It's Glenn Miller, he was from my time, when we had great music." He smiled and asked me if I'd had breakfast and I told him I had.

"Let's have a bit more of it," he said, and we drove into downtown to a very old drug store with a great soda fountain and booths. "My daddy took me here when I was a boy your age. Some things you always love."

He knew the waitress, and ordered a plate of ham, grits, and eggs for himself, and I got a large Coke and piece of blueberry pie.

"Perfect thing for a young man *after* breakfast," he said and winked. Then he said: "I want to talk to you alone, man-to-man. I'm a judge and I can do that."

I smiled or tried to. There were times when Judge Blakely could scare me; he seemed so solid, big, and grown-up. I wondered if Robby sensed that; I'd seen them get along fine, but never in any kind of genuinely warm way.

"Your father's in huge trouble," he said. "I don't know how to say this, and I wish I didn't have to, but people are going to try to make an example out of him. He represents a change in the South, and people hate changes, especially big changes. Southern people want to drag their feet when it happens. I love the South, I grew up here, but there are people who are glad your father got caught in this thing, and they're going to try to—"

"Hurt him?"

"Son, they want to do much worse than that. It's killing me, too. Your father's a good man, but he made some very bad mistakes. He tried to protect people, some of the very people who're charging him with larceny and some other . . . well, some other bad things now."

My face tensed up seriously. "What's larceny?"

"Basically, it's taking something that's not yours. In the business world, it becomes an issue of knowing what *is* yours to take—and that's pretty slippery ground."

"Maybe Dad thought it *was* his to take?"

"Let's say people might have convinced him of it, but it wasn't the truth. Frankly, I think a lot of it came from his associate, Mr. Geyer, and that Robby's protecting him. But you mustn't ever tell anyone I told you this. You've got to be a *very* big boy now."

"What was the other stuff?" I asked.

Grandpa frowned, and now I regretted asking it.

"It was using tainted money that came from . . . let's just say it was a very *bad* source of money. I don't think your dad was even aware of it. But other people became aware, and now they're trying to *crucify* him."

"I see," I said. It was hard to hear this, but at least someone was telling me the straight dope.

Grandpa and I didn't say anything else for a few minutes. His face relaxed and my Coke and pie came. I drank some of it and thought: finally I know *why* kids aren't any more honest than adults. We're not taught to be. Except of course for some of my friends like Tim. No wonder Storch had called him a cocksucker. *And* Nathan. And of course Arthur and even his friend Alfred Johnson, who'd always seemed really honest to me. Suddenly I smiled at Grandpa and he smiled faintly back at me, but he had no idea why I was smiling. It was because I'd decided kids *were* more honest, at least the honest ones were.

A moment later, Grandpa's plate of ham, grits, and eggs arrived. He buttered his toast, and took a bite from it.

"Sure you don't want any more to eat. I can't eat all of this."

He pushed his plate toward me and I had a bite of the ham. It was very good, served with a slice of warm pineapple. He smiled warmly at me.

"What are we going to do?" I asked.

"I'm going to take care of you and your mom and your sister. Your dad was able to save a little money—he put it in your mom's name—and you have the house. The hard thing though is going to be Robby. So you have to show him a lot of love. It's not always easy for a boy to love his father the way he loves his mother. A dad always seems like a stern character, but the truth is he has to be, to protect you all. That's his role in life. To protect his family, even if he sometimes doesn't know what he's protecting them from."

I pushed his eggs back toward him, and ate more of my pie. Then I felt like I had to ask him something. Alfred Johnson made me think about it.

"Grandpa, why do people hate colored people so much?"

"Oh boy!" he sighed. "That's a big question, son. I think they don't hate them as much as they don't know them, and that's a big part of what's always been true here. When I was growing up, there was actually more mixing of the races than now; you didn't have all-white suburbs. But everybody always feels that way: that things used to be better. My family did well for itself, as we had for years, but I used to see little colored kids playing at the side of the road and I would play with them sometimes. We had colored maids and even a colored driver then. So I was raised by them, like whole generations of young Southern children were. But there was always a place where the races did not meet or mix—like a sexual place—and that always scared people. My generation was so polite they couldn't even talk about it. Now we can talk, but not a lot. Your generation will probably do better. And you won't fear and hate each other; I really hope that."

He finished as much of his ham, toast, eggs and grits as he could, paid the bill, then we drove back to pick up Grandma and the three of us drove out to Isle of Hope. Grandma Betty wore a pink suit and pearls; Grandpa was wearing wash pants and a crisp white shirt, and I was in dungarees and a t-shirt, but I still felt very grown up. I was so proud that Grandpa had really leveled with me, something that nobody else seemed to be doing. When we got back to the house, Grandma gave Josephine the day off. She said that they'd stay with us, and do everything and drive me into school on Monday. She and Grandpa went up to the veranda and smoked cigarettes and drank scotch, and looked at the trees and the water beyond them.

I stayed downstairs with Liz and wanted to tell her so much what was going on, but was afraid to. She was just a kid, after all, and wasn't ready to know what I already did.

Mom spent most of the rest of the next week in Valdosta. I could tell that the local papers and even the TV news were full of Dad's story. I didn't want to hear it from them or even want to read it. Mom had stopped taking the paper— "It's just lies," she said. "Lies and more lies." I was pretty much convinced that Mom was right, and made sure that Liz didn't look at the local six o' clock news before dinner. But a lot of the boys at school were giving me strange looks, like I had just fallen in from space and I was sure that their parents were talking about my dad.

Brother Alexis took me aside often and asked how I was doing. We continued my bar mitzvah lessons, and I felt good about that. My grandparents picked me up and took me to school. I could have stayed with them, but I think they felt bad about uprooting us, and as long as Josephine could stay, everything was OK. They trusted her completely. I did my homework and made sure that Liz did hers. Finally, on Thursday, Mom came back. She looked very tired, like she hadn't slept the whole time. I went up on the veranda to talk with her, after she had left her bag in their bedroom.

She had poured herself a drink and was smoking a cigarette. She looked at me and smiled.

"I used to love coming up here with my friends, just talking and having a drink. God, you look big, Benjy. Did you grow in the week I was gone?"

"Tell me about Dad." I said, without answering her question.

"He's doing—" She stopped herself. "The judge gave him seven years. The lawyer said he might be able to be out in four." She started really crying. "God! You can run over somebody in a car and get less time. It's like they wanted to destroy him—why, Benjy? I just don't understand *why*."

"Maybe he represents something," I said. "He represents change and they hate it. The same way they hate colored people, or people like us."

She pulled me to her, and I sat on the arm of her of chair.

"What do you mean, *like us*?"

"People who don't fit in anyplace."

"But you fit in, darling. You fit in at Holy Nativity, and places where you want to fit in. You're really good at it."

I smiled. Perhaps she was right. To fit in, all you needed was somebody who made you feel like they liked you: Like the O'Neills, Tim and his brothers, and my other friends at Holy Nativity. I thought about Arthur; he never had anyone, not anyone he completely believed in.

The phone rang. Josephine answered it, and came out to the veranda and told Mom it was for her. There was a phone close by inside, and she took it. All I heard her say was, "Yes . . . yes . . . do we have to blow this up to *hell* right now? Sorry, but can't you see what we're going through?" There was silence for a moment, then I heard her say, "Ma'am, this is just not the right time to tell me this."

She came back really shaking.

I asked her what was going on, thinking that it had to be something in Valdosta. But it wasn't.

"That was Rabbi Silverman's secretary—remember that old lady? She told me that you weren't at synagogue last Saturday, and the rabbi is 'reconsidering' your bar mitzvah. I have no idea how they could blow all this up, except it must have to do with your father. Why didn't you go, Benjy? Grandpa and Grandma would have driven you there, or you could—oh, crap, I don't care. They can all go screw themselves! I'm so sick of this and I'm sure you are, too. I don't blame you for not going."

"Did she say anything else?" I asked.

"Yeah, she said I could call the rabbi and try to make other plans. Like we might want to have it at the Reform Temple. This means I've got to call Andy and talk to him. He's big with the synagogue people. Maybe he can do something. I'm too tired right now to even think about it. Your dad had planned on not being convicted, so that he could make it to the service. I don't even know if he can make it now. I don't think they let men out of prison to go to bar mitzvahs, even their own son's. And he'd probably have a guard with him. Imagine, at the synagogue! Hard to imagine, right?"

"Yeah," I said, but that was not what I was thinking. I was thinking this was just about fear. That was exactly what Grandpa had been talking about: only about fear.

The next day, I approached Brother Alexis and told him that I needed to talk with him soon, alone. We agreed to meet in his classroom after his last class. I knocked on his door. There were no other boys there and I approached him.

"What is it, Benjy? Are you getting nervous about the big day?"

I couldn't answer him at first.

"So what is it?"

"I'm not sure there's gonna be a big day," I said.

"Why? You've put so much effort into this."

"So have you," I said. "Everybody has, but it doesn't seem to work. The synagogue wants me to keep going t' services like I'm a regular Jew and I'm not. The rabbi's secretary told Mom that they don't want to schedule the bar mitzvah."

Brother Alexis pointed to a chair and I sat down. He sat down with me and thought for a moment.

"Then can you have it at another place?" he asked. "I know the rabbi at the Reform Temple. We've been to some ecumenical things regarding race in Savannah. Not that a lot got done. Mostly it was to keep ourselves from being scared, I mean those of us who feel that integration is good, and who don't give in to the usual idiocy that if God had wanted us all to mix together, He would have made us all of one color—stuff like that. You ever hear things like that?"

I wasn't listening. My Dad was in jail, and race only meant one thing to me: I'd hated that man on the bus because he was a bully, and that was all. He could have been one of the bullies I knew at school. That was what race meant to me: it meant being bullied by people who were convinced they could do it.

"What do you think we should do?" he asked softly, putting his hand on my shoulder. Suddenly it hit me. I don't know why, maybe just being close to Brother Alexis.

"Can we have it here?"

"What a crazy idea!" He smiled. "Your bar mitzvah at a Catholic school. Benjy, what would everyone think about that?"

"I don't care. I fit in here—in this really funny way I do. And people wouldn't stare at my father here, and like you said, you know the rabbi at the Reform Temple. You can borrow a Torah from him and some yarmulkes and some other things we need."

"I meant we could have the service *at* the Temple. It would be a lot easier. The men and the women sit together, and the services are less formal there."

"No, I *want* to do it here!" I said, becoming more excited. "We can say all the prayers we need to and just show the Torah. We can invite the boys here I want to invite and my grandparents, the Blakelys, they're not Jewish, see, and maybe the rabbi at the Temple could come and organize things a bit."

"You're amazing. Did you have all this figured out before you came in here, Benjy?" he asked, grinning.

"No, but when you mentioned the rabbi at the Temple, I thought, you're the *real* rabbi I want. I mean religion is just a matter of what story you believe, isn't it? And all the stories eventually just become one story—I mean about people trying to be good to each other, isn't that true?"

"Well, God does come into this," he said. "But—" he paused.

"What?"

"All the faces of God—what we want from God and how we see God—it really all becomes one Face. I think I believe that, Benjy. Just, please, don't tell anybody else I said that."

"I won't, I promise. I'd say 'Cross my heart,' but that doesn't work I guess. So you'll speak with Father Greer, and see if we can do it on the Saturday when it was supposed to take place?"

"Sure, I can. But we may have to change the date to early November, since it'll take a while to get things organized and the Parents Committee of the school was planning a tea the weekend of your bar mitzvah. Also, President Kennedy is making a trip to Texas around that time. Some people have talked about going to San Antonio to see him, before he goes on to Houston and Dallas. San Antonio is a really Catholic city; Dallas isn't. So we think he might be able to schedule a couple of minutes with us. But I think we can do it, just before then."

He smiled at me, shyly.

"You're some kid," he said. "I've never met anyone like you before."

I felt myself blushing as he looked at me with his dark eyes that seemed to gaze through me, all the way down to . . . what? That place where Robby was waiting, and Arthur Gomez . . . and maybe God himself? I wasn't sure, but suddenly I wanted to hug him. I felt really starved to do that; I'd wanted so much to hug Robby, but now he was gone.

19

The Bar Mitzvah, Or "I Am Confirmed"

The most amazing thing is that everything worked out, though it took a lot of preparation, much more than I'd ever realized. When I told Caroline, she smiled immediately, like she thought nothing unusual about having a bar mitzvah at Holy Nativity. As she put it, "It's all part of God's big party, so what difference does it make who caters it for Him?"

Brother Alexis spoke to Father Greer and whatever happened between them I wasn't told, but Father Greer agreed to do it and said that a large common room the school used for receptions would work well for it. He had a meeting with Caroline—I was not invited—but Mom came out of it happy that Father Greer had agreed to everything. She was less pleased that the school expected a substantial "donation" to do it.

"This means I'll have to go to Andy Geyer for the money," she told me.

"But you'd go to him anyway," I said.

"That was when we were going to do it at the big synagogue, and you know how conflicted I felt about that. Now, I'd actually *rather* go to my parents, but I *am* going to Andy. He may have a conniption about your bar mitzvah being at Holy Nativity Military Academy—Greer wants us simply to call it your *confirmation*, rather than use the Hebrew term on the invitations—but that's going to have to be Andy's problems. Believe me, Andy's caused us enough problems as it is."

I remembered what Grandpa had told me. So of course I wanted to know more.

"You've mentioned that, Mom. What d'you mean?"

She hesitated, then said, "I can't tell you."

"Why not?"

"Cause you're a kid!"

"Is Andy behind all this?" I persisted. "I mean, Dad being in jail?"

"He is," she said. "But I'm not sure how *far* behind it. They've kept me *almost* as much in the dark as they have kept you."

Mom's attitude didn't help; in fact, it made me feel terrible. It wasn't so much that Dad and Andy were lying to me, as much as that no one would tell me the truth—except for William Blakely, my grandpa. And he wasn't telling me everything, because he didn't know it. Maybe Dad *was* guilty— I'd heard whisperings about Jews at the school in Isle of Hope: Jews were deceitful and not to be trusted; they would "jew you down for a quarter." That was really horrible. Once Tim said that at Holy Nate, then looked funny at me and stopped himself. Finally, he apologized to me, and said he'd never say it again.

"You're not that kind of person," he told me. "But then you ain't a real Jew."

That made things even worse, because if I wasn't a "real" Jew, what was I? Maybe I wasn't one, even though sometimes I felt it so deeply inside. But I knew I was Robby's son—*that* I had no doubts about, and nothing would ever stop me from loving him.

Mom had invitations engraved downtown at a small stationary store. They were really beautiful with little pieces of tissue in front of them in the envelope, announcing:

The Confirmation of Benjamin Rothberg
Son of Leon Robert Rothberg and Caroline Blakely Rothberg
on the second Saturday in November
at Holy Nativity Military Academy

with the address of Holy Smokes, the time, and also a smaller envelope inside with our address in Isle of Hope for RSVPs.

Andy came into Savannah a short time afterwards. He approached me with this strange, scattered look on his face, then grabbed me and pulled me into his arms.

"Boychik, you are something else!" he said. "You've made your old man so happy."

"I have?"

"*Very* happy. Leon doesn't care where you have your bar mitzvah, as long as you have it. We're going to make sure a notice goes into the Savannah papers. We'll let these damn Jews—sorry for my language—know what we're made out of."

"Is that necessary?" Caroline said, coming out from the den. "There's been enough about us in the papers already."

Andy straightened up and looked at her.

"Yes, Caroline, it's necessary. I know what's been happening here. As long as Leon was in a position to help people they were all over him. I put him in that position, I know it. The two of us made a lot of *gelt* and everybody in Savannah was peachy with it. But now that the *dreck* has hit the fan, they're scattering like flies after a flushing. I hate it. We should have had Benjy's bar mitzvah at the synagogue, not at a Catholic military school. But—"

"I want it there," I said emphatically. "It was my idea."

Andy's face darkened. "And you just *let* him do it?" he said, looking at Caroline. "You didn't try to deal with the rabbi at all?"

"She—" I was furious. I could barely speak.

"Shut up!" Andy shouted. "You're letting this kid decide this, Caroline?"

"*I hate you!*" I screamed.

He slapped me.

I was really crying now. I ran to Caroline.

"Don't you ever do that again," she said to Andy.

He drew away, and fell into a chair.

"If I ever talked to my father like that—"

"You're not his father," Caroline said calmly.

Andy started crying. "I've got to be, you know that."

"You can't," she told him. Then she told me to go to my room. I looked at her blankly.

"Just go," she said. "You don't have to know everything."

I felt horrible. I had been crying, and so had Andy. I'd never seen a grown man cry except for my father, and Andy wasn't my father. A short time later there was a knock on my door. I didn't answer it, but Andy walked in.

"Can I come in?" he asked.

He was already there, but asked anyway. I nodded.

"You really hurt me. I know you didn't mean it when you said 'I hate you,' but you hurt me. I love your father like you have no idea, and he loves me. I saved his life in Korea. I pulled him through it. He was falling apart; luckily he got wounded and sent home. The two of you—" He paused for a second, like there was something else he wanted to say, but couldn't quite say it.

I watched him closely. Finally he said, "There's something Jewish men have that non-Jews just don't have, no matter how smart or stupid we are. It's like we're brothers."

"I'm not really a Jew," I argued. "My mom's not Jewish. I know I can't have that thing."

He pulled me into his arms. We were on my bed. He smelled of Andy Geyer sweat and cheap cigars, but I didn't care. I almost liked it.

"You've got it. I don't know how, but you've really got it. This totally Jewish soul's in you. *Shtimme.* That's what Jews call it. And you've got it."

"What is it?" I asked.

"It's like there's so much behind you that you can never talk about, but you know it's there. It's always there. It's like why we look east to Israel. It's the land where it all comes together, even here in Savannah, Georgia. It all comes together there."

"I'm not sure I want it all to come together," I said. "I like my friends at school, and they're not Jewish."

"But they'll never understand you. They'll never be able to see all the way down into you. Do you see that, Benjy? Even with Caroline as your mother, there will always be a part of you that will be Leon's little Jewish boy."

"I want him home," I said.

"I know that." He started patting my head. "He'll be able to come to the bar mitzvah, I promise you. I dealt with the judge about that. He's in minimum security. There'll be a guard with him. He's getting some humanitarian help, let's just say."

"Did you have to pay people off?"

Andy nodded. "It never hurts."

He smiled at me, and then lit up a cigar. He stood up.

"Your mom and Josephine made us dinner. That's wonderful. I don't get a real home-cooked meal that much anymore. Want to walk with me downstairs? I know I'm not your father, but I'm your friend. You'll let me be your friend, won't you?"

"Sure," I said.

"Good," he said.

He ruffled up my hair, and then we went downstairs.

* * *

The next several weeks became busy and then even busier. The strangest thing was that presents started to arrive at the house, delivered from downtown stores: something like twelve sweaters and three fountain pens and a bunch of ties and lots of books, mostly about Jewish history, which seemed kind of strange, but also a copy of Leon Uris's *Exodus*. I guess that had become prime bar mitzvah material. I'd wanted a typewriter, a new bike, and a chemistry set, but didn't get them. I did get some money, in cash, in envelopes that came in the mail; Caroline put them away secretively with a wink.

"You never know when you're going to want this for mad money," she said smirking. "We can go to movies, or even some New York shows if they come to Savannah."

"Why don't we go to New York?" I asked.

"Why don't you get through this year at school first? Things are getting very tight with money, Benjy. That's something you've got to understand."

But I did understand. That's why I was happy when Tim O'Neill's parents sent me a check for fifty dollars, a lot of money. It was made out to me, and Caroline told me that she'd open up a bank account with my name on it. That by itself made me feel grown up. Tim was constantly curious about the bar mitzvah. He wanted to know if it meant that I could not sin afterwards without going straight to hell.

"That's what happens when you sin after Confirmation," he explained.

I told him I wasn't sure that bar mitzvahs worked the same way.

"Then what are they for?"

"It means you're a man."

"Oh, c'mon. You can't drink, vote, or get laid—OK, maybe you can do that, but it's a long shot. So how come you're a man at thirteen?"

"I guess way back then, it meant you could do all those things, and you're counted as one of a *minyan*."

I explained what a *minyan* was.

"Oh, I get it. It's like a quorum," Tim said. "We studied that in civics. I guess the good thing is that you got to spend a lot of time with Brother Alex. He's neat, idn't he? Y' think he fools around?"

Everything with Tim seemed to get back to that. It was after school and nobody was around. "You mean like we do?" I asked. "I told you, Brother Alex is not that kind of guy."

Tim only shrugged. "I know some monks do it, and others—like Brother Ulrich, they'll take anything they can get, or grab." He hesitated for a second, then said, "I heard a rumor. Actually, Neal heard it around the locker room. Neal could hardly believe it, but he heard it."

"What?"

"Ulrich—Dorris the Dummy—got Horace the Homo down in that bathroom."

"*Wowwww!*"

"I know. Seems Joe Flauwerty found out from Ken Ferris. It happened 'cause Storch's parents were away, so he invited Flauwerty in to look at his dad's copies of *Playboy*, and they started drinking beer and whatnot, then Storch let it out. He made Flauwerty promise, but Flauwerty's got a mouth like a' open sewer— that's my mom's line about people who can't keep secrets—because everything comes out of it!"

"So what's going to happen?" I asked. "Will Storch's parents raise a fuss, or do something?"

"God, you *are* a fuckin' Jew. Nothing's *gonna* happen. It's like a code: you don't rat on it or the whole thing falls apart. My brothers clued me into that by the time I was eight or nine. Still, there's something evil about doin' it with a monk like Mahoney."

Before I knew it, the Saturday of the bar mitzvah arrived; we had scheduled it for one o' clock so that Rabbi Mendelsohn, the Reform rabbi, could be there. The caterers were already in the kitchen at Holy Nativity, and several of Mom's Salty Dog friends like Lucy Boyd and Jane Wilson were at the school, help- ing the caterers out and trying to keep Caroline from going crazy. Everything was already set up for the service, with a box with yarmulkes, and some prayer shawls, or *tallitim*, from the Reform Temple, and plenty of prayer books. A small platform had been set up at one end of the spacious room, with rows of chairs in front of it. On the platform was the small Torah scroll in its brightly- embroidered covering, and there were arrangements of fresh flowers all over, some of them covering up old pictures of saints; so the place looked wonderful, as if it had been waiting all along for my bar mitzvah to happen. Andy drove me in, beaming all over himself. I was in the same Alfred Roote outfit Mom had bought me, cleaned and freshly pressed so even the buttons looked new, and I felt good about everything.

People started arriving, first lots of Jewish people who had been friends of my father, and some of the kids from the synagogue, like Allen Streitt of course, who came with his whole family, including Nathan who looked at me and smiled eerily, as if we now recognized each other for the first time. Faye was there with her parents, and some other people I didn't recognize, but I guessed Andy might have invited them. Josephine was there in a really elegant outfit, with several of her friends who'd come by the house at various times. Then there were my friends from school—like William Manion, Mel Harris, Alfred Johnson, and Arch Flanders, and other guys from my classes, and some bigger guys like Eugene Whitman. And of course the O'Neills—even Mr. O'Neill, who that weekend wasn't away on business. My grandparents came in, with Betty Blakely looking nice in a blue suit and a small mink stole and Grandpa in a dark suit with a light gray tie, looking like the judge he was.

We were almost ready, but Robby hadn't arrived yet. I ran up to Andy.

"Where *is* he?" I whispered. "Where's Dad?"

"They drove in. I hope they didn't hit traffic."

"We can't start without him!"

"You gotta start, Benjy. You can't just get all these folks here and not start. It's not right. Your dad'll show up, I know it."

I joined Brother Alexis on the platform. He was going to welcome everyone and explain how the service had been arranged. He was wearing a white yarmulke and his gray Sebastianite robes that I could tell had been especially cleaned and pressed; they had a real newness to them.

"I want to thank you all for coming to Benjamin Rothberg's confirmation, or bar mitzvah," he began. "I've done some research on bar mitzvahs and learned that in past centuries they took many forms in different countries. For instance, sometimes there is almost no service involved, and sometimes there is. Sometimes the boy is simply brought up to the *bimah*, the platform here, and he says his name and is blessed by the congregation in the person of the rabbi, and that's it. In America, he gets to read the part of the Prophets that pertain to the Torah reading for this week, and he actually leads the congregation in many of the prayers. Benjy has done a great amount of work—"

I don't remember another word Brother Alexis said, because right then I heard a noise in the back of the room and, craning my neck to look, saw Dad enter with two state policemen in full uniform. I wanted so much to race up to him but I couldn't. I looked into his eyes, and he looked at me; we were both beaming. He was wearing one of his suits that looked like it could use a trip to the cleaners, and also seemed several sizes too large, he was so thin.

Rabbi Mendelsohn came up to the platform and started the service, and I joined in at the places that I was prepared to recite or sing. I was nervous at first, and I tripped over words in a couple places, or even forgot what I was supposed to do. But after that first five minutes or so, I was OK. I kept looking over at Robby and Caroline, who were sitting together. The state police stood at the door in the rear, and it might have been possible to forget they were there—I tried to—but then I forgot about everything except what I had to do, to get through reading my portion of the Prophets. Rabbi Mendelsohn started by giving people an idea of what was being said, then I started chanting it and everything became smooth sailing or like walking down a familiar street. Even my earlier nervousness seemed to reinforce me with energy, and I didn't make any more mistakes.

When I had finished, Rabbi Mendelsohn held up the Torah, and called my name up to it to make a prayer over it. It's called an *aliyah*, which means "to come up," and it really marks the transition into adulthood, because you never get an *aliyah* until you are bar mitzvahed. Brother Alexis had told me that. The rabbi then called Brother Alexis's name, and Brother Alexis said the same prayer over the Torah. I thought this was peculiar, since Brother Alexis had definitely not been bar mitzvahed. Then I realized that at Holy Nativity Brother Alexis could certainly count as part of the *minyan*, so it was OK.

Suddenly I asked the rabbi, "Can my friends come up for an *aliyah*, too?"

He thought for a second. "Do you know their names in Hebrew?"

"No."

"That's OK. Why don't you just go down and get them, and I'll show them what to say?"

So I left the platform, and grabbed Tim O'Neill and his two brothers, and Manion and Mel Harris, and Eugie Whitman and Alfred Johnson who was there with his mother who wore a wonderful hat. I didn't grab Arch Flanders, because I was sure he wasn't old enough, but all the guys came up to the platform, and Rabbi Mendelsohn took them, two or three at a time, to the Torah and went through the prayer of blessing with them.

"*Baruch atah Adonoi, eloheynu melech haolom, asher nosahn lahnu Toras eymess, v'chaiyei olam nahtie . . . Baruch atah Adonoi nahsein ha Torah.*"

They were all thrilled, especially Alfred Johnson who seemed really surprised and kept smiling at me.

What I really wanted was for Robby to come up and bless it. But he didn't, and I was afraid to ask him to. I was afraid to pain him anymore, because I knew that just getting there had been a hard enough struggle for him. While the boys were blessing the Torah, I looked at him. He had his head in his hands for a moment; Caroline had her arm around him, and Andy was sitting on his other side. I knew that I had to stand up very straight. I had to be glad just that my dad was there. And he'd have to go soon, and I knew it.

Next I was to deliver my short speech. I wasn't sure that I wanted to do it, really; what I wanted to do was get my bar mitzvah over with, and go and see Robby. But Brother Alexis nodded to Rabbi Mendelsohn, who stood back and nodded to me. I cleared my throat. Suddenly nothing was going to come out, then it did.

"I want to thank you all for coming to my bar mitzvah," I said. "And most of all my parents for preparing me for this day—" I was supposed to say something about God, but I decided I needed to say something else. "And Brother Alexis, too, and my friends at Holy Nativity. And . . . everyone else who will help me to become a man."

Brother Alexis looked embarrassed at me. This was not the speech we had prepared, but it was truly what I had wanted to say.

We said the last prayer, the Kaddish, the prayer that you say to sanctify God, and also to mourn the dead. Brother Alexis had told me that Jews believe that you sanctify God to mourn the dead because "the dead are with God." He liked that idea, just the simplicity of it. Then we sang one final song that Dad joined in, and it was over. I watched him close his prayer book, and I bolted over to him.

I wanted to leap into his arms, but I couldn't. I had to be a man, a *mentsh*; I knew it. So I hugged him. My head came up to his chin. I was almost as tall as he was, like I had grown since I had seen him.

He couldn't say anything for a moment, then said, "You did wonderful, Benjy. I was so proud of you . . . you have no idea how proud of you I am."

I wanted to kiss him. It was so hard not to cry, but I had to greet a whole lot of people and shake hands and pretend that everything was totally normal for a bar mitzvah.

Mom smiled, and took me aside for a second.

"I can't believe what this has been like," she said.

Liz was next to her, and kept holding on to me. I crouched to hug her.

"You're a real man now," she said. "You'll just think I'm a dumb little girl."

"No, I'll never believe that."

Allan Streitt and his parents came up. He shook my hand, grabbed my shoulder, and then hugged me.

"This is as wonderful as Allan's bar mitzvah," Mrs. Streitt said.

"Better," Mr. Streitt nodded. "I didn't have to pay for it."

"He's only joking," she said. "Nathan, come here. Congratulate Benjamin."

Nathan ignored her, so I went over to him.

"Thank God we're away from them," he said relieved. Then he smiled at me, winking. "You're something, boychik. I really like your friends. They're cool. We should go out in my car again, I'd like that."

He winked at me once more, and left as Alfred Johnson's mother approached me. She was visibly moved and held my hand and told me what a "wonderful blessin' it was for my Alfie t' do this!" She took out her handkerchief and dried her eyes. I thanked her a lot for coming, and went back to my parents.

"How long have you got here?" I asked Dad.

"About another hour. That's all. I can have a drink, they told me."

"You need to have something," Andy said. "Actually, I need one too."

Andy went over to Rabbi Mendelsohn, and handed him an envelope, and by that time everyone was at the other end of the commons room, where tables had been set up for the reception. Rabbi Mendelsohn lifted his glass.

"I'd like to propose a toast to Benjamin Rothberg and to his family. *L'chaiyim!*"

Everyone said "*L'chaiyim*," even the O'Neills and the other boys and their parents.

I joined Dad and Mom who were sitting down. I didn't know what to say to Dad, except that I was glad to see him and that I was doing OK and how much I loved Holy Nativity.

"I'm glad I did this here," I said.

"So am I," he said. "You did this for me, I know it. I'll remember it always."

A lot of people came up to him, including Father Greer who told Robby that I would always have a place at Holy Nativity and how proud they were of me, and that boys like me made the school as good as it was. Robby only nodded. A short time later the two state cops came over to him and he stood up and walked out with them. I'd been talking to Tim and his brothers, and I saw them go out and started to rush over to them, but Mom stopped me.

"Please don't, Benjy," she said. "It'll only make things harder for him. You really have to be a man now."

That night back in Isle of Hope, I felt very big and alone. Everything had been wonderful on the day of my bar mitzvah; I was surrounded with people I cared about. Still, there was this gap in my heart. I thought about calling up Tim, or even Nathan Streitt. I wasn't sure why but I felt close to Nathan. But there was really one other person I wished had been there, and I could imagine him getting up to say an *aliyah* himself, or even the Kaddish.

Arthur Gomez.

I didn't know what hurt the most, that Arthur could not be right there with me, or Dad. He seemed so gone now, almost as gone as Arthur.

I went out to the veranda and saw Mom with Liz cuddled up on a divan in sweaters, looking at the stars. The night was chilly and clear. At least there were no mosquitoes or gnats.

"You were wonderful!" Liz said to me. "Everybody was really proud. I never knew there were so many Catholic Jews around."

"That was my line, Benjy," Mom said. "She stole it from me!"

Mom was having a drink. I asked her if I could have one. She said, "You're not that grown up. But wait a year or so, and we'll see."

She told Liz it was time for her to brush her teeth and get ready for bed. Liz didn't want to go, but did, tromping off to her room.

"What are we going to do now?" I asked Mom.

"You're going to continue going to Holy Nativity, and we're going to be able to keep the house—at least for a while. Andy and my parents have money for us, and Robby has kept some money in a bank in New York. That's hush-hush, but it's there for us if we need it, and we probably will."

"Maybe I should get a job," I said. "I can bag groceries or deliver papers."

"You don't need to, not yet. You just have to believe in your father. He'll get out in a couple of years. I mean, they let him come to your bar mitzvah—it's not like he's a murderer."

"He didn't look very good."

"He's not in great health. But who would be after what he's been through?"

"What wrong with him?"

"Something between a broken heart and worrying yourself to death. I guess just . . . a lot of stuff."

Suddenly she put on that distant smile that used to bother Robby and I'm sure completely disarm him. She ruffled up my hair.

"Thanks for being a great kid," she said. "Right now I want to smoke this cigarette and look at the stars. And maybe you should get to bed, too. That's an order, young man!"

I went to my room, and got into bed. So, they weren't going to tell me *anything*—I was supposed to revert to being a kid, even though Mom had told me already that Dad was sick. I thought about Nathan and what he had done to me on the way home: I was no longer a kid, that was for certain. Would I want him to do it again? I smiled as an idea came to me: The good thing about not being a real Jew *or* a Christian was that I didn't have to worry about a whole lot of disapproval. Tim was right; I'd been spared a lot. As much as I felt that I never belonged, I also couldn't be hurt—at least not by what would drive so many other boys into fears of hell and damnation.

I reached into my jockey shorts and felt myself going "tumescent." What a great word for getting hard. Now I knew that as long as no one crazy really caught me, I could engage in the full splendor of—anyway, stuff I was certainly going to learn about. I licked my hand and used the moisture. Things went a bit hazy; I was deliciously tired. I wished Tim had been next to me and we had stolen some of his parents booze; then something happened I'd never expected.

I saw Robby's face in front of me. That face he'd had at my bar mitzvah, drawn and yet beaming at me. I felt enveloped in his presence, and stopped what I was doing.

I sat up in bed, and felt utterly alone; singular; myself; cut off.

Suddenly I felt a blast of wind blow through the room. I shuddered.

There was Arthur, standing up on the bed, naked. I grabbed his legs and held them. He ran his fingers through my hair, and knelt down so that my head was now on his chest. I could hear his heartbeat. I was crying but without any tears.

"I love you," I whispered.

"I know. Thank you, thank you."

He rose slightly so that my face was at his navel. I could feel the slight remains of his umbilical chord stroking my nose, his lovely, silky brown warmth. I could smell him, fresh as life. I took him into my mouth, kissing him, loving him, and felt him vibrate all the way through me like a shaft of energy, of light.

Then it was over and I fell asleep.

20

The Death Of The President

The next week at school, I felt like I was in this amazing haze. Things did not bother me so much because I realized that I belonged at Holy Nativity, despite any of the facts of my birth. That is, it didn't bother me that I was not a Catholic or even very much of a Jew, but was suspended somewhere between the attractions of Christianity (like going to chapel with the other boys and getting to sit next to Tim while he whispered dirty things to me) and the freedom of being Jewish (like no one telling me that sex was a bad thing—I certainly never got that message from either of my parents). I felt great and even kids like Storch and his crew knew it.

One day Storch approached me. He hadn't bothered Tim or me for a long time, but something must have put lead in his pencil again, as far as being a jerk was concerned.

"I heard about your bar mitzvah, you kike!"

I looked at him and smiled. He was definitely a low worm. I looked at him calmly. "Jealous, 'cause you weren't invited?"

"Sure," he answered sarcastically. "I heard a lotta guys liked it. They're pussies, anyway."

I shrugged and started to walk away. He grabbed my arm hard. I let him, but looked coldly at him, making him realize that *I* had let him.

"You got balls," he said as he released me. He extended his hand to me and I took it.

"OK, I admit it," he said. "You ain't pussy."

I nodded and shook his hand. We were alone for a moment with no other kids around. I looked at him in his slightly rumpled uniform, and felt like I had never really looked at Storch. His small mean eyes hit the floor of the hallway, then they looked up for a second and he walked away.

* * *

On November 21, some of the teachers and parents from the school did go to San Antonio, a very Catholic city, to see President John F. Kennedy, before he went on to Dallas, which was not. They saw him and were delighted that they got to shake his hand at his hotel during a brief rest before he went on to his other stops in Houston and Fort Worth. They invited him to Savannah, which had not voted for him, but they wanted him to know that he had a lot of well-wishers there. The next day they got back on a plane and flew, via Dallas, to arrive home in the midst of, perhaps, the worst news of their lives.

Kennedy had been shot in the city in which they had changed planes. He was dead: The almost endlessly charismatic, first Catholic president of the United States was dead. Father Greer made an announcement on the loud speakers at school.

"Young men of Holy Nativity Military Academy. I have—" He stopped to keep from choking up. "I have terrible news for you. The president of the United States has been killed in Dallas, Texas. I want you all to go home and listen to your radios and your parents and pray for the soul of our president, John Fitzgerald Kennedy."

Every door in the school flew open and boys were all over the place, but without making a sound. It was like a film with the sound off. Then I heard this agonizing muffled sound of guys in uniform trying to choke back tears.

I saw Pat and Neal O'Neill outside on the raised lawn above the sidewalk in front of the school. Pat had collapsed and was sobbing; Neal was crouched next to him, saying something but I couldn't hear. Suddenly there was this huge noise from all the boys breaking silence and talking at once, trying to figure out what to do. It was only about two o' clock. There were no buses outside or people to pick them up. Tim came up, and just looked at me with this stunned face. Brother Alexis came out. His eyes were very red, but he was able to go up to everyone and tell them that they could call their parents in the office, and that some school buses were on the way.

"Who did it?" Tim asked. "Who cudda done it? Somebody who hated Catholics or Negro people or anyone they didn't like and were scared of?"

"I don't know," I said.

"A lot of people are scared," Neal said loudly, raising himself to his full height. "And they hate so much. It makes me so angry!" He knelt down to Pat again, and whispered something to him, and Pat got up. Tim hugged him and then Neal did.

"I'm sorry," Pat said. "I wanted so much to meet John Kennedy. I wanted to shake his hand and tell him how much he meant to me personally—I mean, Catholic and president of the United States. I wanted to tell him how proud he made me as an American—"

He stopped talking.

Neal asked me if I wanted to ride back to their house and call my mom. I told him she was picking me up at three; I'd wait for her. Neal had the car, so they left. Soon the entire school was empty, but I didn't mind it. I wondered how Brother Alexis was doing, then Caroline appeared. She had been crying too. I got into the car, and we didn't say anything for several minutes.

"They found out who did it," she finally said, before starting it again. "Some nut job named Oswald. Lee Oswald. The whole country's gone crazy. I never thought I'd live to see something like this. I guess everybody in the school must be taking this really hard. What a blow to them all—the first Catholic president murdered."

Later I heard that some kids in the public high schools were cheering when they heard the news. Kennedy had been a symbol of so many things the South hated: Harvard Yankees, Catholicism, and racial integration or the specter of it. The weekend was declared one of national mourning. Brother Alexis called the house of every kid he taught to make sure they were OK. Caroline was impressed.

"You're so lucky," she told me, "to have a man like that teach you."

"I thought you didn't trust them," I said.

"I trust him now."

The next week the school held a memorial Mass for Kennedy in the chapel. I sat next to Tim and Arch Flanders. Neal and Pat were sitting with other boys in the junior class. Sometimes Neal would look over at me and nod, but Pat only stared straight ahead; I wondered of course what he was thinking. It was like there was this shadow drifting across his handsome face. I could see its darkness intensify over his eyes, reminding me of the black cloud I'd seen on the faces of those men in Isle of Hope, whom I felt were in danger. It was terrible what hatred could do to people, though at that moment I was only beginning to understand it.

The school choir sang some very beautiful music. They had invited in a group of singers from our sister school, St. Agnes's, so there were genuine girl sopranos instead of just young boys. By this time, I was kind of worn out. I wanted the world to become normal again, even if it would take a long time to do it.

More Jewish Friends, And Basic Kissing

The rest of the year went better. I became closer friends with Allan Streitt. We went out on double dates to downtown movies, with Faye Jacobson and Allan's new girlfriend, a kind of slightly chubby Jewish girl named Sue Strickler. Sue was always very well dressed; she wore what everybody else was wearing, sometimes even before they wore it. Her mother subscribed to a lot of women's magazines, and would go up to New York and buy stuff for Sue at stores like Bonwit Teller and Lord and Taylor or Saks Fifth Avenue. Sue would tell us where everything came from, and Allan would pretend to be embarrassed, like it was not cool to do so, but then he would try to do stuff to Sue, like feel her up at the movies. She was always on a diet, and when we went out to eat, she would say that she wasn't going to eat anything, but always did. Allan would wink at me, and then feed her from his plate, with his fork.

I thought that was totally gross, but then I realized that boys and girls were supposed to do that, it was part of the dating thing.

Mom was really glad that I was doing this, and she would drop us off downtown and then pick us up—it was a lot for her to do, frankly—and sometimes chauffeur us around to other places as well. Allan's father didn't want to do it, he worked too hard he said, and his mother was always too busy with Jewish women's clubs and keeping the house in the perfect condition that was expected of her. She complained constantly which was something I decided must be a Jewish mother thing; Caroline never complained—God, was I happy for that. Allan told me that my mom was "completely amazing. Like, I've never met a mom like yours. How do you stand it? She's so beautiful!"

I guess I was used to it, and the fact that Mom smoked in the car and listened to rock music, and sometimes, when she went with us to a restaurant, everyone forgot that she was my mom, at least for a time. But I think she needed this. She needed to forget about Dad for a moment, and worrying. Her friends still came up to the veranda to drink Salty Dogs, but they didn't spend as much time; by the end of the school year, they had just about stopped. The only one who came was Jane Wilson, and Mom told me that she was getting bored with her.

"All these women want to do is gossip about things that don't mean anything to me. They're still bothered that the queers are moving into Isle of Hope. Who cares? It's not like one of them has made a pass at *you*. They haven't, have they?"

I was embarrassed to hear Caroline talk like that. She could tell it, and apologized.

"I keep forgetting that you're not a total man yet, despite your bar mitzvah. I like it that you're still a boy. I hope you understand stuff about girls. That's something Robby should be around to tell you." She stroked my cheek and detected a slight bit of stubble.

"Golly Moses! In a while, you're gonna have to start shaving."

When I stroked my chin and smiled, she said, "*That* I can tell you about, having lived with men my whole life!"

A few weeks later, she gave me my first razor and a can of Gillette shaving cream. We went up to the bathroom Liz and I used, and Mom showed me how to get the razor warm with water, wet my face, and let the lather soak in, then she guided me with the razor until I felt comfortable about it. I had not wanted to start shaving, because I'd heard that once you started you never stopped. Still, I knew that by next year, the older kids who were officers would start looking at me, and would tell me to shave whether I wanted to or not.

The person I didn't see was Nathan Streitt. I learned from Allan that he had been sent off to a special boarding school near Baltimore for "difficult" teens. When I asked Allan why, his face clouded over, and that smile that stayed around most of the time left it. We were in his bedroom. Allan was sitting at his desk playing with his microscope. He told me he had decided to be a doctor; his mother was ecstatic.

"My brother's an asshole," he said, turning to me. "I wish I had a brother I could—"

I wanted to say "love," but didn't think I could. Older brothers were always a problem, unless you lucked out like Tim O'Neill had. I was glad I didn't have one. The closest thing I had was Robby, even though I didn't know it then.

"Depend on?" I offered.

"Yeah," Allan answered. "All I can depend on Nathan for is to give me grief. He likes you though. I don't know why, but he does. He used to talk about you before he got sent away; he said you were really smart and cool. He'd never say anything like that about me."

"I'm sorry," I told him. I wanted to say, "You must really love him a lot," but I didn't. Jews were always supposed to have to something profound behind them that they couldn't talk about, but I never felt that Allan did. He was a nice kid, a really *nice* Jewish boy, but he seemed flat to me. On the other hand Nathan, who wasn't anyone's idea of nice, certainly had a deep secret side. I could not say anything else to Allan about him. I couldn't tell him about what had happened when Nathan drove me back to Isle of Hope, nor did I want Allan to know how much I'd been thinking about his brother—how I even had dreams about Nathan. I'd seen his face in them, and that smile that looked at me in a way no kid or grown-up had ever looked at me—like I was grown up, way more than I knew.

By this time I'd gotten to first base with Faye Jacobson, and even to part of second base, even though, officially, we still weren't going together. This happened at a party given by one of Allan's friends. They were all Jewish kids, except for me; that is they were all *all-Jewish* kids—and it was in a house in a new, very Jewish development in Savannah, that looked like it should have been someplace else, like maybe in a movie set in Southern California. It went on for about an acre of stonework, glass walls, and teak wood, with a six-car carport attached, all under Cinemascope-big, Hollywood lighting.

"People like this give Jews a bad name," Mom said when she drove me up to it.

"Why?" I asked.

"Because you're not supposed to show off your money this way, certainly not in the South; at least not in the South I came from. My parents would have had a conniption. We didn't let people like this into Dad's gulf club."

"Maybe that's why they feel they *have* to act like this."

She blew some smoke out the window.

"Would you stop being so effin' smart? I'm not being anti-Semitic. I'm just saying you don't have to tell people *instantly* how much money you've got. Are there going to be parents at this party?"

I told her there would be, and she didn't go in to find out. She was going to a movie downtown, and would pick me up in three hours.

That meant I had to act fast. I was dressed up in a nice shirt, but no tie. I knocked on the door. A fifteen-year-old boy named Scott Schneider opened it. He had a lot of glossy black hair, really nice skin, but a nose that looked like a toucan's. Somehow though, that did not stop him from being good looking.

"You must be Benjy, Allan's friend. Welcome!" He started giggling. "Hey, Allan. Your *goy*-friend's here!"

Allan arrived, red-faced and out of breath. He glared at Scott.

"I'm glad you're here, Benjy. Don't act like a *putz*, Scott."

"I said *goy*-friend, not *boy*friend."

"I'm neither," I said to Scott and shook his hand, pretending I'd heard nothing that should bother me.

If there were parents around, they were not to be seen, but the place was so big that they could have been in some back room, watching old movies on TV, without knowing if the front of the house were on fire. Maybe they'd see a fire truck. They had a maid on duty, in uniform. She was about forty, slightly overweight, and most of the time she ignored us, which was just as well. She made sure that the ice bucket was filled and ashtrays were emptied. Allan had been in the den, making out with Sue Strickler. One of the reasons why he looked so rosy was that he had lipstick smears on his face.

I got a Seven-Up from a table set up for it. They had real alcohol, but I decided it would be stupid to have any; I didn't want anyone to smell it on my breath, especially Mom who was like a bloodhound with alcohol. Faye arrived about fifteen minutes later. She looked wonderful with her hair all done up in a French twist, like girls were doing then. She was wearing a very grown-up pink dress with thin straps that emphasized her young figure. She smiled when she saw me.

"I was hoping you would be here," she said.

When I asked her if I could get her a drink, she said she really wouldn't mind having something "stronger." I got her a light Seven-and-Seven. I knew my parents used to offer that to friends. I poured an even lighter one for myself; when I brought them back, Scott Schneider was talking to her.

"I guess you know this one from Allan," Scott said.

"I met him at Allan's bar mitzvah party," Faye said. "I think he's really nice. He has nice manners."

"I think he's a *faigele*," Scott said, smirking. "Hey, are you a *faigele*? Is that why you're with Faye?"

Allan heard this, and got really pissed off.

"Scott, I don't know why you need to act like such a shit. Is it that your parents have too much money?"

"At least they got it—" Scott stopped himself cold—and apologized. "I'm sorry. Allan's right. I acted like a *shmuck*. Been hittin' the gin." He held up his glass, then put his other hand on my shoulder. "You're a fine guy, Benjy. Even for someone going to Holy Nate. A den of—anyway, I hope you have a good time tonight. Let's put on some music. How about the Four Seasons? Ya'll like them? Or Smoky Robinson?"

He went over to the stereo and put on the new Four Seasons album with Frankie Valli climbing into stratospherically high falsetto ("Walk like a man, talk like a man, walk like a man, my so-uh-uh-un"). Now I felt like I really had to do *something*; there was just no way around that "walk like a man, my son" business: the message was too clear. Allan and Sue and Faye and I went back to the den, and found some places on the couch to settle into. Before I knew it, Allan and Sue were going at it. Faye looked, though, very cold and turned off. Her eyes hit them and she winced.

"Why don't we just leave?" she asked me. "I'm sick of this."

I panicked.

"I can't. My mom's picking me up in three hours."

"I meant leave the den—and these two. You'd think they were married or something, or soon going to be."

She got up and took me by the hand. There were about six other couples doing what Allan and Sue were doing in various parts of the house. She knew the lay-out of the place and which rooms to avoid, like I guess, the parents' bedroom, or whatever room they were hanging out in.

"How do you know Scott Schneider?" I asked her.

"They're Jews. It's Savannah. We all know each other. I mean most of us know most of everybody else, except for people like you out in Isle of Hope. The only people who live out there are gentiles. I never understood why you do it."

"My dad wanted to live out there. I think my mom likes it. She has friends out there."

Faye smiled.

"Yeah, they all get together and drink martinis, I bet. Very dry."

"No," I corrected her. "They drink Salty Dogs."

"What?"

"It's gin and grapefruit juice, with salt in it."

She made a terrible face. "It sounds so . . . gentile. My parents wouldn't drink anything like that."

"It's good. Really," I explained.

"I hated what Scott said to you. He's such a *shmuck*. His dad owns a couple of discount stores and some other places in the colored section downtown, so they always say about the Schneiders they have *shwartze gelt*. I guess a lot of Jews get their money from colored people, one way or another. I feel bad that Scott's so self-conscious about it, but as you can see it's made them rich."

I could. I asked Faye what Scott had meant with the crack about Allan's parents, and their money.

"Everyone knows the Streitts got their money by buying up property cheap and reselling it fast. Mr. Streitt's kind of like a shark, but nobody talks about it since he gives a lot of money to the synagogue and stuff like that. Anyway, I'm glad Allan said what he did. Scott can be just *ridiculous* at times."

She looked at me suddenly brightly, smiling and gazing directly into my face. To my surprise, we were right in front of a door. We opened it—

And found ourselves alone in a small maid's pantry with counters, two stools, and a refrigerator, that led on to a lit patio. I explored the refrigerator. It glowed with soft drinks, beer, and several bottles of Beefeaters Gin, including one that was open. I found two glasses and quickly poured us two fingers of the gin and added tonic to it. I'd seen my mother do this enough. I turned off the small lamp on one of the counters, so that all the light came from outside. I sat on the stool and sipped some of the gin-and-tonic. It tasted bitter, but I decided I could get used to it, stupidly forgetting the threat of any kind of smell on my breath.

Faye sat on the stool next to me. "This is great," she said smiling. "I feel very grown up. Do you like feeling that way?"

I shrugged innocently. "I dunno."

"But you're so mature. My mom said that at your bar mitzvah. Your dad's in jail. You've had to grow up. You're not like these other kids; I know it."

I kissed her—that was what I wanted to do. As in not the way I'd kissed Tim but *really* kissed her, on her mouth like the way I had kissed Nathan, but even more seriously. Her mouth tasted nice, very fresh. My heart started pounding; I—like blanked out for a second. She drew away from me.

"Hold on, just wait," she said. "I like acting grown up but—"

She kissed me; I don't know why. Maybe she had lost that argument with herself.

We made out for a long time and I forgot everything, even the drinking. She ended up sitting on my lap on the stool, and let me put my hand inside her dress and edge two of my fingers inside the back of her bra. She let me softly touch her there for a while.

Suddenly, Allan's head popped into the pantry.

"For crying out loud! This is where you are! Schneider started doin' really shitty, dumb-ass things and his parents want us to leave."

"What'd he do?" Faye asked, quickly rearranging her dress.

"Drank too much, started falling all over the place, broke a lamp—the *shwartze* told his parents. They're in the living room now. Schneider's in his room—you should have seen his dad! I thought Mr. Schneider was going to take his belt off and whack him right in front of everyone."

"Scott *does* act stupid," Faye said.

"Yeah," Allan said, exasperated. "And they sent Nathan away! 'Course he's older than Schneider by three years. What time's your mom coming for you, Benjy?"

I looked at my watch.

"Not for about another hour."

The three of us went into the living room where Sue was waiting, sitting in a chair in front of Mr. and Mrs. Schneider, who were both standing. Mr. Schneider was wearing a white shirt and black slacks with suspenders. He was almost totally bald, but had the same nose as Scott. His wife was thin, Miami-tanned, and plain looking, but wearing a lot of make up, kind of á la Elizabeth Taylor in *Cleopatra*.

"I'm sorry this has happened," Mr. Schneider said. He had an interesting accent. It was definitely not Southern like Caroline's, but not exactly Yankee, either. It was more like Robby's accent when he was being Leon. "I apologize for my son. Some kids, you just give 'em too much and they don't know what else to take from you. As far as I'm concerned, I've taken about as much as I can—"

"Norm," Mrs. Schneider said. "I know Scotty didn't mean to behave the way he did. He got carried away. Kids do that sometimes. It was as much our fault as anyone's. We should have been out here."

"He didn't *want* us out here, Vivian. I trusted him! Not anymore! Worst thing is we had to hear it from the maid. Thank God Jessie was around! Listen, if any of you kids need to stay till your parents get here, fine. But no more party, I mean that."

Allan thanked him, and told Mr. Schneider that our parents were coming in an hour, and we were going to the Big Clock. I put on my best pleading face.

"Just don't tell my mom about Scott's drinking," I begged the Schneiders. "I wasn't drinking at all. Neither was Faye."

"I should get you to lie like that for me," Allan said on the way over to the Clock. "I couldn't lie like that if I had—"

"That's because you're Jewish," Faye broke in. "*All* Jewish."

Her words stung me, but I pretended not to hear them.

Everything timed out perfectly. We were back at the Schneider's house just before Caroline drove up, so I didn't have to worry about her finding anything out.

"How was the party?" she asked when I got in the car.

"It was OK. How was the movie?"

She pulled me to her and kissed me on the cheek, getting a good sniff.

"There *was* drinking, wasn't there?"

"No," I said.

"Come on, Benjy. I been around that block myself. '*OK*'? No kid thinks a party's '*OK*' unless he's got something to hide—and I can smell the gin on your breath."

"All right. It was splendid. A perfect success."

She shook her head, and pretended she hadn't heard me.

"How was the host?"

"He's an ass, but Allan Streitt's good. I like him and the other kids I knew there."

"That's good. Did you get to see that girl?"

"Yeah, Faye was there."

"Did you kiss her in a closet, or something like that?"

"God, Mom! D'you have to know everything?"

"Sure, that's why people are called *adults*. We have to know everything. The terrible thing is that we don't." She sighed. "The movie stunk out loud, but it had Clark Gable in it, so I could stand it. When I first met your father, I thought he looked like Clark Gable, in a kind of Jewish way."

I needed to change the subject away from me.

"Is that why you fell for him?"

We were soon on the way out to Isle of Hope. She lit up a cigarette and lowered the window some. She didn't answer me; I wondered why not.

"He was the only honest man I'd ever met," she said finally. "He made me feel like I was smart, not just some Southern debutante who's always treated like she's retarded. If you want to know the way to a woman's heart, treat her like she's smart, not stupid. You'll meet some *dumb* girls—just like there are lots of dumb guys—but Southern men are always taught to treat women like they're retarded. They think it's part of the chivalry thing—'You don't have t' think 'bout nothing, darlin'. Just let me do all the thinkin'!'"

"So why didn't you know more about what Dad was doing?"

"There you go again, being a smart aleck. Mostly, because I thought if I just kept my head buried in the sand in Isle of Hope, everything would be OK. There was also the Jewish thing. He wanted to keep that separate, private. He never asked me to convert, and, frankly, I never seriously gave it a lot of mind. He and Andy seemed to have the Jewish thing together and it went with the business thing. I know that all sounds crazy."

"No, it doesn't."

"Good, I'm glad you see that. So—"

She threw out her cigarette butt. I had seen enough Smokey the Bear commercials to hate that, but ignored them.

"So, what?

"Between us," she continued, "your father and I had the Jewish thing, the Southern thing, the business thing, and finally you kids—especially you. I don't think Liz is going to care about being Jewish, or even half-Jewish. She'll end up like me, just happy to be alive and enjoying herself, and love some guy."

She said a few other things, but I had stopped listening. I realized Liz would be a regular person, not like I was. She would not be acting anything; she'd just be herself. I wondered: was I *acting* with Faye? Inside, I didn't want to feel that I was; I wanted to feel that it was all real and that I could tell Faye anything—except of course about Tim, and Nathan.

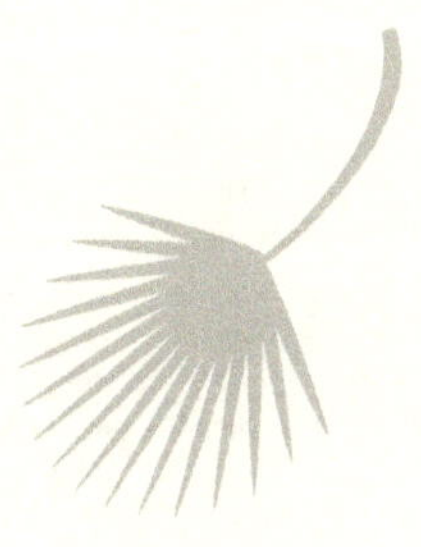

Part Three:

In the Shadow

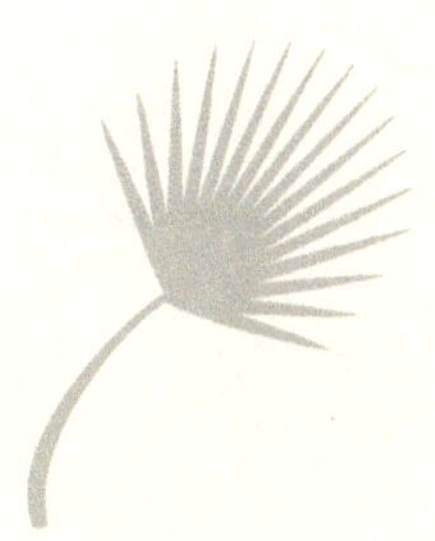

A Visit To My Father

Winter came and the holidays, and it was really hard knowing that Robby wouldn't be with us. He wrote to me sometimes, but not very often. Usually, the letters told me little about his life in prison. Here is an example of one.

Dear Son,

I think about you a lot. Don't grow up so fast that when I get out I won't recognize you. Things are OK here. They treat me all right, but the food is not much. I've learned how to make a license plate and work in a laundry. There's only one other Jew in the whole place. A young guy named Arthur Levy. He's from Atlanta. He won't tell me why he's here. I guess that's his business. I think drugs were involved. Your mom has told me you're seeing a nice girl, and you go to parties. Great! I was worried about you being in an all-boy school—how'd you meet girls. But you have my brains for that. I'm so proud of you. What I want is to see you married and having kids and being happy. That is my great wish.

Love,

Your Dad

I wanted to ask him about Arthur, and if it was really possible to love someone after they die. I wanted to ask him what his life was like in prison. Did anyone try anything "funny" with him. Did he have any friends? What did he think about all day?

But I didn't. I wrote to him about what I did at school, and the school Christmas pageant with some Catholic girls from St. Agnes's in it. Tim called them the Sisters of Satan, because a lot of the girls weren't exactly lookers, or even all that nice. At least Tim thought so. Pat and Neal sometimes dated them, and Neal said they kept their legs closed up tighter than Fort Knox. I sang in the pageant and it was OK; it did not bother me singing about Jesus. I figured by this time that Jesus was like everyone's friend. He was in heaven with God and Arthur and even Moses, and what difference did it make whether he was an angel or God's son, or just another person? What was important was that, even in a bad world you believed in human goodness, and that God could help you become that way. I had read *The Diary of Ann Frank*, and despite everything she believed in human goodness, so of course I wanted to believe in it also.

Summer came and with it the end of the school year, and I decided I did not want to go on retreat. First, because it would remind me too much of Arthur, and second because I wanted to visit Robby. Brother Alexis said that made a lot of sense to him.

"After what you've been through, I can understand, Benjy. Going to see your father—that's truly a sacred act. I'm glad you want to do that."

Now I had to convince Mom. She argued that I needed to stay with Liz; they didn't like having kids visit; it was too depressing. Finally, she said, "Robby doesn't want you up there, Benjy. You don't know what it's like for him. If you come, he'll just feel worse."

"But Andy sees him, doesn't he?"

"That's different. He has to. Andy's supporting us—Andy and my parents." I felt horrible. She saw it on my face, and gave in. "I'll see what I can do. Your Dad's allowed a couple of phone calls a month. They're during the day, when you're in school. I'll tell him that you want to see him."

The next time she spoke with him, Mom told Robby how much I wanted to see him, and Robby agreed that I could come, and Liz would stay at the Blakelys.

Dad was in a place above Atlanta, almost in Tennessee, a full day's drive away. (I had a hard time calling it "the prison," except in my own thoughts.) Mom and I hardly spoke on the way up. Mostly she played the radio and smoked; I could tell she was anxious about the visit. Georgia is such a big state and I looked out the window, watching the landscape change through the drive, from the big dark oak trees around Savannah to the scrubby pine forests further instate. We passed through little towns, and some bigger places like Augusta. It started to feel very hot without the marsh breezes we had in Isle of Hope. Suddenly I missed it, and realized why Mom loved it, being by the water, with all the boats and even the shrimpers, and the beautiful white houses that caught the breezes. I think that was why my dad liked it too, being away from everyone in Savannah, Jewish or not.

We stopped for lunch at a roadhouse off the highway. We got a booth and Caroline went into the dark bar to get a drink. A waitress who was a lot older than Mom and wore a lot of bright make-up with teased-up hair ambled over.

"Hi, Buddy," she said cheerfully. "What-cha gonna have?"

I looked at her unsure because she didn't offer a menu. She must have realized that, and brought one over, as Mom came out of the bar with a Tom Collins. The waitress gave her a funny, sideways look.

"Ma'am, you didn't need t' go in there by yourself and leave yer boy here alone. I cudda brung it back for you."

"Sorry," Mom said. "Guess I was thirsty."

"Don't pay it no mind! I'll come back in a sec' and see what you folks want."

She sat down across from me and lit a cigarette. There were no ashtrays on our table, but she grabbed one from another. "What kind of hell hole is this?" she joked.

The kind you usually wouldn't bring a kid to, I thought, but said, "Dunno. You ever come here before, when you went to see Dad?"

"No, darling. I haven't. Anything pleases you on the menu?"

I told her, and asked her what she wanted.

"Just your company. I'm fine with the Tom Collins." She held up her drink.

"That's not much for lunch."

"Hey, I'm supposed to be taking care of you!"

The waitress came back. "Would ya like another one o' those, Ma'am?"

"Sure. I'd like it. And he'll have a hamburger and french fries—"

"That's *dee*-lux!" She really emphasized the "dee" part.

"Yes'm. I'm sure it is. He'll have that and—bring him a milk shake."

"We don't make no milk shakes, but I can bring 'im a Coke."

She left to put in our order; Mom looked at me for a moment.

"Thank you for thinking about me, Benjy. I don't have a lot of appetite right now. See, the fact is, your dad wasn't crazy about you coming up. He feels so embarrassed by all this. He wants to protect you from it. He's an honorable guy, with a genuine sense of honor and it's hurt by this."

"Did he really break the law?"

"Let's just say he and Andy bent it the wrong way and it snapped." She lit another cigarette. "God, I feel like I'm going to explode. I need that other drink badly!"

We listened to honky-tonk country songs on the jukebox while we waited. Most were about guys who'd lost their girlfriends or the other way around. A song called "Hello Walls" came on, and Mom sang along with it—*"Hello Walls, how things go for you today? Don't you miss her since she upped and walked away?"*

"I like this guy. His name's Faron Young," Mom said. "For years I thought they were saying, 'Fair and Young.' I guess that described him. He was so good lookin' when he was younger, they called him the 'Hillbilly Heartthrob.' That song pretty much describes the way I feel right now."

Some men who looked like truck drivers came out as a group from the bar and stared at us. One man was paunchy and sun-wrinkled, wearing dirty khaki pants. He gave Mom this broad, buck-toothed smile. I hated him. The waitress finally brought Mom's drink, and also my burger, fries, and Coke. When she was gone, I pushed the burger at Mom.

"You really need t' eat something, Mom. Have just one bite, please."

It wasn't much of a bite. She put the burger down and went back to her second Tom Collins. It was in a tall glass with a bright red marischino cherry on a toothpick, sitting on the ice cubes in it. She fished the cherry out and ate it.

"See, I am getting something."

We checked into a motel surrounded by hills and highways, close to where Dad was. It was the end of the day, and we would not be able to see him until the morning. There wasn't a pool or anything else there, and most of the people coming out of the rooms were women and some teen-agers—all white, but that was to be expected. We watched TV for a while. I'd brought *The Sound and the Fury*, and tried to read it. Mom left me in the room and went outside and walked for a while. I wasn't getting very far with Faulkner, it was like he was trying hard to confuse people, then Mom came back in.

She looked really bad. Like she had been crying. I asked her what was wrong. She sat down on the side of her bed.

"I want you to pretend that everything's OK with Dad. I mean, no matter what he looks like. Can you do that? It'll mean a lot to him, that you don't see how bad off he is."

I told her I could.

"Good, Benjy. If you can do that then this trip won't hurt him so much. Just tell him that he looks good, and that you're really glad to see him."

She went into the bathroom and got herself ready for bed. A few minutes later, I did the same thing. In bed, I saw that she was still smoking, so I made sure that she was asleep and her cigarette was out before I fell asleep.

After some guards made sure that we weren't carrying anything bad in, we were led into a large room with tables in it. There were about ten people there, mostly women and some kids, and Mom and I were assigned a table. Robby came in a few minutes later, wearing a uniform with a number on it. Except for the numbers, he could have worked in a service station and worn the same thing; there were no stripes on it like in the movies. At first, he didn't know what to do or say, then he hugged me. He was so thin I could feel all of his bones. It shocked me. He looked pale and gray and his eyes, which had been so beautiful, looked sunken deep into his face, and very red.

"You're lookin' really good, Dad," I said and smiled.

He smiled back, not the smile I remembered that seemed to shower light all over, but the smile of someone who's shrunken, sick and defeated, barely surviving a terrible time.

"How are you, Benjy?" he said, trying to sound cheerful. "How's school? You keeping your grades up?"

"It's great," I said. "I have nice friends, and they're—"

"I'm glad. Mom told me you've been seeing girls. That makes me happy. I want you to be with a family of your own one day. That's the most happiness a man can have; there's nothing like it."

I told him my grades were fine and I was doing fine with girls and everything was—"Fine." I wondered if he knew how much I was lying, and how painful it was to lie, especially to lie to him. He asked me to hug him again, and wait outside the room so he could talk to Mom.

I left the room, and sat in the hall in a row of chairs with a guard nearby. The area was painted in a color between dingy-dismal gray and earwax yellow. Two other kids, maybe ten or eleven, sat near me. One was a girl wearing a pretty yellow school dress, the other a boy in jeans. We had nothing to say to each other, and didn't talk. I felt like shit. That was the only word for it, like

I should not have been there. It was nothing like I'd imagined it was going to be, with both of us really happy to see one another. The worst thing was hating to lie so much to my father.

The guard came up to me and gave me a smile. "Yer Daddy's in there?"

"Yes, sir."

"Hard on you kids. I got kids of my own, and if I was in there, I'd wanna see 'um. But it ain't easy. Never is."

When Mom came out, we had to go through a room where they made sure we weren't taking anything out—what, I had no idea—then we went back to the car.

"You did really great, Benjy," she said, as we started off. "Thank you."

I had to ask—"What's wrong with him?"

"He hasn't been well."

"What's he got?"

"We aren't sure. Nobody is right now. We're hoping he'll be OK until he gets out. Or they'll let him out early."

"Is he going to die?"

After a moment, she said, "I'm praying to God he won't die."

On the way back I wanted to see Tim. I wanted to see him and Neal. I wanted to see Allan and Nathan and Faye, and even Alfred Johnson and Arch Flanders and Bill Manion, and Brother Alexis; I wanted to see anyone who'd make me feel good about being myself and far away from the place where Dad was. Sometime after a couple of hours of driving, I told Mom I needed to take a nap, and climbed into the back seat and lay down. I closed my eyes; the sun cast shadows of clouds or trees across my face, which I could discern even through my eyelids. I saw Arthur. He nestled down right next to me and held me. I could feel his breath on me, and his warm skin.

"I love you, Benjy," he said into my ear. "I'll take care of you, I mean it."

"I love you too," I told him.

"I know. I knew it all along."

I'm not sure how long I was asleep, but when I woke up it seemed that we were closer to the middle of the state and then to home. Mom turned on some pop stations on the radio and we sang along to songs and she ran her fingers through my hair and smiled.

I didn't say anything else to her, but suddenly I felt better. She noticed it, but I had no idea how to tell her why.

"I'm glad you wanted to see your dad," she said to me as we approached the house. It had been hard for her to talk about it; I knew that. "It meant a lot to him, I could tell."

"Is that what you and he talked about when I was away?"

"Mostly it was about money and how to deal with it. And also—"

"What?"

She exhaled, like she was blowing smoke out, but she wasn't smoking.

"The future, Benjy."

"Are you and Dad going to separate or something like that?"

"God, no! When you're older, you'll see that the future is not always the nicest place. Right now, for you, it means getting to do more of what you want. Isn't that what the future means to you?"

I smiled. How did she guess?

23

Other Men Like Nathan Streitt

I was approaching fourteen, and that seemed grown up already. There were times when I felt that I had outgrown Tim, even though he was my best friend, then other times when I realized how much I liked him. The rest of the summer I spent time with the Blakelys, and of course with Mom and Liz. The three of us went to the beach at Tybee Island a lot. Sometimes I'd walk off by myself just to think—what was life really about? It seemed so big and I felt so small in it. I was growing up, but I wanted the process to speed up so that I could feel…well, just a bit more in control. There was a section of Savannah Beach where a lot of Jewish people stayed, and one day I strolled up to it and saw Nathan Streitt.

He was by himself, lying on a beach towel with some sun tan oil, a book, and a cloth bag I guessed had a change of clothes in it. He smiled at me. I'd never seen him in just a bathing suit. He had bony shoulders and thin legs, and his narrow chest had a funny cave-in to it.

"How ya doing?" he asked, leaning back on his elbows. He invited me to join him.

I sat down. "I heard you were sent away," I said.

"To this *hospital,*" he answered. "Except you weren't supposed to call it that. My parents figured I had a break down. That wasn't the real problem, though."

"What was it?" I asked.

"Not sure I can tell you."

"Why not?"

He pushed himself up and smiled. "God, you're some kid. You get right down to it. Cause polite Jews don't talk about things like this, especially in Savannah, Georgia. That's *why.*"

I popped the elastic waistband on his bathing suit.

"Maybe I'm not so polite," I said. "And I'm only half Jewish. You know that.

You made a big deal out of it."

He touched me lightly on my chest.

"You don't know what I'd like to do to you right here."

"Shut up. Now, tell me, why'd they send you away?"

"They wanted to straighten me out—in other words, turn me into a regular *boychik*. Instead of a boy-chick. If you know what I mean."

"You don't seem like a *boy-chick* to me. You seem like a—"

"Regular boy? You know that's not the truth. Where's your mom?"

I pointed down the beach. He got up.

"Why don't you introduce me to her? Tell her I'm Allan Streitt's big brother and you met me at his bar mitzvah party and I'd like to drive you home. We can talk more then."

When I got up, I realized I was almost as tall as he was. Now I did feel grown up, and smiled directly into his eyes. We walked down the beach to Mom and Liz. Mom seemed to take my meeting Nathan very casually. She watched me as I gathered my clothes into a small bag to change in later. When Nathan was out of earshot, she told me to be careful.

"Watch how he drives," she warned. "Don't be afraid to tell him to slow down."

Nathan had the same Karmann Ghia convertible that he drove me home in before.

"Want any shades?" he asked me as I got in.

"Shades?"

"Sunglasses?"

I smiled. "OK."

He brought a pair out from the glove compartment. I looked at myself in the rear view mirror in them. The sunglasses were a wonderful, deep-coated black, like the kind aviators wore. I felt immensely glamorous, handsome, and mysterious and not at all like a kid who hadn't turned fourteen yet. Nathan smiled at me, still bare-chested in my bathing suit. It was dry, so I wasn't uncomfortable. He put his hand on my chest for a second, then we were off. It was great driving top down on the familiar streets of the beach, past set-back bungalows and stores. I didn't feel at all self-conscious, although some people looked strangely at us, but I figured they simply wanted to stare. Nathan had changed into a pair of dark Bermuda shorts and a white, completely unbuttoned short-sleeved shirt; he was driving barefoot. He looked really cool; I stole looks at him. We turned onto the long causeway drive back from the beach, lined with palm trees, and suddenly I could have been in California or Tahiti, or on some exciting TV program set in one of those places.

"How's your mom doing," he asked. "I mean, with everything happening with your dad?"

"She's OK." I said, looking at him while he drove.

"My mom and dad don't get along. Guess you figured that out."

"They seem OK."

"Only seem."

I put my hand on his knee. I wanted to, I didn't know why; maybe because Nathan was close to the same age as Neal O'Neill, and I might have done the same thing to him.

"You'll a real flirt," he said to me, smiling and glancing at my hand.

"What does that mean?" I asked. I left my hand on his knee.

"It means you make people want to kiss you, even if you're not aware of it. There are kids like you; they're naturally seductive. But they can't figure out why people respond to them the way they do. Did you ever think about the way people respond to you?"

"I don't know what you mean."

He put his right hand into the waistband of my bathing suit, and felt my cock. His hand felt instantly warm to my dick that was still cool from swimming, even though my suit was dry.

"I mean like that," he said.

"You should watch your driving."

"You mean I should slow down?" he asked with his hand still in my bathing suit.

I looked at the speedometer, and told him yes.

"I'm not just talking about my driving," he said.

Now he'd lost me. I wasn't sure what seductive meant, either. But I knew I couldn't ask Caroline about it, or even Tim. I wondered if I'd been seductive with Brother Alexis. Maybe it was just something I couldn't turn off. I needed to know more.

"Tell me about being seductive," I said, and withdrew my hand from his knee. "You know a lot about it, I guess."

"Some boys just have it," he answered, and smiled, glancing at me. "You have it, and I fall for it. Ever heard of the book *Lolita*?" I nodded—it was one of those things I wasn't supposed to read, especially at Holy Nativity. "Lolita's twelve, and *very* seductive. You're older than Lolita, Benjy. Tell me, do the guys at your all-boys school fool around a lot?"

His hand left my bathing suit, and moved up to my chest. He started softly stroking my left nipple. I remembered what Tim said about nipples getting harder. I felt extremely nervous. Even driving fast down the highway from the beach, I was sure someone could see us in the car. I grabbed his hand and placed it on my knee.

When we'd driven a few miles more, past Fort Pulaski, an old Civil War fort, he said, "There's some place I want to show you. You might find it interesting."

There was a narrow road off the highway that led to a landing in the middle of more marshes, thick with stumpy pines and palmettos. Nathan drove slowly down the road, until a hidden parking lot became visible. A building at the end of it was completely obscured from the highway. He parked his car in the lot.

"What's this?" I asked.

"It's a bar, called the Cove."

"I'm too young to go into a bar, unless they have a restaurant. Sometimes Mom takes me into those. I get a Coke and she has a real drink."

"Do you ever drink a *real* drink?"

"Sure," I said.

"Good. I want you to put your clothes on—and keep on the glasses."

I wriggled out of my suit and he touched me while I did it, making me hard. I felt crazy suddenly, like I was no longer a kid but I knew I was. I thought about the time I'd wanted to touch Arthur on his bed, and now Nathan was touching me. He was so wild, and mean at times; I was scared of him, yet I wanted to get close to him. When I was dressed, he put on his sneakers and mussed up my hair so that it fell across my face. Then he kissed me with his tongue in my mouth. I'd never done before, not even with Faye, but I accepted it.

The Cove was very dark inside, even though the sun was still out. There were three guys sitting at the bar, and a very fat man attending it.

"Hi, you guys got ID?" he asked.

"I do," Nathan said. "But my friend doesn't drive. He's jus' gonna have a Coke anyway. We'll drink at a table."

"OK, but do it quick. And I want to see your ID."

Nathan showed him a piece of paper with a name on it. A Georgia driver's license was notoriously easy to fake, and even I could tell it was phony. Tim told me that Neal and Pat had had phony ones for years to sneak into bars with.

Nathan ordered a screwdriver and got me a Coke. We sat in the back, in a really dark spot, and I realized that as big as I was already (because of Caroline's height), in place like this I could pass for sixteen—but not for twenty-one.

"Congratulations," Nathan said. "This is your first gay bar."

"My first what?"

"A bar for queers. You know, *faigeles*, guys light in their loafers—stuff like that."

I wanted to run out. I got up, but Nathan stopped me.

"It's OK," he said. "I'm just joking. Everybody knows you're *not* a *faigele*. Or light in your loafers. I am, I know it. Most of the people who come in here, you couldn't tell what they are on the outside; I mean the outside of the bar. Or the outside of them. But you're smart. I have a feeling you know how much people lie, especially down here. I mean down in Savannah. The Jews lie to each other, and lie to non-Jews. The *goys*, they live off lies. The black people, they're the only—"

Suddenly a man came up to us. He was short, with really black skin, even blacker than Josephine's. He was about Robby's size, but his chest was twice as big.

"Hi, Nathan," he said, grinning broadly and showing his teeth. I noticed that two up front were missing. "Hi ya doin', boy?"

"I'm fine, Moe." Nathan looked at me. "*Randy*, this is Moe. Moe's a friend of mine. We met about a year ago in Forsythe Park. He was cruising around and we liked each other fast."

Moe ran his fingers through Nathan's hair and smiled.

"I like your friend Randy," Moe said. But he's *real* jailbait. Ya got any idea what kinda trouble he is?"

"We're gettin' outta here in a minute."

"Wanna come back to my place? We'll just be cool and have a drink."

Nathan looked at him with this full flowering of a smile, and I realized suddenly what he meant by being seductive.

"Not now, Moe. But thanks for the offer. I gotta get Randy here home. I promised his mom I'd take care of him."

"You do that, Dah-lin'. He's one sweet boy. I know a lotta guys who'd just *lu-u-uv* t' love him."

Moe winked at me, and went over to the bar. The words just flew out of me, as I whispered, "He's a *shwartze*."

Nathan's eyes clenched shut, then he opened them.

"Don't ever say that word around me again, Benjy. Negroes are the only cool people here. Cool, good, and accepting. My parents wanted to have me put away for life—or something like it. Moe explained to me that I'm all right. He and some of his friends got me to survive this shit. In Savannah, you got colored guys and white guys and they meet in a bar like this."

I remembered the Grocery Store; I asked Nathan if he'd ever been there.

"The cops just closed it," he said. "They'll close this place in a couple of months. They don't raid the bars here, just close 'em. They're scared they're going to find someone like the mayor's son in one. It's hard—fucking hard. I thought about killing myself when I figured out I was a queer."

I looked at him intensely. "You *did*?"

What could I have done for Arthur? I'd done nothing. I had just lied to him about girls. I'd been too scared. I got up feeling horrible. "We need to go," I said.

The light was starting to drain outside, but it still felt bright after being in the Cove. We got into the car. I was crying. Nathan pulled me to him.

"What's wrong, Benjy?" he asked.

"I think a kid I know killed himself."

"Sorry. I am, I mean it."

He leaned over and cupped my chin in his hand and gently kissed me. I was glad this time.

"Would you be happy if you didn't see me again?" he asked.

"No. I'd be really *un*happy if that happened. I like you, Nathan."

He took my hand and brought it for a second up to his lips.

"Good." He started the car. "I wish I could tell you what my parents tried to do to me. But I got smart. *Hip*, like the Negroes say. I wouldn't let them do it to me. I wish I could have done something for your friend. What was his name?"

"Arthur. Arthur Gomez."

"Nice name. I guess he wasn't American."

"He was Puerto Rican."

"Puerto Ricans are American. A lot of them live in New York. They have a hard time of it. Was Arthur smart?"

"He got a scholarship to Holy Nativity. His dad works on a fishing boat. He drank a lot and used to beat Arthur."

I couldn't stop crying. I leaned over and buried my face in Nathan's shirt, until we left the back road and were approaching the main highway. There a group of speeding teenagers blew their horn at us and gave us the finger. They charged ahead of us and disappeared.

"That was close," Nathan said. "They could have run us off the road and killed us. It's one of the problems of going to the Cove—most people don't even try to go in the afternoon. It's safer at night, but my parents get mad if I'm out too late. I've decided to leave home in a year. Too bad you can't."

I didn't want to leave home. My parents weren't like the Streitts. I loved Caroline and Robby and Liz. I was just afraid what they'd do if they found out any more about me. Then I realized something: maybe I didn't know a whole lot more myself. Maybe I'd end up with a girl like Faye Jacobson, and get married and make Robby happy. I was thinking about that when Nathan reached over and touched my hand.

"I'm glad you want to see me again, but you don't have to do it soon. Just give yourself some time and then call me if you want to. I'm glad you told me about Arthur. I am."

I offered him his dark glasses back and he said, "Why don't you keep 'em? I can always get another pair. The one thing my parents are good about is giving me money."

We didn't say a whole lot on the way back to Isle of Hope. Nathan put on the same kind of songs on the radio that Caroline liked, then switched to a Negro gospel station and sang or hummed along to everything. I asked him to stop the car as he was about to turn into the driveway.

"Thanks for the glasses," I said. "They're really cool."

I leaned over and kissed him on the mouth. I didn't do any tongue thing—that was still creepy to me—but I stayed on his lips for a few seconds.

"You are some kid," he said, then drove me up to the house. He walked in with me to say a brief good-bye to Caroline.

"He seems like a really nice guy," Caroline said as he drove off. "But isn't he… kind of *old* to be your friend. I mean he's still a teenager, but—"

"I'm mature," I reminded her. "Nathan knows it."

Mom nodded. "That you are, Benjy. No doubt about it."

24

School At Fourteen

School started again, and I was fourteen. I felt like a totally different person from the kid who had entered Holy Nativity just two years earlier. Brother Alexis himself looked at me differently. He smiled at me in a more serious way. He asked me about my summer, and I told him about visiting Dad but nothing about Nathan Streitt. It was the O'Neill twins' last year and I saw them a lot, and they acted differently around me too. Like, suddenly I was closer to their age than Tim was, even though Tim was about a year older than me. Tim seemed now like a kid to me. I was a more of a *grown-up* kid. For the first month or so of school, we kind of avoided each other; it was hard to have even a moment alone at Holy Smokes, anyway. Then one day in October after lunch, Tim invited me to sleep over that weekend, and I just shrugged and told him I didn't want to do it.

"We don't have t' fool around," Tim whispered. "Maybe you done outgrowed that."

I didn't want to tell him that I'd outgrown *him* and wasn't interested in fooling around anymore, but it was true. I was interested in something else, but I wasn't sure what it was. Maybe I wanted it to be involved with Faye Jacobson, or a girl like her. Still, what Nathan had told me about surviving—that you had to have somebody else to help you to do it—just kept popping into my head. It killed me that I hadn't been the *person* to help Arthur. I could barely hold it in how much it hurt. Maybe I shouldn't have taken that much weight on my shoulders, but I felt it sometimes.

"I don't know what I've outgrown," I told Tim, and looked away from him. When I looked back at him, his face was hanging down. I could tell that I had hurt him. I felt like a shit.

"OK," I said. "Let's do it."

He smiled and put his hand on my shoulder. I wriggled away from it, not because I didn't want it there, but because you could never tell who might see you.

In fact, Joe Flauwerty and Ken Ferris suddenly popped up, just like that. Flauwerty had been promoted to sergeant first class and was wearing stripes on his shirt. Tim and I were never promoted. Neither of us cared about the military part of military school. Ferris had that look of a hungry weasel spotting a fish—we called him "Feral Ferris," because he was so ...*feral.*

"You girls havin' a meetin'?" Ferris asked.

"Yes, *sir!*" Tim said, and spit right at Flauwerty. Now that Flauwerty was promoted, he had to act more like a brown-nose; he backed away and grabbed Ferris.

"Leave 'em alone," Flauwerty ordered. "We don't beat up queers anymore. Not on school time. We'll look for you *after* school."

"You ever touch me or Rothberg and I'll have my brothers kill ya," Tim said.

"Ya brothers ain't gonna be here *after* this year," Ferris warned. "Whatcha gonna do then, squirt?"

I ignored Ferris, but looked Flauwerty straight in the eye—he was easier to deal with than Ferris, who was still a bullying dope. I was bigger than Tim, and knew that if I had to, I could look tough. Or at least act as cool as Robby had told me how to be.

"Why don't you just wait and find out?" I snarled to Flauwerty. "I thought you guys and Storch had grown up some. Guess you haven't."

Flauwerty's eyes hit the cement. He backed off and walked away with Ferris closely following. My body loosened up.

"What was that all about?" I asked Tim, who knew more gossip than any other kid at school.

"Storch is on probation. We're not s'posed to know it, but if he screws up one more time, the brothers are gonna throw him out of school. Neal told me."

"Did Storch beat up somebody we don't know about?"

"I dunno. Neal won't tell me anything else. We can talk about it this weekend, if you still wanna come over."

"OK," I said. I felt cheerful again. I liked the O'Neills, and it did seem stupid of me not to be close to them, even if Tim was still a kid: a *real* kid.

We had to be a lot quieter this time in Tim's room, because his father was around. We were sitting on his bed in our jockey shorts.

"I think my parents were gonna get a divorce," Tim said. "They were real close to it."

"I thought Catholics didn't do that."

"They ain't s'posed to, but lots of 'em do. They just call it an annulment." He laughed. "Like you can annul a marriage after you have six kids."

"What happened?"

"Neal knew what was going on, that Dad was seeing this woman in Augusta. He'd go up there and see her on 'business.'"

"How'd Neal find out?"

"He's smart. He actually talked to Dad about it. Neal likes Dad because they drink together. Pat is more Mom's boy. Y'know, he takes the Catholic shit seriously and he's quiet and likes girls but won't fuck one till he's married. So Mom loves him." He put his hand on my bare shoulder. "You went t' see your dad in prison, didn't ya?"

"How'd you know?"

"I could tell. You're so grown-up now. Even Mom sees it. We all see it. It's cause you had t' grow up, right?"

Maybe Tim wasn't as much of a twerp as I'd thought. He knew I was grown-up. I pulled him to me and kissed him hard, right on his lips. He jumped away from me.

"Why'd y' do that? That's so—queer!"

"Cause I felt like it. Maybe I'm—OK, I don't know what I am. But if I want t' do stuff like that, who's gonna stop me?"

Tim's whole body shook, like he was keeping from either laughing or shuddering.

"*Who?* Flauwerty, Ferris, Storch. Brother Dorris the Dummy—guys like that."

I suddenly laughed.

"And you think they *don't* do it? They're all scared of something, cause maybe Storch is the biggest queer of 'em all. Kids used to call him Horace the Homo, right?"

"That was a joke, Rothberg. Everybody's a homo at Holy Nate, at least till we figure out something else t' call 'em. They're all homos, 'sept you and me, and sometimes—"

"You're not so sure about me. But isn't that what killed Arthur? People saying stuff like that? And his dad, and him being so alone and everything?"

Tim turned away from me and started choking, like there was something stuck in his throat. I pulled him toward me and just looked at him. I wanted to hold him, even kiss him again, but I didn't. He got out of bed, found a Kleenex and blew his nose. He got back into bed, and drew his knees up and rested his head on them.

"What is it?" I asked. "I'm sorry I brought up Arthur. Is that it?"

"That's only part of it, Benjy. There are a lot of secrets in this world, and I can't tell you all of 'em."

"What does that mean?"

"It means, leave Arthur alone, OK? And don't kiss me anymore. I don't want you t' kiss me now—not anymore. I mean it."

"OK," I said. "I just wish people weren't so afraid, that's all."

"Is that *all*? I wish you'd shut up, and I wish I wasn't scared, too."

I put my hand out to him, but drew it away. We kept our jockeys on and laid down to sleep. But I couldn't. I wondered what was really going on, and who knew what—about Arthur, or even about myself. I watched Tim as he settled into unconsciousness, his eyes closed, his breathing deeper and more regular. Did I *really* seem that much more different than I had last year? Maybe meeting Allan and Nathan Streitt had changed me as much as meeting the O'Neills. Kissing Tim had been risky. Sure, it was OK to jerk each other off, or even suck each other a bit, but going as far as real kissing—that was supposed to be something you only did with girls.

But I had done it with Nathan, and I'd liked it.

Something *was* different at breakfast the next morning. There was a starchy formality in the air. Mr. O'Neill was looking at the Savannah papers, and Mrs. O'Neill treated him like he was more of a guest, like me, than a member of the family. It was like he was there, but there was no telling how long he would stay. Pat and Mrs. O'Neill made scrambled eggs. Neal winked at me a lot and smiled, like we had some secret between us; I wondered if what I had done with Nathan had somehow changed the air itself and become known only to Neal. He got up to get some more orange juice and put his hands on my shoulders as he passed. I didn't flinch. Maybe he'd seen the same thing in me that Nathan had seen. I wondered if Neal had read *Lolita* also.

"How's everything at the O'Neills?" Mom asked when she picked me up.

"OK," I said.

But she could tell it hadn't been, and asked me what was wrong.

"Tim told me that his parents almost got a divorce."

"With all those kids! How crazy can they get? But they aren't, right?"

"Sure. They aren't."

"Good. You need both parents around as long as you can have them. I learned that when I was a girl. I'm learning it now as a parent."

"How's Dad?" I asked. "Have you been able to speak with him lately?"

She hesitated for a moment, then said, "He's been sick, Benjy. Really sick."

We came to a traffic light. She pulled a cigarette out of her purse and lit it with the car lighter. Her hands shook.

"I just keep putting off telling you. It's hard enough for me to talk about anything. One day I hope you'll understand all of this, but I don't want you to grow up so fast that you need to understand it now."

I looked out the window. We were getting closer to Isle of Hope. I could smell the approaching salt in the air, and feel the marshy landscape around me, flat but filled with the dense, choking presence of ancient trees and Southern island vegetation. It reminded me of something going back hundreds of years; I could imagine people in very old clothes living here. When I'd been really small, it scared me sometimes, like Death itself was chasing me into the closing grip of the past.

"What does he have?" I asked, coming back to the present.

"Can we talk about it when we get home? I can't drive and talk about it now."

25

I See Robby Again

We were in the den with the door closed. I had some iced tea in my hand and Mom had a scotch. Liz was with Josephine.

"He has cancer," she said.

I put the glass down on a small table in front of the TV set and could see its gray reflection in the blank TV screen. Even my own reflection looked gray.

"Is he going to die?"

"They're moving him to a hospital in Augusta soon. He's been at a hospital where they take—uh, men in the prison. But the hospital in Augusta is for veterans, and they're releasing him to them."

"Does that mean that if they release him from the hospital, he can come back home?"

She started shaking, then crying. I got up and took her hand, and sat next to her on a settee.

"I haven't even thought about that," she said between sobbing. "There's a beautiful cemetery with a Jewish part to it, called Bonaventure. It's on the other side of Savannah from us. He wants to be buried there."

"When can I see him?"

"In a few weeks. It can't happen right away because of all the paperwork and stuff to get him into the VA hospital. But I'll drive you to Augusta, and Liz too, though I'm not sure about Liz. She's awfully young still. She's a baby."

"If we don't take her, she'll feel terrible. I know it."

She nodded her head. "You're right."

"Do Grandpa and Grandma know about it?

"They know. Daddy is going to keep us in this house, and your father has some money that he has been able to hold on to. Andy Geyer promised me that you'll have enough money for Holy Nativity."

"What good is *his* promise?" I blurted out.

 She pulled me to her.

"I know you're angry. I understand. I was so scared to tell you this because I was afraid; how were you going to get through the rest of your year knowing this is happening? How are you going to be a kid, with all of this on top of you?"

I started crying, and I didn't want to. "I can't be a kid," I sobbed.

"You've got to be. You've got to have some part of you that's still a boy in school. I would feel terrible if you didn't. And so would your father. He didn't want me to tell you at all."

"Not at all? Then he would just die and I wouldn't know it until—"

Neither of us could say anything for a couple of minutes. When I calmed down, I said, "I'll be OK at school. I have a lot of things to think about. I guess we won't see him until the middle of November, is that right?"

"Yeah," she said. "At the beginning of the holidays."

The days passed, and then the weeks. It got colder; you could feel that aching chill of damp that hits the low-lying coastal areas of the South. It felt as if once the sun was no longer around, even the pines and the big old oak trees were shivering from the unaccustomed snap of cold in the air. I hated to study, but made myself do it, and then finally felt better that I had forgotten what was going to happen soon and could simply think about Caesar's military adventures in Gaul (*"Gallia est omnis diuisa in partes tres"*—I could say it by heart) or French verbs (after the fifth or sixth tense, I usually got lost), or how to keep geometry from driving me crazy. I wanted so much to tell somebody something, but couldn't do it. I couldn't tell Tim or Neal, or any of the other kids around me. They might ask stupid questions that I didn't want to answer.

I decided to talk to Brother Alexis; I trusted him. He gave me a note to get out early from my last class, geometry, to meet him in his office. Of course my geometry teacher was none other than Brother Ulrich, whose explanations of geometric problems often tied themselves into knots. I heard from Tim that Brother Ulrich had actually majored in music, *church* music, but had little talent for that either, so he ended up in Mathematics Education. I'm sure that if he had to teach arithmetic to fourth graders he would have been fine, but not geometry. He was a revolting, impatient teacher. Since I was learning almost nothing from him, I had to rely on my textbook and tried to cram it all in as hard as I could, which was driving me crazy. While the class was working on problems, I got up and gave him Brother Alexis's note.

"What's this about, Mr. Rothberg? You *need* to see Brother Alexis? *Why?* Geometry has to come first, d' you understand?"

I knew he was getting back at me for what had happened in the library basement, even though that was months ago. I tried to be suitably deferential.

"With your permission, sir, I need to see Brother Alexis." I lowered my voice to a note above a whisper. "He's giving me some counseling."

Brother Ulrich lowered his voice too, but still growled.

"What kind of counseling? You're *not* Catholic."

I didn't want to answer. I could hear the boys behind me starting to talk.

"Well? What's your answer, Mr. Rothberg?"

Now, I was really pissed. I put my head almost into his face but kept my voice low.

"Brother Ulrich, if you don't let me go, I will go to Father Greer and explain *everything* to him."

Ulrich rose up at me, slamming the palm of his right hand down onto his desk and drawing his lower teeth up his top lip. Without saying another word, his eyes directed me towards the door, and I left.

"So what's happening?" Brother Alexis asked when I reached his tiny office, where we sat almost knee-to-knee. "Something here, or at home? I want you to feel free to talk to me, Benjy."

I started crying. He reached for some tissues and gave them to me.

"It must be really bad," he said. "I hope it's not because of school."

"My father's dying."

"Oh, dear God."

"He's got cancer. They're moving him from jail to a hospital in Augusta. I'll get to see him and then he'll die."

It was the hardest thing I'd ever said in my life.

Brother Alexis stood up and walked behind me, placing his hands on my shoulders. I was so happy that he was doing this; I didn't want him to stop, but he did.

"Does he have a rabbi he can talk to, or someone he can pray with?"

"I don't know. I don't know what he's got."

"I wish I could give him absolution. I wish I could pray with him. But I can't.

Would you like me to pray with you?"

I hesitated, then nodded.

"Our Father who art in Heaven," he began. "Hallowed be thy name; Thy kingdom come, Thy will be done on earth as it is in heaven. Give us this day our daily bread; and forgive us our trespasses as we forgive those who trespass against us; lead us not into temptation, but deliver us from evil."

"Isn't there more of it?" I asked.

"This is the Catholic version. The rest is called 'the Doxology,' and Catholics don't say that. It wasn't part of the original Matthean prayer. There has been some discussion to include it, but we haven't done it yet."

"But that's the part I like the best," I said. "Thine is the Kingdom, the Power and the Glory, forever and ever, Amen."

Brother Alexis smiled. "It does gives you something to look up to, and I guess look forward to. If you want to say it, you can. You're not Catholic."

I grinned. It felt good to grin; he put his hand on my head.

"I'm so sorry you're going through this. Maybe when you see your father you'd like to say the Lord's Prayer with him. It's very comforting."

"It's not a Jewish prayer."

"Do you know one that you can say, like the *Shema*? That's the basic prayer, isn't it?"

"I can say that. I wished I believed in Jesus. I wish he could just come down here and hold me and tell me what to do."

"It doesn't happen that way, Benjy. Believe me, I wish it did. You have to accept him in your heart as God Himself, as part of God, as a part of God that cannot be divided from God, and also, if you're Catholic, with his mother, the Blessed Virgin. Could you believe that?"

"I don't know," I said, then added, without even thinking about it, "But I'd like to try."

"I don't think this is the right time for you to make that statement. But maybe you can think about it later. I'd be happy to help you with it then. People do convert from one faith to another. You have to find something that makes you feel whole, makes you feel like you have finally found yourself. That's what Jesus is about, finding yourself."

I got up. I didn't know what else to do. I was afraid I'd started crying again just because I was so tired suddenly from even thinking about Dad and God, and what was going to happen when I saw him, and that I had to feel something that I had no idea how to feel: that my father was not simply leaving me.

"You're a fine boy," Brother Alexis said. "Please come and see me again before you see your father."

I did, and Brother Ulrich didn't make a big deal of it anymore. I would see Brother Alexis once a week and tell him about myself. I omitted the stuff about Nathan, because it seemed impossible to tell him any of that, and also about Tim and Neal. He talked to me, too. He told me how destroyed he had been by John Kennedy's death; Kennedy had meant everything to him and now the first Catholic president was gone. It had tested his whole faith in the world, but he came to realize that goodness still had its place. Sometimes I just let him talk. It was easier for me to listen to him than to try to figure out what was permissible for me to say.

One afternoon he told me about his growing up in a village outside of Montreal—and revealed to me his baptismal name, Robert Grainger. He was glad, he said, to be named for St. Alexis, the patron saint of pilgrims and beggars, because he knew he'd be leaving his birthplace, and he'd been born into a poor family with many brothers and sisters. He told me how French Canadians never got the justice they deserved from the English government.

"It's kind of like being Jewish, but not as horrible," he explained. "There was no Hitler for us, just the idea that we'd never be as equal as the Anglos were. That's why I've always understood the underdog—like colored people are in the South. I like the fact that at this school, we don't have the usual Southern attitudes. I was really glad you decided to come here, Benjy."

There were moments with Brother Alexis when I felt that he was fighting some impulse to hug me or hold me closer to him. None of the other brothers I knew at Holy Nativity were like him. With some of them, it felt as if under their gray Sebastianite habits there wasn't an actual body. Tim used to joke about it, the way he told me that Brother Alex "had a big one, but what would a priest do with it?" He'd joke about the other monks: "I wonder if they squat to pee." It was coarse. Neal wouldn't even talk like that, and certainly never Pat.

Sometimes I wondered if I was being "seductive" with Brother Alexis? Was that why he had this feeling for me? Of course, I had no way of knowing, or even imagining asking him anything like that, but over the next several weeks, before the trip to Augusta, I started to feel better. It felt as if there were some other element inside me giving me real strength, and not allowing me to feel so alone. Caroline sensed it; she would talk to me now like I was an actual adult, calmly telling me things about how she had met Robby and what he had meant to her and how she had never thought she would ever feel that way about another person.

Finally we went to see my father. Everything about the trip was strange when you think about it, and I still think about it. The weekend before Thanksgiving, Mom got word through Andy Geyer that we could go. Augusta was about a three-hour drive from Savannah. However, she was still not sure about taking Liz.

"She's too young," Mom said to me in the den. We talked in the den a lot now, because we were sure Liz couldn't sneak in and eavesdrop the way that she and I used to do behind the doors to the veranda. "I'm not sure what this will do to her."

"But what will it do to her when we just tell her that Dad's dead?"

"I don't know," she said. "Children are supposed to be resilient, aren't they?"

We decided to take her. Each of us would have a brief time alone with Dad and then the three of us would see him together. Andy had warned us that Robby's energy level was very low. He was on a morphine drip for pain, and sometimes he would lose his temper and start screaming.

"That's normal with cancer patients," Caroline told me. "Don't think of him as being really like your father. But don't think of him as *not* being like your father, either."

I tried to figure out how to do this. No matter what, it would have to be possible.

We dressed up for the trip; I put on the same clothes I had worn for my bar mitzvah, Liz was a in a very pretty pink dress, like a party dress, and Caroline wore a beautiful navy-blue suit that her mother had bought for her. We looked like we might have been going to something downtown at the Civic Auditorium, when some kind of opera or other cultural thing came in on tour. I remembered being taken to the Philadelphia Orchestra when I was about nine. They played a long piece by Tchaikovsky that I got lost in, but Dad loved it. I was dressed up. Afterward, Dad told me how grown up I had been, and hadn't squirmed or yawned or anything. The best part was that he took me out for ice cream afterwards. It made me understand that every real event should have ice cream at the end of it, but kids always think that way. I thought about that on the way to Augusta as Mom smoked and drove, and we listened to a stream of pop songs on the radio and she didn't cry. Andy was already there, and had reserved a room for us at a hotel, since after seeing Dad we'd need to spend the night.

Liz asked about the hotel. We'd gone on vacations a couple of times and had spent nights in hotels. She liked them, with all these grown-ups doing things for her, like carrying the luggage or bringing in breakfast in the morning.

"It's a nice hotel," Mom said. "President Eisenhower used to stay there when he played golf in Augusta. Do you remember President Eisenhower, Liz?"

"Ike?"

"Good girl. We'll only spend one night. Then we need to go back home. You guys have school, and—"

She stopped speaking.

"And what, Mom?" Liz asked.

"We can't see Dad a lot," I said. "He's sick, and tires out easily."

Liz's small face clouded up.

"How sick?"

The three of us were all in the front seat. I turned and held my sister's hand.

"He's very sick, Liz. We're going to see him to cheer him up. But you can't spend a lot of time with him or make him tired. Those are the rules."

She started crying now and I felt terrible. Then we saw some cows outside, and I pointed them out to her. She stopped crying and watched the cows go by, and then some pigs and chickens and a farm. There were billboards and some of them were almost funny, like "SEE ROCK CITY," and I read them out to her, then we made up a game to see if she could read them before they disappeared. Mom started singing "Old McDonald," and that helped. Finally, Liz fell asleep and we were in Augusta.

Andy met us in the hotel lobby and we went up to the room, then he drove us to the hospital. It was exceptionally dreary, that's the only word for it, but busy; there were lots of Army guys there and some Air Force and Navy people. The receptionist gave us a hard time about Liz, because she was underage for visiting, until Andy stepped in and said something to her that Liz and I couldn't hear. After that, the three of us were allowed up. We waited outside the room while Mom went in to see Robby, then she came out and brought Liz into the room for a couple of minutes. When they came back out, Liz was smiling, as if Daddy had joked with her.

"He'd like to see you," Mom said to me.

He was in a double room with a white curtain between Robby and the other bed. For a second, he looked like he was asleep. He opened his eyes and looked at me, smiling.

"Hi, Dad."

He held out his hand and I took it. It was all bone and veins, so was his arm. Even his face looked like that, but his eyes—his beautiful dark blue eyes—still looked alive, like the father I knew. I looked into them and became lost in them; it was like I had gone back into a time when none of this had happened. Then I saw the rest of his face—his nose, his sunken cheeks. He had lost a lot of his hair and what was left was now white. His eyes closed and his face tensed with pain. His hand squeezed mine tightly.

"Can you call the nurse in?" he asked. I turned from him, but he still had my hand in his. "No, wait a second," he said. "Just wait."

The pain must have gone away, because he smiled again. He released my hand and told me to sit down, and I did in the only chair I could see. It was pulled up close to him; maybe Mom had sat in it earlier. He looked down at me, calmly, from his bed.

"I just want to look at you," he said. "How's school?"

"It's OK. I'm so glad you sent me to Holy Nativity."

"I thought it would make a man out of you, Benjy. Or an adult. That's about the same thing most of the time. Are they treatin' you OK?"

"Yeah, they are."

"But you're still a Jew, like I am, aren't you?"

I nodded. It was true. I was a Jew, just like he was, no matter what.

"Your Mom's the most wonderful woman in the world, but there are things she never understood about me and I know it's the other way around, too. I guess that's the way it always is with men and women, but with us it was—well, more so. The important thing is that she brought you to me. You're like her—a lot, and like me."

I nodded again. Suddenly I couldn't think of another word to say. I got up and held his hand again. I didn't want to cry. That look of pain shot through him again.

"I should get the nurse," I said. But he grasped my hand.

"Wait a second. Just wait. They asked me if I wanted t' have a chaplain visit, and I told 'em I wanted a rabbi. They said there was one; he's supposed to come by later today. Remember that prayer I taught you when you were small?"

"Yes."

"I want to say it with you. Will you?"

"OK."

He began the *Shema* prayer, and we said it together:

>"Hear O Israel, the Lord is Our God
>
>The Lord is One."

I stopped saying anything, but Robby continued and finished by saying, "The Lord has brought you to me, and that's the only thing that's important."

I was crying. I couldn't stop the tears. I bowed my head and Robby sat up closer to me in his bed.

"It's true, Benjy. It's the only thing."

There were tissues near him; I blew my nose. Now I was scared. I wanted to say something but had no idea what.

"It's OK," he said, like he was reading my mind. "The only thing I regret in this life is that I won't get to see you grow up. Believe me, that's all."

I nodded and looked at him; it was like everything else had disappeared except his eyes and his face. I didn't feel frightened anymore. I leaned over and he kissed me on my cheek. He had no smell except hospital disinfectant. It was like he had already given up his body, he was so thin. Then that pained look came back on him.

"I'll go get the nurse," I said, and he let me go.

Mom was outside with Liz; I told her that we needed to get the nurse, and she left me with Liz. We sat in a row of chairs in the hall.

"Is he gonna die?" Liz asked.

"I don't know," I said. "Dad's very sick."

She looked at me very gravely and seriously, and nodded, like she now understood everything: Maybe even things that I didn't understand. There was no telling with kids.

Mom came back with the nurse who walked past us to Dad's room.

"She's going to give Dad something to go to sleep. I think we'll have to leave."

"Will I get to see him again?" Liz asked.

"I don't think so," Mom answered.

"I wanna see him. Please. Can't I?"

"He needs to sleep," I said trying to be mature. I wanted to see him too. But I had a feeling that that would not happen.

Mom lit a cigarette. There were no ashtrays, and smoking was not allowed, but she did it anyway.

"I'll ask the nurse when she gets back," Mom said.

An orderly, a young red-headed guy in white, came up to her and reminded her about the cigarette. He told her there was a place to smoke down at the end of the hall. He brought her a small metal bowl to put her cigarette out in. She thanked him.

"It's OK, ma'am. Lotta wives need t' smoke up on this floor. I know wha'cha goin' through. These your kids?" Mom nodded. "They're fine-looking kids. Your dad's a nice man. We all like him up here. They're bringin' a rabbi in to see him later. He wanted one, I hear."

"That's good," Mom said, her voice so strained it was hard to recognize.

The nurse came out, and Mom asked if we could go back in. She said it was OK, that Mr. Rothberg was sleeping. We stood at the door of the room and just looked at him for a moment, then left.

Andy was downstairs in the lobby waiting for us. He was smoking a cigar.

"How is he?" he asked.

"Sleeping," Mom answered.

"He sleeps a lot. It's better that way. I'm glad you and the kids could come and see him. It's a mitzvah, really." He looked at me. "It's one of the great mitzvahs, Benjy. You know what that means? It's one of the great responsibilities of you being a human and a man."

"Don't I count?" Mom said, half-jokingly.

"Of course you count. It's a mitzvah for you, too. But now that Benjy's been bar mitzvahed it's important for him to know. That meant the whole difference to your dad, that you got bar mitzvahed and he could attend it. I want you to know that."

I thought about Arthur Gomez. Where was his mitzvah? I wondered.

"Can I get you guys some supper?" Andy asked. "There's a good steak house in town. They have hamburgers for the kids."

"Sure," Mom answered. But I could tell she wasn't hungry, and all she wanted was a drink and a cigarette.

The steak house was called Cobb's, named for a Confederate general. It had pictures of golfers, baseball players, and President Eisenhower and Vice President Nixon on the walls. There was also a picture of John Kennedy, playing golf, and of Lyndon Johnson. The L.B.J. picture did not show him playing golf.

"I don't know if he ever set foot in Augusta," Andy said. "But I guess they gotta have his *ponem* in here too."

"What does that mean?" Liz asked.

"His face. Johnson has one of those faces that can't do anything but tell the truth 'cause it's too ugly to lie with."

Mom laughed really hard. I think she really needed to. The restaurant was noisy and smoky; we were seated in a back table, away from a lot of the noise. The host was a white man, but the waiters were all Negro men who acted extremely courteously.

"Mr. Andy," our waiter said. "You here with yo family?"

"Yeah," Andy said beaming. "They *are* my family."

Andy dug into large steak that came with a baked potato and a salad loaded with garlic dressing. He had two scotches. Mom drank a Tom Collins, and picked at her salad. Liz had hardly any of her burger and I had about half of mine, along with some french fries with it. I watched Mom try to pretend that we were at a normal gathering with a friend. All of her ambiguity towards Andy came out; he was now running the show and she hated it. Andy paid the bill, and drove us back to the hotel.

We were all in one room, with Liz in a small cot that the hotel had brought up for her. Mom was in a large bed, and I was in a smaller one. Everything felt very forced and artificial; those were the only words I could use for it. I went into the bathroom and brushed my teeth, then got into bed. All I wanted to do was sleep, to get away from everything. But when I closed my eyes, all I saw was Dad's face.

After I did manage to sleep, I woke up some time later—I had no idea when— but I heard something that sounded like leaking water. I turned towards the big bed and it was Mom crying. I got out of bed in my underwear and went over to her. She looked at me, and sat up in bed.

"Oh, Benjy. What am I going t' do? This is not fair to you. You should be having a regular boyhood now. Like other boys have."

I sat down on the bed and took her hand.

"We'll get through this," I said. "I've got to be a *mentsh* now. I know Dad would want it."

"I love you," she said. "I'm glad Liz is asleep. I'm going to take a sleeping pill. It's the only way I'll get to sleep. Tomorrow I've got to go back to the hospital with Andy. There are things we've got to go over; I want you to stay here with Liz."

"Does that mean I won't get to see him again?"

"Probably. It's a lot of strain on him to see all of us. He's in a lot of pain, and the only way they can do anything about it is just to knock him out. You can understand that."

I went back to my bed, and listened to Mom's breathing until I was sure she was asleep. I thought about what Nathan Streitt might say to me about telling the truth—Mom was telling me the truth—and then about my grandparents the Blakelys, until my head felt too heavy to stay awake.

We had breakfast the next morning in the hotel's dining room, then Mom went off with Andy and I was left with Liz. We played games and watched soap operas in the room. Then Andy checked us out of the hotel and we drove back to Isle of Hope. The trip was so somber, I hardly remember it. I felt that everything was like a movie and I was merely watching it, watching everything along the road pass by.

The next two weeks or so went by in the strangest kind of suspended motion. Mom drove back to Augusta several times while Betty Blakely stayed with us. I got the feeling that Andy Geyer was always there with Dad; he was devoting his life now to Robby, or Leon. He would call Mom and sometimes speak to me, putting on his gruff exterior. I would pretend that we were just two guys talking to each other, and mentioning a third guy, my father. That was the only way to get through it.

At the beginning of the second week of December, while the whole school was getting ready for its Christmas pageant and celebration, Mom talked with me in the den. She told me that Dad was presently in a coma.

"There's nothing I can do for him now," she said. "Nothing. He doesn't even know I'm there, or even if Andy's there. Sometimes I think we appear to him like we're in dreams, that's all."

"You're not going to see him?" I asked.

"I don't think I can. I'm just so worn out."

I decided I wanted to appear in the Christmas pageant as one of the shepherds. I mean, they were Jews anyway, right? There were several directors and organizers of it (it had to be a major event at a school called Holy Nativity), and Brother Alexis was one of them. I was happy to have that time with him. I had told him everything that was going on about Robby—about the trip to Augusta; that time was running out; everything that I could. We were after school in the midst of the second rehearsal. It had begun as a cold, miserable, rainy day, when he took me aside.

"I need to see you in my office," he said and led me there by the hand. I felt like every kid in the world was watching us, even though they weren't.

He shut the door to his small office and sat down at his desk, putting his hands on his face for a second.

"Your father died about two hours ago," he said softly. "Your mom called and asked me to tell you. She said it would be better if I told you. I'm so sorry, Benjy."

He got up and hugged me. He felt so huge next to me. Maybe I just wanted him to feel that way. It took a moment for everything to sink in. He asked me if I wanted a lift home, and said that he would drive me himself.

"Your mom can't come. She's too upset; I understand. I'm glad I can help you. I think this was why I joined the religious life—that and God. I wanted to serve God. I'm really sorry, Benjy."

For a moment, Brother Alexis started crying too. I could hardly believe it; then it was over. He went back to the auditorium and told Brother David, the pageant's music director, that he was taking me home.

We left by a side door, away from the other boys, and found a school car in the parking lot. I'd never been in a monk's car before, although I think that they all got to use this one. I noticed that the back seat was filled with pamphlets and stuff about Holy Nativity; maybe it was dropped off at churches and other places. I sat in the front seat with Brother Alexis who was now in his black suit. I thought about Dad and the last time I saw him. I was glad that we had our talk, and had gotten to pray. I told him about praying the *Shema* with Dad.

"I'm glad you could do that, Benjy," he said.

"He told me that God had brought me to him."

"He did," Brother Alexis agreed. "Your father and I both believe that. I believe God also brought you to me, Benjy. One day maybe we'll both understand that."

Suddenly I felt really close to Brother Alexis; it was a good feeling and I wanted to keep it all the way back to Isle of Hope. I don't remember if I said anything else or if he did. He was steering with his left hand and I took his right hand and held it; he pressed my fingers into his. I looked out the window while the scenery of everyday Savannah skipped by and the sky appeared to be delicately clearing as evening fell. As we approached the marshlands, it became more of a Southern fall/winter along the Georgia coast, with the coolish light gently lowering against palm trees and oaks thick with Spanish moss and dense hedges of camellias surprisingly still in bloom, their bottoms wrapped in burlap against the cold. I loved the scarlet and pink ones and crisp, veiny white camellias in all their variations of petals. By the time we got back to the house, it was dark out.

Mom came out to greet us. She looked haunted, like there was someplace else where her real face, which was so pretty, had gone. She was wearing a dark skirt, a white blouse and a sweater. Most of the time my mom liked to wear pants, but not now.

"I'm so sorry," Brother Alexis said, extending his hand to her.

"Thank you for bringing him home," she said hoarsely. "I just couldn't drive in right now. My parents are here and I didn't want them to leave me."

Grandma and Grandpa came out; Grandpa put his arm around me.

"It's gonna be all right," he said to me. "Just you watch. Everything will be all right."

Mom invited Brother Alexis in. He spoke to her privately in the den for a few minutes, while my grandparents took me and Liz into the dining room, then he came to say good-bye to me. I walked him to the door.

"If you don't want to be in the Christmas pageant, we'll certainly understand," he said."

"No, I want to be in it," I said. "I need to."

"Good," he said, and hugged me, then left.

Betty Blakely had prepared a supper for Liz and me. I was hungry and ate a hot dog and a little of the potato salad. Liz just played with her food. Suddenly she started crying.

"You mean he's not *ever* gonna come back?" she asked Grandma.

"He's with God," Grandpa said. "God will take care of him now."

I got up and went in to see Mom who was still in the den. I asked what Brother Alexis had said to her.

"He said he would do anything necessary for the funeral. That was really nice of him. I don't know anything about doing this. Andy said he'll take care of the arrangements. It's going to happen in a couple of days, because you know, Jews don't do a viewing."

"A viewing?" I asked blankly, not quite comprehending the idea of it.

"You know, it's when they show the body at a funeral home, or even at home like they used to do."

Suddenly I remembered what Tim had said about his own grandpa.

"God, that sounds so gross," I said.

"It does because you're young," Mom said. "But sometimes you're just not ready to give somebody up and bury him. When you get older you'll understand, but you've understood so much already, haven't you?"

26

The Funeral

The funeral was in three days, and Andy did do everything. It was at Whipple's, a funeral home where I learned that all the Jews in Savannah had their services. This time the synagogue and the rabbi didn't give anyone a hard time and because of my bar mitzvah lessons I could pretty much follow the service. There was a notice in the Savannah paper, so some of my friends from Holy Nativity came, including Mr. and Mrs. O'Neill and the twins Pat and Neal and Tim; also Father Greer came with a small group of teachers, and of course Brother Alexis. Allen Streitt and his parents came, and so did Faye Jacobson with her parents; but Nathan Streitt did not.

The rabbi gave a very flowery speech saying that Leon Rothberg, like all humans, had his faults but that God takes our faults and uses them to achieve His own will and perfection. He could have said that about anyone. Then he talked about "the children," meaning myself and Liz, and how we meant everything to Leon and were his hope for the future. After that, everyone who could said *Kaddish*, the prayer for the dead, and then we drove to Bonaventure Cemetery, the large cemetery filled with big oak trees, where it turned out my father had bought a large family plot years ago in the Jewish section.

Andy stood next to me while Dad's simple wooden casket was lifted out of the hearse by six men from the synagogue's burial society. I was trembling, really scared; it was as if my whole future were dying too. At fourteen, I felt that Robby was as much a part of my future as the rabbi had said I was his. He was at the center of my own path into adulthood, genuine, recognizable adulthood, and now he was gone. But also, undeniably, there was Death itself, standing within the shadowy groves of the cemetery, waiting to obliterate me, too, with its darkness. I understood that my father's death could not help but portend my own mortality.

The casket was lowered into the ground, then the men took turns shoveling a ritual portion of dirt over it. The rabbi approached me.

"Would you like to do that, as a favor to your father?" he asked.

"If you don't want to, you don't have to," Andy said.

"No," I said, my voice shaking. "I will."

I went over to the men, and was handed a shovel. I scooped up some earth and looked down into the hole at the cover of Dad's casket with its large, raised blue wooden Jewish star. I tossed some of the dirt on top of it, and then put the shovel aside—and suddenly felt sick. It was just too much to feel at one time. I tried to hold myself together and stand up straight. Suddenly I thought … what if dying were only like slipping into an embracing sleep? I saw Robby's tired face, with his blue eyes closing. What was there then, to fear in it?

Andy approached and hugged me, crying terribly. I'd seen him cry once before, when we'd fought about having my bar mitzvah at Holy Nativity, but never like this.

"You don't know how much I loved him!" he sobbed. "He was such a *mentsh.*"

Mom walked over to us, with Liz and the Blakelys. We got back into the Blakelys' car and returned to our house, where Betty Blakely had arranged a reception for everyone at the funeral. Rabbi Silverman was there. He spoke a lot to Andy, then came over to me and shook my hand.

"You're quite a young man," he said. "I wish you'd come to synagogue more. You need to say *Kaddish* for your father. The mourning period goes on for three months, and you need to come in and say it."

Andy had been drinking a scotch, and overheard. "I'll make sure that he comes in," he said. "You can bet on it."

The rabbi shook everyone's hand except my mom's. He made almost no effort to speak to her except for a few words at the cemetery. Then he left.

"That sonovabitch," Andy said to me, aside. "Just 'cause Caroline's not Jewish, and a woman, you'd think he had a license to act like a *mumser*. Your dad was worth six rabbis, remember that."

I nodded and went off to speak with the Streitts, Faye, some friends from school, and finally Brother Alexis, who was talking with a group of other brothers from Holy Nativity.

"We were saying this is certainly different from a Catholic funeral," he said.

"Jews are more austere."

"Yes," Father Greer said, nursing a scotch. "They save everything for the weddings, I guess. Since some of us don't have weddings, the Catholics have to spread it around to funerals."

I smiled. It was good of them to joke. I needed to smile, even to laugh. Tim, Neal, and Pat came up to me. Tim was very upset.

"Losing your dad," he said. "I can't even talk about it."

"We're really sorry," Pat said.

"We are," Neal added. "We feel like you're a part of our family. We love you, Benjy."

He hugged me; it meant a lot to me. Then Brother Alexis asked to speak with me before he left with the other monks.

"I've asked permission to counsel you," he told me. "I hope that's all right. I think you'll need it for a while. We'll set up a time once a week for you to come in and talk with me. How does that sound to you?"

I told him that it sounded fine, and I held his hand for a moment when we shook hands.

I didn't go to the synagogue to say *Kaddish* for my father. I just couldn't face it. I felt like a stranger there and I just didn't want to feel that way. Brother Alexis said that was fine and I could say *Kaddish* in front of him. The prayer actually doesn't mention the dead; it merely praises God's name and what He does and how He's the head of everything. We said it together.

> *Yis'gadal, v'yis kadash shmei raba.*
> May his Great Name grow exalted and sanctified.
> *Y'hei sh'mei raba m'varakh l'alam ul'al'mei al'maya*
> May His Great Name be sanctified for ever and ever.
> *Y'hei sh'lama raba min sh'maya*
> May there be abundant peace from Heaven
> *v'chayim aleinu v'al kol yis'ra'eil v'im'ru*
> and life upon us and upon all Israel. Now say:
> "Amen."

I actually enjoyed saying it; I found it comforting, especially saying it with Brother Alexis. The first time I did, I cried a lot and he waited until I stopped, putting his hand on my shoulder until I felt better. We talked a lot and he told me more about growing up in Canada as one of six kids and how it was just expected that he'd enter religious life.

"I liked it," he said. "There was this huge sense of belonging to something. I guess you can understand that, most people do."

I did; I felt that way at Holy Nativity, even not being Catholic.

"And," he continued, "I wanted to offer something to God. It's hard to put that into words. But at the beginning it was very exciting."

"Is it now?" I asked.

"I don't know; sometimes I feel like I'm just playing a role," he said. "But there are real parts to it. Maybe I shouldn't be saying that to you."

"That you're playing a role? That's OK. I know what that's like. I did it at the school I was in at Isle of Hope, before I came to Holy Nativity. I was trying to be like everybody else. Here it's not so difficult because there are so many guys who—"

I wasn't sure what to say.

"Yes, it's not hard here," Brother Alexis said. "We try to let students be themselves. But their good selves, Benjy. Just remember that."

At the end of our first counseling sessions Brother Alexis would shake my hand or put his hand on my shoulder, never hugging me. He would look into my eyes for a moment and I felt better. But somehow it only made me realize how very deeply I missed Robby—it was difficult to say how much because I was barely aware of who Robby was, and exactly how much he had meant to me. Maybe I was still too young for that, but Brother Alexis, sadly enough, was not going to take his place.

27

The Christmas Pageant

I did take part in the Christmas pageant. I needed to—I needed to have a definite feeling that I belonged at the school; it was one of those things that still connected me to the world, now that some of my own world had fallen apart. We had one final rehearsal with the girls from St. Agnes's. They arrived in their short skirts and sweaters and every guy made a big deal out of it, whistling and joking. Even if you didn't exactly feel that way, you were supposed to put up a show—but not in front of any of the Sebastianites, who got mean if they saw it. I met a very pretty, sweet-faced girl named Laura Murphy who was playing Mary the Virgin. She had pale skin with almost no freckles, a lovely soft pinkness in her cheeks, nice breasts, a tiny waist, and she cursed something terrible when no one was looking.

"So you're the Jewish kid?" she asked, her eyes flashing at me.

"Yeah, half-Jewish."

"You're damn cute to me!"

She smiled at me. Her smile had a lot of voltage.

"Thanks," I said, blushing.

"How d' Jews make out?"

We were walking into the auditorium, and I realized that anyone could hear us.

"Not like porcupines," I said softly.

"That's good."

She smiled again. She pretended to whisper something in my ear, but instead stuck her tongue into it. A direct signal of tingly nerves shot through me. No girl had ever done anything like that before! I was in my uniform, and I'd heard that Catholic girls went crazy over boys in military school uniforms: it just did something *hormonal* to them.

At the end of the rehearsal, Laura asked me for my phone number before joining the other girls on the bus back to St. Aggie's (as it was called). I gave it to her; Tim was later beside himself.

"She really asked *you* for your number? Man, you're so lucky!"

I just grinned. "Maybe it's because I'm a Jew and seem different to her."

"You're different alright! I can tell her that."

Tim punched me lightly on the shoulder. I had no idea what I'd do if she called. I felt as if I was really going with Faye Jacobson; that is, as much as I was going with *any* girl.

The pageant was held at the end of the week, on a Sunday evening. Mom came with Liz and our grandparents the Blakelys. The auditorium was packed; I was extremely apprehensive, even more nervous than I'd been at my bar mitzvah—close to peeing-in-my-pants on edge. I had no idea why, except maybe it had something to do with leftover feelings from my father's funeral—all of those emotions were still there—or maybe it was just a form of *hysteria*, something I couldn't even control. I'd heard that girls got *hysteria*, and I can't tell you how bad I felt about it, but I did.

The pageant began with all the boys marching in in uniform, class by class, while the Holy Smokes choir sang rousing Christmas music like "Silver Bells" and "Jingle Bells," joined by some St. Aggie's girls with even higher voices. Then Father Greer gave a benediction, followed by the other brothers and some of the older boys reading prayers.

While that was going on, I was backstage putting on my costume. There were boys all over the place, nervously supervised by Brother Simon, who taught French III and did theater stuff. Laura Murphy came over to me in her blue B.V.M. outfit, looking intensely wonderful, like she was *born* to play the Blessed Virgin Mary, despite the fact that Mary was Jewish and Laura definitely was not. Laura looked more like a statue of the Virgin or a very nice painting of her, not some homely Jewish girl who'd simply might have been Jesus's *actual* mother.

"You're the only person here who looks like the real thing," she said with a wink. "Wanna make out?"

I blinked. "*Whaa?*"

"We got 'bout three minutes 'fore this fuckin' thing starts. There's a closet next to the dressing room. Come on!"

A second later we were in the closet with the door shut and she was kissing me like I'd never been kissed before by anyone, male or female. Suddenly she stopped short and pulled some gum out her mouth.

"Sorry," she whispered.

"Z'OK," I said.

We had three minutes, which did not *exactly* do a lot towards calming me down. Was I supposed to do something with her costume on? There was a knock on the door.

"Shit," she whispered.

The knock got louder. I opened the door. There was Brother Simon, his eyes ablaze.

"Get out!" he ordered. "And never do anything like that again! I want both o' you on the stage *immediately*!"

Brother Simon had a distinctive voice, like an English actor trying to approximate a Southern accent or the other way around. Mom had heard him once and had described it as High Priest Pansy. She told me to watch out for dark corners and broom closets with Brother Simon—and now I had been in one, with Mary the Blessed Virgin. I couldn't help but smile.

We got on stage just as the pageant started. There was almost no dialogue; we were simply supposed to move around at certain times as the choir sang songs and the boys read from the Gospel about the birth of Christ. There was a manger with a baby doll wrapped in swaddling clothes, actually it looked like a small mummy. Towards the end, Laura was supposed to pick the thing up and show it to the shepherds and to this tall dorky boy named Andrew Ryan who was playing Joseph, to the Three Kings, and to some smaller boys who were just there for show. The smaller boys had extra make-up on to make them appear more Mediterranean, not quite so Irish or Anglo-American. The Three Kings were all lost in their big beards, and Andrew Ryan had red hair that was covered over by a hood. I, as Laura said, did not need extra make up. She on the other hand looked exactly as the Virgin Mary looked in pictures: pale, blushing, and extra-glowing. Some of that was caused by rouge and lipstick and I realized after touching my face that I actually had some of it on me from our moment in the closet. I could only imagine what Tim would have said, and I was glad that he was too old now to be on the stage as one of the small kids, a role he had played for years.

The showing of the doll Jesus was followed by a tableau of the Kings giving presents, with Laura smiling, nodding, and acting *very* modest, like . . . well, a virgin. Nevertheless, I noticed that she kept catching my eyes and smiling into them, like we had this intense secret, although to be frank I wasn't sure what it was. I still felt that I wanted to be involved with Faye Jacobson, and Laura was definitely not Faye.

The last person to speak was Father Greer, who gave a benediction, that we had dedicated this whole thing to the infant Jesus and his beloved Mother, and to the Saints and God the Father. Then, exactly as we had rehearsed it, the choir exploded into "Come All Ye Faithful."

It seemed louder than anything I'd heard before. Maybe it was just the way it hit my ears, with Brother Peter hammering away at the notes on an old upright Steinway, but for a moment I felt that it had taken over my brain. We had been coached by Brother Simon on how to proceed next. First the small boys would leave; then the Holy Family, with Mary holding the Christ doll; then the Three Kings; then the shepherds. We would depart the stage through the stairs down into the audience, walk up the center aisle, and process out as the choir, led full-force by Brother David, sang every verse of the song with Brother Peter's ever-louder piano rising to the occasion. I watched all this happen, until only we four shepherds were left on the stage—then suddenly I spaced out, unsure of what to do.

Melvin Harris, my clunky squad leader and one of the other shepherds, almost tripped over me, knocking me right out of my trance with his elbows.

"Rothberg," he whispered emphatically. "We haven't got all day!"

I started across the stage to the stairs, then it happened. I'd been so nervous—I started crying—because I realized for the first time, in my deepest heart, that my father was *really* dead. He wasn't ever coming back. The finality of this stopped everything; I could barely move. Harris was now walking behind me, nudging me down the short stretch of stairs with his clenched hands, but I felt like I was made of wood. I don't know how long the feeling lasted—maybe only a minute, maybe even less—but it seemed that I was no longer at Holy Nativity at the end of the Christmas pageant. I was deep within something else, something unnamably profound.

And past the stairs and up the aisle, all I could hear were the same words repeating themselves over and over again in my ears:

Come and behold Him,
Born *the King of Angels*

O come, let us adore Him,
O come, let us adore Him

O come, let us adore Him

Christ, the Lord.

The words felt as if they were drifting in from very far away; I was not even close to them because inside I was so extremely silent. I felt like I was floating, just hovering on some cloud of energy that was not my own. I had stopped crying, then I saw Brother Alexis sitting in the audience, looking at me and smiling, but I felt that he was there now in that very same space with me, along with Dad, and, at the end of the slightly raised aisle, surrounded by pure light, waiting for me, was *Arthur*.

I could see his face, but only for a second.

Born *the King of Angels*—

King of . . . *Angels*—

Then it was over. The singing. The pageant. We were supposed to stay at the entrance of the auditorium for a moment as the people—mostly parents, families, and friends of kids—streamed out.

"The idea is to make the birth of the Christ child real," Brother Simon had told us. "So stay in character, kids. Then I want you to return backstage through the rear entrance. Just show yourselves, then disappear."

Laura smirked at me as the parents started flocking in. I saw Mom, Liz, and the Blakelys, then followed the pageant cast back through the rear entrance to the backstage area.

Harris approached me. "What happened to you? Did you fall asleep?"

Tim had snuck in and was now standing next to me. "Too much excitement," Tim explained, grinning.

Harris only threw up his arms and disappeared.

"You musta gotten something offa Laura Murphy, you lucky sonovabitch," Tim said. "Everybody knows she makes out faster than a dog in heat. Lemme tell ya though, she ain't no dog."

I shrugged and Tim dashed out to join his parents.

I quickly changed back into my uniform. As if by magic Laura Murphy appeared, looking younger in her St. Agnes's uniform than she had as the Virgin Mary, maybe because she had on less make up, just a bit of lipstick.

"Lemme introduce you to my boyfriend," she said. There he was, this gangly kid in a tie and sports jacket who looked about fifteen.

"I'm Weeks," he said. "Dan Weeks."

I shook his hand and told him my name.

"You looked great up there," he said. "Like a real shepherd."

"He did, didn't he?" Laura asked, then she was all over Dan, almost but not quite as much as she'd been all over me. A second later, her parents approached us, and she dropped Dan's arm and started acting like a Catholic school girl *should*, or at least would want her parents to think she acted.

I got out and joined my family who were still at the front of the auditorium. Mom looked happy or like she was trying hard to be. She had been drinking more and staying up late. She'd also been taking pills that her doctor had prescribed for her. Liz seemed to be the happiest. It was like she had this little switch that she could turn on and become happy again. We went out to dinner at Johnny Tate's, a steakhouse Grandpa Blakely liked that was all done up for Christmas. He had two scotches and a steak. Mom had several mixed drinks, including a Rusty Nail and a Salty Dog. Who could forget names like that? When I got old enough to *really* drink, I decided I wanted to drink Rusty Nails.

Mom ordered a steak sandwich and only ate half of it. I could tell that Betty Blakely was concerned about her. Now I felt bad about being in the pageant, like it was too early for Caroline to be out in something like that. She was still in this fog of grief, the one I was trying hard to come out of. That had to explain why I had walked up the aisle of the auditorium feeling like a piece of wood, and had that vision—had that been simply grief, too?

The good thing about the Blakelys was that they could always find things to talk about, especially Grandpa who loved *regurgitating* politics. (That was Mom's term for it. "Your grandpa's regurgitating politics," she'd said during various points at past meals. Grandma would give her a determined stare, and say, "Caroline, must you use that kind of language at the table?" Betty firmly believed in old-school manners at the table. Once I'd heard her say to an old lady friend: "If I can't have decorum at my table, I don't want to set one!" Mom was not like that, especially after she'd had a couple of drinks.)

"Your dad would have been really proud of you," she told me while she played with her sandwich. "But I'm not sure about the shepherd thing. He didn't believe in any of that, you know."

"He believed in human goodness," Betty said, primly. "And that's what Jesus is about, isn't He?"

"The hell if I know," Mom said. "If He was so damn good, how come He took Robby from me, and stuck him in that goddamn jail for something he didn't do, and made him sick as hell?"

"That's enough, Caroline," Betty said firmly. "Not in front of the children. Please, think about what you're doing to them."

William Blakely pushed himself away from the table.

"I need to use the bathroom," he said and got up.

"Look what you've done to your father," Betty said with a kind of sweetness that always had a knife in it. "You've upset him."

Mom looked at her drink. Liz and I pretended that nothing had happened.

I excused myself and went to the men's room, too. Past the swinging door, there was a little lounge area where men could smoke. I saw Grandpa there, but he wasn't smoking. He saw me and pulled me to him.

"You just learned a great lesson about women," he said. "They *can* attack each other when the chips are down. Your mom's been through a lot. I wish my dear wife didn't act the way she did." He smiled at me. "Why don't you go in the gent's and do what you need t' do and then we'll go back together?"

When we returned to the table, Mom and Betty seemed to be on better terms and Liz was smiling again. She was a little girl who knew how to keep herself happy; I envied that.

That night, before going to sleep, I thought about "Come All Ye faithful" and *King of Angels* and seeing Arthur and Dad. It was all telling me something;

that maybe I needed to know more about Jesus. At my next counseling session with Brother Alexis, just before Christmas break, I asked him what Jesus meant to him.

"I'm glad you asked me that, Benjy," he answered. "Jesus, please understand, is *useful*. He means huge numbers of things to huge numbers of people. But to me, as a Catholic, He is the total miracle of existence. He is what is *behind* existence; I believe that with all my heart. He is human consciousness brought to its highest form."

"What about the other forms?" I asked. "I mean, forms without Jesus? My father didn't believe in Jesus."

"Well, Benjy, Catholics will say other things, but—and this is strictly between us—I don't know about it."

I smiled; it was wonderful hearing that Brother Alexis, who did know so much, did *not* know some things. I told him about my vision at the pageant, and asked him if he thought Arthur and Robby were really there.

"That was beautiful, Benjy. What's important is that they were really there for you."

"Do you think they joined Jesus, the King of Angels?"

Brother Alexis closed his eyes. A wave of concentration, of tension, ran across his face. Finally, after a minute he looked at me. "Yes, Benjy. They've joined the King of Angels. They are part of Him."

"Thank you," I whispered.

I knew I shouldn't do it, but I got up and touched his shoulder. He took my hand and held it.

"I should thank you, Benjy. You're helping me make a decision."

"About what?" I asked cautiously.

"My life." He released my hand. "You should go now. Our session's over, Benjy. I'll see you again in three weeks, after Christmas break."

"Three weeks?" That seemed like such a long, long time. I wondered why he wanted to skip a week, even after the break. But he only nodded at me, and I walked out.

As Caroline drove me home, I wondered about the strange end of our session and the skipped week. It seemed like a long time to wait—it had been Brother Alexis's suggestion that we meet every week. Had my touching him been *seductive*? Maybe any kind of touching was just not right for a monk—not *kosher* as Robby would have said. I could hear him telling me: "Benjy, the guy's truly sacred. You have to treat him like he's a real *mentsh*."

I smiled suddenly; Caroline noticed it. "Something's making you happy," she said. "What is it?"

"Dad and Arthur are with Jesus," I said.

"If only," she sighed, exhaling some smoke from her cigarette.

"You don't believe it?" I asked.

"Whatever floats your boat, Benjy. I'm having a hard time floating mine, but I guess you must know that. Now it seems we're up Crap's Creek with money. I'm just hoping we can stay in the house. Grandpa and Grandma are scraping cash together for it. See, the house now belongs to Andy."

"You're joking?" I said.

"'Fraid not. When your dad was really sick and realized he was going to die, he transferred the title to him, and made me do it, too. He thought, that way, when people started coming out of the woodwork with your dad's debts, they couldn't demand the house, because it wouldn't belong to us anymore. Andy agreed. Nice Christmas present, isn't it?"

"So what will Andy do?"

"He's promised to do nothing, as long as we can keep up with the payments. I'm thinking about getting a job, but I don't have a single skill in the world. I was only bred to be a wife."

"Will I have to leave Holy Nativity?" I asked. Caroline told me I was paid up till the end of the year but not any further, and a scholarship was pretty much out of the question. Too many deserving Catholic boys were waiting for one. "I could get a paper route," I suggested once again.

"Sure, that would pay for about two weeks at school," Caroline said sadly. "I don't want you to do that. I want you to study hard, keep making friends, and have a good life. That's what Robby would have wanted."

"Is there anything else we can do?"

"I could remarry, but let's don't get into that. Your dad had a little bit of insurance, but not much. And since he was a wounded veteran of the Korean War, I've applied for some veteran's widow's benefits, but that's pretty small. I'm thinking about going back to school to get a real estate license or at least learning to work in an office. I just hope I can fake it until I do it."

As we approached the driveway, I asked her what she meant by "faking it."

She didn't answer for a moment, but parked the car. Shaking at the wheel, she started crying and reached into her purse for a tissue.

"I've been seeing a psychiatrist while you're at school—this has been horrible for me, Benjy. Not easy for you, but just hell for me. I feel like I'm cracking in two, and I don't know how to put myself back together." Her mascara was running. "I must look a mess," she said. "I don't want Liz or Josephine to see me like this." She dabbed her face with the tissue, which was now streaked with the mascara.

"You look fine," I said, wishing I could say something really smart to unlock some mystery of money or love or life.

But I couldn't. We stayed in the car until she collected herself, then went inside. Josephine was cooking dinner and it smelled wonderful, crab cakes with collard greens and rice. She had made biscuits that were wonderful. I grabbed one, piping hot from a plate in the kitchen, and put butter on it. The phone rang and I answered it with my mouth full of biscuit.

"Benjy?"

"Uh-huh."

"Hi, it's Nathan."

"Nathan? *Nathan*!"

"Yeah, man. Who else? I been away again—another boarding school this time. But it's Christmas break. Think you can get away this Saturday? I'll take you to dinner. I know a great place."

"Sure," I said. "I'll ask Mom."

He said: "You do that," and I put the phone down and found Caroline in the den having a drink. Suddenly I had a thought: maybe I shouldn't tell her *exactly* what was going on.

"It's Allan Streitt on the phone. He wants to know if I can go out with him and some of his friends this Saturday. Dinner. Is that OK?"

"How will you get there?"

"His brother will pick me up."

"Will there be adults there?"

"His whole family."

She looked up at me and smiled. "Sounds great. What time?"

I went back to the phone and asked Nathan, then went back to Caroline and told her seven o' clock.

28

A Date With Nathan

I was dressed up, in my tie and jacket with a wool scarf and a pair of nicely pressed chinos, when Nathan picked me up. I'd asked him not to come up to the house, and I was waiting at the end of the driveway, next to the road. It was dark out and cold and I was shivering a bit, but I didn't mind. There was something about this evening that seemed both very grown up and exciting to me, like we were two *big* guys having dinner out. I'd never had a *real* one-on-one date before and for a moment I wondered if you had a "date" with a guy, did it count as one? When I saw the lights on Nathan's car, I got so excited that I realized instantly that it was.

Nathan opened the passenger's side door for me. He was wearing a beautiful navy blue overcoat but no tie. He looked great, with his very dark hair and smooth skin. He smiled at me and I realized what great dimples he had.

"I'd glad you could come," he said and leaned over and kissed me. I didn't expect that. I felt shocked for a second. He looked at me as I sat down.

"Sorry," he said as he drove off. "Maybe I shouldn't have done that."

"Suppose somebody saw us from the road?"

He smiled at me, modestly. "Tell 'em I'm your cousin. Kissin' cousin."

"I'm not queer," I said.

"Yeah, I know. But you're very seductive, and you know that. And I told you how seductive people invite others to kiss them."

I had no idea what he was talking about. Then I remembered Laura Murphy at the Christmas pageant, so maybe Nathan had a point. Without thinking, I put my hand on his knee. It just seemed like a thing to do. He told me stuff about himself as he drove. The boarding school that the Streitts had sent him to was called the McClelland Academy for Young Men. It was like a military school, just not as much fun as Holy Nativity.

"You wear a tie and jacket and you get demerits for farting. I mean that literally; fart and they give you a demerit. My parents thought this would 'straighten me out,' but the truth is the school is pretty queer. Guys fool around all over the place. They just put on a big he-man show whenever they can. Or, I should say a *Hebe*-man show. A lot of the boys are Yids. Their families couldn't get them into big-time WASP prep schools, so they got them into this. It's in McClelland, Virginia, an area mainly known for tobacco. So the boys smoke like chimneys."

"But you don't smoke like a chimney?"

"Naw, hardly smoke—a vice I don't need. Would you like to sleep with me?"

"I'm fourteen. That doesn't bother you, Nathan?"

"I like younger men." He let out a big guffaw. "I'm just joking, Benjy. Like Mo said, you're jailbait. But it doesn't mean I wouldn't want to suck your dick every now and then. Who wouldn't?"

"God, who taught you to talk like that?"

"Some of my older friends. You'll meet one tonight. We're going to the Pink House. Ever been there?"

No, I said. But I'd seen it. It was a fancy restaurant in downtown, close to the old squares and the river, in an elegant two-story house, painted pink and surrounded by azaleas, with big stone columns outside. It went back to the days when slaves served the food. At least that's what I thought.

"The bar's very gay," he said. "But we won't be at the bar. My friend Myron Lewis is going to meet us. The meal's his treat."

"Why is that?"

He exhaled very impatiently.

"Don't ask, young man, why people want to buy you dinner. Just accept it."

The Pink House, as I expected, was very swank and glowing with Christmas decorations. It was not the kind of place that kids went to casually on a date, unless they were going to spend some real money. But I did notice a smattering of teens at some tables with adults I assumed were their parents. A very old lady with pink-colored hair met us at the door. She wore heels and a dark silk dress with small flowers printed on it and a huge white Christmassy corsage with little bells and stuff covering most of her very large chest.

"My, young men! Don't we look handsome t' night! Do ya'll have reservations?"

"We're guests of Mr. Lewis," Nathan said. "He's at the bar, I believe."

"Of course, he is! Let me bring you t' your table and I'll go 'n' get him!"

She brought us to a table that was towards the rear of the room. Soon a waiter came and presented Nathan with a glass of wine.

"Mr. Lewis wanted you to have this. I'll bring an iced tea for the other young man."

"Can I have a Coke?" I asked.

As I watched the waiter disappear, suddenly a new group of well-dressed people arrived in the room—and among them were Neal and Pat, with dates. I thought my eyes would pop out. This must have been a special evening for them to pony up for a place like this; I guessed it was part of their Christmas celebration. I didn't want them to see me, especially Neal. There was no telling what he'd say to Tim. But it was too late. Neal saw me and winked at me. I cautiously waved back.

"Who are they?" Nathan asked.

"Guys from school."

"Ah, Holy Nativity jocks. You've got good taste, kid."

At that moment, Myron Lewis appeared. He was a *lot* older: maybe twenty-eight or even thirty. He had a scrawny neck and thin shoulders and a little paunch above his belt. He smiled at me in a strange way when Nathan introduced us, like he was staring all the way through me. Mom called it "a carnivorous smile." She said, "Some people have it."

"Are you one of the Chosen People, too?" Myron asked after he sat down.

"He's only half a Hebe," Nathan said smiling.

"Nathan, that's not the nicest thing to say t' our young man," Myron was still displaying that electric eel smile. "So both of your parents are not Jewish, I assume?"

"My father was, not my mother."

"Was? Is he still alive, or did he convert?"

"No, he didn't convert," I said sadly. "He died a . . . short while ago."

"I'm so sorry," Myron said, turning off his smile. "I lost my father too. He died when I was eighteen."

"I'm sorry, too," I said.

"He killed himself," Nathan put in matter-of-factly.

"Prone to agonizing depression," Myron explained. "He couldn't come out of it. Let's talk about something else." His eyes zoomed through the room and landed on the O'Neill twins. "My, there are a lot of good-looking young men here tonight."

"Benjy knows them. They go to his school. Holy Nativity Military Academy."

"Military school boys! Can you invite them over, Benjy?"

I panicked. Nathan saw it on my face.

"No!" Nathan said firmly. "Benjy's friends are with dates—girl dates. You remember *girls*, Myron. Benjy is not going to ask them to come over."

"Oh, you *are* being difficult t'night, Nathan." Myron opened the menu. "Anything you guys especially interested in?"

It was one of those menus that never seemed made for real kids, but when the waiter came back I ordered fried chicken and Nathan had lamb and Myron had something called "Boof something." I learned later that it was just beef, from a cow. As we were eating, Myron kept ordering more wine and encouraging Nathan to have some. Nathan didn't want to drink any more because he was driving, but Myron insisted, and poured more wine into his glass.

I didn't like this. I could tell Nathan was getting drunk and I didn't want him to drive me back to Isle of Hope that way. The road with all of its sudden twists and turns was famous for killing drunk drivers and their passengers, and I was sure I'd have a hard time explaining it to Caroline if we got into any kind of trouble. Myron got very giggly and started telling jokes about Negroes, but Nathan shut him up fast. Dessert was very nice though, custard served in tall, elegant glasses, and small cakes. Myron had some coffee and so did Nathan. That seemed to sober them up.

"I hope you guys are going to come back to my place for a night cap," Myron said after he had paid the bill.

"I'm not sure, Myron. It's getting late," Nathan told him.

"You're not that much of a baby, neither of you. I insist. I took a cab over here and I need a lift home. You know it's only about half a mile from here."

Nathan reluctantly gave in. On the way out, I saw Neal smiling at me. He was with a new girl I'd never seen. She had blonde hair and a small waist and was very pretty. Pat was with his old girlfriend, Mary-Kay Walsh, a dark-haired, quiet girl; they had been going together for a while. Suddenly, Neal got up and strode over to me.

"How you doin', Benjy?" he asked.

I told him I was OK, and introduced him to Nathan and Myron. Neal shook Myron's hand firmly, like there was nothing the least bit different about him and, in fact, nothing *that* different about two teenage boys with a man old enough to be . . . maybe their young uncle? But I noticed Pat was looking away from us, like he didn't want to know anything that was going on. That seemed just like Pat; he and Mary-Kay were whispering something, and, frankly, I didn't care a lot what it was. I was convinced Pat was not getting anything off Mary-Kay; Tim had already assured me of it.

Soon we were out of the Pink House and on the street, lit with old-fashioned street lamps, that looked like they were left over from the time of the restaurant. Everything in downtown Savannah had this old-timey quality to it. Sometimes it was unsettling, like you were no longer in the year 1964, but in eighteen-something and death was all around you because it was so long ago. That's how I saw the past then: filled with death. Then I felt this cold jolt of fear running straight up my spine. A group of teenage boys were gathering in on us, and I could tell they weren't the kind who'd hang out at the Pink House.

"Hey, queers!" one shouted. "Got any *Christmas* money, faggots?"

Nathan walked faster toward his car; Myron hurried to catch up. I didn't know what to do. I felt like I was stuck somewhere—maybe in the year eighteen-something, or back in Isle of Hope, with the boys' voices sounding like the men who worked on the boats, who'd frightened me with their harsh talk about guys like Myron.

Ten or twelve steps behind Nathan and Myron, I froze. The boys were beating them up. I watched blood trickle out of Nathan's nose onto his blue overcoat. Myron crouched down, his hands clutching his head while the kids punched and kicked at him as they reached into his pants pocket and pulled out his wallet. I wanted to shout, but couldn't. The words wouldn't come out of me. I stood in an eerie, isolating silence amid antique street lamps faintly glowing between pools of darkness, and those big twisted tree shadows, chest-deep azalea bushes, and cracked sidewalks.

A tall, skinny nightmare-scarecrow of a boy out of a horror movie shouted, "Kid! You a queer, too?" and jumped at me. I bolted away, scrambling towards the Pink House. When I realized I wasn't being chased, I stopped and looked back, barely able to catch my breath. The boys had disappeared. Nathan was bent over on the sidewalk, holding his sides. Myron lay on his stomach on the concrete, his hands gripping his head.

I got back inside the Pink House and walked quickly past the chubby lady with the corsage to Neal and Pat, who were standing with their dates, helping them put on their coats to leave.

"I gotta talk to you," I said to Neal and pulled him aside. "Some boys—"

"You got jumped, didn't you? Where are your friends?"

I told him they were on the sidewalk outside.

Neal told Pat to wait on the portico of the Pink House, and he and I hurried towards where Nathan and Myron had been. They were gone, but there was blood on the sidewalk.

"This area can get pretty rough after dark," Neal said to me. "Especially for guys like that Myron character. How'd you meet up with somebody like him?"

"He's a friend of Nathan's."

"I *see*," Neal said knowingly. "I guess he likes kids. Your friend Nathan seems OK, but that Myron's a creep. No wonder he got beat up."

We went back into the Pink House, and Neal announced to his brother and the girls that he was going to give them a lift back to his house and then take me home. The girls, both wearing Christmas corsages, looked very concerned at me. On the way to Neal's car, I spoke to him in a low voice so no one else could hear, "I can have Mom pick me up from your place. I hate for you—"

"Let me take care of this, Benjy," he said firmly. "I don't want your mom to ask you any questions you can't answer." He smiled, winking at me. "Believe me, Pat and I have both been in that situation."

I felt better when he said that—and needed to. I knew I'd lied to Mom; I'd been with Nathan who'd been drinking; and then with Myron, who was a *bona fide* queer. It was all awful. So Neal drove Pat and the girls back to his house and dropped them off, then we took off together to Isle of Hope. I was really happy he'd done this. I felt terrible about Nathan, and asked Neal what he thought might have happened.

"I guess he drove that Myron guy home, or maybe even to a hospital—you don't want the cops involved with this kind of stuff. A guy like Myron tried to fool around with me and I almost killed him. It's just natural. You don't want some old queer pawin' you. Some guys do it for money."

"They do?"

"Sure, it's the world's oldest game. Girls do it with old farts; boys do it, too. I'm glad I don't know any kids who do, but I know about it. If you see some kid starting to show a lotta dough he didn't get from his folks, you can pretty much bet he's in on the game. It doesn't make a difference what the kid looks like, as long as he's a kid. Those old queers love kids. I dunno why—maybe they're just nuts."

Now it *almost* made sense—Nathan had been getting money from this Myron character—but why did he need to drag me along with him? Suddenly, I hated Nathan. I decided I'd call him and let him know that I didn't want to see him again, but not for a day or so. I asked Neal to stop the car at the foot of the driveway.

"I guess your mom's waiting up," he said. "You haven't been drinking, have you?"

"No. I'm too young to drink like Nathan does."

"Keep away from it as much as you can. It's fun, but it's dangerous, believe me."

We were still in the car. He shook my hand, then pulled me to him and hugged me for a moment. I loved the way his dark Irish hair felt next to my cheek.

"I needed to do this," he whispered. "For Arthur's sake."

I pulled away from him.

"Arthur?"

"Yeah." His voice was strained.

"Why Arthur?"

"Because I couldn't help him."

I wanted to say I felt that way too, but I was afraid I'd start crying.

"The truth is," Neal explained, "nobody's figured out how he died. But all the grown-ups have written him off. They wanna believe he killed himself—except, being Catholic, they can't admit it. I don't believe it, Benjy."

"Did you tell that to Det. Whitaker?"

"Sure. But Father Greer and the other teachers don't want to know about it. They just want it t' disappear, like Arthur did."

"He didn't disappear for me," I said sadly and got out of the car.

Mom was waiting in the den. She had a drink in her hand and was smoking a cigarette. She wasn't looking at TV or reading.

"Hi," she said. "Did you have a good night?"

I told her I did. She asked me how Allan Streitt was, and I said fine. She asked me about girls at the party, and I told her some story about them, making up stuff that did not happen. It was easy; maybe the fact that she was half drunk helped. I was just happy that I didn't have to call her to pick me up. That would have been bad for everyone, and worst for myself. How could I explain to her that I'd been out to the Pink House with Nathan and his queer friend who was paying for us? Was this also part of being *seductive*? Was Nathan trying to "do something" for Myron Lewis regarding me? I remembered what his friend Mo had said, that lots of guys would just "*lu-u-uv* t' love" me. I'd hated the way he'd said that. He made it sound so dirty; maybe just from the fact that he was black—I really wasn't used to being around colored people except for Josephine; how could I be in Savannah, Georgia?

I couldn't sleep. It had been such a strange crazy evening. I remembered Neal and Pat at the Pink House with their dates—all of their soft movements and the decorations and the way the boys flowed around the girls, like doing a dance with them, even without the dancing. Just the way they led them to the table and stood while the girls sat, then sat down themselves and smiled. They looked as if they were in a wonderful Christmas dream. Everyone's eyes were sparkling simply from being there, knowing that this moment was theirs.

I had not felt like that. I had felt like I was *acting* grown-up with Nathan and Myron, but not like the moment was mine. It wasn't mine until I was in the car alone with Neal, and what he had told me, and the way he had hugged me before we parted. I wanted to feel that hug again and stroke my face against his hair; that sweet, immense, delicious closeness, that hug of Robby and Arthur, and. . . .

Now I was with him. Arthur, in his white sleeveless t-shirt, just like when I had been with him in his bedroom. But I was touching him. Touching his face, his shoulders, his chest. He had pulled his T-shirt off, over his head, and was hugging me bare-chested. This instance of that light brown-skinned light, coming from him, like the light from stars, the light from many, many Christmases past, like the distant glimmering jewels in a crown, touching me.

Then it was over. Arthur was gone. I missed him; I could feel missing him.

I decided I had to ask Brother Alexis about him, as soon as I could.

* * *

Despite my anger at Nathan, I called him the next day, Sunday. I'd told myself that I wouldn't call him for a few days, and then I'd tell him to drop dead; but I didn't wait. Mom was in the den pretending to watch TV while drinking, and Liz was with Josephine taking a walk outside. It was a pretty, sunny-wintry Southern day, with that kind of humidity in the air that snaps at you, like a little ping on your skin. I knew that the sun would be up only for another hour or so. I called him upstairs from Mom's room.

Mrs. Streitt answered the phone. I told her who I was, and she told me Allan was out of the house.

"He's playing racket ball with his father. They both want to lose weight."

"I want, uh, to speak with Nathan," I explained. "Is he there?"

"Nathan?" she said after a funny pause. "I thought you were Allan's friend. He's closer to your age, right?"

I panicked for a second, then remembered something Robby had once told me: "In business, it's important to let people know only what you're most *sure* they should hear."

"He promised once to help me with some homework." I said confidently.

"Homework? Benjy, Nathan doesn't even help Allan with *his* homework."

"It's for English. He's read a lot more than I have."

"That's true, he does read," she said thoughtfully, as if the idea had suddenly come to her. "*Hold the phone.* I'll see if he's in his room. He came in late last night and I haven't seen him all day."

She put the phone down with a clunk. I heard her take several steps then shout, "Natey!"

There was silence. Finally someone picked up the phone.

"Huhhhh?"

Nathan sounded like he was underwater, hoarse and very hung-over.

"It's Benjy. What happened last night, Nathan? I went back t' the Pink House to get help. When Neal O'Neill and I came back, you were gone. Both of you." After a long icy silence, I asked, "Can y' talk?"

"Sure, I got a phone in my room. Dad gave it to me for my birthday a few years ago. Some cops came, Benjy. They took Myron to Memorial Hospital and I got back into my car. I told the cops some colored kids tried to rob us. If I had told 'em the truth, wudda been too many questions. Colored kids, and the cops don't ask anything. I'm glad you're OK. Your friend took you home? Good."

"What was going on last night, Nathan? Why did you want me to meet that guy Myron? He's a creep."

"I have a bad headache, Benjy. I can't answer your questions right now. Sorry you think Myron's a creep. I guess us creeps gotta stick together around here."

"You thought he'd be interested in me, didn't you?"

"Jesus, fuck-no. I like you, Benjy. Myron paid for dinner. It's a nice place and I wanted to take you out. Didja really think I was tryin' to pimp you out to Myron?"

Pimp. That was the word. Neal didn't use it, but it made sense. I'd never heard anyone use that word in front of me, but remembered hearing one of Mom's drinks-on-the-veranda friends use it. I even asked Mom about it. She wanted to know where I'd heard it and I told her at school.

"It's someone who purveys girls for sex, Benjy," she explained. "Some men will pay women to sleep with them. A pimp is a sleazy guy who provides them. My, you *are* becoming an adult!"

"Were you?" I said to Nathan. "Trying to pimp me out? It's like that Mo said, guys would *lu-u-uv* t' love me, right?"

"You remember that? Mo was only jokin', Benjy. God, you don't know what's going on. If the cops get to my parents, they're really going to have me fucked up. In a place like Georgia, they could have me sent to a state mental institution, like Milledgeville. Ever heard of that place?"

I had. Kids used to say, "You're so nutty, you belong in Milledgeville." But I didn't think they'd do that just because you—then I thought about it. Nathan was right. I felt genuinely shitty. Like a whole pile of crap had fallen on me.

"Sorry," I said. "I hope they *never* do that."

"You and me both. My parents, 'specially my dad, would give me the third degree. They'd want to know how come I know somebody like Myron. 'He's a *homo*-sexual, isn't he?' They always make you think that 'homo' and 'sexual' are two different words. Like you're not simply sexual, you're just '*homo*.' I don't want to spin down again to the point where I want to kill myself, Benjy. I need guys like Myron. I need something that's not totally all by myself here. Can you understand that?"

"I'm glad you're OK, Nathan. I mean, not in the hospital."

"Thanks. I'm glad you called. I really want to see you again. Can I?"

I didn't have to think about it. "Sure."

"Can I say something to you?"

"What?"

"I love you."

"Don't—you do? Why?"

"You're not like anyone else here. I felt that way as soon as I saw you at Allan's bar mitzvah party. That's why I acted like such an asshole. I gotta admit it now."

"You were an asshole." Then I realized something. "I love somebody else," I said.

"That girl Faye?"

"No. Arthur Gomez. He's dead."

"I understand," Nathan said. "I'm glad I could tell you, Benjy. I need to take a shower and try t' act presentable to my parents so they think I'm normal again. It's a real act, but I can do it when I need to."

I hung up the phone, and almost a second later Mom came into her bedroom and asked whom I was talking with. I told her Allan Streitt and she asked me why I needed to talk up there and not downstairs.

"We were talking about girls. You know how boys act sometimes."

She smiled at me.

"That's great Benjy. Your dad'd be so happy. He was always worried about you and that boys' school, that you wouldn't get to meet the right girls. But you do, right?"

She had a drink in her hand and cigarette. The drinking and smoking had aged her in the last year. But it had been a horrible year, with Dad's problems and his dying. Sometimes I felt like I didn't know her anymore, or had I only made it impossible for her to know me? I had heard some of the guys talk about hormones and how they started to rush into you at my age. Like they caused you to have a boner when you didn't want one, like when you got up in front of a class of all boys—and the guys could see it, and they'd laugh right at you so you felt like a complete jackass. But this was different. Mom didn't know *me*, but I could tell that sad, terrible things were going on with her. I could see it right in front of me. She looked as if someone had added a thick layer of paste to her face, and in the paste were lines that weren't there before, lines that went down to her neck and even farther. I had never seen my mother without any clothes on, but I wondered how far down her body the lines really went—how far down, and how deep?

29

Counseling With Brother Alexis

We spent Christmas with the Blakelys. When my father had been alive, Christmas had been a pretty awkward situation even though we had a tree, just for Mom and Liz, and also for Josephine, who helped decorate it. My father put up a silver menorah, and he said the prayers for it and lit the candles. Sometimes I would watch him, or even light the candles after he said the prayers. This year we didn't have a menorah and I missed it, but Mom said that just the thought of it would make her cry. I got a Sears bike from the Blakelys, and also a small portable Remington typewriter. Liz got a doll, but I could tell that she was already outgrowing dolls. She looked and it, smiled, and a short time later put it away.

I was happy when school started again, but nervous going into my counseling session with Brother Alexis, especially after our last one. I didn't want to get too close to him again; I was afraid of getting into some situation like I had with Nathan Streitt—one of being seductive when I wasn't really sure what it was. Mostly what I had on my mind was Arthur; I needed to know what had happened to the investigation of his death. Why had Det. Whitaker stopped coming by the school? Had they reached some kind of resolution of the case? Had Arthur really killed himself?

Brother Alexis asked me how I'd been. I told him I was OK. What else could I say?

"Are you still thinking about joining the Church?"

I told him yes, I had thought about it sometimes. And, yes, I believed there was a King of Angels, just like in the song.

"That's wonderful, Benjy. Our Lord Jesus Christ is the King of Angels. He is the incarnate Word of God, God's promise to us made real and of flesh. I'm glad that you are beginning to believe that."

"But if he's the King, don't kings have successors?"

"Not this king, Benjy. Christ is eternal."

"But isn't the blood of the King in other people, people who are close to Him, who should be close to Him?"

"Whom are you talking about?"

"Arthur Gomez."

A pained expression twisted Brother Alexis's handsome features. At first he seemed angry, then upset. I'd seen that look on Robby when things happened that he couldn't account for. I had hated it because I'd always thought he was angry at me.

"Why are you bringing up Arthur Gomez, Benjy?" Brother Alexis asked sharply. "What happened is really none of your business."

"I'm sorry," I said.

I started to get up out of my chair, but Brother Alexis grabbed my hand—his office was so small you were never more than a foot from him—and made me stay put.

"We need to put the situation behind us, Benjy. God doesn't want you to dwell on that kind of death. It was God's will. I truly believe that, do you understand me?"

He still had his hand on me, gripping me hard.

"Let go of me!" I said, suddenly hating him—I never thought I could do that.

"I want you to put this behind you. Please, *will* you, Benjy?"

He eased his grip, but he still had me. I remembered what Caroline had said about watching out for the men at Holy Nativity. What was Brother Alexis going to do to me? My head sunk miserably into my shoulders.

"I'm sorry," he said, releasing me. "But the investigation into Arthur Gomez's death has ended. The school was satisfied that it was a tragic accident and the will of God, and only by accepting the mercy of God can we understand it."

"Is that the same mercy that took my father?"

Brother Alexis sprang up from his seat, so upset that he looked like he wanted to kill me. I jumped towards the door but he stopped me, locking me in his arms like a wrestler. He was crying. Tears were streaming down his face.

He let go of me. I reached up and placed my hand on his head, like I would have done with Robby if he'd been in that kind of condition. Brother Alexis leaned his head towards me; I stroked his hair for a second. We both sat down.

"I'm sorry," he said. "I shouldn't have done that. You're an amazing kid. You have answers I don't even have. I wish I knew where you got them."

"Do you think I'm seductive?" I asked.

"*What?*"

"One of my friends thinks I'm a seductive person. He said I make people want to kiss me."

"He's crazy!—Seduction is a sin in the eyes of the Church. In the Garden of Eden, the Serpent seduced Eve into going against the will of God."

"But wasn't that how humans got knowledge?"

He looked at me, and I saw that he was no longer angry, but something else. Maybe, pleading.

"Yes, it was, Benjy. Maybe your friend really means that you have some knowledge that other people would like to have, or you are not afraid of knowing anything. Isn't that the truth?"

"Maybe."

I straightened up in my seat. I'd never thought of myself in that way, but perhaps it was true. Maybe Nathan thought I was seductive because I wasn't afraid of him. Scared sometimes, who wouldn't be—the whole queer thing scared me. I was scared guys would think I was a queer and hurt me, or Robby might be angry, or Caroline. But maybe knowledge itself was fairly . . . well, *queer*—coming straight as it did from the Serpent itself.

"I'm not afraid," I said firmly. "I *do* want to know what happened to Arthur."

"Why?"

"Because I loved him. I know that now. Maybe I'm not supposed to, but I did."

"It's OK. You loved him as a friend."

I had to say it to somebody, and not just to Nathan—I knew this was the time.

"I didn't *just* love him as a friend. I understand that."

"Then maybe you need to get help with these feelings, Benjy. They are not the right ones to have, especially here at Holy Nativity."

"Have you loved me?" I asked.

"No, not in that way!—I think this session is over and I don't think we need to have any more of them."

I looked at him straight in his eyes. I knew he'd been lying to me, just as I had been lying to Mom, Mrs. Streitt, and even my dad. I wondered if this seductive thing included lying as well as knowledge. Suddenly I felt stronger. I could imagine Nathan being in Brother Alexis's tight office, telling me what to say and how to say it.

"I want to know about Arthur's death. And I'm going to find out."

"You're only a kid, Benjy. You really need to think before you start talking."

His eyes riveted me fiercely. I remembered that look from the first time I'd gazed at him at the swimming pool. Brother Alexis could be very threatening, but I didn't turn away from him. He was right. I was *just* a kid, but I was not going to back down.

"I will find out, Brother Alexis. If I have to ask everyone in Savannah, I'll find out."

The color drained from his face.

"Will you?" he asked, looking so much older now, like Mom did.

"Give me a week," he whispered. "Come back in a week and then I promise, I'll tell you what I know."

I was on pins and needles for the rest of the week. Sometimes I'd see Brother Alexis in the hallways in his Sebastianite habit and he would give me this *look* that could be described as either "Get out of my way!" or "Why have you *put* yourself in my way?"

I became afraid even to say hello to him. Monks, especially in their flowing robes, had this intimidating way of walking, determined as a fireman on the way to a four-alarm. Maybe they were trained in seminary, but it said: "We mean business!" Brother Alexis had been different; I was used to seeing him linger and talk with guys, joking with them. Not anymore. I decided I should start thinking about my next point of action.

I called Morris Whitaker after school, and actually got him at his desk.

"Yeah, Benjamin Rothberg—you're one of the kids from Holy Nativity. What can I do for you, young man?"

I paused for a second. "I'm calling, sir, to find out what happened in the investigation of the death of Arthur Gomez. Was anything determined?"

I thought "determined" sounded professional, instead of only "What happened?"

"It was determined that he died of natural causes, in an accident. He drowned."

"Uh . . . how was that *determined*?"

"The medical examiner did a routine autopsy. He's a doctor, y' know—sees lots of drownings—what the body looks like. Lungs, stuff like that. I can't go into details with a child your age."

"I'm fourteen years old, sir. That's not a child."

"You're still a minor, and you're asking me to divulge private information that really only the family of the deceased should have access to. If you get me a Letter of Consent from that boy's parents, then I can do something."

"I don't think that's going to happen," I said. "His parents barely speak English. At least his mother doesn't; his father drinks."

"Sounds like you knew a lot about this kid. Everything except how he died, and I'm telling you the investigation is closed. *Finished*. I talked with Father Greer and he was perfectly accepting of the conclusion that Arthur Gomez drowned. He didn't ask for anything else, and the boy's parents didn't ask either."

"So he didn't kill himself."

"Might have. Drowning's drowning. If you jump in the water and drown, it's very hard to tell if you did it on purpose or not."

"But it wasn't a lot of water."

"That's hard t' say, Benjamin. He was found in a lake. He might have got in and got tired and just drowned. But you can drown in a bathtub. People have done it before, young man. Especially, if they've been drinkin.'"

"He wasn't drinking."

"I didn't say he was. Now I think it's time for you to go home, do your homework, and get on with the regular business of being a normal teenager. What d' you think?"

"Yes, *sir*," I said super-politely and hung up.

I realized then that something was fishy, *super-fishy*, despite the *superficial* efforts at investigating Arthur's death. I thought back. Who was at the retreat more than a year ago? Tim O'Neill and his brothers, Pat and Neal. Alfred Johnson. Bill Manion. Melvin Harris. Arch Flanders whom Horace Storch loved picking on.

Storch! If anybody knew, it had to be Storch. He was there with his sidekick Ken Ferris, but not Joe Flauwerty. I wondered if anyone had even talked to Storch; it seemed he was nowhere in this story. But he had to be lurking somewhere around it.

Storch no longer scared me. If anything, he just turned my stomach. It was a knee-jerk reaction, like the slight wave of nausea you get after a rollercoaster ride. As much as you don't want it, it's still there. You can't hate somebody for so long and still feel even vaguely relaxed about talking with him.

I decided to ask Tim what to do. Tim had the low-down on so many guys at Holy Smokes; if I needed to get some real information from Storch, he'd know how to do it. I pulled him into an empty corner of the hallway between periods, where nobody could hear us.

"Are you crazy?" he said. "You wanna ask Storch what he knows about Arthur's death? Why? Ol' Arthur's in heaven now, where he oughta be, and all good Catholics want t' go."

"Tim, Arthur didn't even believe in the Eucharist. He was as Catholic as I am; actually less—did I tell you I'm thinkin' about joining the Faith?"

"You're nuts," Tim whispered. "You have such a good thing goin'. Why'd you want to end up with that whole bucketful of guilt we carry? You don't even have Jewish guilt *or* Christian guilt. You're perfect, so keep at it."

"Because I believe there *is* a King of Angels. And Jesus is it."

"That's just a song, Benjy. You sing it at Christmas, before you drink too much eggnog and try to get laid. My brothers been doin' it for years. They love Christmas and eggnog and girls. Even Neal does."

"Why'd you say that?" I asked, looking at my watch. Change of class would be over with in about another minute.

"Cause."

"Cause what?"

"Cause he goes for guys as much as he goes for girls. Just don't ever mention that I said it or Neal'll kill me."

"Was he with Arthur when Arthur died?"

"I can't tell you. But I can tell you this. Brother Alexis is leavin' the school. He's given his resignation to Father Greer. It's hush-hush, but Mom found out. Didja know his real name's Robert Grainger?"

I felt really sad.

"Yeah, I knew it. When's he leaving?"

"In another week."

30

News About Brother Alexis

That did it. That was why he had said wait until the next week. Brother Alexis wanted to give himself time to get out. I wondered what excuse he had used to resign with? Was he leaving the Sebastianite order itself, or just the school? All kinds of thoughts filled the rest of the day. I wondered if I'd had any role in it. Now I had to corner Brother Alexis again. Mom was coming to pick me up at exactly three, which meant I'd have to wait a day to see him again.

When Caroline picked me up, I had to pretend that I knew nothing, but it was hard for me to conceal it on my face. She didn't look very good herself, trembling, her face *ashen*, like the white ash of a cigarette, one of the many she smoked and discarded.

"Are you OK?" I asked her after we'd been driving a while.

She had the radio on low, with her favorite pop music on. The Jaynetts, a girl group, were softly singing, "*Sally don't you go, don't you go downtown.*" Mom liked that song; it was about girls warning other girls about danger. She turned it off.

"Why'd you ask?"

"Because you're looking…pretty bad."

"Sorry. I should have washed my hair and maybe put on some fresh lipstick."

"It's not the lipstick. What's wrong?"

"I told you I've been seeing a psychiatrist," she said, lighting another ciga-rette. "It's just not something I want to talk to a child about."

"I'm not a child," I said, feeling like I had to repeat that line over and over again.

"You are to me. That's one of the problems of being a mother; your kids are always children. I know you know a lot, probably more than I want t' know about. You're a boy, and I know what boys are about, that's why I wish your dad was still around. When I was your age, I hardly knew where babies came from. The first time I had my period, your grandmother Betty took me aside and told me it was God's promise that I would have children after I'd found the perfect husband and Jesus blessed us. Your dad wasn't perfect. I was crazy about him, but he wasn't perfect—and if having a period is God's promise, all I can say is *shit* on it."

She looked at me and smiled; we started laughing, really laughing. Suddenly I wished that we'd both been having a drink, like Salty Dogs or Rusty Nails or even just lemonade.

"You're wonderful," I said and kissed her on her cheek.

"No, I'm really pretty foolish. And I'm really scared. You don't know how scared I am, Benjy. We've got to go. I've got stuff to do at home, and you've got homework."

At home we had a very quiet meal, but I could tell something was wrong. Even Josephine acted like something was wrong. I told Mom that I would be late the next day, because I had a meeting with Brother Alexis.

"He's the good-looking priest?" she asked. "At least he's fun to look at."

Caroline was having a drink at the table; it looked like bourbon in the glass. She was taking pills now too. She took one from a prescription bottle and downed it. I knew nothing about medicine like that or what it did to you, or how it mixed with alcohol, but I didn't like it. Afterwards she had a more distant look, like she was gazing at us from a far-away window. She tried to smile, but even her smile seemed far away. I could tell that Liz was aware of it. She and I left the table and went upstairs. Mom always stayed to cleaned up with Josephine.

"Is Mom OK?" Liz asked. "Why does she look like she's trying hard to like us?"

"She loves us," I said. "But things haven't been easy here."

"Cause of Dad?"

We went into my room, and I shut the door.

"I think Mom's sick," I said. "But you can't tell her that I told you this."

She clouded over. "Is she gonna die?"

"No, but we have to be nice to her, and not expect things t' go easy. Can you do that?"

She nodded, and a few seconds later went off to her room. Liz seemed so flexible. She wanted to be happy, the way kids always do. It made me wonder when I had stopped being that way.

At about ten to three the next afternoon, I knocked on Brother Alexis's door. "Come in," he said, but looked startled when I entered. He was wearing black pants and a plain white shirt. Piles of open boxes in his small office left hardly any room for the two of us.

"I thought I told you not to come back for a week," he said glaring at me.

"You're leaving," I said.

"How do you know?"

"I heard it from one of the kids."

I was going to say something about all the boxes, but he said, "How'd he hear it?" then he added, "Who cares? It's a fact; I *am* leaving. I wanted to talk to you before I left, but only *just* before I left. Now you're here, and the truth is I don't know what to say to you."

I pushed myself through some of the boxes to the other single chair in the office and sat.

"What do you want t' say?" I asked.

He looked at his watch. "Is someone coming to pick you up?"

"I told my mom I'd be late."

He folded his arms in front of his chest. "Can you still call her? I'll drive you home. I don't want to talk here."

I dialed the phone in his office, and got Mom just before she was ready to leave the house. She was happy I was getting a lift. It was evident in her voice she wasn't doing well.

"This is what I want you to do," Brother Alexis said. "Leave the school and walk three blocks south on Talmadge Boulevard. There's a gas station, I'll pick you up in ten minutes."

I felt strange doing this, yet at the same time it seemed almost natural. This was certainly no different from being with Nathan Streitt. Close to the gas station was a bus stop; I waited there, so he could see me. Although it was still winter, it was a sunny, almost warm day. A few minutes past his ten, he showed up in a car I didn't recognize and I got in, without asking him about it.

"Is there someplace you'd like to go?" he asked.

"I don't know," I said.

"Dumb question, isn't it? You probably have as little idea where to go as I do."

"There's a small park near the Pink House," I said. "It's a restaurant down—"

"Yes, I know what it is. Have you ever been there?"

"Sure, I've been to the restaurant with some friends."

"No, I have another idea," he said. "I think this is better. Why don't we just go by the riverfront, to Factors Walk? It's nice to walk along those cobble-stoned streets, and if anyone sees us, we'll say we met by accident."

We drove over, and he found a place to park under some big live oak trees. We got out and started climbing down the old steep stone stairs from the street to the river level, where we found a bench alone, overlooking the water. It was much chillier down there, but we were both wearing coats. I zipped mine all the way up. We could see distant ships docked on the river, and there were some old warehouses behind us, built directly into the bluff above, that were now used for offices and small stores. Brother Alexis stared for a while at the river.

"This is the most difficult conversation I think I've ever had," he said, "and it's with a fourteen-year-old kid." He sighed, and went on, "Arthur didn't kill himself. You were right. I knew what had happened and I just held on to it. Several of the other teachers at the school also knew, and *they* held on to it. I would have let it eat me alive had you not pushed your way into it. But I suspected you would do that; I suspected your father would have made you do it, if he had lived. I got the feeling he was one of those few truthful people, and you inherited it from him. Some of our clergy are not that way, despite our vow to tell the truth. We have faith, that's the truth, but I'm not sure faith is enough."

"How did he die?" I asked.

"One of the boys killed him."

Even though I was cold, I felt like I was nailed to the bench. I was scared to ask, but I had to.

"Who?"

"What difference does it make, Benjy?"

"You know it makes a difference. I've got to know."

"If you know, it can destroy the school."

I edged closer to him; I didn't want to speak loudly. A group of twenty or so people came by, tourists enjoying the sunny day, looking at the waterfront. I waited until they disappeared.

"He was at the lake with Neal O'Neill," I said. "Neal had a close friendship with him. Was that part of it?"

"No—yes—*of course* it was part of it. Brother Ulrich knew about that friendship. He had become, I guess you could say, *close* with some of the kids who were troublemakers. He always said, 'It's the troublemakers who need our help, not just the good kids. We have to be there for God's black sheep, as well as the white ones.'"

"So who did it?"

"Horace Storch, and his buddy Ken Ferris."

Somehow I'd suspected it all along, but hearing it took my breath away.

"Ferris, Storch, and Brother Ulrich were all at the retreat. They started taking walks along the lake. Late one afternoon they spotted Neal and Arthur canoeing together, and Brother Ulrich commented on it; he asked Ken Ferris to watch out, to see if 'anything unusual' was going on between Gomez and O'Neill, for the sake of the 'reputation of the school.'"

"But doesn't everybody know what Brother Ulrich does, down in that basement of the library?"

"Just some people," Brother Alexis admitted. "Anyway, even if *everybody* knows *something*, only *some* people will talk about it. A day or so later, Storch crept up on O'Neill when he was giving a blowjob to Gomez. They were in the bushes by the lake, thinking they were alone and out of sight."

"God … " I said barely above a whisper.

"Storch hated O'Neill, and you know what happens when a bully has any kind of weapon in his hands. But O'Neill threatened to kill Storch if he said a word to anyone. This spooked Storch, and to top it off O'Neill grabbed him and hit Storch a couple of times hard in his stomach—so no blood was shed. Then O'Neill lit off, leaving Gomez behind, terrified. He tried to leave, too, but Storch grabbed Arthur and held him back—and just at that moment, Ferris popped up. Then the two of them tortured Gomez together for a while in the water, until Arthur was worn out. That's when Ferris left; things were getting too 'touchy' for him. Ferris had always been Storch's sidekick, but never any kind of a ringleader. After Ferris was gone, Storch was in a state of total rage. He dragged Arthur into the lake, and held him underwater until he drowned."

"Arthur was all alone," I said, choking back tears. "After Neal left him, there was no one there to help him." I gave way to crying. I hated doing it. "He could swim," I said. "I saw him swim. I—"

Brother Alexis handed me a handkerchief; I used it to dry my face.

"He was completely worn out, Benjy. When he and Neal got caught, that left him really vulnerable. Sex does that. Arthur wasn't a small guy, but I'm sure he felt abandoned and he knew what would happen if his father found out. It wouldn't make a difference who did what, just that he'd been caught, and how far back it all went."

Back to me, I thought. Mr. Gomez would connect it back to *me*. I could barely breathe. I remembered Tim saying, "Arthur just *gave up*." I felt like I was drowning now, too. I needed to put some sense into all of this.

"What about Detective Whitaker. Did he learn about any of it?"

"No, but Father Greer did. He had a talk with Brother Ulrich, who knew everything, because Storch told him. Storch at first said that Gomez had made a pass at *him* in the bushes, but that's just a pile of rot. I'm sure Gomez wouldn't have done that; he hated Storch. Maybe that was Storch's real problem. Nobody could stand him except for his little gang. I'm not even sure his parents really like him, but they could make a fuss. Storch threatened that if any of this came out— in *any* form—he and his parents would make sure that it destroyed the school. You only need one real homosexual scandal at a boys' school to destroy it."

I could see the pain on Brother Alexis's face.

"We knew that," he continued. "Nobody really talked about it among the faculty, but we knew. It was one of those things that keeps you from talking when you need to talk. That's the reason why people go to Confession, to say things they can't say anyplace else. But there's no Confession for the whole school. There was only this huge silence around Arthur's death. A silence no one could break. I could tell Father Greer was eaten up by it; he knew about Brother Ulrich and what he was doing in the basement. But Ulrich had the goods on Greer, too. Once when he'd been tippling some himself, he let it out to me, 'If Greer ever tries to touch me, I'll expose him as a drunk and a child molester.'"

"Was he?" I asked.

"He drinks, but he's no child molester, I'm sure about that. But once something like that gets out, it's hard to put it back in the box. I started to think about all of these things and how I fit into the Church. I'd never even questioned it before; it just seemed right that I'd become a teaching monk. My parents are good French Canadian Catholics, and you can probably guess what kind of kid I was—maybe I was even somewhat like you."

I looked at him, puzzled.

"I had a lot of secrets," he went on. "And it seemed like the best place to keep them secret was in a religious life, where I not only had God on my side but I could show people that I could talk to Him in a very special, intimate way. The Catholic Church is good about that. We understand God and saintliness, and the Nature of Grace: things that people yearn for. We also understand a brotherhood linked together through God's direct calling, and goodness—a goodness outside human sin and pettiness. It's a hard calling, Benjy. Mother Church has been doing that for almost two thousand years, sometimes doing it very well. It's just that at other times, humans fail. We're simply *too* human."

"Are you going to leave the Church?"

"I might. I can't say right now. But I'm definitely going to leave the school and go back to Canada."

"What should I do?" I asked.

"Nothing. I've told you: it will destroy the school if this gets out. If you push for this investigation—that is, if the police accept anything you say about Arthur's death—then Father Greer will have you expelled. They won't allow the school to be destroyed by this."

"Maybe you can take me home now," I said, standing up.

I felt like I had been hit super hard in the chest. How could I look at anybody now, anybody I was close to, like Tim and his brothers, or Manion or Harris or Alfred Johnson or even Arch Flanders, and certainly my other teachers at Holy Nativity? The worst part was that Storch and his gang were still around, still bullying, just being a little bit more careful about it. And knowing that Brother Ulrich and Father Greer, and everything at Holy Nativity Military Academy, would simply go on in its own genuinely decent way, while everything indecent was covered up.

Brother Alexis and I didn't speak much on the way back to Isle of Hope; I felt locked inside myself. I missed Robby. He would have said something to me that would have made sense of the situation, like, "Whatever you do, don't hate yourself. Jews don't hate themselves."

Suddenly the words just came out of me.

"Do you hate yourself, Brother Alexis?"

"Call me Robert," he said. "I'm really Robert Grainger. Yes, sometimes I do *hate* myself. For keeping all this a secret. Why'd you ask?"

"I just thought of my dad. It seemed like he'd ask a question like that. I don't think he hated himself ever."

"He was lucky. Strangely enough, I think self-hatred makes you stronger. It keeps you grounded on the earth."

I nodded, and thought: is that what keeps someone tied to a place like Holy Nativity? "You're going to leave the school?" I asked. "Isn't part of being grounded staying there?"

"You do have a Jewish brain," Brother Alexis said smiling. "I hadn't even thought about that. Maybe you're right. Self-hatred can go only so far, even for a Catholic."

It was getting dark. I liked the drive out to Isle of Hope at twilight, as the light faded into night. I made myself stop thinking about all of this, and thought about my homework, my mom, the next time I'd see the O'Neills, and how much I wanted to go back to the beach when the weather turned warm. I thought about Nathan Streitt and how much I wanted to see him again, despite everything that he was; we'd go swimming together and I'd feel like an adult around him again.

"I'll write and tell you where I am," Brother Alexis said as he stopped the car in the driveway. "I want to know you when you're an adult. I mean that."

"Thanks," I said.

"You've been given an amazing gift, Benjy. Somebody told you who you are at a very early age. I'm not sure if you're aware of it."

He leaned over and pulled me to him and hugged me, kissing me on my cheek.

Mom was waiting for me in the living room. "How's Brother Alexis?" she asked, as she smiled at me in a distant, pained way.

"He's leaving Holy Nativity." I said.

"He is—they didn't throw him out, did they?"

"No. Why'd you ask that?"

"Monks live in a pretty secret world, Benjy. It's hard to tell what they're all about. My dad had a funny run-in once with one. He told me about it after I'd grown up. He was a kid and a priest had come into his school to give Bible lessons, of all things. He was Catholic and a lot of the kids were from Irish homes, it being Savannah and all. To make a long story short, the priest got him alone after school and tried to feel him up. He pretended that he was just patting Dad on the stomach, but the pat got lower and lower. Your granddad said it was because they didn't marry. They had to go after anything they could get."

"They're married to God," I insisted.

"Sure. But isn't that kind of queer? *God* being a man."

She lit a cigarette and smoked it nervously.

"I dunno," I said. "Maybe some men just like God. They think about Him and need Him, really need Him."

"You miss your father, don't you? So do I." Suddenly she was sobbing; I didn't expect it then. "I've stopped believing in God. Why would He take your father? He got wounded in Korea and worked so hard for us. Then he got caught for some stupid crap because the rednecks down here wanted to—" She stopped herself. "I'm sorry, Benjy." She was coughing and crying at once. "They wanted to *crucify* him!"

I thought about what Grandpa had told me. "Like Jesus?"

"Yeah. Another Jew." She got up. "You need to eat some dinner. Liz is with my folks. She's staying there tonight."

We had some chicken and a salad Josephine had prepared for us in the kitchen. Mom had three or four scotches and finished with a Rusty Nail. I hated watching it. By the end of the meal, she was barely able to focus her eyes or walk. I had to help her up to her room; I felt stupid. I should not have been doing that. It didn't seem right.

In bed I kept thinking about Arthur and Nathan, and of course Brother Alexis and what he had said to me about someone telling me who I was. I couldn't figure out what he had meant; I still couldn't figure out who or *what* I was. Was I Jewish or not Jewish or—the next thought I didn't even want to allow—or like Nathan? Was I really seductive without knowing it, like Nathan said? Was that what Brother Alexis was telling me?

I tried to think more about it until, quickly enough, sleep descended on me like this wonderful comforting blanket, and I was at a beach, swimming in clear blue water with Nathan, Brother Alex, and Arthur. They were all around me, being deliriously playful; they'd stopped thinking about anything except having fun. We were splashing around, and the fine spray of the water was so pure you could see directly through it, like crystals splitting the sunlight. But soon the spray got faster and denser, until it was flying straight at me, blinding me.

Then Horace Storch stood in front of me, alone.

"I'm gonna get you, Rothberg—*Rat* Man!" he screamed, grinning at me with the expression of an enraged, razor-toothed dog. He charged after me, pushing me down into the water. I kept coming back up, but the tide gushed furiously into my nose, eyes, and throat until I could take it no longer. Storch was moving around me too fast to avoid him. He jumped on me full force with every muscle in his body, and held me down in the water, his hands tightening around my neck, strangling me. I couldn't even cry out for someone to save me. Everyone I had hoped to count on was gone. No one was there, not even Robby who I was sure was in heaven. Where was *He*? Where was the King of Angels?

Nowhere.

My eyes popped open. I was slammed awake by a loud thud in Mom's bathroom.

31

Mom in Trouble

I jumped out of bed in my undershorts and raced to her. Caroline was in her nightgown, unconscious, the side of her face pressed onto the tiles. Her teeth had cut into her bottom lip; it was bleeding. I knelt trying to wake her up. There was a bottle of sleeping pills on the sink but I wasn't sure how many she had taken. I couldn't wake her. I ran back into her room, and phoned the Blakelys. The phone rang and rang. Finally Grandpa answered.

"Yes?" he said groggily.

"Mom's had an accident!" I cried. "She's in the bathroom on the floor. What should I do?"

"I'll be right over. I'll call the police—I know half the cops in Savannah. If the ambulance arrives before I do, ask the cops to stay with you and I'll pick you up."

I went back to Mom and tried to wipe the blood off her lip with a cold washrag. She was breathing softly. The ambulance came faster than I thought it would; two attendants dressed in white hurried out of it with a stretcher. They were both young white men. One was big-bellied and very tall with short, dirty-blond hair trimmed in a flat-top, and deep zit-scars on his face. His name was Billy. He smoked a cigarette which he kept dunking into his hand and putting the ash in his white coat pocket. The other, named Ray but called Red, was shorter and thinner. He had wavy red hair and freckles across his nose. I led them both up to the bathroom. Billy told me to wait outside while they strapped Caroline down. I didn't want to leave Mom, but did. I sat on her bed, and listened to them in the bathroom discuss what to do with her.

"Wanna try t' wake her up, Billy?"

"Naw."

"Sure? I hear she belongs t' a big ol' judge."

"Makes no diff'rence. All these women is alike. Used t' causin' trouble.

Come on, let's jus' get her done."

"Billy, if she dies we gonna get fucked!"

"Red, stop y' goddam whinin' and git this done. Move her arm over here, and don't you touch nothin' y'ain't s'posed t' touch. Understand?"

"Think she's gonna swaller her tongue?"

"Put the damn clamp on it, Ray."

Two policemen arrived with Grandpa, and one of them ducked into the bathroom. Grandpa looked terrible; his shirt was untucked, his hair messed up. He ran over and hugged me, repeating, "My boy, my boy."

Billy, the bigger one, came out of the bathroom. "You know anything about these pills?" he asked.

"She was taking them to sleep with," Grandpa said. "I don't think my daughter tried to kill herself. But she's been under a lot of strain lately."

"Sorry to hear that, Judge Blakely," the police officer said. "We heard about your son-in-law. It's sure sad."

"We gotta pump her stomach when we take her in," Billy said. "That's the way it's gotta be done."

"I guess so," Grandpa said sadly. "No matter what, that's the way it's *got* to be done."

He looked at me as if he had just revealed something I wasn't supposed to know. Billy motioned to my grandfather and took him out toward the bathroom door. Grandpa returned to me.

"I want you to just stay here," he said. "They're going to take your mother down to the ambulance."

"Can't I see her? Is something wrong?"

"She's going to be OK, Benjy," he said. "They just think it's better if they do this themselves. That way if something *does* happen, you're not in the way."

I stayed in the bedroom with Grandpa and one of the policemen while the other one and the two ambulance attendants took Mom downstairs. I could hear them talking to each other about not bumping into anything. The door to the bedroom was left open; I stood up and craned my neck around as much as possible, while Grandpa held me. I could see Mom's face for only a second. She was still unconscious, strapped down, with a large clamp on her tongue. She looked very pale, almost gray. Her hair seemed damp.

Grandpa held me like I was still a child, and told me not to cry. I knew I wasn't going to. I felt removed from all of this, as if I were too far away to cry and still in some kind of dream, even if the Horace Storch nightmare had seemed so much more real than what was actually going on here.

Grandpa drove me back to his house and left me with Grandma, then told us he had to go to the hospital to fill out papers. Grandma looked very disapproving, like this was just too much for him.

"I need to go, Betty. They need to see me there, so they'll treat her as well as she's going to get treated. You know how hospitals are."

He gave her a look that made me understand that this was as much as he was going to say in front of me. I'd seen that look from adults too many times. Grandma took me up to a room that had been Mom's room, where I used to stay sometimes. Liz was asleep in her own room that had been a guest room. Grandma said some things to me about breakfast and closed the door.

I took off my clothes and got into bed in my undershorts. I was very tired, but couldn't sleep. I felt alone and strange, like I was a stranger now even to myself, even in the Blakelys' house. I kept thinking about the conversation I'd had with Brother Alexis that afternoon. It ripped away so many of the secrets around Arthur Gomez's death, and around Holy Nativity. I guess the fact that I was a non-Catholic going to a Catholic school set me up for it. There would always be things that other people, say, the O'Neills, would hold true and keep close to themselves and believe; and I couldn't believe them, even as much as I wanted to believe in something.

But I could not believe that God could be served by Arthur's death or the way that the truth behind it had been hidden. It seemed that there were so many secrets in the world that I was in: the secrets of colored people and white people, and guys like Nathan Streitt and Myron Lewis, and that man Moe I'd met in the Cove, and Louie, the bartender at the Grocery Store; they all seemed to swirl above my head in this current of secrets, or a secret current itself that led me, soon enough, back to Robby, and then to Arthur.

I felt they were both looking down on me, and bestowing real comfort on me. This had to be my *own* secret; that in this threatening world hiding all sorts of things, I had them on my side. I decided that no matter what people told me or how much they tried to shut me up, I'd still have them. Especially Arthur—I could never forget the time we spent talking in his room, and how much I wanted to get closer to him, closer than I could possibly allow myself to be.

I didn't get to see Mom for three days. I went to school and Grandpa dropped me off and picked me up; Liz was still in school in Isle of Hope, so it was much harder getting her there. I overheard my grandparents talking about transferring her to a school in town, so I realized that something was going on. I got Grandpa alone and asked him what was happening to Mom.

"She going to be OK," he said. "It was an accident what happened to her. She fell and became unconscious. When you see her, try to cheer her up. She feels pretty bad about letting you kids down. One day when you have kids yourself, you'll understand what I mean."

"When are we all going to be back home?"

"That's hard to say, Benjy," he answered. "Your mom's had a difficult time of it. We think she's going to have to go off for a while. There's a hospital out of town, over in Augusta not far from the place where you father was. It's for people who've had emotional problems. We feel we should send her to it."

Mom had a room by herself in Memorial Hospital. I could tell that she was in the mental wing because the Blakelys, Liz, and I went through several locked doors to see her. Liz and Grandma were asked to stay in the lounge area, which was just a room with some sofas and chairs in it. Grandpa and I went to her room. She was sitting in a kind of easy chair. She stood up and I hugged her. Her face looked completely worn and haggard. She was wearing regular clothes (I guessed Grandma had brought them to her) and lipstick, and her hair was combed. But she looked sleepy. Her eyes were open, but I got the strange feeling that her mind was someplace else.

"I'm so glad to see you," she said, hardly above a whisper. I told her I was glad to see her, too. "How's school. Are you making friends? Are the Catholics OK?"

What was she talking about? I had been at Holy Nativity for almost three years. I glanced back at Grandpa and he nodded to me.

"We shouldn't wear your mom out," he said.

"I like having him here," Mom said. She smiled, and for a second looked like her beautiful self again. "Is Liz here? I want to see her, too."

"She's in the lounge," Grandpa said. "The nurse will bring you over to her."

"Good. I didn't want to see her in this room. She's still a child. You're both still children."

Her face folded up again, the smile gone. She started crying softly, and blotted her eyes with a tissue.

"It's OK, Caroline," Grandpa said. "We understand, don't we, Benjy?"

I nodded; I wanted to understand. The nurse, a young woman, came in and gave Mom a pill, then escorted her by the arm slowly towards the lounge. I took her other arm. Grandpa walked behind me. Suddenly he touched my shoulder and I let go of Mom's arm. She and the nurse went ahead, down the hallway that smelled of hospital disinfectants. I heard soft moaning sounds come from the rooms and saw a few patients walking slowly about in pajamas, some of them smoking. Grandpa pulled me aside.

"Let your mom have a moment alone with Liz. Betty won't interfere. This is really hard on that little girl. You're bigger and can understand some of it, but she doesn't understand any of it."

"She does," I said. "She's really smart."

"That's worse," he said. "Because even *I* don't understand it."

"What don't you understand?"

"How things can get so messed up. I'll tell you more about it later."

"When?"

"Just later. What you have to understand right now is how much your grandmother and I love you. We loved your dad, too, despite everything."

There was a chair in the hallway, and he sat down like he had this huge weight on him. After a moment, he got up and we joined Mom and Liz in the lounge. Grandma was not near them, sitting by herself.

Liz was shining with this Christmas-morning smile that seemed completely real. I'd seen that smile with Robby and some of her friends. It was like she hated for people to know she was unhappy. Liz and Mom were talking about dresses and dolls and Liz's friends at school. It was as if nothing had happened, and both of them were not pretending but were just someplace else completely real to them. It made me smile, too. I wondered how sick Mom could really be, and how much she needed to be sent off to a hospital, if she could still be that way with Liz.

The young nurse told her that the visit was over. Mom hugged Liz, and then I saw it. She returned to the same face I had seen in her room. The only thing that remained like before was her lipstick. She was no longer bright and animated with Liz, but lost someplace I couldn't reach.

"What's going to happen to Mom?" Liz asked after the nurse had taken her back.

"She's going to have to go away for a while," Grandpa answered, sounding formal and knowing, like a judge. "You and Benjy will come live with us."

"Why can't we just stay at home with Josephine?" Liz asked. "I want t' do that!"

"No, dear," Grandma said. "You kids can't. It won't be so bad. We'll do all sorts of nice things. We'll go to movies, and see places and I'll make sure you're happy, and—"

"You cannot stay at home with Josephine," Grandpa Blakely repeated. "It's out of the question. Your mother needs help after the death of your father. You have to understand that, Liz. There will be some changes in your life. But they won't be all bad, we'll make sure of that."

There were changes. Liz had to transfer to a school in town. My grandparents spoke briefly to us around the dinner table. Grandpa Blakely said that we should not worry about anything.

"We're going to do everything we can for Liz, so that the new school is fun," Grandma said.

"But all my friends are in Isle of Hope," Liz protested.

"You'll make *new* friends, Sugar!" Grandma Blakely said almost too sweetly. "I promise. And I'm gonna buy you some *new* school clothes, and we're gonna enroll you in nice dance classes and even in riding school. Do you want t' learn how to ride a horse? Your mom was so good at it when she was your age!"

"Sure," Liz said, smiling even though she was looking at me.

"Good," Grandma said. "Why don't we go up to your room and make some plans? And we'll watch some TV, too."

The Blakelys nodded to each other, and Grandma led Liz off. William Blakely looked at me for a moment, took a drink of water, and began talking.

"Benjy, things got *really* bad towards the end of your father's life. He'd hoped he could leave you with enough money to take care of you all, and that his friend Andy Geyer would take care of his affairs for him."

"He knew he was going to die, didn't he?" I asked.

"It happened faster than he thought it would. Your father went kind of crazy trying to make money and he turned to Mr. Geyer for help. The truth is Mr. Geyer has not turned out to be the best person for that kind of trust."

"What do you mean?" I asked.

"He cooked up the schemes that ended up putting your father in prison. And he owns your house now. Robby put it in Andy Geyer's name so your mom would not be liable for his debts. I don't know the whole details. It was between Mr. Geyer and Robby. The whole time I was a judge here in Savannah, I never had a case like this. We didn't have this kind of chicanery back then: business was pretty straight forward, crooked maybe in a Southern way—people would take land away from their relatives and kick Negroes out—but this was a whole different kind of situation, involving loan schemes and credit and certainly that factory in Valdosta. Those people in Valdosta didn't know what they were signing, and it ended up closing the factory down."

"So what's going to happen?"

Grandpa looked as if it was hard for him to talk.

"Mr. Geyer," he finally said, "is going to sell the house. He'll give your mom a portion of it, about a third of the price after the mortgage is paid up. He says he's also had to pay so many legal fees and expenses."

"What will we do then?"

"You'll move into town, into a less grand place certainly. I'm not sure about Holy Nativity, but I think we have enough money to send you there for a while. I wish you could graduate. I think Robby would have liked it. Maybe I can take out a loan."

"Don't," I said firmly. "I don't want to stay there."

He took my hand and held it.

"Think about it," he said, his eyes cloudy. "Just think about it."

I did think about it, and a few days later, after Brother Alexis had left, I saw Neal hurrying down the hallway. I caught up with him and told him I wanted to speak with him.

"So speak," he said grinning broadly at me as he kept walking briskly.

I grabbed his arm and made him slow down. "Not here," I said softly. "I want to speak with you about Arthur Gomez."

He stopped dead. "Can't you just let him alone? He's dead. There's nothing you or I can do about it."

"Yes, there is. I need to talk to you, Neal. I've *got* to talk to you."

The color drained from him. As much as Neal liked others to believe he was cool and on top of everything, he wasn't, and now I could see that.

"You wanna come over this weekend, and you and I can talk? We'll go for a drive. I guess you don't want Tim around for this."

"Yes," I said. "You guessed it."

A Meeting With Neal

I got Grandpa Blakely to drive me over on Saturday. It was a nice day, with a lot of sunlight. You could feel spring coming. Soon it would be Easter, and that meant a lot to Catholics and to Jews, who celebrated Passover at that time. Easter in Savannah was really beautiful, just this blazing riot of azaleas and other spring flowers. The parks would be like walking into a Technicolor movie. I was looking forward to it. I needed to look forward to something, because staying with my grandparents made me feel as if I were in a goldfish bowl. I couldn't feel at ease with Betty Blakely, but sometimes I could with Grandpa, especially after he'd had a drink or two.

Tim met me at the door.

"So you wanna talk with Neal, right?"

"Yeah," I was already self-conscious.

"Z'OK. I know you need to get something off your chest, and Neal's good with that." He called out "Hey, Neal!"

A minute later Neal, looking super-cool in a pair of tight blue jeans and a bleeding Madras button-down, hurried downstairs and motioned for me to come outside. We got into his car, or the car he shared with Pat when they went out together.

"Where you want t' go?" he asked.

I told him the Big Pig, a drive-in I liked that made great barbeque sandwiches and had nice large Cokes with lots of shaved ice.

"Got any money?" he asked.

I had about three dollars, which was enough for two Cokes and two burgers. Neal said fine and drove there, but didn't say much in the car. After we parked at the drive-in, a carhop with teased blond hair with dark roots took our order. Her face looked like a mask. She was about thirty, old for a carhop, and flirted with Neal, who grinned at her automatically.

"I know all about what happened to Arthur," I told Neal after she left.

"What?" he asked bluntly. "*What* d' you know?"

"That Storch killed Arthur. Brother Alexis told me before he left."

"That shitass!" Neal exploded.

"That's no way to talk about a monk."

"Fuck you and you ain't even Catholic!" Neal turned away from me. "How d'you know how t' talk about one of 'em? You got any idea what they do, when they ain't givin' out Communion?"

"I don't think Brother Alexis would ever do that."

"How d'you know?"

"Did he?"

"I always thought he wanted to. I could just tell it."

"Tell what?" I asked.

Neal put his hands over his face, as if he had just dropped the entire Cool-Guy impression he wanted the world to have of him. I felt bad for him. We shouldn't have been at the Big Pig; it was too easy for some other dumb kid to see us—everybody went there, and Neal was not exactly acting like the boy he pretended to be. Suddenly I felt that I knew what he was really like; I was happy I knew.

"You think Brother Alex was attracted to you, or me?" I asked.

"Don't act like such a pussy!" he said, glaring at me. "You *knew* he was. He was *crazy* about you! I could see it when he looked at you. A lot of people are; I knew it from the moment Tim brought you home. But I didn't mess with you, like I did with Arthur. He was different. He was a wonderful kid. I—"

"What?"

"I loved him. But don't you *ever* tell anybody."

"I won't tell. But why didn't you speak up about his death?"

Suddenly the carhop came back with the burgers and Cokes. She smiled at Neal and Neal went back into his cute-teenage boy act that he did so well. But when she was gone, I could tell he was happy to be rid of her. He handed me a Coke and burger, and sipped his Coke.

"I couldn't speak up," he said, looking at me. "You don't understand; you're not Catholic. There are things about this that are deep inside the faith."

"A kid's murder?"

"I mean *not* destroying the Church, or the school or the people in it. I'm a good Catholic. I receive Communion. I go to Confession. But I know how twisted up so much of it is, especially if you're looking at it from the outside."

I nodded; I *was* looking at it from the outside.

"When you're Catholic," Neal explained, "you go inside this special holy place and they give you *everything*—and no matter how bad you are, they'll forgive you. You stop existing; you're not yourself anymore. It's like being in heaven except that it's here, with all the *love* they offer you and the rules and the experience of Christ and Mary and the Saints. They're all so fuckin' perfect, and you can share in that. You can believe in it and share it, no matter how *bad* you really are."

"So they have you?" I said.

"Yeah. It's like that."

"It sounds like they have to kill you," I said. "In order to keep you alive."

"Only a fuckin' Jew'd say that. But it's true—in a way. They have to be able to *fuck* you up in order to *un*fuck you up. That's when they give you Absolution—and you feel so much better afterwards that you don't mind it. In fact, you crave it. It's like—how can I say it?—they wound you. They create a pain inside you and then they dig at it and gouge it out until you start to feel that the only possibility of salvation—of safety, you have—*is* that wound. It's like all those pictures of St. Sebastian—arrows comin' out of him all over the fuckin' place but he looks so calm. *Beatific.* It hurts like shit, but at least you know *where* it comes from. Yes, I knew that about Arthur's death, and I knew that there was no way in hell anybody could tell the truth about it."

"Did Tim know, or Pat?"

"No way in hell. Did Brother Alex fuck you before he told you?"

"NO!" I said too loudly. I lowered my voice. "Brother Alexis never touched me, except in a nice way."

"Did he tell you the whole thing? What happened in the bushes?" Neal looked at me with a pure flame in his eyes.

"Yeah."

"Damn!—no matter *what*, I'm not queer, Benjy. You are, I know it."

"Sure. You just like to mess around."

"Who doesn't? The monks and priests do it all the time. Brother Alex must have found out from one of the other goddamn brothers. That turd Ulrich has his shitty dick in God-knows—Sorry for the language." he tried to calm down.

"I want t' do something, Neal," I said, taking a deep breath. "They can't just let Arthur's murder go away."

He grabbed me by the back of my neck, squeezing as hard as he could. "Don't you say a fuckin' word to anyone. I swear t' God, I'll kill you. The cops'll come and question me again. It'll get back to Pat and follow Tim forever. You got any idea what that'll do to us, and t' my parents?"

He let go of me as the carhop came back.

"It sure looks like ya'll ain't as hungry as two growin' boys should be?" she said, seeing our untouched burgers. "You want me to pack these up for you t' take home?"

"That'd be fine, ma'am," Neal answered.

She took the tray away, and I could tell she was putting a little extra sashay in her walk just for Neal. His eyes narrowed at her, then he looked back at me.

"I betcha she'd like it if I fucked her," he said. "Women like that—man, are *they* trouble. Pat and I are graduating soon, then we're going to Georgetown University in Washington. It's a great Jesuit school. I want t' get away from all of this, and from Savannah."

I nodded at him. "I won't say a word, Neal," I said. "I promise."

He smiled at me and put his hand on my cheek.

"I'm surprised Brother Alex didn't try something with you," He said, and took his hand away. "Maybe he's just a good guy."

The carhop came back with the burgers in a paper sack, and I gave Neal my three dollars. He gave me back two, handed the woman some money and then we drove off.

A Meeting With Andy Geyer

I kept my promise for the next week or so. I felt like I was living in a charade, in that hardly anyone at school knew I was living with my grandparents. Brother Alexis was replaced by a Diocesan priest (that is, he wasn't a Sebastianite) named Paul Peeley, a short, chinless man who was instantly dubbed "Peeless Peeley." Peeley never seemed to smile or engage you directly in the eye. I noticed him talking with Brother Ulrich on several occasions, and wondered how close they were to each other and what that meant. I started calling Ulrich "Mahoney," like a lot of the boys did.

Mahoney had a definite way of looking at me, like he was taking all of my clothes off and cutting my heart out. I saw him talking with Storch and his group of ghouls—my new word for them; I got Tim and Manion to call them ghouls, too—putting his hand on their shoulders and smiling at them like they were among God's chosen children. Maybe they were. And maybe Neal and Brother Alexis (I still had a hard time thinking of him as Robert Grainger) were right and I should have just minded my own business.

But I couldn't. Arthur's murder replayed over and over again in my head. I thought about it during classes, with my teachers accusing me of daydreaming. And at night in my room, my nightmare returned, except now Storch was holding Arthur down. I kept seeing Arthur struggling and dying in the water, with Storch aided by Ferris and Mahoney. I counted Ferris and even Joe Flauwerty among Arthur's killers now, and was sure Mahoney must have given them the *courage* necessary to keep quiet. I knew what they all said about *queers*—that not a single one of them had the right to exist. I kept seeing Nathan on the sidewalk that night with blood on him, next to Myron Lewis. But the worst thing was seeing myself there with them and knowing I could have been beaten up, too. That was the thing that made me really cry at night.

And I kept thinking about the black girl on the bus who'd told me, "You didn't need t' do this."

But I did. I had to. It was part of me; and part of Robby, too.

And even Arthur.

A few days before Passover, I got a call from Andy Geyer. "I want to wish you a happy *Pesach*," he said.

"Where are you?" I asked.

"Savannah. I'm staying in the DeSoto Hotel downtown. I love this place. It hasn't changed since God-knows-when."

"How'd you know I was here?" I asked.

"Listen, boychik, I been in touch a lot with the Blakelys. They're great people. They're doing a lot for you."

"They're my grandparents."

"Like I don't know? I wanna see you. Or, let me make it plain, Benjy. I *need* t' see you. Can I?"

I saw him the next day. It was easy for me to get to the DeSoto. Now that I was staying in town with my grandparents, I could take a city buses. The old hotel was in the middle of a block that looked like a small park. Andy was waiting in the lobby. He led me out to a veranda that circled most of the ground floor, with thick beds of blooming azaleas outside. We found two cane rocking chairs to sit on beneath slowly circulating ceiling fans. A gray-haired colored waiter in a white jacket came out; Andy ordered a bourbon-and-soda for himself and an iced tea for me.

"I usually don't drink bourbon 'sept when I'm down here," he said smiling that Andy Geyer crooked smile that never seemed to light up very much. He started sipping it after it had arrived. He signed for it and gave the waiter a dollar bill. The waiter thanked him and left.

"Do you want some peanuts? Are you hungry?" Andy said.

Suddenly I felt very adult, like I did with Nathan or Brother Alexis, and sometimes even with my mother.

"I want to know what you *needed* to see me about," I said sharply.

Andy looked hurt. He could do that very fast; I wondered if that was only an act, too.

"I needed t' see you cause you're Robby's son, and I loved Robby. I also needed t' tell you that your mother's a lot sicker than you think. And I need to sell your house."

"*Why?*"

Now I wasn't sure how adult I could be.

"Caroline's been hiding a lot, Benjy. Your father's death drove her to a break down. But, believe me, she wasn't doing too good before it. Your mom's going to be in a hospital for a long time—maybe six months, maybe even longer. I don't know where all the money's coming from to keep her there, and to pay for the house."

"I thought my father left—"

"It's gone. And the Blakelys are living off old money. You know what old money is like in the South? You have a house, but you gotta pay taxes on it; so you have enough money to hire a *shwartze*, and maybe go out with the garden club ladies and that's it. Your mother lived like a debutante, like a *shiksa* princess. But there was no *gelt* in the castle."

"What about Holy Nativity?"

"You can spend the rest of the year there, then you'll have to go a public high school, like normal kids do. It'll be OK, because when your mother comes out of the hospital, you'll live in town anyway."

"So, even with the sale of the house, I—"

"The house is mortgaged to the hilt, Benjy. I'm telling you this because nobody else will. They can't talk about money in the South, it's worse than talking about sex. Speaking of which, are you seeing any girls?"

"Sure, I am."

"Who—is she cute?"

"Her name's Faye Jacobson. She's very cute."

"But you're not—you know?"

"I'm fourteen years old."

"So, in the Old Country people married at that age. I had aunts who were fourteen when they got married back in Poland. They're all dead, like Robby's people. Leon—your Robby—was so damn alone. He had a couple of distant cousins up in New York, but he was a lone boychik. That's what put us together back in Korea. Two *Yidden* with nobody really."

"I don't trust you," I blurted out.

He looked stunned, like I had now slapped *him*. "That's a damn crappy thing t' say, Benjy. You really hurt me. I shouldn't let a fourteen-year-old kid hurt me, but you do."

"I still don't trust you," I said.

"Go fuck yourself—God! *Sorry!*"

His eyes teared up again; he looked like he was just holding himself down. He took out a handkerchief from his back pocket and wiped his face and blew his nose.

I just stared at him, feeling very cold. It was hard for me even to understand what he had said; I felt stupid. I wondered what the Blakelys would say, what story they'd try to tell me because I was a kid. Suddenly I thought about them and Father Greer and the detective all in one boat: All of them lying either to protect me or protect somebody else; or else just not wanting to admit that the truth existed.

The only one who did was Nathan. And he was a queer.

"I need to go," I told Andy. "I need to get back to my grandparents."

"Do you hate me?" he asked, his voice strained.

"No."

"It's OK if you do. I mean it. Your father really loved you, like you can't even imagine. That's the one message I have for you. One day somebody will love you just that way, maybe a wife. But if it happens, you'll be very lucky."

The waiter reappeared but Andy put his palm up, to keep him away. He walked with me back into the lobby and offered me money for a cab, saying he would have driven me home, but he had to get out to Isle of Hope to meet with a realtor.

"The market's kind of down," he said. "I hope we can get out of this alive. Don't tell your grandparents what I've said. They'll try to tell you something, so just try to believe them. Or make them think that you do." He smiled. "Just remember your Jewish *kop*, and keep your thoughts separate from what most people expect. See, down here, people just think *exactly* what they think people want them to think. But you're different. You're Leon's son, I know it."

34

A Date For A Movie

About a week later, I got a call from Allan Streitt. Surprised, I asked him how he knew that I was living with the Blakelys.

"Word gets around," he said. "Everybody at the synagogue's a *yenta*. We know your house is up for sale in Isle of Hope."

"You do?"

"Sure. Realtors and Jews talk a lot. Listen, why don't you come over this Saturday? I'm having some kids over, we'll go out afterwards, see a movie or something. Faye'll be there."

I told him I'd have to ask my grandfather to drop me off.

"My mom'll pick you up. I think there's something she wants to ask you in private. Would you mind?" I asked him about what? "I can't say. She just wants to talk to you."

Now I was really curious, and then I realized that it would have to be about Nathan. I thought about calling him and realized that I couldn't without his parents knowing. I decided not to think about it too much. I had enough to think about with what Andy Geyer had told me. Mostly I thought about my mom and how I couldn't get to see her. I'd written her a couple of letters in the hospital in Augusta, but she just answered with postcards that said things like, "I miss you a lot. I'm getting better. Love, Mom."

Toward the end of the week, I ran into Tim in the hallway. He looked at me in this very funny, kind of sideways-way and walked past me. I stopped him. He tried to get away.

"What's goin' on. You mad at me?" I asked.

"Shit-yeah!" he blurted out.

Suddenly Joe Flauwerty appeared. "You two queers havin' a love spat?"

"Sure," I said. "Like the kind you have with Storch. We all know you give the

326

best blow job in the school, Flauwerty."

"You know *what*?!"

He rushed up against me, and I punched him so hard in his shoulder that he screamed, "You fuckin' turd!"

Immediately Father Peeley came out into the hallway, in his black habit.

"I will not tolerate this sort of language for one moment," he said, riveting his eyes on me, which was really unusual because Father Peeley never looked at anyone directly. "What is the meaning of this outburst and why this peculiar type of expression?"

"He was blaspheming," Flauwerty said, suddenly grinning.

"About what?" Peeley asked.

"He questioned the Virgin."

"Rothberg did no such thing," Tim said. "I was right here. Flauwerty was just butting into a conversation he had no right to butt into."

"They're both lying," Flauwerty said. "They're both homos!"

Father Peeley frowned and rose up to his full height, which was hardly taller than Tim.

"This level of exchange is not desired at Holy Nativity, Mr. Flauwerty—or any other Catholic school. Such back alley conversation is not desired here. Is that understood? All of you, clear out of the hall immediately."

Flauwerty hurried off.

"So, what's keeping you?" Father Peeley asked Tim and me.

"We were talking when he interrupted us," I said respectfully.

Peeley looked directly at my chest, then turned around and walked back into his room.

"I'll say this, Benjy," Tim admitted, "You ain't scareda no priests."

"Why are you so pissed off at me?" I asked.

"I don't know what you said to Neal, but it sure *weirded* him out."

"I'm not going t' say a word about it here," I told him. "Next Storch'll come up, and that turd Ferris."

"They been actin' like they own the school again. I think it's 'cause now they know they have Dorris the Dummy on their side."

"I'll call you," I said quickly.

"You wanna come and have a sleep over?"

"I'm gettin' kind of old for that."

"Then we'll just go out for a Coke. Now that you're in town, it's easier, right?"

I told him sure and shook his hand.

"My, you look handsome!" Anita Streitt said when she picked me up at seven in her big pink Oldsmobile Starfire. I was wearing a nice tie and a smart robin's-egg-blue sports jacket that had belonged to my grandfather when he was younger; I was big enough for it. She was in a tight-fitting dress that actually matched the pink of her car, plus a lot of jewelry that sparkled like headlights.

"I just wanted to talk with you for a second in private," she said as we drove off. "I hope it's OK."

"About what, ma'am?" I asked in my most sugary tone of voice.

"It's about my other son. Nathan. Y'know we have a lot of trouble with him. He's a troubled young man. There's no two ways about it."

"I think he's nice," I said.

"That's good. He can be. He can be a very nice person, when his troubles aren't getting the worst of him. He's prone to depression, and he can do some strange things. And he has some *strange* friends. Did you ever meet one named Myron Lewis?"

"No, ma'am," I said. "Is he about my age?"

"No, dear. He's an adult. And we think he's a pervert. Do you know what that word means?"

I looked perplexed. "It has something to do with your brain, right?"

"Perhaps, dear. It has more to do with—well, stuff *way* below the brain that I can't talk to you about. It's adult stuff, and even though you're a mature young person, you are not an adult yet."

"I guess not, ma'am. Where is Nathan?"

"We had to send him off again—he threatened to kill himself. We found out about this Myron Lewis character. Nathan visited him in the hospital after Mr. Lewis was beaten up by a bunch of hoodlums—that is, well, the kind of kids who beat up perverts. It seems Natey told the cops a cock-and-bull story and they didn't believe it. So they got in touch with us—since no matter how you slice it, Nathan's still a minor. He's below the age of twenty-one. It's sad that our son has got himself mixed up with people like Mr. Lewis. Savannah's a good city for the South, but it has a dark underside, if y' know what I mean."

I pretended that I didn't and just looked at her blankly.

"I'm sorry," she said. "You're too young to understand these things. I guess this is kind of an adult conversation for you, isn't it?"

"Where is he?" I asked.

"We sent him to a hospital in New York, to try to straighten him out."

I felt like my heart was breaking. "That's a long way off," I said stupidly, like it was the only thing that could possibly come out of my mouth.

"It's where we're from. Nathan and Allan grew up in Queens till we moved here after Isaac figured out a way to make more money in Savannah than he could ever make up there. It's a trade-off. There's no culture down here and the people are backward. But you probably know that already."

"What will they do with him?"

She hesitated. "Ever heard of electro-convulsive therapy? It's also called 'shock treatments.' It's been known to work wonders in cases like Nathan's. We want the best for him, I hope you understand that."

"I see," I said, then just smiled like a kid would, and talked about the weather. I realized what Andy meant then about the "Jewish *kop*." I would have it to use it, even with Jews. Faye was at the Streitts' house, looking very pretty in a flower-print dress with a small white Peter Pan collar. She seemed very fresh and appealing with her bare arms and a sweet innocence in her face. She reminded me of some young teen star like Natalie Wood.

"It's nice to see you," she said, smiling. "I hear things haven't been going very good for you lately. I'm sorry."

"They're not," I said. "But I don't want to talk about it. You're looking really pretty."

She thanked me. "I hear you're living with your grandparents? They're not Jewish, are they?"

"They're my mother's parents. The Blakelys aren't Jewish. But they have Jewish friends."

"Does it confuse you, I mean being half Jewish and half not?"

I shrugged and tried to smile.

"I'm not confused. I'm just myself. Both my parents let me be that way, most of the time."

"How about the other times?" she asked seriously.

"That's the time when I have the most fun," I said wickedly, and giggled.

Her face went really sour, like I'd made a dirty pass at her. Or maybe that just wasn't the sort of thing nice Jewish boys were supposed to say to nice Jewish girls. I thought about Laura Murphy, the Virgin Mary who, I had a feeling, wasn't. Laura would have taken what I said right and laughed with me.

"Do you know what movie we're going to see?" I asked to change the subject.

She told me no, and then we tried to pretend that nothing had happened. There were several other kids at the Streitts, some with licenses. So we drove in two cars to a Shoney's out on Victory Drive. I sat next to Allan and his chubby girlfriend Sue Strickler, not Faye, and had a burger, a Coke, and a piece of strawberry pie. Allen and Sue reminded me of a salt and pepper shaker set; they resembled each other so much in size and facial appearance. Then we went to a movie downtown that did have Natalie Wood in it, and I sat next to Faye. I put my arm around her; it just seemed like the correct thing to do. I could tell she wasn't too happy about it at first; then she warmed up to me and placed her hand on my knee. It felt really good there.

Then her hand edged up to my thigh, and—as the guys say, I popped a boner. I was really embarrassed. I watched the screen, afraid to move for any reason, hoping she didn't notice it. I tried to think about something far away, anything *not* exciting, but all I could think about was Nathan and what Mrs. Streitt had told me. I had this horrifying thought. Suppose "word" got out about *me*, and people tried to put me in a hospital? I saw myself in a straitjacket, straining to rip my arms and hands free from it. Then I realized Caroline would never do anything like that to me. *Never.* She'd always be kinder and more loving than the Streitts. Anyway, she was *in* a mental hospital.

Now I could get up. I asked Faye if she wanted anything from the concession stand. She said she'd like a Coke. I managed to slide in the dark past all the people on the row. An usher opened the door for me. Out in the light of the lobby, I felt better.

Suddenly I didn't want to see the movie because all I could think about was Nathan and what he must have been going through. Why were people so stupid, so unable to see that Nathan was a good person who tried to be honest about everything? He had been honest about me when he'd first met me—not very nice, but honest. I went to the concession stand and got a large Coke for Faye and a roll of Necco Wafers for me. When I got back I asked Faye in a whisper if I had missed anything.

"Just me," she said.

"Good."

She put her hand back on my knee, then slowly moved it up to my thigh again. I took her hand and held it, afraid I'd return to that situation where I couldn't get up.

"This is nice," she said.

I squeezed her hand, then let go of it and pretended to watch the movie; she dropped it into my lap and softly stroked my thigh.

Now I wondered if she was just playing a game. All guys talked about girls who cock-teased you until they got what they wanted, like to go steady or get your class ring. I was too young for any of that, although I knew guys who went steady, like dumb Mel Harris who was going steady with a dog from St. Agnes's. He thought it was a big deal, but we all laughed because she made the term "ugly as sin" look good. She was kind of fat, bowlegged and flat-chested, but then he was no prize himself, even with his rich lawyer father. Caroline used to say that God made couples like that for a purpose, but "they shouldn't reproduce, although they *always* do."

I smiled just thinking about that, which would give anyone a complete hard-off.

After the movie we all went back to the Streitts for coffee and cake. Nobody talked about Nathan at all; it was like he had died. I wanted to ask Allan about him but knew I couldn't. Scott Schneider was there, but he was the last person I could ask. He would have made some disgusting comment like "Y'mean the homo?"—even in the Streitts' house, about their son.

I had a private moment with Faye, and we began kissing. It was really nice, although not nearly as nice as kissing Laura Murphy or even Nathan for that matter. This made me feel really bad, like I wanted it to be different. I could imagine marrying a girl like Faye, although her parents would probably put up some fuss about me not "really" being Jewish. So, as Robby would have said, I put some "real English" behind kissing her and I could tell that she was pretty turned on by it. I was good at it, I knew it, and I felt good about that, too.

I felt good about everything, like someone has just turned on the happiness switch and it floods you with it. I stopped thinking about Nathan and everything; I was just kissing Faye Jacobson, this pretty girl, and everything about doing it was perfect. Scott Schneider came by and saw me, and smiling gave me an index-finger-and-thumb-together circle sign. It said, "You've got it here, kiddo." Scott was a *shmuck*, but sometimes you want shmucks to like you, too.

When I got into Grandpa Blakely's car he asked me if I'd had a good time. I told him I had.

"Did you spend some time with some girls?" I nodded. "Isn't that great? I remember when I was your age and I spent time with girls. Nothing feels like it. Know what I mean?"

I wondered if he was talking about boners, but I said yeah anyway.

"Does she want to see you again?"

"I think so."

"Take it slow. Just think of girls as being like icing on the cake. Too much icing can make you sick, but cake with no icing—pretty bad, don't you think?"

I wished I could have talked with him about Nathan, but knew I couldn't.

"How's Mom?" I asked.

"Things are working out for her," he said seriously. "But it's a slow process. It's slow for all of us, Benjy. We have to get used to your father not being here, and for real changes in our lives. I want you to know I'll always be honest with you. Your father lived in his own special world, but sometimes that world was not the way the real world is."

"What does that mean?" I asked.

"Mr. Geyer has sold your house, and that means that your mom and you kids will have to live someplace else when she gets out of the hospital. It's not going to be as big and wonderful as your house in Isle of Hope was."

"Can't we just live with you and Grandma?"

"It would be better if you don't. Your grandma and I are getting old. We don't even know how long we can be in that house. But let's don't think about it right now. We'll just wait until your mom gets out of the hospital."

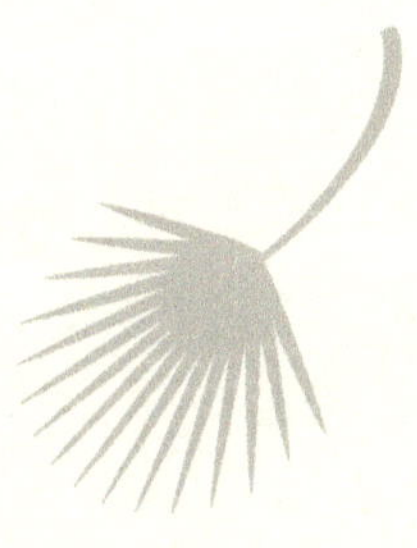

Part Four:
Within the Light

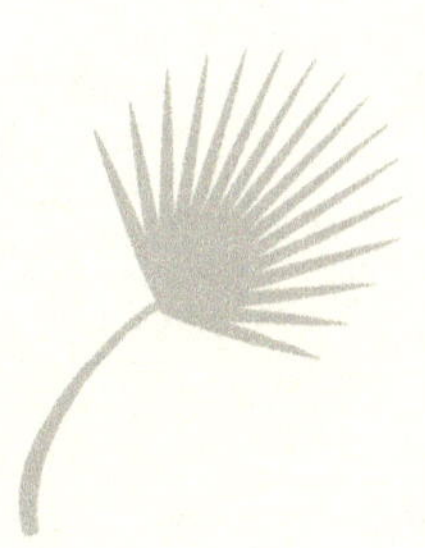

35

A Meeting With Tim

Exactly a week later, the next Saturday, I took a bus over to the O'Neills to go out and have a Coke with Tim. He smiled at me at the door; I could see that his mom was at home, but not his twin brothers. I was glad—I didn't want to run into Neal there. Mrs. O'Neill gave Tim fifty cents, and we walked out. There was a nice drug store with a soda fountain a pleasant walk away down Victory Drive, a broad avenue lined with palm trees and greenery. We were both wearing shorts because it was getting a lot warmer, the way Savannah did in the spring.

"I've got a hard-on," Tim announced, grinning at me.

"Why?" I asked.

"Dunno. Maybe just 'cause it's fun to have one. You got one, too?"

"No!"

Right there in broad daylight, he ran his hand down the front of my shorts. Victory Drive was a busy street, with cars speeding down it, and there was no telling who could be in one of them.

"Stop that," I said, really annoyed at Tim.

"I'm just playin' with you," he said. "That's all, sorry."

Then, suddenly I popped a boner too. I don't have the world's biggest dick, but it was popping right out there in front of my shorts. Cars were stopped at a red light and I could feel people looking at us. I *saw* them looking. I wanted to get off Victory Drive as soon as we could.

"Why don't we go in there?" I asked and pointed to a small park with a playground close by.

"I thought we were getting Cokes?"

"They can wait."

"You're embarrassed?" he asked. "'Cause of your dick?"

"Just leave it alone. Let's go to the park."

The park had wooden benches and picnic tables. We sat at a picnic table; Tim sat next to me and tried to feel me up under the bench. I hated him doing this, even though he was only joking around. I knew there were things I could not do with Tim that I might want to do with somebody else—like really kiss him, or even go down on him for real—but it was just not possible.

"So," he said. "What'd you say to Neal that got him so upset?"

"We talked about Arthur."

"Can't you just leave it alone? I told ya, Arthur's in heaven. Simple as that. It's where all good Catholics go."

"But he wasn't a good Catholic, and I know what went on when he died. I know all about it."

Tim's whole appearance changed completely—his face fell—I wondered how much he knew. He put both his hands on the picnic table and stopped looking at me. For a second, I thought he was just going to walk away.

"No one's s'posed to know it," he said, turning back to me. "Who told you?"

"Brother Alex—maybe he's Robert Grainger now. He told me just before he left."

"The whole thing?"

I nodded. "How d'you know?" I asked. "I thought Neal told no one."

"I put two and two together, or one and one." He grinned nervously, briefly. "I figured something happened while Neal was with Arthur. I knew Neal was sweet on him, and let's be frank: Neal goes both ways. He ain't a queer, but he likes guys—I mean foolin' around with 'em. And I figured Storch and his ghouls had somethin' t' do with it, just the way they been actin'."

"You figured this all out on your own?"

"Sure," he said smartly. "But it ain't goin' any further, Benjy. This could destroy the whole school if it got out. You wanna get the investigation goin' again, don't you?"

"Of course I do. I owe it to Arthur."

"You don't! God has forgiven Arthur. He's forgiven everybody."

"Why should God forgive Arthur?"

"'Cause Arthur wanted to die right there."

"How would you know that?" I insisted. "Neal must have told you *something*. You didn't figure it all out by yourself. Did you, Tim?"

Tim paused. Some little kids, maybe six or seven, passed by with their moms on their way to the slides and swings at the other end of the playground. Their moms smiled at us.

"Hi ya'll doin'?" one mom asked.

"Fine, ma'am," Tim answered, putting on his dimply smile until they'd left.

"I got it out of Neal one night," he admitted. "I got him drunk and started playing with him and he told me. I think he'd kill you if this got out, and if he didn't, somebody else would."

I put my head down on the table, burying my face in my hands. I couldn't help crying.

"You gotta stop this," Tim said. "Somebody could see. They'll think you're a pansy."

"That's *all* they think about!" I said, rising up. "Anybody who ever tells the truth is a pansy, a homo, or a queer. Light in the loafers. He sucks *nigger* dicks. It's always something bad. I can't just forget about Arthur. He was murdered."

"You gotta, Benjy. If you was Catholic, everything would be OK. You'd go to Confession, but God would forgive you, the same way He's forgiven Arthur."

"But who forgave Storch and Ferris?"

"They were just part of God's will, Benjy. Poor Arthur wasn't gonna survive anyway. Don't you know that? His old man was close t' killin' him. He was this poor Puerto Rican kid who got into a good school, but his luck ran out. My parents felt terrible for him, but nobody's gonna destroy us because of Arthur Gomez."

"Then you feel you can live with this?" I asked. I'd stopped crying. Now I felt pretty lucid. I had to know.

"Any good Catholic could live with this, because inside the Sacred Heart of Jesus, it *is* forgiven. There is no more 'eye for an eye,' there is only forgiveness. We're just kids. We have to be forgiven."

"I see," I said.

"You still want that Coke?" he asked, his face bright like only Tim could be.

We got up and walked to the drug store and looked at magazines, like *Argosy* and *Playboy*, until one of the clerks shooed us away. Then we sat down at the counter and had two Cokes.

"You still thinkin' about becomin' Catholic?" Tim asked me.

"No, I don't think I'll ever be able to figure it out."

"It's kind of like bein' a Jew. You really have to be born this way. My mom knows some converts, and they never *really* make the change. Either they try too hard, or not enough."

"Why is that?" I asked sucking down the last of my Coke through a straw.

"Because if you're born Catholic, you don't really believe all this stuff, you *are* it. It's part of you, and even when it ain't part of you, you still find this place where it protects you. Where no matter how bad things get, you can go to it—like the Kennedys. They lost Jack and Joe Junior and a lotta other things, but the Church takes care of you in it's own funny kind o' way. If you ain't Catholic, it seems—well, weird. The statues, and the nuns and the faggoty priests in dresses. But once you know it and become part of the mystery, you can live with anything. Even if you hate yourself sometimes."

So that was the secret.

"I see," I said quietly. "I'm glad you could tell me this."

36

The Graduation

My mom came out of the hospital a few weeks later, earlier than Andy had predicted. Still it was hard to recognize her. She was no longer the striking blond woman I remembered who sang along to pop songs on the radio and sat upstairs on the veranda drinking Salty Dogs with her friends. Most of her friends had disappeared. Her face was lined; her hair was gray and she didn't color it. We moved to a walk-up rental apartment in an older, run-down section of town, in an upper story of a peeling wooden tenement that had not changed since the Depression. It had cockroaches in the shower, and a kitchen where the smell of generations of grease never disappeared no matter what Mom did to it. Grandma and Grandpa oversaw the move, but so much of our stuff had to be sold or put into storage that it felt like we'd never lived another life before. The only thing that remained for me of the "other life" was going to Holy Nativity. Everyday I reminded myself how much joy Robby had got from that, and how much I had liked it at the beginning, after I left public school with the redneck kids who acted like I was some kind of zoo animal to go to a Catholic military school, full of smart, caring monks like Brother Alexis and the assortment of boys who went there.

I felt at this point that I had to tell myself a deeper story, one beyond the fact that we had come down so far in life. I thought about Robby a lot, what he would instill in me, how he would have handled things—even if I *was* only creating a fiction. But didn't Robby create his *own* fictions? Maybe he had needed to do that to survive. But I felt that Robby was urging me to have some kind of backbone, and not give in to sadness and loss. So what if we were no longer in the big white house by the water in Isle of Hope that he'd had to work so hard to keep us in, with a maid and the nice cars Caroline and Robby Rothberg once drove? So what if I'd not be able to return to Holy Nativity at the beginning of the new school year—what else could I do? What else would Robby *want* me to do?

When I was doing my homework or just staring into space sometimes, I'd hear Arthur's voice saying, "I never had a friend like you." There were times when I wanted so badly to touch him that it hurt. When I was alone or in bed, I would touch myself and pretend I was touching Arthur's firmly soft chest, or his back, or his throat, running my fingers lightly over his skin and feeling its golden-brown silkiness, so different from Tim's pale skin. Or Faye's, which seemed like it might be covered in pearls, but still was not like Arthur's amazing, magical skin, that skin and all the feelings under it, that were now in my dreams, even my waking ones.

There was also kissing him, and I did kiss him in my sleep. And kissing him became infused with the experience of kissing Nathan, Nathan who had told me that he had loved me, even though I could not accept it. How could I? And be labeled a *queer* and sent off to God-knew-where, even though I knew that Caroline would never do that to me? She was still smart; she had a Jewish *kop* of her own. Liz was going to a public school nearby. It was filled with rough kids from the area, all white, because it had not been integrated yet.

"I hope she doesn't end up dumber than dirt like those kids," Caroline said to me. "They don't know what life is really like, that it takes all kinds of colors to make the rainbow and humans are only part of those colors. You know that, don't you?" I nodded. "I don't regret anything about your father. I loved him. I just regret that I wasn't strong enough to do what I had to do to get him out of this."

"What would that have been?"

"I would have sold everything—and got us back up North."

I wondered where she'd got that idea. Andy would have called it another dream. He was up North now, and wrote us letters every now and then. He was getting married to an older woman named Clare Stein who had an apartment in a place called Brooklyn Heights. I had never been to Brooklyn. It seemed kind of savage; I remembered movies about it with gangs and juvenile delinquents. Despite our coming down the social ladder, Savannah still seemed more gracious and livable. I had no idea that Brooklyn had parks and museums and was actually another city attached to New York. To me the whole world seemed like it was bordered by water and the past. But that would soon change.

The school year was quickly ending. At the end of the last week in May, Father Greer asked me to come into his office to inform me that it looked like I would not be returning to Holy Nativity the next year.

"Usually by this time parents have filled out a form with a deposit," he explained. "I don't see any form of this kind from your mother or your grandfather Judge Blakely."

"I guess that's the truth then, sir," I said.

"We're sad to see you go, young man. We've enjoyed having your presence here. You have added a—" He paused. I wondered what he was up to. Now that Robby was no longer donating anything extra to the school, what did he really think—what had he *ever* thought of me, really?

"Could I apply for a scholarship, sir?" I asked, filling in the pause.

"You could, Benjy, but I have to tell you, those usually go to promising Catholic students from impoverished families, like poor Arthur Gomez. He was attending Holy Nativity on a full scholarship. Terrible what happened to Arthur, but I'm sure these things are God's will, and—"

"Who are we to question it?" I interjected.

"Exactly, Benjy. Who are *we* to question it?"

"I questioned it," I said, my eyes rising to his.

"Then perhaps, young man, you don't believe in the will of God as strongly as we do."

For a moment, my eyes scanned around his office, to the picture of St. Sebastian, then they returned to him.

"Nevertheless," he said, almost cheerfully. "We've been happy to have you here as a student at Holy Nativity. And at the end of the term, we'll send your mother a complete transcript of your classes and grades, so you can make a smooth transition to whatever school you prefer next to attend."

He got up and shook my hand; I rose and gave him a quick salute and left. I didn't want to tell anybody else that I wouldn't be coming back, but Tim knew, his mother being on the Parents' Committee. At recess he took me aside and told me how sorry he was and shook my hand.

"It just ain't gonna be the same without you, Rothberg. Jesus, Storch'll be here and you won't."

"But we can still be friends, can't we?" I said.

"Sure," he said, but I knew he didn't believe it. Once I was out of the uniform of Holy Nativity, there would be a barrier between us, a barrier even higher than my being half-Jewish.

The last event of the year was graduation, and by custom, every boy in the school would attend it. It was like the summer retreat or the Christmas pageant, the idea being that it wasn't just a thing you did, but it brought you closer to God and the school. There were eighty boys in the graduating class, a scant number compared to a larger public school, and among them were Neal and Pat O'Neill who were there with their parents, as were all the other graduating boys.

The ceremony was held in the afternoon in the school auditorium, which wasn't air conditioned; so the idea was to get it done quickly. The school choir sang a Catholic hymn and then "America, the Beautiful." A white-haired priest named Father Gagnon, whom I had never seen before, from the big Catholic cathedral downtown, gave the invocation. Then one of the graduates, a tall, awkward guy named William McIntyre with a tight-lipped, Richard Nixon kind of face, gave the Salutatorian's speech. I had a feeling he'd copied it from God-knows-how-many-other graduation addresses; he must have used the word "promise" about twelve times. I realized then that Arthur would never have his graduation, or his promise. I choked up thinking about it, and blew my nose into a tissue I had in my pocket. Tim looked at me and smiled. He was sitting with his parents, instead of with his class.

It became time to give out the diplomas. Brother Peter hammered away as usual at the piano, something that sounded like "Pomp and Circumstances." I watched as the graduates' names were called, and they marched up to get their rolled up certificates. I really wasn't thinking a whole lot, even when Pat O'Neill got up to give the Valedictorian's Address.

"I want to thank all of you," he began. "But mostly my teachers and my parents for making this day happen. This is a day when we realize how close we all are—and how blessed we all are—to have a future in this country. Despite our differences we are really all one people, all close in the same Faith, all believing in the same God whose Son gave His life for us on Calvary, that we may be joined in eternal life, all—"

I will never know what happened to me then, but something did. I jumped up and shouted, "What about Arthur Gomez? Where is *his* eternal life? Why has there been *no* investigation of his death? No *real* investigation, no—"

I was stopped by Storch on top of me, calling me a "Jew bastard!" At least three cadets in stiff uniforms from the graduating class were pulling him off me and hitting me at the same time. I dunked down into my seat, but there was no way I could get escape. And from what? What could I really get away from? I looked up. Pat O'Neill was shaking on the stage, and Neal beside him looked like he wanted to kill me. Father Greer appeared next to me, and everything quieted down.

"Mr. Rothberg and Mr. Storch! In my office right now!"

I hurried out of the auditorium, with everyone booing and throwing whatever they could at me, followed by Horace Storch, held in check by several teachers including Brother Ulrich, who was definitely on Storch's side, and Father Paul Peeley.

"I should murder you, you fuckin' Jew bastard," Storch kept saying while Brother Ulrich tried to shush him up.

I saw Ferris racing toward us. "He never got over his fairy friend," he said. "They all stick together, these homos!"

Suddenly I felt really good—like you can't imagine how good. If only it *were* true. If only queers did stick together, no matter who or what the queers were. The funny thing was that I wasn't even scared. What else could they do to me? They'd talk about me, maybe, until it was forgotten, or whitewashed and covered over like they'd done with Arthur, until I was just another name in a file. When I went over to the big public school in the fall, I'd have a reputation for being a troublemaker, but maybe in a larger school that wouldn't be the worst thing to have.

Father Greer, in his full military uniform, escorted me into his office alone and shut the door hard behind him.

"I want you out of this school immediately, Mr. Rothberg," he said without sitting down. "You've already had your finals, so we can't keep you from them. Still, I could hold back your transcript for this kind of disruption."

I would not let him intimidate me. "My grandfather'll sue you," I said. "He's not Catholic and he's not scared of you."

"You're an insolent young man, Mr. Rothberg. I want you to leave *now*. You're an offense to Catholic education."

"Thank you, sir," I said smartly, and turned to the door.

Storch and Ferris were sitting on a bench outside, with Brother Ulrich and Father Peeley standing over them. Peeley nodded to me curtly, then turned and disappeared. I stood up straight; I was now on my own.

"I'll kill you!" Storch screamed at me.

"Like you killed Arthur Gomez?" I said.

"You cocksucker! You're a cocksucker!"

The word no longer bothered me. I smiled. I was going to say the truth, and nothing would stop me.

"You're a murderer, Storch," I said calmly, and looked at Brother Ulrich and Ferris. "And they *both* know it."

They both looked away from me. Storch's shoulders were squeezed all the way up to his chin, he was so tense. I could hear his strained breathing, like air mixed with a gallon of snot.

"Shut up!" he exploded, spewing spit all over. "YOU COCKSUCKER!"

Ferris didn't say a word; but neither could he look at Storch or the old monk. I could tell that what I'd said had finally hit him: that his buddy Storch had murdered Arthur and Brother Ulrich knew about it. He looked like he was ready to pee in his uniform.

"I've got t' leave," he said, starting to get up. But Storch grabbed him, and jerked him back down on the bench forcefully. Ferris remained there as Storch buried his face in his hands, convulsing with sobs.

"There, there," Brother Ulrich said softly, trying to calm Storch without actually touching him. "Be quiet, Horace. It seems all of you boys have had more than enough t' say, and none of it's goin' t' bring back poor Arthur Gomez. As far as this school's concerned, it was only a tragic accident. He drowned all by himself. Now he's right with God. That's the only thing that counts."

I looked at Ulrich—Dorris Mahoney—leaning over Storch, who was trying hard to pull himself together. Storch lifted his red face up to Ulrich.

"It's…it's…God's will," Storch cried, choking on his own thick tears. "God's will."

"It was," Ulrich intoned softly.

"Even you don't believe that," I said to Brother Ulrich.

"GET OUTTA HERE!" Storch screamed.

"Just leave it alone, Horace," Brother Ulrich said, edging a bit closer to Storch. "Soon he'll be out."

Ulrich looked at me and smiled. Our eyes locked on each other. His smile was so chilling, so destructive, that it embodied everything I'd hated at Holy

Nativity and could not overcome. For a second, I wanted to run out as fast as I could, but Mahoney stopped me with a motion of his hand.

"The only satisfaction I'll get out of this," he said calmly, "is knowing that you're going back to your *own* people ... no matter who they are."

I nodded—how funny. I almost started laughing. He was right.

"I am," I said. "And I'll find them."

"Good," Mahoney said. He lowered his face to Storch and Ferris, then shot his eyes back at me. "Now get the hell out."

I did—and left, trying to avoid people as much as possible—dashing out a side door, away from the parking lot, thinking I'd be alone. But I wasn't. The first person I saw was Neal O'Neill. He must have been following me, and I was scared now, not simply because of what Neal might do to me—and anything including murder seemed possible—but because of my own feelings for him that I couldn't shake. I'd never forget how Neal had driven me back to Isle of Hope that night after the Pink House, and how he'd made me feel when I was so fleetingly close to him—as if that moment in the car, out there in the marshes with its own softness of light, *was* mine. The O'Neills would cut me off completely now. But Neal didn't look terribly angry, just distant, like I was no longer worthy of his fury. As if, not being a Catholic, I was now outside even his own version of hell. He approached me and grabbed my arm, but not very hard.

"Stay here, Pat wants to speak to you," he ordered, and left me.

I could have run, but knew I shouldn't. I'd destroyed Pat's glory, his Valedictory moment. I owed it to him to stay. I was sure Robby would have told me that, and in this he was right. It was definitely part of the moral teachings of Holy Nativity.

Neal came back with Pat, and Pat approached me. His face was so dark that I couldn't see his eyes, sunken under his wrinkled brow, and his fine, beautiful black Irish hair. I felt like we were two knights meeting alone on a battlefield, with only Arthur watching.

Suddenly his eyes emerged from the darkness, and he slapped me as hard as he could across my face, knocking me back into reality. What *knights . . .* Arthur?

"Do it again," Neal ordered. "Hit him again!"

Pat's fist smashed into my stomach, with his whole body behind it. I crumpled to the pavement, close to throwing up. Pat crouched down and looked at me. He was crying, openly.

"You did the right thing, Rothberg," he sobbed.

"Shut up!" Neal said as loud as he could without screaming. He pulled Pat up away from me, and hugged him while Pat cried.

"I hope you're satisfied," Neal said, and spat at me. "I hope you're fuckin' satisfied."

I was very happy that Caroline had not been at the graduation. She wasn't in the mood to go to public situations like that anymore; they had become embarrassing to her. I didn't tell her anything about what happened. She seemed to be in a haze that I could only penetrate at times, mostly when she snapped into focus about something that irritated her. If I needed a dose of actual reality, I'd go to Grandpa Blakely, and he wasn't as honest as Andy Geyer had been with me, although the fact was I still didn't trust Andy.

I didn't call Tim to apologize, which is probably what I should have done if I had been a real *mentsh*. I could only imagine the way Tim must have felt afterwards. But it just wasn't possible. In all probability, Robby would have said to me, "You don't screw your friends, Benjy. Why'd you have to do something so painful to people who were nice to you?"

On the other hand, my father had always been truthful with me, or as truthful as he felt he could be, since in his eyes I would remain a kid forever. I guess that's what makes us love our parents, no matter what; they still see innocence inside us, after it's gone. I knew mine was gone, as gone as it could be at close to fifteen. I was a teenager, all raging hormones and flat-out, unmissable boners walking down the street. The good thing was that the Streitts, also, had not been at the graduation (they were Jews, why would they go?), and neither had Faye Jacobson.

I knew that Faye went to Chatham High School, and I'd see her next year. Maybe we'd start going steady—I'd need a steady girlfriend at a large public high school. I knew I'd be lost there, just another kid; the school had just become integrated, and I told myself that I'd make friends with some colored kids, because that was something I'd become used to at Holy Nativity.

The thought that I'd not be going back there really hit me the first few hot days of summer. There were not a lot of kids around, and the kids who were there were a lot rougher than I was used to. They reminded me of the redneck kids from Isle of Hope, just more grown up. Or was it that I had grown up? I was challenged to fights on the sidewalks and called a queer and a sissy just for walking down the street with Liz.

"Why do they hate you?" Liz asked.

"I dunno. Maybe because we don't look like them?"

"We don't look like anybody, do we? You look like Dad and I look more like Mom, but we still don't look like anybody else."

I told her that was fine. Eventually some of the kids stopped calling me names and we became friends; that is, we could talk to each other in that ambling Southern way, and smile and just walk off in other directions. I was starting to feel bad about such things and then the phone rang one afternoon at the end of June. I answered it myself.

"It's me, Nathan," the voice said.

"You're back!" Obviously he knew where to find me, which made me happy.

"Yeah. They did enough shit to me. They decided I had turned around. Let me pick you up. We'll go to the beach."

I told him that was great; he knew I wasn't living in Isle of Hope anymore.

"My folks have been talking about it," he said. "They keep telling me you're living with *goyim*."

"And I wasn't in Isle of Hope?"

"You were living with rich white people out there. Now you're not. You know how Jews in the South are, money trumps religion."

"What does *trump* mean?"

"It means—hell, I'll explain it later."

Nathan Again

Nathan picked me up a short time later in a small gray Chevy sedan that looked older, and more beat up than his sporty Karmman Ghia. Nathan also looked older. He had gained a little bit of weight and had lines around his eyes and mouth. His hands shook, and he licked his lips as if his mouth were constantly dry.

"You look good. How are you?" he asked, after I got into the car and he'd lit a cigarette.

"I'm OK."

"Really?" He put his hand on my bare knee. I was wearing shorts and he was in jeans.

He started the car again and we headed off for the beach. I told him everything, about what Robert Grainger had told me, and what had happened at the graduation. It was wonderful to have someone I could talk to and be honest with.

"I can't believe you did that," he said. "You're fantastic. I wish I had your balls. I'd leave my parents, and this fucking town. I'd go live in New York in the Village, or Chicago or someplace like that."

"Your mom told me you'd been sent away."

"I sure was. She found out about Myron, and connected you with that evening. I guess she wanted to know if I'd done anything to you."

"I told her no. It's none of her business."

"Good. Why don't we go to Hilton Head, it's deserted? There's hardly anyone there. We can talk."

"I can't be away that long. I told Mom I was going off with you to the beach."

"We'll go to another beach then, near Wormsloe Plantation. Ever been there?"

Wormsloe was an old plantation, now mostly in ruins, left over from colonial times; originally they had tried to raise silk worms there, thus the name. I'd never been there before, even though it was close to Isle of Hope. I'd heard it was still private, but Nathan assured me that no one would bother us. I'd learned about the plantation in a Georgia history course that basically left out Jews and colored people. While Nathan drove, I sat back and watched the beautiful trees, the quiet old homes, and repeating glimpses of the water, and realized that I *would* leave here someday, and go someplace where no one questioned who I was.

The place we parked could hardly be called a beach. It was just some rocky sand on an inlet of water that lapped right up to palmetto trees and tall stands of swamp grass. I got out and took my bathing suit and towel. Nathan had a towel, but no suit. We found a shady, secluded place and spread out the towels.

"We could swim naked here if we want to," he said.

I told him I didn't.

"I guess you're scared," he said smiling. "I've learned not to be scared anymore—at least not *too* scared. Basically, my parents wanted to punish me; that was the first thing, I think, that went into their heads. You know how Jews are? Everything's a punishment from God, so humans have to be a part of that."

"So they sent you away just to punish you?"

"The more I think about it, the more it seems that way. My parents really believe God punishes Negroes by making them black." He smiled, and went on. "And I guess God punished me by making me queer, so they had to add their own two cents. The things those people in New York did to me! Drugs. Shock treatments. But I lucked out. I met this young social worker there. He told me that the biggest problem I'd have being queer is hating myself, just because other stupid people do. 'You need to be honest with yourself,' he told me. 'And if you are, you'll learn to like yourself, which you should.' When he said that, it was like somebody just turned on a light."

"I like you," I said.

"Do you?"

He leaned over and kissed me and I let him. He put his hands inside my bathing suit, and I told him not to do that.

"Why?" he asked.

"Cause I'm not sure I want you to."

"OK. But what makes you not sure?"

"I dunno. I like it when you kiss me though."

"I like kissing you. Are you scared?"

"I feel like I'm too different already," I admitted. "Next year when I go off to Chatham High School, the kids'll already know I came from Holy Nativity. They'll think I got kicked out just because of Arthur Gomez. Y'know how kids talk?"

"You'll be strong," he said. "You've already got some idea of who you are and those other kids don't have a clue yet. All they can do is mouth what they think their parents want to hear. They'll hate the same people their parents hate and think the same things. But you are *different*. You're already your own self. That's why people are so attracted to you."

It was true: there had to be something different about me, even though I wasn't exactly sure what it was. Suppose I didn't *have* to be afraid of being different, even if it were only inside me that I didn't have to be afraid. I smiled at Nathan and pulled his face to mine and kissed him. Really kissed him, like I couldn't remember kissing anyone before, not even Faye.

"You've really got me excited," he said.

His jeans had a bulge in the crotch.

"Why do you think people are queer?" I asked him. "What makes them that way?"

Nathan looked at me seriously, and thought for a second. "I don't know. I just know that most of the time you can't tell if someone's that way, even if you think you can. Except maybe 'screaming queens.' Maybe you've heard of them; I'm sure you even know kids who are one hundred percent sissy—you aren't, but you must know them."

"I've never met one."

"Don't worry, you will. They always have girlfriends to cover up with. Anyway, most of the time you can't tell. Some guys come off a hundred percent normal, and then suddenly you find out they're queer as a three-dollar bill. But I think it's kind of like magic; suddenly we're there when you don't expect it— like that social worker. His name is Sam Levitts. He's gay, but he couldn't let me on to it. But I could feel it and it was wonderful, just to have him there at that hospital. When I got there I was so depressed I couldn't even walk, so of course they decided to give me shock treatments. What I really needed was someone to throw me a lifeline. Sam got me off the shock treatments."

"I wish I could have saved Arthur."

"You're really in love with him, aren't you?"

"Is that what being in love is like?"

"It's like magic, too. It's sad and beautiful. And people are scared of it, just like they're also scared of magic. Real magic, the kind they can't explain, without even a magician involved. That's why they're so scared of homosexuality, there's no magician around and they can't explain it. They try hard, but they just can't do it. Maybe we're all magicians."

"But the magic?" I asked. "What does it do? It doesn't keep us from being hurt."

He smiled at me, I loved his smile. It seemed to come directly from his heart, like Robby's had.

"Maybe it *trumps* everything," he said. "Even money. God has got to be in it someplace, because ultimately, it keeps us from being scared."

Ah, now I understood what he had meant by *trumps*. I had to ask him something. "What'll you do when you get old and you don't have kids?"

"Allan'll have kids. I'll be their Uncle Nathan; maybe you'll have kids with that Faye girl."

"I don't think so," I said.

He smiled at me. "Why not?"

As an answer, I unzipped his jeans and began to get them off him. He started kissing me again. Then before I could do anything else, he took up the towels and we found a place further back in the trees. I wasn't scared anymore, at least not at that moment. I felt that my brain was completely open, and everything around me was entirely a part of me. It was strange to feel that way at almost fifteen, but I did. I could say what we did but I don't feel that I should. But nothing we did was anything I didn't want, and after it was over—after he had brought me to climax and I had his semen on me, on my chest and even some in my mouth—all I wanted to do was hold on to him.

"We'd better go," he said. "Do you want to swim? It'll wash everything off."

"Will you swim, too? We can do it naked."

We did, and it was wonderful until we heard another car come up and knew that we'd better run to our towels as soon as possible. I rushed back into my swimsuit and Nathan jumped into his jeans. The car parked and a plain-looking white couple emerged with their two small kids, a boy and a girl. The man was balding and tall in tan pants and a T-shirt and had a wrinkled face that looked like a hawk's. His wife was much shorter and pregnant.

"You boys like swimmin' here?" the man asked warily.

"Yes, suh," Nathan said, putting on a heavy Southern drawl I'd not heard before.

"Well, you jus' bettuh watch y'selves—they got rattlers in these woods. They come out and'll bite y' hard when y' not lookin'! Understan' what I mean?"

He kept giving us that knowing hawk-smirk that was more threat than anything he said.

"Uh do, suh," Nathan drawled.

The man just squinted his eyes at us and said, "Janey, get them kids back in the car. We ain't stayin'." The kids put up a fuss, but she pulled them back in, and they drove off.

"Guess they must live in some swamp around here," Nathan said, suddenly laughing. "I thought this place was deserted. I came here with Myron once. We didn't do anything though. I wonder if that guy saw us in the water."

It was time for me to go back. I told Nathan that I wanted to see him again, that we could go to the beach together or do something else. I really needed to have him as a friend.

"I can't see you a lot," he said. "My parents will start to put two-and-two together and get worried that I'm doing something with you. You know how my mom is. I'm going to leave here as soon as I can and go off to college. But I'll make sure you can always reach me, I mean that."

Before we left Wormsloe, he kissed me again. I felt kind of beachy-sunburned and salty and he did too. I loved being next to him, with the fresh beach feel and the saltiness, the smell of the pines around us, and the water close by. I was sure I'd love that feeling for the rest of my life.

I saw Nathan one more time that summer. I had gone over to see Allan, and Nathan was home. We pretended nothing had happened. He went upstairs and at a certain moment I excused myself to go to the bathroom and walked into his room.

"I'm glad you're here," he whispered. "God, I'd love to kiss you."

"I know," I said. "But not now."

I smiled at him and walked away. I was glad I got to do that.

Then I pretended to be a kid again with Allan, just an almost regular, half-

Jewish kid. We went out to the Bijou, a soda shop a few blocks away, and had Cokes. Faye and a girlfriend of hers joined us. I smiled at Faye and she smiled back, and I got up and kissed her and realized how much I enjoyed it. There was something fresh about her and sweet, and I wanted so much just to be a part of that. The way, I guess, all kids want it.

38

A Part Of Arthur Again

A few weeks before school started again, I got a transcript of my grades from Holy Nativity. I had done all my work and passed all my classes with mostly excellent grades, except for a few Bs. There were no teacher recommendations on it, nothing that said to my new teachers, "You'll be lucky to have Benjamin Rothberg as a student." I tried to imagine what might have gone on at Holy Smokes after I left, but it all seemed so far away to me. Even the O'Neills now seemed far away.

Then one morning a week before school started, there was a knock on the door. Mom told me that she wasn't expecting anyone, so I went to answer it. It was Arthur Gomez's father. For a moment I hardly recognized him. I told him to come in.

"Can you come out with me for a while?" he said. "I wanna talk to you alone, about my son."

I told Mom I was going out to the library and wouldn't be home until after lunch. She was watching soap operas on TV. Sometimes she did that for hours, and then would try to do some housework. We had no maid anymore, and the house never looked very clean but no one cared. She smiled at me and got up.

"Be careful," she said. "Make sure you have a dime to call me."

"I wanna take you on my boat," Mr. Gomez said proudly in his car. "I'm not drinking anymore. Some guys I know decided to go up North, and they let me buy their boat cheap. D'you like boats?"

I told him I did.

The small fishing boat was docked on an inlet not that far from Isle of Hope. When we got on it, he asked me if I had lived out there.

"How'd you know?" I asked.

"Arthur told me. He told me a lot about you. See, I did ask. I wasn't drunk

354

all the time and bad to him."

Soon we were out on the water, but not that far from the shore. I could even see our old house, just the top of it, very white through the trees. It made me think about Dad and the way Mom used to be, and about Liz and how we used to hide behind the doors of the veranda and listen.

Mr. Gomez put his hand on my shoulder.

"I know you been through a lot, son. One of my friends works in the kitchen at Holy Nativity. He's how we first got Arthur in there. This friend, Juan, he told me what a good school it was and how the brothers were great to the boys and how it would help Arthur become a man and do good in this country."

Mr. Gomez looked like he was ready to cry; I felt very bad for him.

"He also told me what you did at graduation. Juan was there, see? You have guts, *cajones*. I'm sorry I wasn't there. I knew they didn't do any real investigation into Arthur's death. Thinking that my son killed himself drove me crazy for a long time. He was my beautiful son. I wish I'd been a better dad to him."

"I wish I'd been a better friend," I said.

"You loved him, right?"

I hesitated, then I said, "Yes, I did love him."

"That's what's important. You can try to explain everything in the world, but what's important is that you loved him. Do they know who killed him?"

I looked at him. Suddenly knowing anything made no sense to me.

"No," I said. "They don't."

"I wish I could find out. I'd kill 'em."

"Maybe you will one day. But they'll die anyway. All I know about God will punish them."

"You're a smart kid," he said. "Arthur told me that, too."

"He was really smart himself," I said. "And really nice. I miss him a lot, like I miss my dad."

"I read in the paper he died. If you ever want a dad or just somebody like that, let me know. I'll take you out in the boat whenever you want me to. You loved my son and that's the only thing that's important to me."

I thanked him, and he drove the boat past the end of Isle of Hope, which was as beautiful as I had ever remembered it. Even the name of it was so beautiful—Isle of Hope, "I'll-a-'ope"—like Calliope; it kept repeating in my ears, like music. Then he turned the boat around and drove back to the dock. I got out first and looked at the water and the dock, feeling like the whole landscape I had passed had just seeped into me. I missed Robby so much that it was suddenly painful, like a stab directly in my heart. I never thought I'd miss him so much. The intensity of it was impossible even to fathom, and yet it was mixed with this strange sense of relief that he would never understand what I was, or even be able to name it. Still, I knew that I was his son, and in any place in this world that was the whole glory of it.

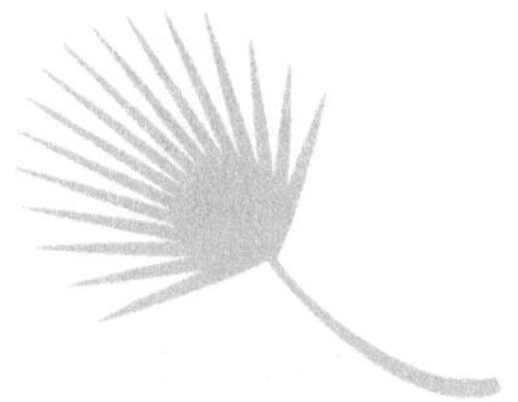

Coda

I entered Chatham High School and, as I expected, word had got out about what happened at Holy Nativity. I guess it was inevitable. There were rumors, I was sure, that I was at best weird and at worst queer. Most kids stayed clear of me, but I had developed a hard enough shell to protect me and I wasn't sure I wanted to let in anyone I didn't completely trust. Then, as is also inevitable in a reasonably small town, one afternoon in downtown Savannah I ran into one of my old classmates. Alfred Johnson was in his Holy Nativity uniform, but looked like he had grown up a lot. He was very happy to see me.

"I miss you so much, Benjy," he said. I smiled at him and he looked sheepishly back at me. "I loved your bar mitzvah. Gettin' to bless the book."

I shook his hand, but he didn't want to let go of me. He told me some of the gossip from Holy Smokes. Brother Ulrich had finally "retired," after another boy had complained to Father Greer about Mahoney luring him downstairs to the bathroom in the basement. Word about it had finally got through the school, and the kid's parents were too powerful to be ignored. Father Greer made a tearful announcement on the public address system about Mahoney's leaving, saying how "sincerely Brother Ulrich would be missed by generations of Holy Nativity cadets blessed by his dedication." Storch had also left, mostly at the insistence of Father Paul Peeley who firmly disliked him. Storch had been discreetly "pressed" to leave; the school couldn't exactly throw him out. Ferris and Flauwerty were still there, but since neither was a ringleader they stayed mostly to themselves.

I asked Alfred what had really happened to Storch.

"He started actin' strange, fallin' apart, gettin' so angry he s'ploded. Everybody noticed; there was talk he was seeing a headshrinker. That's what Tim O'Neill said, and he always knows everything." (I nodded.) "Anyway, Storch's parents jus' up and left town. He told people his father'd been transferred t'nother city, but I wonder. Ferris had started talkin', and tho' nobody could *really* talk about it, we knew Storch had done *something* to Gomez, and it was horrible. We all jus' knew it, 'specially the guys who liked Gomez. So if Storch didn't kill him outright, he sure killed him enough!"

"It's what I wanted people to know," I said. "But none of us helped Arthur, not as much as he needed it."

"I admired what you did at graduation, but I was too scared t' do anything. I'm at Holy Nativity on a full scholarship too, so—"

I told him I understood. As we said good-bye, we looked at each other for a moment, and instantly I wanted to be back in uniform again, to be like other guys back at Holy Nativity. I thought about what I had been with Tim, and Neal and Pat, and my other friends there. But that was all gone. It was like trying to bring my father back, trying to be there alone with him on the veranda, when he was Robby or, even Leon.

Later, as fall drifted into the rainy Holiday Season, that difficult time when Robby died, two letters arrived in Savannah. The first came from Montague Street in Brooklyn and was addressed to Caroline Rothberg and to me. It was from the woman Andy Geyer had married.

Dear Caroline and Benjamin,

It is my terrible duty to tell you that Andy Geyer passed away last week. He had been having some health problems and complained about short-ness of breath walking up the stairs to our place—we live in a third floor walk-up here in Brooklyn. We rushed him to the hospital after he could not make it up the stairs and fainted. He'd had a stroke and never recov-ered. I know that he loved you and Robby very much. He talked about you all the time. We made plans to come and see you so you could meet me. He felt very bad about the misfortunes that happened to your family, and was afraid that you, especially Benjamin, blamed him for them. Sometimes fate just plays out its own hand, and it did it terribly for Andy, too.

I hope at some point we can all meet. I'd like that very much. If you are ever in New York, please give me a call. I'd love to have you over here in Brooklyn and we can have a great talk.

Yours sincerely,

Claire Geyer

* * *

Strangely, Caroline took it very hard; despite her mixed feelings about Andy, he was another link with Robby as long as he was alive. She told Liz about it and Liz started crying. Andy had been a favorite of hers, and in his joking way always knew how to make her happy. So much had occurred already in Liz's short life, and even her inborn resilience was starting to fray. To cheer us up, Caroline took us out for lunch. We went for sandwiches at a drug store, since we couldn't afford much else. All three of us had Cokes.

"I want to say a toast for Andy," she said, lifting her glass. Liz and I looked at her. "Come on, lift your glasses up. Pretend it's champagne. We want to say something for him, right?"

Liz smiled and lifted her glass.

"Tell Andy that I miss his cigars, and the funny way his cheeks felt, and the way he—"

"He what, darling?" Caroline asked, lighting a cigarette and blowing out the match.

"The way he laughed at all the silly things I said," Liz said. "Nobody else would. Only he would."

I had to work hard to keep from crying. I blew my nose into a paper napkin to keep from tearing up.

"That's a good toast," I said, clearing my throat, and kissing Liz. I didn't kiss my sister that often. I'm not sure why but I didn't.

"Yes," Caroline said. "It's a good toast."

She and I looked at each other, and it was like everything I couldn't say was being said; I would never miss Andy the way I missed Robby, but later sometimes it would be hard to separate the two of them. I could hear Andy saying, "Boychik, I'm proud of you, and so is Leon." Suddenly I realized that Andy had understood me even better than Robby had, and that was why I had hurt him so much. He knew how much I had to hide, but we could never talk about it.

The second letter arrived a few weeks after that. It came from someplace in Quebec, and was addressed only to me.

Dear Benjy,

I got your address from Brother Donavan, who managed to get it from Miss Pilkin. I've been wanting to write you for a while, but things have been pretty unsettled with me. I am back in Quebec, where I come from, and everything seems wonderfully familiar except the weather—way too cold. I wanted most of all to tell you what a fine boy you are and how much I loved teaching you. I felt especially close to you, but I wanted you to know that that closeness was a natural part of me preparing you for your bar mitzvah, and also of teaching you. There was no other component in it, certainly none that would need explaining to anyone else. But I am very glad that I got to disclose the secret that I shared with you, about the death of your friend Arthur. Keeping that secret was destroying me. And it was certainly destroying my faith, not only in the other brothers at Holy Nativity, but in my calling itself.

Therefore, I want to tell you, and no one else there in Savannah, that I am leaving the order of Sebastianite brothers in which I had been professed. I'm not sure what I'll do after this, but I am leaving that religious life. However, I am exploring other avenues of faith because I believe that one of them will soon enough call me.

As for you, Benjy, I hope you will always stay in touch with me one way or another, and that you'll always question anything that will keep you away from God, as you know Him. And also, please, I want you to know that I'll always remember the great lesson you've taught me.

It is that *all you have is what you are*.

Yours truly,
Robert Grainger

THE END

Perry Brass

Originally from Savannah, Georgia, Perry Brass grew up in the late 1950s and early 1960s, equal parts Southern, Jewish, economically impoverished, and very much gay. To escape the South's violent homophobia, he hitchhiked at seventeen from Savannah to San Francisco—an adventure, he recalls, that was "like Huckleberry Finn with drag queens." He has published sixteen books and been a finalist six times for LGBT Lambda Literary Awards in poetry, gay science fiction and fantasy, spirituality and religion. His novels *Warlock* (2001) and *Carnal Sacraments* (2007) garnered Ippy Awards for Best Gay and Lesbian Fiction from the Jenkins Group/Independent Publisher, the most competitive book awards program in the world; his non-fiction bestseller *The Manly Art of Seduction* won a Gold Medal Ippy Award in 2010. *Carnal Sacraments* was also a finalist for a Best Book of the Year Award from *ForeWord* magazine.

He has been involved in the gay movement since 1969, when he co-edited *Come Out!*, the world's first gay liberation newspaper. In 1973, with two friends he started the Gay Men's Health Project Clinic, the first clinic for gay men on the East Coast, still surviving as New York's Callen-Lorde Community Health Center. In 1984, his play *Night Chills*, one of the first plays to deal with the AIDS crisis, won a Jane Chambers International Gay Playwriting Award. Brass's extensive collaborations with composers include the poetry for "All the Way Through Evening," a five-song cycle set by the late Chris DeBlasio, that recently lent its name to the title of a feature film on young composers who died of AIDS, directed by Rohan Spong; "The Angel Voices of Men" set by Ricky Ian Gordon, commissioned by the Dick Cable Fund for the New York City Gay Men's Chorus, which featured it on its *Gay Century Songbook* CD; "Three Brass Songs" set by famed composer/pianist Fred Hersch; "Five 'Russian' Lyrics," set by Christopher Berg, commissioned by Positive Music; "The Restless Yearning Towards My Self," set by composer Paula Kimper, commissioned by Downtown Music Productions, choreographed by Sasha Spielvogel; and "12 Musical Figures," set by Gerald Busby, composer for Robert Altman's influential 1977 film *3 Women*.

Perry Brass is an accomplished reader and authority on gender subjects, gay relationships, and the history and literature of the movement towards GLBT equality. He has taught numerous workshops and classes in lgbt writing and publishing, and on the hidden roots of gay culture. He lives in the Riverdale section of "da Bronx," but can cross bridges to other parts of America without a passport.

A note about the cover art by Wes Hempel

Wes Hempel is a distinguished painter, more information about his work can be found at his website, www.weshempel.com. We'd like to thank Wes for his generous use of "A New Beginning."

Helping LGBTQ Youth

There are now numerous organizations that help lesbian, gay, bisexual, transgendered, and questioning youth to feel less isolated, to deal with issues of bullying or parental rejection and neglect. Research has found that 40% of all homeless youth are LGBTQ, but many youth who live at home also need encouragement and support. There may be an organization in your area that works with lgbt youth, but here is a short list of several I feel are worthy of our support.

GLBT National Help Center (for youth and adults) National Youth TalkLine Toll-free 1-800-246-PRIDE (1-800-246-7743; http://glbtnationalhelpcenter.org)

I'm Gay Now What: an international online community for lgbt teenagers. (http://www.imgaynowwhat.com)

Hetrick-Martin Institute, New York City. Crisis Line: 1-866-488-7386 (http://www.hmi.org/)

GLSEN: Gay, Lesbian, and Straight Education Project (New York office number: 212.727.0135; http://www.glsen.org)

The Matthew Shepherd Foundation, Denver, Colorado. 303.830.7400 (http://www.matthewshepard.org)

Lost 'N' Found Youth, Inc, Atlanta nonprofit agency actively working to take homeless LGBT youth off the street. (www.lost-n-found.org; emergency hotline: 678.8-LOST-25)

Free to Be: LGBT Advocacy and Youth Services, Huntsville, Alabama 35810 (www.glbtays.org; (256) 425-7804)

Other Books by Perry Brass

Sex-charge

"...poetry at its highest voltage..."

—Marv. Shaw in Bay Area Reporter

Sex-charge. 76 pages. $6.95. With male photos by Joe Ziolkowski.
ISBN 0-9627123-0-2

Mirage *groundbreaking science fiction*

An erotically-charged gay science fiction classic! An original "coming out" and
coming-of-age saga, set in a distant place where gay sexuality and romance is
a norm, but with a life-or death price on it. On the tribal planet Ki, two men
have been promised to each other for a lifetime. But a savage attack and a blood-
chilling murder break this promise and force them to seek another world, where
imbalance and lies form Reality. This is the planet known as Earth, a world
they will use and escape. Finalist, 1991 Lambda Literary Award for Gay Men's
Science Fiction/Fantasy. This classic work of gay science fiction fantasy is now
available in its new Tenth Anniversary Edition.

"Intelligent and intriguing."

—Bob Satuloff in *New York Native*

Mirage, Tenth Anniversary Edition. 230 pages. $12.95. ISBN 1-892149-02-8

Circles *the amazing sequel to Mirage*

"The world Brass has created with Mirage and its sequel rivals, in
complexity and wonder, such greats as C. S. Lewis and Ursula LeGuin."

—*Mandate Magazine*, New York

Circles. 224 pages. $11.95. ISBN 0-9627123-3-7

Out There *Stories of Private Desires. Horror. And the Afterlife.*

"...we have come to associate [horror] with slick and trashy chiller-
thrillers. Perry Brass is neither. He writes very well in an elegant and easy
prose that carries the reader forward pleasurably. I found this selection to
be excellent."

—*The Gay Review*, Canada

Out There. 196 pages. $10.95. ISBN 0-9627123-4-5

Albert *or The Book of Man*

Third in the *Mirage* trilogy, and decades ahead of its 1995 publication date, *Albert* predicted gay marriage and the division of America into progressive "blue" states and conservative "red" ones. In 2025 the White Christian Party has taken over America. Albert, son of Enkidu and Greeland, must find the male Earth mate who will claim his heart and allow him to return to leadership on Ki.

"Brass gives us a book where lesser writers would have only a premise."
—*Men's Style*, New York

"If you take away the plot, it has political underpinnings that are chillingly true. Brass has a genius for the future." Science Fiction Galaxies, Columbus, OH. "Erotic suspense and action . . . a pleasurable read."
—*Screaming Hyena Review*, Melbourne, Australia

Albert. 210 pages. $11.95. ISBN 0-9627123-5-3

Works *and Other 'Smoky George' Stories, Expanded Edition*

"Classic Brass," these stories—many set in the long-gone seventies, when, as the author says, "Gay men cruised more and networked less"—have recharged gay erotica. This Expanded Edition contains a selection of Brass's steamy poems, as well as his essay "Maybe We Should Keep the 'Porn' in Pornography."

Works. 184 pages. $9.95. ISBN 0-9627123-6-1

The Harvest *a "science/politico" novel*

From today's headlines predicting human cloning comes the emergence of "vaccos"—living "corporate cadavers"—raised to be sources of human organ and tissue transplants. One exceptional vacco will escape. His survival will depend upon Chris Turner, a sexual renegade who will love him and kill to keep him alive.

"One of the Ten Best Books of 1997,"
—*Lavender Magazine*, Minneapolis

"In George Nader's Chrome, the hero dared to fall in love with a robot. In *The Harvest—a vastly superior novel,* Chris Turner falls in love with a vacco, Hart256043."
—Jesse Monteagudo, *The Weekly News*, Miami, Florida

Finalist, 1997 Lambda Literary Award, Gay and Lesbian Science Fiction

The Harvest. 216 pages. $11.95. ISBN 0-9627123-7-X

The Lover of My Soul *A Search for Ecstasy and Wisdom*

Brass's first book of poetry since *Sex-charge* is worth the wait. Flagrantly erotic and just plain flagrant—with poems like "I Shoot the Sonovabitch Who Fires Me," "Sucking Dick Instead of Kissing," and the notorious "MTV Ab(solutely) Vac(uous) Awards," *The Lover of My Soul* again proves Brass's feeling that poetry must tell, astonish, and delight.

"An amazingly powerful book of poetry and prose,"
— *The Loving Brotherhood*, Plainfield, NJ

The Lover of My Soul. 100 pages. $8.95. ISBN 0-9627123-8-8

How to Survive Your Own Gay Life *An Adult Guide to Love, Sex, and Relationships*

The book for adult gay men. About sex and love, and coming out of repression; about surviving homophobic violence; about your place in a community, a relationship, and a culture. About the important psychic "gay work" and the gay tribe. About dealing with conflicts and crises, personal, professional, and financial. And, finally, about being more alive, happier, and stronger.

"This book packs a wallop of wisdom!"
—Morris Kight, founder,
Los Angeles Gay & Lesbian Services Center

Finalist, 1999 Lambda Literary Award in Gay and Lesbian Religion and Spirituality

How to Survive Your Own Gay Life. 224 pages. $11.95. ISBN 0-9627123-9-6

Angel Lust *An Erotic Novel of Time Travel*

Tommy Angelo and Bert Knight are in a long-term relationship. Very long—close to a millennium. Tommy and Bert are angels, but different. No wings. Sexually free. Tommy was once Thomas Jebson, a teen serf in the violent England of William the Conqueror. One evening he met a handsome knight who promised to love him for all time. Their story introduces us to gay forest men, robber barons, castles, and deep woodlands. Also, to a modern sexual underground where "gay" and "straight" mean little. To Brooklyn factory men. Street machos. New York real estate sharks. And the kind of lush erotic encounters for which Perry Brass is famous.

Finalist, 2000 Lambda Literary Award, Gay and Lesbian Science Fiction
"Brass's ability to go from seedy gay bars in New York to 11th century castles is a testament to his skill as a writer."
— *Gay & Lesbian Review*

Angel Lust 224 pages. $12.95. ISBN 1-892149-00-1

Warlock *A Novel of Possession*

Allen Barrow, a shy bank clerk, dresses out of discount stores and has a small penis that embarrasses him. One night at a bathhouse he meets Destry Powars—commanding, vulgar, seductive, successful—who pulls Allen into his orbit and won't let go. Destry lives in a closed, moneyed world that Allen can only glimpse through the pages of tabloids. From generations of drifters, Powars has been chosen to learn a secret language based on force, deception, and nerve. But who chose him—and what does he really want from Allen? What are Mr. Powars's dark powers? These are the mysteries that Allen will uncover in *Warlock*, a novel that is as paralyzing in its suspense as it is voluptuously erotic.
Warlock. 226 pages. $12.95. ISBN 1-892149-03-6

The Substance of God *A Spiritual Thriller*

What would you do with The Substance of God, a self-regenerating material originating from Creation? The Substance can bring the dead back to life, but has a "mind" of its own. Dr. Leonard Miller, a gay bio-researcher secretly addicted to "kinky" sex, learned this after he was found mysteriously murdered in his laboratory while working alone on the Substance. Once brought back to life, Miller must find out who infiltrated his lab to kill him, how long will he have to live—and, exactly where does life end and any Hereafter begin?

Miller's story takes him from the underground sex scenes of New York to the all-male baths of Istanbul. It will deal with the longing for God in a techno-driven world; with the persistent attractions of religious fundamentalism; and with the fundamentals of "outsider" sexuality as both spiritual ritual and cosmic release. And Miller, the unbelieving scientist, will be driven himself to ask one more question: Is our often-censored urge toward sex and our great, undeniable urge toward a union with God . . . the same urge?

"Perry Brass has added to the annals of gay lit."

—*Book Marks*

The Substance of God. 232 pages. $13.95. ISBN: 1-892149-04-4

Carnal Sacraments *A Historical Novel of the Future*

In the last quarter of the 21st century, Jeffrey Cooper has made a Faustian pact with the global economic system running the world. No matter what age he is, the system will secretly keep him young and razor-sharp, as long as he can stay on top of his job and keep profits high. But Cooper has a problem: work stress and the congested, hyper-competitive life around him is killing him. Can he keep his stress level a secret from the system itself, his co-workers, and even his own seductive "daddyish" German therapist who has told him that when all else fails there are "angels" in the world who can save him, and often we don't know who they are?

But one, in the most violent form, will appear in Jeffrey's life. At first, he seems to be the Devil himself, offering every kind of excitement, even offering Jeffrey back his own lost soul—but will this younger, extremely mysterious and attractive man end up killing Jeffrey, or saving him?

> "Layered with philosophical elements, fascinating descriptions, and a clear focus on character overall, Brass' latest work is one of the most unusual novels I've read in years."
>
> —*Bay Area Reporter*, San Francisco

> "Exotic locations, high-powered wheeling and dealing and excursions into this new world's dark underside . . . make this a book that captures the imagination and will not let it go until the last page."
>
> —*Out in Jersey Magazine*

Carnal Sacraments. 312 pages, $16.95, 2008, ISBN 978-1-892149-05-3

The Manly Art of Seduction *How to Meet, Talk to, and Become Intimate with Anyone*

Winner Gold Medal Ippy Award from Independent Publisher, Gay and Lesbian Non-Fiction, 2010

"Men are not supposed to be seductive."

Perry Brass heard this while young, so of course it gave him an open field in a kind of behavior that can be exciting, fulfilling, and satisfying. If you feel you're always waiting for someone else to make the first move—if you're traumatized by your fear of rejection and don't have a clue how to open a conversation or expand the terms of a relationship, *The Manly Art of Seduction* is a must-have. Brass explains male territorialism, and how it keeps men locked inside themselves. He talks about making decisions yourself, and how these decisions can be used to make seduction possible—even easy. He deals with the monster of rejection, and how to use mind pictures and exercises to rejection-proof your psyche. At the end of most chapters are questions you can use to tailor this book to your needs, seeing your own progress as you come to master this art.

Although seduction is a part of our commercial environment, Perry Brass has brought it to a place where we can find spiritual and inner nourishment, and where the chronic aloneness of much of life can be changed into a state of delight and deeper sexual and emotional connections.

"Relationships between men can run the gamut from brief connections to long-lasting commitments. This book demonstrates how to break through fear and old patterns to increase your seduction skills and decrease missed opportunities. No matter what kind of connection you might be looking for, the advice offered here is helpful, sharp, and pulls no punches. But the tough love is served with style and humor."

—Dave Singleton, author of
The Mandates: 25 Real Rules for Successful Gay Dating

"A first-class primer for every taste,"

—Richard Labonte, BookMarks,
nationally syndicated column about LGBT books

"Filled with useful, practical advice, this guide is likely to make gay men feel more in control . . . Although he touches on common advice like tapping into shared interests, Brass also explores deeper concepts like valor and territorialism, and his stunning chapter on rejection should be a must-read for everyone in the dating scene."

—Elizabeth Millard,
ForeWord Reviews, January, 2010

"What Brass does so well is guide a man in how to get from the initial meeting all the way to the first date and beyond. But the brilliance of the book is that you can actually read it from the perspective of the person being seduced. The 'seductee' can see just how open and vulnerable the person approaching them is being, and also see what types of responses they might end up getting back. The seductee might then see himself and begin to understand how his behavior might be affecting the situation. And in that, he might learn how to let down his own guard, and allow that connection to take place."

—Kevin Taft, Edge Magazine: Boston, March 1, 2010

The Manly Art of Seduction, 200 pages, $16.95, ISBN: 978-1-892149-06-0
Ebook ISBN: 978-1-892149-10-7
Also available in a SmashWords edition.

All Perry Brass Titles Are Available At Your Bookstore, Or From:

Belhue Press
2501 Palisade Avenue, Suite A1
Bronx, NY 10463

E-mail: **belhuepress@earthlink.net**

Please add $2.50 shipping for the first book and $1.00 for each book thereafter. New York State residents please add 8.25% sales tax. Foreign orders in U.S. currency only.

You can now order Perry Brass's exciting books online at www.perrybrass.com. Please visit this website for more details, regular updates, and news of future events and books.